STANCHIONS HOLLOW

NIGHTMARIST

STANCHIONS HOLLOW

NIGHTMARIST

BY

A.B. DAVIS

ISBN-13: 978-0-578-99239-6

First edition, October 2021

The text type was set in Adobe Garamond Pro
Book design by A.B. Davis

For the **DREAMERS**, who sleep in peace,
because of the *NIGHTMARISTS*, who keep the dark at bay.
And for all who do not yet believe.

CONTENTS

CONTENTS

PROLOGUE

The riders in flight plummeted from the night sky like bombs in free-fall.

They barely avoided collapsing the roof they harshly landed upon, and rapidly sized up the gruesome scene of victims strewn before the black figure.

Shrieking between the gravestones of the dark churchyard, a man's mouth hung agape, his bloody face stretched with terror. His legs were mangled to cripple him, and his arms helplessly felt for the other two out-of-reach bodies: a crumpled blond woman, heaped facedown at the base of a cracked gravestone, and a small boy, sitting up with a blank but tear-stained expression.

No more than six or seven years old, the boy watched in silent disbelief as a shimmering, bluish-white light was siphoned from his chest, and flowed into the bone-white fingers of the black figure.

"Liam," Will began, "*what* in this world...."

In a flash, Liam dismounted the growling entity he flew upon and called out.

"Quickly, now!"

Will hopped onto the slate roof at Liam's command, and the third rider, Eralynn, followed. Together they dropped into the slick grass, their winged mounts plowed into the side of the black figure, and Liam tackled the boy to safety.

Running over to the mangled man, Will hastily turned his bloody face skyward.

"Good Lord, Liam," Will swore. "Why, it's Christopher!"

Eralynn jerked her head over, looking at the man now dead.

"Christopher *E-Errandi?*" she said with a dry sob. "That means...no, *no, NO! That's Misty!*"

She turned toward the crumpled blond woman lying nearby as the dark figure recovered.

"GET IT!" Liam yelled.

Will cracked his neck, double-knocked his sparking brass knuckles together, then held his closed fists steadily out in front of him. Bright red light instantly blazed from the metallic knuckles, and the side of the church, gravestones and dark figure were saturated with crimson rays.

But the dark figure remained unmoved, and as the red light illuminated it they saw that it wasn't covered with a physical cloak, but was shrouded by rippling black smoke. Only visible within its opaque darkness was a skull-like face, staring out without expression.

"Eralynn!" Will yelled urgently. "Help!"

Will turned his fists outward like keys in a lock, and the steady red stream changed to a fiery orange and yellow. Yet the figure remained still, unmoved and unwavering in the new light.

"ERALYNN!" Will yelled again. *"Come ON!"*

The young woman wiped the tears from her eyes, turned away from Misty, and shouted.

"Somn... S-Somnüs!" she cried out. *"Somnüs! Pæcief!"*

The strange words only lingered in the air, ineffective against the dark figure.

"Flaring and Lulling *aren't working*, Liam!" Will called. "What is this?"

At Will's question the dark figure stirred, and moved through the light of his still-shining knuckles. Shuddering as two black, tendril-like arms took hold of his fists, Will's eyes slackened out of focus, and a smile stretched across the skullish face before him.

"*Mary? Vi?*" he trembled uncertainly. "But, how are you here? You *shouldn't* be here…. No, go — run! RUN, GIRLS!"

Will's mouth pried itself open at whatever he was seeing, further and wider than its limit. The ligaments of his jaw snapped apart with a loud popping sound, his throat gurgled, and his eyes rolled backward until they were pearls of white.

"*SOMNÜS! PÆCIEF!*" Eralynn shouted in panic. "SLEEP — STOP!"

Will was thrown into the church, and the black tendrils next grabbed Liam. Just as Liam's eyes widened into the smiling face of the dark figure, a new voice cried out.

"That's *enough!*"

Liam was cast aside, and the dark figure turned. The blond woman was standing, her left ear dangling by sinew, bits of her scalp stuck to the gravestone behind her, and fractured bones poking through the skin of her leg and forearm. Her gaze scanned the cemetery until she saw the boy.

"*Seventy sevens* is my price!" she fell to her knees, pleading. "Seventy sevens' worth of time for the boy, and I will give you the location of the true key!"

The white face grinned, and then spoke through cracking vocal cords and rattling teeth.

"*Seventy. Sevens.*"

Rising from her knees with effort, the woman limped forward a step.

"Stanchions…." she said morosely. "*Stanchions Hollow.*"

The woman turned to the boy, and Eralynn saw her face fully: half of it stricken beyond grief, and the other peeled away entirely. Eralynn gasped at the meaning of what she saw and understood.

"Take care of him, Eralynn," the woman whispered, *"and I beg you...he can never know...."*

STANCHIONS HOLLOW

NIGHTMARIST

EYES IN THE CROWD

Grimmond Scylent's face could hardly hide his dread as he dragged his feet up the sidewalk, walking toward the handfuls of students he'd been lucky enough to avoid since early June.

The same ones that had begun avoiding him nearly ten years ago, when his parents died.

Not tonight, he thought. *Please, for once, just don't let it happen here....*

He deeply rued his agreement to attend the party. From the sidewalk, he looked on at the throng of teenagers filling the wraparound porch. A sea of sweaty hands waved in the hot evening air like an angry mob, fingers twisting back and forth to the whirring, robotic techno that Grimmond despised.

Boom-ch, boom-ch-ch, wa-wa-waaahh!

Other Boston neighborhoods would've called the police on the music that shook the trees, but Grimmond didn't expect the whole of Short Branch to be shut down. Each house on the street was alive with partygoers that weekend: the last weekend of August, the last Saturday before school started back up.

He turned up the front path to the house, looking sideways at the formerly well-manicured lawn, now littered with empty cigarette packs and beer bottles, as well as a pair of neon yellow boxers. This wasn't Grimmond's crowd. He'd never had one, anyway, but frustration with the boy beside him, Patrick Gusset, gathered steam.

Patrick was the nearest thing Grimmond had to a good friend, and he shouldn't have pressured Grimmond into coming. Tonight of all nights, something just hadn't felt quite right to Grimmond since leaving his house, and he hoped dearly for once that his instincts were wrong. He tried to breathe deeply, gritting his teeth as he booted an empty bottle into the grass.

"Why'd I let you drag me into this, Patty...." Grimmond grumbled, thinking he wouldn't be heard.

Patrick looked over, grabbed Grimmond's arm before the porch stairs, and yanked him toward a tall cluster of urine-scented bushes.

"Because we *had* to, Grim!" Patrick shouted over the music, eyes wild as he jabbed a stubby finger in Grimmond's chest. "HAD TO! Junior year starts Monday, and we're not gonna be weirdos *anymore*! You hear me?"

Patrick said *they* were weird, like it was a package deal, but Grimmond knew that it was only himself who truly fit the description. He'd been marked by gossip and rumors long before Patrick transferred to his school, freshman year. Yet Patrick stuck close, even if it wasn't what Grimmond always wanted — and even if most of the rumors surrounding Grimmond were true.

"It just feels a little *off* here —"

Bada-boosh, bada-BOOSH!

"What?" Patrick said loudly.

"BAD VIBES, man!" Grimmond shouted. "Feels *weird* tonight!"

Weird for Grimmond Scylent meant something different than it would for other teenagers. Patrick knew some of Grimmond's story, but not all of it. No one knew what really happened that night, nearly ten years ago.

Not even Grimmond's godmother, Eralynn.

Patrick waved a hand in the air, casually dismissing Grimmond's concern, then gestured to the flopping newsboy cap balanced on his head. Its unflattering appearance seemed well worth it to him, as it gave him the extra few inches of height to reach Grimmond's brow.

"How do I look?"

"Like you sell sheep!" Grimmond answered, annunciating each word to be lip-read through the noise.

"You want it?" Patrick offered. "Might hide your hair a little better."

"No, I'd sooner jump off the top of the —"

"Okay, fine!" Patrick cut him off and nervously rubbed his small hands together. "Well, get your game face on, then. Tonight's your shot with Stella. This is technically her brother Alan's college kick-off party — you remember Alan, right?"

Despite his own sense of warning, Grimmond had been coaxed to the party in the sole hope that Alan's younger sister would be there, the pretty girl for whom he'd tucked away his feelings since math class that spring. One of the last people among a few hundred, in fact, that was still friendly to Grimmond at school. And he allowed Patrick to bully him into thinking he had a chance with her.

"Alan Matterson, who graduated three months ago?" Grimmond asked in mocking incredulity. "The same punk who shoved me into the deep end of the pool in third grade after I told him I couldn't swim?"

Patrick issued a flat stare, unhappy of the reminder that he and Grimmond hadn't been friends since birth.

"Yeah Patty, I know this is the Matterson's place. I just feel *wrong*, being here — like I've been taking a test, and my time is almost up!"

You're missing something, Grimmond.…

He snapped his head to the rustling bushes beside them, but quickly averted his eyes from the couple within. His senses were now jumping into high alert. How was he to explain to Patrick the strange urgency within him? He didn't want to say more than he already had and risk sounding like a scared child.

"You're gettin' old tonight, Grim!" Patrick shouted. "But I don't think you're out of time just yet! You said we'd give this a try, yeah? It's only one hour!"

Grimmond nodded, loathing himself and his promise to remain at the party for sixty minutes all the more.

"*Right*," Patrick sucked in a breath like he was about to dive underwater. "Let's go!"

Grimmond waded up the stairs with the dreadful feeling of entering hostile territory, immediately fighting the urge to plug his nose. Alcohol and body odor combined forces to become day-old seafood, and battled against the fog of cigarette smoke wafting overhead.

"Wait right here!" Patrick shouted as they entered the house.

Grimmond stood just inside the open doors as Patrick hurried off, and exhaled with only slight relief when the ceiling didn't collapse on him. He wiped his sweaty palms on his jeans, forcing his feelings down, forcing himself to be normal for once. What had he been so worried for?

But something *was* wrong — Grimmond knew it with certainty, like a needle pricking his soul.

He'd had the chilling feeling a thousand times in his life, in the same way he knew gravity was real, but couldn't be seen. That summer, the feeling had proven true and worse than ever before. He looked across the dance floor, squinting from the flailing bodies to the sickly green mist hovering near the ceiling. Seeing nothing out of the ordinary, the tight knot inside him nearly loosened, until his sweeping gaze stopped upon the lone girl.

The *dead* girl, dancing grotesquely in the corner of the room.

Grimmond caught his breath, struggling to keep his heartbeat from racing out of control. Her rotting face and dimly illuminated eye sockets narrowed back at him, unblinking. Now, he understood — it was going to be one of *those* nights. Mouth askew and gnashing horrifically, the girl's sallow skin dripped from her face like wax, her gaze ghostly silver flashlights as she stumbled toward him.

Grimmond smacked a hand to his eyelids, and with the other reached for the plastic baggie in his back pocket.

This is why you don't go to these things, you IDIOT! Grimmond berated himself. *Don't panic, don't freak out — just snap OUT of it!*

A clammy grip yanked on his arm, and Grimmond's heart jumped into his throat. He wildly opened his eyes to gauge his fight-or-flight response, but before him was only a smiling Patrick, beckoning him further into the house. Grimmond let out a shuddering breath.

He snapped his head back to the dance floor, but the girl was no longer there. Something worse filled her place: the smell of damp, overwhelming rot. Grimmond's heartbeat continued to pound in his ears. His field of vision was oddly rimmed with bluish-white light, and the faces in the crowd became fuzzy and gray. Would his mental state make him become blind next?

No more...not tonight, please.... No one else can know I'm like this!

Grimmond needed to leave the party, and *soon.* He swallowed hard and rubbed a hand over his heart, willing it to slow as he followed after Patrick.

They passed at least two staircases on the way to the kitchen, and more than several people already making out. Grimmond wasn't glad to see most of them, especially in his state. Only a few had ever been hostile toward him, among whom was Erik Beese: recent graduate, hothead, and currently attempting to grope a senior who still had her wits about her.

A hard smack across Erik's face could be heard over the music.

"Nice!" Patrick cheered, handing Grimmond a red cup as he sipped from his own. "He'll feel that tomorrow."

Grimmond discreetly sniffed his cup, then lowered it without drinking.

"C'mon, Patty," he said with a narrowed glance, "you know better."

"What?" he answered sheepishly. "I thought, *just this once*, since your godmother's working late...."

Grimmond scowled, and Patrick suddenly leaned in, looking concerned.

"Hey — nothing's *screwy* yet, right? Cause we'll go if you need to. Do you need one of your — uh, *you know* — breath mints?"

Just lie.

"No, no," Grimmond said as Patrick winked obviously, "nothing like that. I told you I'd give you an hour, and that's the deal. Then we hit the midnight movies, right?"

"Right-o!" Patrick answered, taking another large swig from his cup.

Grimmond walked to the sink of the enormous kitchen, inconspicuously replacing his beer with tap water. He then hurried back to Patrick, who was already acting as if he'd had several drinks in the last minute, rather than a quarter of one cup.

"You see her smack Erik right on the kisser?" Patrick yelled to a few nearby girls. "Haaad it comin', I think, and serves him right! Dude's got a real attitude. You hear the Sox scouted him for spring training? Yeah, well, they dropped him — just a real attitude, they said."

The pair of girls smiled weakly at Patrick, but went to muttering when they saw Grimmond approach. Grimmond sipped from his cup a moment until he noticed them staring, then walked away to lean against a wall. He diverted his gaze to find Stella in the crowd; and, he hoped, nothing else.

He checked the time on his phone, still shaking the rotting face of the dead girl from his mind.

Fifty minutes to go. Maybe Stella's not here, and we can just leave early....

Forty minutes passed without event, but Grimmond could no longer stand the atmosphere. No one had spoken to him aside from Patrick. He was like a piece of artwork anchored to the wall, one which passing people didn't like but couldn't articulate why. Maybe most of them still remembered him as the orphan who would scream in the grade-school hallways at the things he alone was seeing — something Patrick hadn't been around for.

In the seconds between the changing of songs, Grimmond made his decision.

He took a step toward Patrick, planning to cut their deal slightly short, but a laugh reached his ears. He jerked his head to the far wall to see Stella, tucked within a small crowd of friends. His heart leapt, and the first traces of a smile briefly tempted the corners of his mouth. But just as quickly, they tightened like a zipper.

The boy and girl on either side of Stella shot their empty eye sockets toward Grimmond, mouths suddenly sagged open, red-tinted saliva dribbling out. The eyeless holes glowed dimly silver, as the rotting girl's before them had, and their brown teeth began to rabidly gnash chunks from their own lips.

Still smiling, Stella squinted over at Grimmond, recognizing him. Grimmond quickly turned away, her face having turned fuzzy and gray, and the edges of his vision tingeing bluish-white again with his accelerating heartbeat. What was happening? He shook his head violently back and forth to no avail, then reached a hand over to Patrick. He yanked him by the back of his shirt so hard that most of the amber liquid spilled from Patrick's cup.

"What the heck —"

"Shut *up*, Patty!" Grimmond scolded, breathing hard. "Look, I've got a *serious* problem...."

The drunken Patrick looked over Grimmond's shoulder and smiled widely.

"Stellaaaaa!" he raised his cup over Grimmond's shoulder, twirling him around with his other hand.

"Grimmond Scylent!" Stella slurred, opening into a sloppy, one-armed hug. "Welcome to my hose — my *houmes*. I mean — *uh* — I live here!"

"Hey, Stella," Grimmond waved awkwardly, unable to hear himself over the renewed music.

She might have asked if he was enjoying himself next, but Grimmond wasn't sure. His eyes kept darting over her head, back and forth through the crowd as he looked for blood-gnashing mouths and glowing silver eye sockets. He reached back a shaking hand to his jeans pocket, feeling again the plastic baggie with the pills inside.

"Mine's the *kewl*est room in the house — and probably the *world*," Stella continued over the noise. "I will show you —"

"Can you tell me where the bathroom is, Stella?" Grimmond leaned in, cutting her off. "I've, um, had a bit too much to drink. I'll be right back, though."

Grimmond hurried off in the direction he thought she pointed, his eyes peeled to the crowd. A twinge of anger prodded his gut as he saw letterman jacket number eighty-four, Erik Beese, attempting to grope a new girl. Grimmond passed them by, hoping Erik didn't see him.

He quickly came across a closed door with a long line outside it, but with no time to wait, he zoomed up the stairs to find another. The second-floor hallway opened up to the right, and Grimmond hastily threw open the first door he found ajar.

Both Grimmond and the girl standing in the dark on the other side jumped.

"Get out, or I'll vomit on you," Grimmond warned as he turned on the light.

The girl took a second to process his warning, then hurried out when she realized Grimmond wasn't whom she was waiting for. Grimmond slammed the door behind her and locked it, barely recognizing he had found the second-floor bathroom. He pulled out the plastic baggie from his jeans and dumped one of the little white pills into his palm.

No matter that they were prescription, he'd never risk anyone knowing — Patrick only having found out by accident — and Grimmond decided he'd go to his grave before willingly telling anyone else he was on anti-psychotics. He stared at the pill while his nostrils took steadying breaths, and a moment of stubbornness kept his lips glued shut.

But Grimmond noticed when the porcelain figurine on the back of the toilet glowed orange, and swiveled its head toward him. The old woman in the bonnet grinned wickedly, her cackling laugh pitching from high to low, and echoing much deeper than her stature would allow.

"It's *not* real, it's just in my head," he said. "They can't hurt me...."

Grimmond whispered it like a mantra, trying to be convinced. But the figurine hopped off the toilet and began to rise up, surpassing the sink, and then Grimmond, and then the shower curtain as it filled the room. He closed his eyes and popped the pill in his mouth.

When did it get this bad?

He drank a few handfuls of water from the faucet, and splashed some on his face. He opened his eyes and turned back to the toilet, but the figurine was completely gone; he wasn't even sure if it had been there to begin with.

He shoved the pill-filled baggie back into his pocket and hurried downstairs.

Winding his way back through the thrumming noise to the kitchen, Grimmond saw that Patrick had left his former spot. He checked his phone but hadn't received any texts, even though the hour was up and the agreement fulfilled. And although he'd just found Stella, he was anxious to leave without further incident. Grimmond had never had so many hallucinations in one night.

He hoped the pill in his stomach would stay effective long enough.

Scanning through the crowd once more, Grimmond spotted number eighty-four pinning a girl on the opposite wall, tongue choking her airway and hands blindly groping. The same twinge of anger again jolted Grimmond's gut, harder this time, and his own desperation was overshadowed. He couldn't see who the girl was, but assumed she didn't like the interaction by the way she tried to push Erik off. Even sober, Erik was likely too stupid, and too much of a jerk to have noticed the resistance.

Look away, Grimmond! It's not your concern.... Just find Patrick and you can get out of here!

Grimmond exhaled deeply as he watched the girl try to push Erik away again. He shook his head in anger, slamming his eyelids shut several times. But after each blink Erik was still there, as real as he was a bully. Grimmond's fists clenched. Why wasn't anyone over there stepping in? Did each person expect the other to do something?

Don't you DARE *get involved, Grimmond Scylent!*

For once that night, Grimmond knew he had the ability to fight what he was seeing. Erik was older and bigger, but Grimmond didn't care. He wouldn't be the person who later wished they'd done something, and he was tired of being helpless.

He elbowed through the crowd and reached Erik in a flash, grabbing onto his shoulders and furiously jerking him backwards. Erik tipsily stumbled into a group of bystanders, who barely prevented him from smashing through the bay window.

"That's enough!" Grimmond yelled, his heartbeat picking up with his courage. "Can't you tell she doesn't like —"

"Grimmond?" the girl cut him off in an angry slur. "Whaddinahell — *hiccup* — you do that for?"

Grimmond turned around to see Stella leaning against the wall, wiping her glistening chin. He felt his ears burn red first, followed by his cheeks as his whole head flushed to the shade of a ripe tomato. He tried to keep his mouth from popping open in shock as he looked back and forth, but was unsuccessful.

"Little blue-haired *FREAK!*"

"Nooo, Erik!" Stella stumbled forward. "He's fu — *hiccup* — unny looking, and probably my favorite friend to copy in math cla — *hiccup* — ass, probably even the *world....*"

Stella hadn't been trying to fight Erik off at all as she leaned against the wall — she was pulling him in for more.

Onlookers swelled by the second for the anticipated fight, but Grimmond just wanted to dig a hole, crawl into it, and remain there the rest of his life. He had unwittingly believed Patrick, thinking he had a chance with Stella, and was crushed in return.

I shouldn't have come tonight...what did I think *people did at these parties?*

Grimmond looked back to Erik's fuming stare. He nearly considered an apology, but instead withheld a gasp. There, just past his bully's shoulders, Grimmond saw them again. All three of them, together.

Taking the little white pill hadn't worked after all.

His heartbeat whirled up like a machine. The faces in the crowd rapidly turned blurry and gray this time, but the three rotting bodies stood out the brighter. Their dead eyes burned like dirty lanterns. Red foam sloshed between their snapping brown teeth, and decaying yellow skin fell from their jowls in chunks, revealing the purple glow beneath — like their bodies were made partly of flesh, and partly of light.

The grotesquely dancing girl stumbled and smacked into the floor as she came toward Grimmond, tripping the other two rotting bodies in turn. When the gasping mass of limbs started to pull themselves across the floor, Grimmond turned on his heel and fled.

He shoved through the unrecognizable faces toward the front door. Beneath the green mist he ran, past the dance floor, where the mindlessly flailing Patrick was only found because of his newsboy cap. Grimmond grabbed him, nearly carrying him out to the porch. They almost made it to the front path when Erik came barreling down after them, a large crowd nipping at his heels and looking for blood.

"GET 'EM, Beese!"

"Shave his blue head!"

"FIGHT!"

Before Grimmond realized what was happening, a tight ring formed around him in the grass, and Patrick was pulled away. Grimmond rapidly searched the crowd for the three rotting bodies, glowing in the darkened yard, but couldn't find them.

He breathed deeply to slow his heart, attempting to collect himself before things got too out of hand. Faces in the crowd regained their focus just as Erik pushed into the ring.

"Erik — I'm sorry, all right?" Grimmond yelled over the music. "It was all just a misunderstanding…I don't want to fight you!"

"Save it, you orphaned freak!" Erik bellowed, spitting out his gum and raising his fists. "Think I dunno about you? You think *Stella* doesn't know you've stalked her for months? Well guess what, *freak* — tonight you're done! S'all over for you, weirdo!"

Grimmond raised his hands to pacify the situation, but Patrick suddenly weaseled his way past the front ranks, likewise throwing up his arms to stop Erik's assault.

"WAIT!" Patrick shouted. "You can't! H-he thought you were somethin' else, Erik! He's *crazy!*"

Grimmond's body tensed up, and not from the impending fight.

What does he think he's doing? Grimmond thought wildly.

"Hold your horses, pipsqueak — you're next!" Erik yelled over the jeering crowd, assuming his gladiator-like stance. "What're you talking about, anyway?"

"Grim's CRAY-ZEE, man — I'm talkin' for real, *pill-popping* nuts! He'll tear you apart if you get any closer! Right, Grim? Show him the pills man! Prove it!"

Grimmond slowly dropped his hands, deflated like a balloon, unable to believe what he was hearing. Had Patrick really just divulged his nearly decade-long secret, in full view of half the school?

The cries for blood diminished as the students began to hiss, some giggling, some gawking. Erik blinked stupidly between Grimmond and Patrick, but his lips sneered with derision as he saw the truth on Grimmond's face. Unclenching his fists, the look in Erik's eyes said more than words could.

Patrick had just confirmed every rumor surrounding Grimmond since the summer he turned seven.

None of the rotting bodies or laughing figurine from the bathroom had yet resurfaced, but Grimmond wouldn't have minded if they had, if only to swallow Patrick on the spot. It was all over: the fight before it started, the evening before it ended, and the rest of Grimmond's social life.

Erik disappeared with the dispersing crowd, and Grimmond looked over in time to see the back of Stella's head, wobbling up the porch stairs to the crowded house. He thought he heard her calling for Erik.

"That was *so* close, man!" Patrick laughed boisterously, turning to him and taking an unsteady bow. "You owe me one! Ready to head to the movies? Grimmond — you ready?"

Grimmond's feet had taken root in the grass.

"Grim?" Patrick slurred again, swaying before him. "You good? Let's a-get...*outta heeeere!*"

"Patty, do you have any idea what you've just done —"

"What?" Patrick shouted over the music.

"I said," Grimmond inhaled, *"WHY DID YOU DO THAT?"*

Grimmond exploded, grabbing Patrick by the collar of his shirt and nearly throwing him to the ground.

"First, I find Stella making out with Erik, then you tell everyone I take meds for being crazy? I'm a freak for the *rest of my life* now — thanks to you!"

Patrick's face convulsed, and Grimmond released him, stepping back a few feet to avoid the vomit.

"Grim —" Patrick choked, wiping his mouth with the back of his hand. "Wait...."

"Forget it. I'm done here," Grimmond said. "I think you and I are, too."

Grimmond shoved his hands in his pockets and started down the path to the sidewalk.

"GRIM! I just wanted to be normal for *one* night!" Patrick shouted. "You know? You know what I mean, man?"

"Yeah, Patty," Grimmond whispered without turning around. "I know what you mean."

He turned up the sidewalk and out of sight, leaving Patrick to mutter beneath the rattling music.

"Happy Birthday, Grim...."

CHAPTER TWO

MUSIC TO MEMORY

Grimmond hoped that the night was over, to just think alone for a while.

His shirt was already soaked through with sweat when he reached the Esplanade — the long, paved path along the Charles River. He checked the cracked screen of his phone: free of missed notifications, after midnight, and almost dead.

Why, that's not symbolic at all....

But it made no difference. The ride he would have called for was drunk at the party he just left, and his godmother, Eralynn, would be working at her security guard job until the sun rose. Even if he could call her, he wouldn't have. She'd been behaving strangely toward him that whole summer, acting as if he was dying, and he didn't want to bother her.

Right now he just had to keep his feet moving, hurrying away from what chased him: his own mind. A mind that used to hallucinate in short flashes, no more than once a month, and no more than a handful of times a year. But not that summer.

Now they were more of a weekly occurrence, taunting Grimmond when he least expected it. Piercing orange eyes stared at him from the alleys, cashiers' noses poured bright blood when handing him change, and rattling breaths filled his ears if he closed his eyes too long. But seeing four separate hallucinations in a single night, in the *same* place — that was unprecedented.

He looked over his shoulder, quickening his pace as he replayed the night's events.

His eyesight had never changed before. Never gone bluish-white at the edges, people's faces never fallen out of focus like they had at the party. The putrid smell of the rotting bodies still burned his nose, the way their mouths twitched and gnashed, gargling their own bile, made his skin shudder into goose bumps. Grimmond wasn't calming down; he was growing worse.

What was going on? Could everyone's sixteenth birthdays be this bad?

He hoped fleeing the party would help his mind, the boiling sense of urgency coursing through his limbs, but both had gotten worse in the last thirty minutes. He wondered what was held in store for him on Monday.

Everyone at school would know his secret, if they didn't already, but Grimmond decided he wouldn't deny it. He'd be a complete outcast for the next two years, maybe even longer. He'd have to look for colleges out of state.

But maybe Patrick did him a favor, too.

Grimmond couldn't keep his lucid hallucinations secret another year. Not another month, not another night, even. They had never felt more real; *nothing* had. Nothing except the memory of his parents leaving him, nearly ten years ago. Or rather, the memory of their cold-blooded murder that night.

Eralynn told Grimmond that that night in his memory didn't happen. His mother's face wasn't ripped apart when she was thrown into a gravestone. His father's legs weren't grotesquely mangled by a dark figure, forcing him to scream in pain and watch in helplessness as the strange light was drawn from Grimmond.

The dark figure's face, skull-white, flashed vividly across his mind. Always, when he wasn't sensing his other hallucinations, the skeletal face within the dark figure was there. Watching him, and waiting.

"If that thing didn't steal something from my chest, why does my heart feel weird?" Grimmond would ask.

"Because of the hole," Eralynn explained, "the defect in your heart. We have to be careful we don't get it pumping too hard, for too long. That's why you can't play with the other kids outside, remember?"

Despite his supposed condition, Grimmond never went to the doctor for it. And having hallucinations made it hard to keep his heartbeat in check, even without sports. When Grimmond would run to Eralynn as a child, telling her of whatever moaning monster was tapping on his window, or crawling through the house, she'd always say it was just a nightmare — despite him being wide-awake when he saw it.

"The things you see aren't *real*," she would explain, "just hallucinations from your brain, stewing since the day your parents left."

"If none of this is real, where are my parents if they're not dead?" Grimmond would ask further, seeing her stumble over the words every time she fed them to him. "Why are they gone?"

"Because they couldn't take care of you anymore," she always answered, "and your mother asked me to look after you."

For all Eralynn told him, Grimmond sensed that fact alone was somehow true. But as he grew older, he eventually considered her version of things: that he made it all up to deal with his own abandonment. The idea of the dark figure, the gruesome memory of his parents' murder, the strange light within his chest. And the last part that no one would ever know about except Grimmond and his dead parents.

Maybe none of it ever happened.

It was just his stewing brain that made the hallucinations come alive, like Eralynn said. But tonight, he would do *anything* to turn off his mind. To make it all disappear.

Grimmond's eyes darted between the Charles River and the flickering shadows beneath the trees, past the reach of the streetlamps. He kept his pace just below a jog, aimlessly moving as he tried to beat his mind into submission. The anti-psychotics he took should have been effective, being the highest dosage allowed when the psychiatrist prescribed them in July. It was the first night he had the courage to try them, the woman promising they would be effective immediately.

Why didn't they work? And why are they STILL *not working now?*

Grimmond breathed heavier, his heartbeat accelerating despite his efforts to remain calm. He stopped walking, rubbing the sweat from his eyes to see into the darkness beyond the path. Only, it wasn't dark any longer.

For the first time — and *certainly* not the last — Grimmond hoped that he was just plain crazy.

Alight in the branches of the trees, the glowing severed heads began to appear. Ghostly green, purple or blue light dripped from their necks like haunted will-o-wisps. At first they only moaned piteously, but then they started to float down, accelerating toward Grimmond with their mouths open, and howling as if being freshly decapitated.

Grimmond's feet wouldn't move, every inch of him frozen in horror.

He tried to get out of the way, but was only able to topple backwards, like a falling tree. One of the moaning heads barely missed smashing into his face, a flap of its wet neck skin grazing Grimmond's forehead as he fell.

Gasping, he scrambled to his feet, wiping the ooze from his face as he jumped into the dry fountain nearby. He ran up the stone steps and ducked behind the legs of the war hero perched at the top. To his dismay, the bronze statue turned its gaze downward, empty eyes burning white, and face twisting unnaturally.

"You know why the pills didn't work," uttered a gargled whisper beyond its lips. *"You know why you still see."*

Frozen, Grimmond stared into the cold white eyes, barely able to breathe. The statue spoke, but Grimmond knew that was *impossible*. He watched as thick black liquid dribbled from the statue's mouth, and bits of purple light pierced through the pockmarks on its face.

"You know what is real, Grimmond Scylent," the statue went on, *"like you know your time is almost up."*

"You're *not* real," Grimmond breathed, ducking another floating head as he backed down the fountain steps. "None of this is! You — you're just in my head!"

"Pretend as you wish, but it will not stop the Ending...."

It took a single threatening step down from its plinth.

"Nor will it stop us. Run, while you can, little Errandi...while your heart still beats."

The statue's face stretched even longer, and its triangular hat glowed red like an anti-halo. Then, it unsheathed a rusty sword, the glowing ethereal heads dove like wingless vultures, and Grimmond nearly face-planted as he leapt from the fountain.

He ran faster than he'd ever run before, and his heart quickly surpassed its cautioned limit. The same odd change that came over his vision at the party happened again. His sight blurred bluish-white at the edges, and the dark shapes along the Esplanade sharpened to clearer focus. Streetlamps dimmed, the sky brightened to a shade of nightmarish purple, and the water of the Charles burned radioactive green.

A group of mangy dogs was passed, and several glowing heads soared directly in to invade their bodies. The mutts howled and yipped, until their eyes burned with the same eerie light of their possessors. Grimmond watched in disbelief as their bodies grew as large as wolves, dark coats bristling, saliva falling from their mouths like leaking faucets.

His heart threatened to burst from his chest. An emergency telephone was spotted, and he moved toward it until he read 'Out of Service' in watery white letters.

No one could get here in time anyway, idiot! RUN!

Near the end of the Esplanade, a soft melody was rising from the Hatch Memorial Shell, the amphitheater used for outdoor concerts. Grimmond sprinted the harder toward the crowd of people, and as the music loudened, he heard the sound of snarling diminish. Turning his neck to see his pursuers slowing and changing course, Grimmond stumbled and fell onto the edge of the grass seating area.

He turned back to the path frantically, but the glowing heads and snarling dogs were gone. Several concert attendees turned to look at him, annoyed at the disturbance, but their faces were blurred and grayed, as the partygoers' had been earlier.

"Sorry — sorry," Grimmond said to those nearby him.

Discreetly placing a hand on his pulse, he felt his heartbeat about to push his eyeballs from his skull. He pulled out his phone to call Eralynn — whether she was at work or not — and found the battery dead. He swore beneath his panting breaths and shoved the useless phone back into his pocket.

Regardless of what had just happened, Grimmond found his mood strangely altered as the orchestra now invaded his senses. Though he wouldn't say he enjoyed the dark music, it calmed his pulse, and he watched as the faces of the crowd focused back into lines of color.

I know this song....

Grimmond was entranced into a state of haunted wakefulness that stirred the deepest places of his memory. He remembered the spring when he was six years old, the last time he heard that song, the last night his parents were alive.

Whether his ears were relaying the current music or the memory from nearly a decade ago, Grimmond didn't know. But he remembered where he and his parents sat against a tree at the back of the amphitheater, and remembered standing up to leave before the concert ended.

How could I know any of this, if — according to Eralynn — it never happened?

He could almost see his shadowy memories walking before him, swaying to the melancholy song that played the night his parents disappeared — the night of their murder. He watched his memories cross the street, and decided to follow.

He recalled holding his mother's hand as they jaywalked, and could see his father zipping up his jacket to keep the cool night air at bay. Grimmond even knew the smell of the pizza shop on the corner before he saw it. He followed all the way to the shadows of trees shrouding Boston Public Garden, where the notes of the song were barely heard anymore.

Passing the George Washington statue, he dreamily walked with his memory until he reached the footbridge to cross the water, but found the way darkened by burned-out lights. There he remembered his father, Christopher, picking him up and speaking sternly. Grimmond could almost see his mother's saddened face next to his father's, framed by her streaming blond hair.

This memory — it was the last time he ever remembered seeing either of them. He wondered if right there was where it happened. The night he did something he'd regret every hour of his life afterward. The part that — if it all actually *had* occurred — no one knew about. The pain, the sorrow, it was all so real.... Wasn't it?

At the edge of the bridge, the spell wavered. Grimmond's memory began to fade, replaced by something he hadn't heard as a child, though something unmistakable nonetheless: the tearing, chewing, and swallowing gulps of a large and hungry mouth.

Grimmond tried to shut out the noises coming from across the bridge. He tried to find the music again, to bring back the outline of his parents, to say he was more sorry than they'd ever know for what happened.

For what he did to them.

But the loud moans beneath the sound of chewing were too distracting. Too demanding. The orchestra could no longer be heard, and the flickering memory of his parents was all but erased from his mind.

For a fleeting moment, Grimmond wasn't scared of his hallucinations, but angry with them. Angry at whatever was on the other side of the bridge, taunting him, ruining the first gleaming recollection he'd had of his parents his entire life.

"HELP!" screeched a ragged voice. "*SOMEBODY!* HELP M—"

Grimmond's anger was smashed flat as the voice was choked off.

A dry lump rose in his throat with his elevating heartbeat. He tried to swallow them both back down, but his hair stood on end as if awaiting a lightning strike. A wave of animalistic fear washed over him at the renewed sounds of tearing fabric and chewing teeth across the bridge. He reached for his phone to call the police, but then hesitated.

What if the noises were in his head? Just another hallucination?

And, worse still — what if they weren't?

Grimmond's mind went into overdrive. The horrors of the party and Esplanade were confused against his parents' now-faded recollection. He *knew* the memories stirred up from that gruesome night had to be real, and that the dark figure that killed them was, too. What did that mean about his hallucinations?

Could that statue have been telling the truth?

Grimmond looked around the park for anyone else that may have heard the scream, to verify his torn sanity, but he was alone. No one would be able to help him, and he had to act. Grimmond had to either go into the darkness or run away from it: to choose either bravery or fear.

He swallowed a dose of both, and hurried forward.

Fists clenched, he didn't realize just how dark it was until he got to the other side of the bridge. He swept his gaze from side to side, but didn't see any bodies on the sidewalk. No possessed dogs, glowing heads or haunted colonials. But when the chomps of teeth and tearing reached his ears again, he realized that it was coming from *underneath* the bridge.

Another weak whimper sputtered out, gurgling through a mouthful of hot liquid. It sounded more human this time than it did before, and Grimmond's heart rate increased to the level of a hunted beast.

You can do this. None of it's real — it's all in your head...right?

"Hey! H-hang on!" Grimmond called. "I'm coming!"

Descending the stone stairs beside the bridge in a flurry, he almost didn't see the edge of the pond in time. Trying to skid to a halt, he slipped on the slick pavement and fell hard on his backside. He hoped the stone was only wet from ducks recently exiting the water, not piles of excrement. But when he stood quickly to brush his jeans, they dripped with something warmer than pond water.

Warmer, tackier, and smelling of copper and iron.

Another tearing noise rent through the air, followed by the sucking gulps of a large, wet mouth. Grimmond's voice didn't work anymore, even if he wanted to call out again. Every fiber of his being told him to flee. But he didn't.

He raised another foot forward, and this time it stepped down and squished. With a shudder he slowly lifted his foot, then nudged the bundled, oblong thing again. A trembling hand reached for the light of his phone, but Grimmond cursed himself when he remembered it was dead.

Blindly, he bent down.

His fingers found the sleeve of a wool jacket, and held it high until what was inside slid out onto the pavement with a squelch. Grimmond picked it up. Still warm, still wet with tacky, dark goo, his touch ran the length of something slimy and hard. All the way down until he greeted the gnawed fingers of another human hand.

Grimmond's heart rocketed like he'd been shot with an adrenaline needle.

Stars in the sky quickly returned to their haunted purple glow, and the pond water became the same radioactive green as the Charles River. Shadows sharpened into focus, like Grimmond's vision was beaming bioluminescence onto everything his eyes raked across. But when he finally looked beneath the bridge, he struggled to remain standing.

He first saw the river of blood that dripped from the floating white tennis shoes.

Then, he looked up at the greasy torso of a boy, clutched in the grip of an otherworldly horror.

Sifting with its fat fingers through the shredded body, the horrific creature twisted and turned the boy's innards, like food on a plate. The boy's mutilated head was mostly still intact, still moaning quietly, though Grimmond didn't see how that was possible. He would have wondered more, but turned his own head to the side, and threw up everything inside him.

The creature turned its gaze to Grimmond at last, evil red eyes burning hungrily. It dropped the leg it was about to next tear into and growled low. Grimmond thought he heard laughter somewhere, perverse and satisfied. Was someone else watching?

Turning to face Grimmond fully, he saw that the creature took the shape of a very large, fat human being. Clumps of the boy's clothes and skin were caught in its bared teeth, and its dark red body swished back and forth, like a sack of blood that would explode if prodded by something sharp. It licked its lips and stepped toward him.

"FREEZE!"

Grimmond looked up to the bridge with a jolt as two flashlights blinded his enhanced night vision. Hearing a growl and soft splash, he dazedly looked back down, watching numbly as the boy's body was dragged into the water.

Grimmond didn't even move as the police officer tackled him to the ground.

He was handcuffed before he could wipe the puke from his mouth. Before he could smear the sticky blood off his hands, or the slime of the detached throwing arm that now lay a foot from his face, already stinking like hot metallic yeast.

Grimmond wished he were face down on something other than the damp letterman jacket scratching his face, and now stained red. One that once reeked of cologne, with the large number eighty-four stitched into the back.

Grimmond wished most of all that he hadn't just watched Erik Beese be eaten alive.

THE VISITOR

O ut with it — I'll wait."
Grimmond hadn't said a word the entire way back to the police precinct.

He hadn't said anything, even before the arresting officer read him his Miranda rights while cuffing him. Now he kept his head bowed in the bright room with the two-way mirror, looking at the dried blood on his hands, wishing he could peel his eyes away from them. Blankly staring at his hands made him feel guilty, somehow, even though he knew he'd done nothing wrong.

Another hand smacked down on the table to get his attention.

Grimmond didn't jump, but stirred from his stupor to lock with the eyes across the table. The man introduced himself when he first walked in, but Grimmond was too out of it to hear. He was young, with combed hair, a clean-shaven face, and a look of pure arrogance.

"Five-foot-seven, I'd guess...." the man said with a victorious smirk. "A hundred forty pounds, maybe, soaking wet. Blue eyes, brown hair with some hippy blue streaks in it, skittish but not intimidated. Did I miss anything, aside from your problem with authority?"

Grimmond looked back down to his hands. He couldn't stop thinking of the horror beneath the bridge, the sound of its chewing, and Erik's pleas for help.

"C'mon, kid, we've gotta get somewhere, or we'll be here all night. Your *name*, at least."

"I'm Grimmond Scylent," he answered quietly. "I told you guys when I got here."

"Yeah, I remember you said that," the man leaned forward and interlaced his fingers. "It was just so ridiculous, I didn't believe you. Ya see, when you're a kid and don't have a driver's license yet, we can't find a whole lot on you without your social security number. And you just *happen* to not know that, either, isn't that what you said?"

"Haven't had much use for it, being fifteen and all. Or sixteen, I suppose, in about an hour —"

"Blah, blah, blah," the officer raised his hand like a shadow puppet, mocking him. "Cut the crap. You're the one covered in blood, practically *swam* in it, it looks like, but I'm guessing it's not yours. Oh, and someone seems to have forgotten their arm underneath that bridge. Think they'll come back for it? It's big, probably a white male's, but the skin looked young. Fingers are too mangled to make a print."

The young officer gauged every blink, every breath of Grimmond's as he spoke.

"So who was it? Who's number eighty-four?"

Grimmond swallowed.

"Number eighty-four?"

"*Don't* play dumb again," the officer sneered. "You wouldn't be so rattled if it was a stranger."

You're smarter than you look, Grimmond wished he could say, *but you'd be rattled too, if you saw what I did.*

Grimmond only swallowed again, keeping his eyes on his hands. He couldn't stop thinking about Erik's shredded body, but knew he couldn't admit he knew him. That would lead to more questions, and if Grimmond told the man what he had seen, Grimmond would be in a psychiatric ward by sunrise.

"Shouldn't there be somebody here for me?" Grimmond asked. "Somebody on my side?"

The interrogator's face stretched into a wide grin.

"That's all I needed to hear. Like a hundred guilty people before you, they lawyer up as soon as they can, just like that. You *little* piece of —"

"All right, Daniels," said a much calmer voice. "Take a beat."

The door to the room had opened, and the man who arrested Grimmond walked in, looking quite the opposite of Officer Daniels. His dark hair was disheveled atop a scruffy, sun-deprived face, and the black suspenders he wore were tattered around the edges. Grimmond guessed that he was Chinese-American, second or third generation.

Officer Daniels stood up to leave, giving Grimmond a look that said, *'we're not through, yet'*.

"Grimmond Scylent," the new man offered. "I'm Detective Tippins. Just happened to be near the park tonight when the call came in, saying somebody was screaming for help. Sorry about roughhousing you earlier, by the way, 'thought you might have been the perp."

He walked over to Grimmond and removed the handcuffs.

"Need anything? Coffee? Donut?"

Time for the Good Cop, Grimmond thought.

He looked up at the man's dark eyes piercing through him, the faintest traces of a smile dancing at the corners of his mouth. Detective Tippins had much more experience than Officer Daniels, Grimmond sensed.

"Kidding," the detective said briefly. "We won't have 'em until the shop opens in a few hours, anyway. You know that old place around the corner? Always say 'yes' to the coffee — *great* coffee — but 'no' to the donuts if you know what's good for you. Worse than the drugs on the street, anymore."

Detective Tippins slid over his cellphone to Grimmond.

"Before we get started, you need to call somebody? I saw that your phone was dead."

Grimmond began to reach for the phone, but then hesitated. Did he really want to drag Eralynn into this? How could he tell her that one of his hallucinations had come to life and eaten one of the school bullies? It sounded crazy even thinking about it, and he knew it would sound worse if Detective Tippins heard him say it aloud.

Grimmond pushed the cell phone back across the table.

"No, thank you," he said. "My godmother doesn't get off work for a few hours, and she never brings her phone with her."

"Your parents?"

Grimmond tensed.

"What about them?" he asked.

"Can you give them a call?"

"No," Grimmond said, clearing his throat. "They've been murder — *eh* — I mean, *missing,* for a long time. Not around anymore. They left me with my godmother when I was six."

Detective Tippins grimaced apologetically, and he looked the part.

"I'm sorry," he grunted, "but yes, I saw you wrote that, too. Christopher and Misty Errandi, right? Just wanted to double check."

Grimmond nodded, wondering where the man was headed.

"Well," the detective went on, "I'll tell you I don't really agree with Sergeant Combley, then — the other officer from the park earlier? She thinks you never had parents, because evil isn't born like the rest of us. It's just always been there. Said she saw your eyes glowing in the dark, and that's when we shined our lights on you. I could hardly get her in the same cruiser as you after the scene down there. Good cop, just superstitious."

Grimmond blinked, trying his best to look untroubled under the detective's stare. The man clicked his tongue, drumming his fingers softly on the table.

"I've got a few gallons of blood spilled beneath that footbridge, Grimmond, and half of it got on you," he stated matter-of-factly. "I found you next to a human arm, along with the jacket it fell out of. Our dogs are having a bit of trouble finding a scent based off those two items. Whoever got rid of that body did a good number, I think.... *So,* let's chat. Wrong place at the wrong time, I take it?"

Grimmond wanted to say so, or to tell the man *anything*, but something held him back: the sheer craziness of it all. Detective Tippins shot a quick, knowing glance over to the two-way mirror, then turned back to Grimmond and smiled.

"It's been a long night, Grimmond. Maybe we should give you some time to think. We won't put you in the drunk tank since you're a minor, but we can't release you back to the street without your guardian signing you out, either. There's an older cell in the backroom where the storage is. It's quieter back there, and you won't have to smell half a dozen losers crying themselves to sleep.

"What else? Oh, I think processing has all they need from you, so I'll take you over to the latrine. You can rinse whoever's blood that is off your hands and face."

Grimmond was ushered from the table and escorted to the bathroom, where he was able to wash Erik's blood away. Scrubbing hard in the mirror, he was careful not to stare into his own eyes and risk losing his composure. He was next wound through the police station, avoiding the other visitors for the night, and taken to the backroom.

Detective Tippins opened the door and led the way in.

A few fluorescent ceiling bulbs lit the long room. On Grimmond's right was a labyrinth of cardboard boxes, stacked three and four high, labeled *Christmas* or *Community Events*, or even *Bathroom Supplies.* The dim red light of an emergency exit sign was hung above the door in the far corner, and almost entirely blocked by the unnavigable maze.

Leave it to the cops to have a fire code violation.

"Don't worry," the detective said, noticing Grimmond's stare. "None of it's evidence. Just making the most of the space we have in the precinct right now."

The reality of Grimmond's situation began to sink in still further as Detective Tippins pointed to the middle of three cells on the left wall, door opened and awaiting Grimmond.

"This is you," he said, leading Grimmond in and shutting the bars behind him. "Hate to do this, but we can't do anything else given the circumstances. We'll be checking the school colors of that letterman jacket, along with any student who used the number eighty-four. Don't worry, we'll know something soon. And we'll work on getting a hold of your godmother in the meantime, too."

Say SOMETHING, *idiot! You're about to go away for a murder you didn't commit!*

Grimmond's chest began to swell with panic as Detective Tippins turned and walked back to the door.

"It wasn't me!" Grimmond called out at last. "I didn't do *anything!*"

Detective Tippins stopped in his tracks and swiveled on his heel, shoving his hands deeply in his pockets.

"Denying it to me is a start, but denial to *yourself* is something else. Be clear on which one you want me to think, because I'll be honest — it doesn't look good from my side of things, Grimmond. You're upset — like you might have just done something you regret. You were also found with drugs on you, that you claim are prescription —"

"They *are* prescription!" Grimmond asserted. "They just didn't work the first time! They're anti-psychotics, and I need them back!"

"Not helping your case here, son. Besides, we can't just administer an unlabeled bag of medicine to you, even if you're telling the truth. We need to see the prescription and bottle, first."

"Look," Grimmond gauged his words, trying to stay calm. "I think that *something* killed whoever that was. An animal, maybe, or something like…like a monster…."

Grimmond thought that Detective Tippins would begin laughing, or roll his eyes. He didn't.

"You know Grimmond, I've only ever even heard of *one* other case like this. One of my old cases, in fact, unsolved. Blood everywhere, untraceable DNA, signs of struggle. I saw something fleeing the scene that night, too — more like *flying* the scene — but no one ever believed me. Case went cold, stayed unsolved, because we never knew whose blood it was, and never found any bodies. Same monster, you think?"

"So you believe me?" Grimmond asked hopefully.

"Ah, but *you* were at the scene tonight," the detective smiled wryly. "Didn't have you to take into account last time. Caught red-handed, if you excuse the morbid pun. Can you prove otherwise?"

Grimmond's mind whirled and tumbled as he tried to think.

"I know it's hard to believe," Grimmond said, "but I *think* whatever did this is the same type of thing that killed my parents."

"You said your parents were missing earlier," the man said, shaking his head. "Now they're dead?"

Detective Tippins took a step toward the bars, his face hardening by the second as he stared.

"Don't you watch television, Grimmond? Your public defender will be here soon, to listen to your story. The first step in all this is getting it straight —"

"I'm not lying! I-I remember now!" Grimmond sputtered, bits of recollection barely forming a mismatched jigsaw in his guilt-ridden mind. "My parents were m-murdered! Just outside Boston Public Garden, almost ten years ago!"

Grimmond didn't know he was crying until he wiped the angry tears from his cheeks.

"My dad was taking us to a cemetery, Grain Silo — or *something* — it was called. We got there, and then…and then they were *murdered*, both my parents! And Eralynn says it never happened, but I know it *had to have happened*. Because where else did they go? I've looked for them for y-years!"

Tsk tsk…lying about the details is getting easier, I guess….

Detective Tippins didn't move a muscle. The flickering fluorescent lights glimmered on his face as he stared at Grimmond in silence. Grimmond wildly hoped for a second that the look in his eye was one of belief, and just maybe, he would let him go free.

"Granary?"

"Huh?" Grimmond sniffed.

"The name of the cemetery," the man said with bated breath. "Was it the *Granary* Cemetery?"

"Oh," Grimmond answered. "Um, that sounds right, actually…how'd you know?"

The expression on Detective Tippins' face was strange. His eyes flicked up to the top of Grimmond's head, and a flash of memory danced across his face. He slowly turned toward the door, at first muttering as he exited, and then shouting at Sergeant Combley to bring him an old file.

The door shut with a snap, and Grimmond slumped onto the edge of the squeaky mattress.

For once, he understood his situation was absolutely real. It was only a matter of time before the police discovered that it was Erik's jacket, traced him back to the Matterson's place where he and Grimmond almost fought, and a hundred witnesses would say that Grimmond was deranged. He buried his face in his hands, hopeless, not noticing how the ceiling lights began to flicker on and off.

Why didn't he just leave the bridge when he had the chance? Why did he get involved at the party at all? Both times he was trying to do the right thing — to help someone he thought was in trouble. But if he knew it was Erik Beese under the bridge, maybe he would have just moved on. He *should* have moved on.

No...for all Erik had done, I never wished that *on him.... I'd never wish that on my worst enemy.*

But now his life-long bully was dead, and Grimmond would be the one to pay for it. He sat up to slam his fists against the mattress, only to find the room had been swallowed in darkness. A familiar chill spread through him like a shockwave, warning him, and he jumped to his feet.

He looked beyond his confinement, through the labyrinth of boxes, feeling the waves of fear emanate from his body.

What the....

His stomach somersaulted when he saw the shimmering ribbons of black mist beneath the glow of the emergency exit. When they began to float through the air toward his cell, his heart momentarily stopped. But just as quickly, the ceiling lights flickered back to life, and the black mist faded away.

Grimmond's eye was drawn to the corner above the storage room door: the red light of the video camera blinked off.

Not good.

He fought the urge to cry out for Detective Tippins. What if this was the same thing from the park, now coming for him?

He counted the seconds, knowing the lights would go out again. But before any bulb could flicker, the black mist materialized in the shadows just beyond the edge of the boxes, a gasping and squelching coming from within.

The failing fluorescent lights flickered in rapid succession like a strobe, and in each split second of darkness, the mist approached the edge of the bars. A hollow series of popping bulbs then resounded, and the room went completely black.

Grimmond's vision changed expectedly when his heart revved up like a jet engine. The shadows of the cell, boxes and creature before him sharpened into focus. Impossibly as it was beneath the bridge, he could see through the darkness, and looked upon a wispy body, like a murky cloud of silt disturbed at the bottom of a lake.

A face within the shimmering mist was charred black, with overlapping folds of skin to jitter along with its shaky movements. Slimy optic nerves whipped out from each eye socket, latching onto two bloodshot eyes. Its gaping mouth had hardly any lips to hide its black teeth, or the third eyeball embedded on a long purple tongue.

Grimmond caught his breath, trying to smash his brain with his hands.

"You're not real, you're *not* real —"

"Yes, yes," a feminine voice said in a hoarse whisper, "if one tells themself enough — *slurp* — it must be true! But that has never really worked for one such as yourself, has it?"

The unnerving voice crept into Grimmond's ears, squelching and wet, like a boot being tugged out of mud. He covered his ears, hoping futilely that the jail cell bars would stop its approach.

"Stop!" Grimmond begged. "D-don't come any closer!"

With the amused tut-tutting of an old woman, the shadowy creature walked through the bars of his cell and raked a long, blackened finger across his brow. It felt like ice that had caught fire, stunk like fish and was even slimier than it looked. Grimmond moved to recoil, but stopped himself, wishing for something he'd never thought possible: he *wanted* to feel the creature. To *know* it was real.

A sensation coursed through his body at the creature's touch, his terror filling him with an odd certainty.

"You're…you're r-really here, aren't you…?" Grimmond said, trying to keep his heart from exploding. "B-but before tonight, nothing talked to me! Not one of my hallucina—"

"Ach!" the thing spat loudly. "Enough with talk of hallucinations already — *slurp* — your borrowed time is nearly up, boy, along with your time to play make believe — *squelch* — acting as if a Nightmare can be wished away!"

The thing laughed hideously, black teeth chattering along with the wild eyes protruding from their sockets and whipping about. She went on, her mouth occasionally slurping and squelching for air between sentences.

"Listen well, for someone thought you should know: your seventy sevens have passed. You have less than an hour — *slurp* — the Ending comes tonight!"

Grimmond's mind churned like butter.

"The Ending," he said slowly. "In an hour."

He didn't understand, but the sense he'd had the entire night of time running out — the sense of urgency — came back in a flood. Was that what this thing was talking about? He recalled the statue mentioning 'the Ending' on the Esplanade, as if it was something understood as more than just a word. Something more foreboding than the completion of a novel, or road under construction.

"What are you?" Grimmond asked, his curiosity getting the better of his pounding heart.

"I?" it said in its sucking voice. "I am a humble Nightmare — *squelch* — some call me Kremaya. Others call me the Boogey Man, though I am not he — *slurp* — I came to warn you! Leave now, or you will be worse than dead within the hour."

Grimmond swallowed down his disgust at the stench filling his pores.

"Tell me what the Ending is, first, then…maybe I can leave…."

"The Ending is sent, and the Ending comes! And if the Ending succeeds — *slurp* — you are finished, and emptiness follows — *squelch* — then darkness. Then death. For *all.*"

To Grimmond's great surprise, the cell door swung open before him. But he didn't make a move. Kremaya's shimmering ribbons of black mist shuddered in agitation, and the eye on her tongue narrowed at him.

"The clock ticks — *slurp* — and seventy sevens is up! You must flee — *squelch* — FLEE to the hollow, where Endings won't follow. And there you will see — *slurp* — what you choose to be!"

"I — I can't just run out of here ——" Grimmond protested.

"You will pay for the boy in the park!" she spat loudly, coming close enough for her stinking mouth to be only a few inches from Grimmond's. "Do you not see? They think you ate him — *slurp* — but don't worry, I know it wasn't you."

Grimmond didn't ask how she knew, but decided he didn't see any bits of Erik caught in her teeth. He did feel that it was costing her great effort to not take a chunk out of his face.

"What does 'seventy sevens' mean?" Grimmond asked.

"Ach!" Kremaya hissed through the black ooze of her teeth, beginning to talk faster and with more urgency as her dripping eyeballs stared at him. "Days, weeks, years — *slurp* — open your ears! Nine full years have gone, no more may come —

squelch — not until the veil between the worlds is undone — *slurp* — sew, sew, sew it up good!"

"I-I don't know what that means!" Grimmond whispered desperately. "What are you *talking* about?"

One of Kremaya's optic nerves suddenly elongated, wrapping around his neck. It pushed him back toward the wall as her whispered tone grew even more manic.

"Whether lock or key — *SLURP* — you must choose to be! Ajar becomes rift, rift tears to open — *SQUELCH* — shut the door, seal its edges — *SLURP* — follow the heart unto the hedges!"

The slimy nerve pulsed around Grimmond's throat as she spoke. The other two eyeballs then came right before his face as she calmly went on.

"Are you scared, child?" she laughed wickedly. "Afraid of old — *slurp* — Kremaya? Fear is key to all, you know, but keys turn *two* ways. Lock the door to save — *squelch* — or open the darkest days. You must choose! Open the door or forever close it — *slurp* — sew, sew, sew it up GOOD!"

"W-what," Grimmond sputtered, hands futilely grasping at his throat, "what d-door?"

Kremaya threw him against the iron bars next, the folding skin of her face laughing as she floated around the cell, hideously singing. Grimmond could barely breathe, struggling against the strangling nerve.

"*ACH!*" she spat again. "If the Ending finds you before the door is sealed — *slurp* — then all is lost and the world is dead! If the Ending finds you — *SQUELCH* — you will be forced to watch your worst fear play out before your eyes. You will die watching your worst nightmare unfold — *slurp* — someone thought you should know."

Kremaya released him and Grimmond fell to his knees, gasping as she continued.

"No time — *SLURP* — make up your mind, already! Flee to the Hollow, flee the Ending or die — *SQUELCH* — find the key, shut the door, seal it up or don't!"

Grimmond looked to the camera with its recording light still off. His heart raced, and he was barely able to keep his redlined flight response in check.

"Why are you helping me escape?" he asked, massaging his throat.

"I already said — *slurp* — someone thought you should know. Come!"

The voices of officers reached Grimmond as they passed outside the door of the storage room. Kremaya watched Grimmond, but he didn't cry out, didn't call for help or say that an insanely gasping Nightmare was in his cell, talking about sealing doors to avoid the end of the world.

Grimmond stood up, then took a step toward Kremaya.

"Come!" she called.

Checking the camera one final time, Grimmond raced after Kremaya's mist through the black labyrinth of stacked boxes, all the way to the emergency exit. Before he could warn her, she pushed open the door — and nothing happened. Grimmond noticed the ribbons of thick mist obscuring the alarm on the door. He peeked his head through to see if the coast was clear, and stepped into the alley.

"Your sixteenth birthday approaches — *slurp* — I suggest you hurry, Grimmond Scylent."

Without another word, the black mist and Kremaya faded back into the shadows.

Grimmond started running.

SEEING IS BELIEVING

The shock of escaping the police station took a few seconds to process, and was quickly replaced by a suffocating fear. What had Grimmond just done? And what exactly was that *thing* that helped him?

A Nightmare, it called itself.

Knowing he would shortly be discovered if he didn't move quickly, he stopped only to turn his filthy, blood-stained shirt inside out, and ran toward the subway. He didn't know what time it was, and was rue to discover that the nearby Orange Line had stopped running. A rideshare couldn't be scheduled, since his phone was taken by the police, nor did he have any money for a taxi. Above it all, Kremaya's words rang out in his mind:

'You have less than an hour — slurp *— the Ending comes tonight!'*

Grimmond breathed heavily, trying to calm himself. He turned south and took off at a run. The main road he could follow almost all the way home, he knew, and he *had* to hurry — no matter the danger to his heart. Its rate quickly picked up with his pumping arms and legs, and the night came alive.

Lines of shadow sharpened to dark green, the sky became purple, and faces turned gray in the crowded bar patios. Scattered among them all were glowing heads and bodies — like Grimmond had been seeing all night — dribbling or darting in and out of the green shadows. Grimmond marveled at how the gray faces seemed to be aware of nothing, but he ran all the harder when the glowing things began to notice him.

Could all of this be real?

The Boxford neighborhood, where Grimmond lived, was reached without further incident. He stumbled up the stairs to his house, tried to catch his breath before going in, then made the mistake of looking into the window of the adjacent building. A pair of burning red eyes looked back at him balefully, as if awaiting something. Counting down.

Grimmond retrieved the hidden key to his front door and stole inside. He shut his eyes and leaned forward, hands on his knees.

"I *thought* I heard you come in."

Grimmond nearly jumped out of his skin as his godmother peeked her head from the kitchen, holding a steaming mug of coffee.

"And I thought you'd be at work!" Grimmond gasped, staggering after her.

"Would I miss making your breakfast birthday cake like I do every year? *Please*," she replied, resuming her icing of Grimmond's round cake. "I took the night off. I thought you were going to the movies, anyway. Where's Patrick? Did you have a good time at the party —"

"Eralynn," Grimmond interrupted, still out of breath, "there's something I have to tell you."

"All right," she said without looking up. "What's up? I've got a fresh pot of coffee on. You might like it if you try it — you never know."

Grimmond leaned against the wall, listening to his godmother hum to a song on her phone. With his heart slowing down, he looked into her face and was calmed to see the hard lines that formed it. As usual, her attractive cheeks and eyes were far more tired than those of a woman in her early thirties should be. Grimmond always felt worse, knowing it was because of him.

"Voila!" she said, flicking her brown braid over her shoulder as she placed the last candle in the cake. "Now, where to start lighting them?"

"Eralynn," Grimmond said more urgently, stepping up to the counter, "we have to leave. Now."

"Where to? You're sixteen years old in twenty minutes! We can finally celebrate right on time for once."

She glanced up, taking a good look at his red face and blood-stained clothing at last. Her eyelids flew wide.

"Grimmond — where have you been?" she asked, rushing over. *"What happened?"*

"I just left the police station...in a manner of speaking...."

Grimmond took a deep breath, then allowed the events and emotions of the night to erupt.

"It all started when I got to the party, and it was *too* loud, and my hallucinations came on suddenly, and they were worse than they've *ever been* before — I know I should have just left as soon as I felt them start —"

"Grimmond, *please*, slow down —"

"But there was this girl I liked, so I wanted to stay and talk to her, but then I saw her kissing Erik, and we almost fought until Patrick told him and the *whole* school I take crazy pills —"

"Erik *Beese*?" Eralynn asked. "The bully from school?"

"Yeah, that's the one," Grimmond huffed. "Only, you don't have to worry about him anymore, because he's dead —"

"WHAT?" Eralynn bellowed. "DEAD? What do you mean, *dead*?"

"I mean, I watched him get *eaten* in the park. Then the cops came and arrested me, thinking that *I* had something to do with it! I didn't call you because my phone was dead and I thought you were at work —"

"YOU SHOULD HAVE CALLED!" Eralynn hollered, her face aghast.

"I know!" Grimmond yelled. "But there's more to it than just that!"

Eralynn held up her hands, struggling to find her next words.

"Wait, wait…so the police just *let you go* after all that?"

"No," Grimmond answered with trepidation, hit anew with the magnitude of the crime he'd now officially committed. "Something helped me escape — she called herself Kremaya. I thought it was just another hallucination at first…but she helped me *get out* of the jail cell, and then through the emergency exit without being seen! She said she was, uh — a *Nightmare*. She was real, Eralynn, I know it."

Eralynn's face hardened strangely as she lowered her arms, her fists discreetly clenched. Her voice deepened as she took a step forward.

"And? Why would she do that? Why did a Nightmare help you?"

Grimmond resisted the urge to back away from his godmother's menacing stance, the like of which he'd never seen in their years together.

"Because," Grimmond continued. "She said my borrowed time was up, and that I had less than an hour before the Ending came — whatever that means. Not the first time I heard that tonight, either. She kept telling me to flee to 'the Hollow', but I only fled the precinct because I didn't know what the police were going to do with me! I didn't do *anything* to Erik — you have to believe me!"

"*More than one* Nightmare warned you the Ending was coming tonight?" Eralynn asked dangerously. "Did this *Kremaya* say anything else?"

"Um…she said that *seventy sevens* is up, and if the Ending succeeds, I'm finished. Then she said something about sewing up the veil between the worlds, and I have to choose between being a lock or a key for some door. She was kind of crazy, I think…."

SHE'S *crazy? Do you hear yourself?*

For someone who had downplayed every hallucination Grimmond had ever had, telling him they weren't real, Grimmond found his godmother to be taking it all in stride. He thought he'd have to beg her to believe him, to plead until his face was blue. But naming the Nightmare as he had named it, with no doubts or sideways glances at all: Grimmond sensed that Eralynn knew something he didn't.

Her face became hard like dry plaster, her eyes distant and cold. She picked up her phone and dialed a number. Grimmond was certain she was calling the men in white coats to come and collect him.

"I was wrong," she said quickly. "It's tonight — seventy sevens *did* mean nine years and five months. They killed a boy from school to get to Grimmond. We have to get out of here, *right now*. There's less than twenty minutes."

Eralynn hung up the phone, stuffed it in her pocket and looked up at Grimmond with a blank stare.

"Go pack your suitcase and backpack with as much as you can fit, quick as you can."

Grimmond stared back. What just happened?

"Eralynn? Who was that?"

"There's no time to explain…do as I say, and hurry."

She rushed out of the kitchen, but Grimmond followed after her.

"I don't understand what's going on! Talk to me!"

Eralynn stopped at her bedroom door and spun around to grab him by the shoulders. She shut her eyes hard, exhaling sharply as she spoke.

"Grimmond, you *must listen* carefully," she said weakly. "You're *not* crazy. The pills you took tonight — I never wanted you to have them, because...then you'd find out they don't work for people like us...."

Grimmond stared, frozen, as she squeezed his shoulders tighter.

"What you always see — your hallucinations — they're *not* just in your head like I always told you. They're called Nightmares, like Kremaya was. And Nightmares can be very, very dangerous. I fight them, like your parents used to fight them...."

Grimmond swallowed hard, soaking up the words like a few drops of water on a large and very dry sponge — it simply wasn't enough. He began to sputter.

"You're saying that I'm...I'm *not*...I've *never been* crazy? My parents' death — all of it's real? And you actually *fight* these things?"

"Yes," she released a deep breath. "All of it, yes. Nightmares are *real*. And I'm a Nightmarist — someone who's trained to fight them."

"A *what* —"

"I'm sorry I had to lie for so long, Grimmond. But please, trust me now. We need to go!"

Grimmond followed her into her room as she wildly yanked a suitcase from the closet.

"It's all starting to make sense," she spoke almost to herself. "The Nightmares have been worse than ever this summer...they've been stirring, waiting for the bargain of seventy sevens to be up...we have to get to Stanchions Hollow where the rest of the Nightmarists are —"

"Stanchions Hollow?" Grimmond blurted out. "Is that the place where that *thing* — Kremaya — told me to go?"

"Grimmond — we have to leave before the Ending comes for you. If it's the same thing that killed your parents…well, suffice it to say we're no match for it. I've never fought anything like it before, and I couldn't even touch it back then. There's no time to explain more, we *must* hurry —"

A loud knocking rapped on the front door.

Eralynn stiffened like a warrior, reached into her pocket, and slipped a set of sparkling brass knuckles on her right hand. Then she ran to her bedroom window and ripped away the long curtain rod, flinging the rings off the open end. Grimmond realized that it wasn't a normal curtain rod at all, but a long pole with a blade on the end.

Before he could stop or help her, she crept silently to the front door, stood to the side, and threw it open. Grimmond's stomach leapt at the sight of the stranger on the other side, but Eralynn relaxed.

"Liam!" she exclaimed with relief. "How on *earth* did you get here so fast?"

On the stoop stood a tall man with dark, silvering hair, though he didn't look much older than Grimmond's godmother. Grimmond got the impression that she stopped herself from embracing the man as she lowered her weapon.

"Eralynn," the man said, relief likewise spreading over his face as he stepped inside. "Thank goodness you're both still safe. We'd already arrived when you called. Coach Maurs has a team on your roof, and another atop the old tower across the street. The Dread Map alerted us earlier that something was coming — do you know anything about it?"

Eralynn nodded and shut the door, turning her body toward Grimmond.

"It's the same thing as that night, all those years ago, Liam. It's called an 'Ending', fittingly enough…several Nightmares warned Grimmond themselves about it tonight. One of them named Kremaya helped him break out of jail, warning him to flee to Stanchions Hollow."

"*Kremaya?* But who could send…." he trailed off, seeing the severe look on Eralynn's face. "Never heard of a Nightmare named Kremaya before. Nevertheless, fill me in on the rest as we drive. Grab your things. We'll take Stanchions' transportation, since you two will shortly be fugitives —"

"HOLD IT!" Grimmond yelled, stomping his foot and throwing up an arm. "I'm not going ANYWHERE until I find out what the heck is going on here!"

"Stay calm, Grimmond," Eralynn warned. "Whenever your adrenaline starts pumping too hard, you see the Nightmares most clearly, and we need you sober-minded right now. It's the same with all Nightmarists. There…there's no hole in your heart, Grimmond…."

"*WHAT?*" he roared.

"I did what I must to protect you — to keep you from seeing clearly! Just get your bags, throw some stuff in them you don't want to lose, and come on. We'll never see this house again."

"I just told you, I'm not going *anywhere* until I get some real answers!"

Liam appraised him a moment, his stoic demeanor tested at Grimmond's belligerence. The man took a step toward him, looking ready to clobber Grimmond on the head as soon as shake his hand.

"Please," Grimmond tried again, head spinning, "just tell me why the Ending wants me."

"We don't know," Eralynn said dejectedly. "But something about your parents made it worthwhile for them to be dead, and that same worth likely applies to you."

Grimmond struggled to speak, hearing his godmother openly talk of his parent's death.

"Did it only kill them because they were like you? Nightmarists?"

The two adults exchanged a dark look, until Eralynn turned away, her eyes glistening.

"Grimmond," Liam started, "there's something you must know. Your mother, she —"

"Was an amazingly brave woman," Eralynn finished pointedly, shooting a furtive glance at Liam. "You were protected from the Nightmares for over nine years, Grimmond, by a bargain she struck for you. But now that it's over, they won't torment you anymore — they'll just kill you."

Liam cleared his throat, but Grimmond suspected that's not what the man wanted to tell him.

What was he about to say? What must I know?

"Yes...yes, of course," Liam stuttered, looking between Eralynn and Grimmond. "You are right, Eralynn."

"I pack faster," she said. "I'll be back with our bags in less than five minutes."

Liam averted his eyes as Eralynn left, but then turned back to Grimmond.

"Your godmother was very close with both of your parents," he said slowly. "Your father, Christopher Errandi, was the last descendant of those who created the key and the door to seal the Nightmayr Realm. He was the last — prior to *your* birth, that is. He lived at Stanchions once, he and your mother both. They learned to fight as Nightmarists, as Eralynn and myself did."

Grimmond remained quiet, staring up at the man.

"My name is Liam Stawlart. I run things at Stanchions Hollow, as much as one man can, and I offer you the opportunity to save yourself. Join us at the Hollow, and learn to fight your fears."

"Join you?" Grimmond asked. "But I don't even know what the Hollow is!"

"It is a proving grounds of sorts, among other things," he began darkly. "You know already — most people don't believe things are hiding in the dark. But I tell you, *some* know better. They've accepted their fears, and grown up fighting them.

"Do you wish to be rid of your waking Nightmares, Grimmond? To do something besides cower behind medicine and the backs of your hands? Forget about Boston — come with us and learn to fight."

A glimmer of hope started in Grimmond, hearing something he'd wanted deeply for most of his life.

"Are you saying that the Hollow can get rid of my hallucinations?" he asked. "I mean, the *Nightmares* I see?"

"We can show you how to deal with them properly, yes. They've grown bold recently, and I fear the worst — that something's about to happen, and that it might be taking place already. They haven't just been attacking people who are asleep, but *those who are awake*. Soon, Nightmares won't only be a thing of bad dreams — they will turn the whole world toward darkness. The Dreamers will be in turmoil —"

"Dreamers?"

"People who've from an early age convinced themselves that Nightmares aren't real. Average people, like your friends, who can't see them anymore. Not like we Nightmarists do —"

"You see the Nightmares, too?"

"Yes," he answered. "A single creature of the Nightmayr Realm, when manifested in our world, looks the same to every Nightmarist."

Questions began to pile up in Grimmond's mind faster than he could ask them.

"But…where do they come from?"

"Bad dreams, of course: fears, phobias, hatred, memories of love and loss — these nightmares of humankind fester in the Nightmayr Realm, until they're powerful enough to manifest themselves *here*. They slip back into our world, through cracks in either the veil, or the door made by your father's ancestors.

"The door is shut still, and, though it was lost after being made, there's only a single doorknob, and on our side only. That way, the Dark Naught trapped within the Nightmayr Realm can never find its way out…."

Grimmond thought back to Kremaya's words in his jail cell, and started to think that she wasn't so crazy after all.

'Shut the door, seal its edges — SLURP — *follow the heart unto the hedges!'*

"Are — are you sure it's still shut?" Grimmond asked. "Because I've seen some pretty terrible things tonight —"

"Yes, we are sure it is shut, for now. But think of it as a door made of thin wood, and the cracks in it likewise spread through the veil that separates our worlds. We dare not try to repair either, for fear of making things worse. But the cracks are showing up more often, and growing bigger, though we don't understand how."

Grimmond thought for a moment, his curiosity again getting the better of him.

"You said my ancestors made a *key*, too," he said. "Is the door unlocked? Why not just guard it all the time?"

"We do not know the location of the door, *or* where the key is, Grimmond," Liam explained. "But the key is said to be the cypher, the *clue* that can correctly reseal the door. We are always searching for them both, to seal the Nightmayr Realm for good. Come to Stanchions and prove yourself — prove that you can face the Nightmares. You may help us in our search."

Grimmond started to sputter in protest.

"I can't just…just…."

"Just leave?" Eralynn interjected with a growl as she reentered the room with several bags. "Who are you worried about — Patrick? He's an idiot, telling people you're crazy. And the Ending is after *you*, not him. Leaving would be the safest thing for him."

Grimmond raised his hands, as if soon to be betrayed.

"And how do I know you're both not just playing along with me?" Grimmond asked. "Like you're not about to haul me off to some psych ward?"

"Stanchions Hollow is not a mental institution —"

"Well," Liam let out a bark of laughter, "in a manner of speaking. It holds no one against their will, at least. There, you can decide for yourself what you want to do, but we must hurry if we are to give you that chance."

"Decide what?" Grimmond asked, his willpower waning.

"Whether you'll help us fight the Nightmares that are getting worse," Eralynn said quickly, "before that Ending catches up to you. You saw tonight with Beese — the Nightmares are far more than bad dreams anymore, Grimmond. And anyways, you're wanted for murder, so unless you plan on turning yourself in —"

A loud, beastly roar sounded just outside the front door, causing Grimmond to jump.

"That'll be Coach Maurs," Liam said anxiously. "Time to go!"

Eralynn picked up her bags, opened the door, and hurried down the steps after Liam. With only a moment's hesitation, Grimmond picked up his own bags and raced after them.

At the edge of the sidewalk was a shimmering black car. The symbol of a double, overlaid "R-R" was emblazoned on the hubcap of each tire, and a small silvery figure rested on the hood, cloak billowing behind it like tiny wings. Liam grabbed the two door handles, opening them outward like an old-timey gangster car.

Eralynn threw her bag in the trunk, and then twisted her curtain-rod weapon. With a smooth sliding noise, it retracted to a third of its size and she placed it beneath her seat.

"*Get in*, Grimmond," she commanded.

"Wait, Eralynn."

"Liam, there's no time!"

"This must be the boy's decision," he replied, turning to Grimmond. "I need to hear *him* say it. What'll it be, Grimmond? Just say the haunted words. You may or may not regret them for the rest of your life."

Grimmond thought of the last few hours: of Patrick's drunken behavior, the events on the Esplanade, and the music that stirred memories of the worst night of his life. He thought of holding Erik Beese's arm and the thing that ate him, getting arrested, and Kremaya helping him escape from his jail cell. But his eventful night began to cloud with confusion and betrayal.

He looked at his godmother in the front seat, knowing she'd lied to him his entire life. Grimmond had been petrified the last ten years when he thought Nightmares were only *hallucinations* — was the truth better, or worse?

If I go, could I finally be done with all this?

"Last chance, Grimmond," Liam said. "Make your decision."

From inside the car, a police scanner buzzed to life, calling out Grimmond's description and home address. Grimmond took one last look at the house and neighborhood around him, then turned back to Liam.

"Okay," he breathed. "Let's go."

Grimmond hopped in the car and strapped in, momentarily marveling at the sleek, starlit interior as the doors slammed shut by themselves. He was thrown backwards as the tires peeled away from the curb, but was only truly alarmed when a large head popped up on the dashboard. Casting a dim purple glow, with fuzzy white hair and two shining, golden eyes, Grimmond thought of Ebenezer's doorknocker from *A Christmas Carol*.

"Relax, Grimmond," Eralynn said, turning on softly playing music.

Grimmond swooned beneath the little lights in the ceiling above him, the classical music calming him in the same way the orchestra at the Hatch Memorial Shell had earlier that night. He tried to bring back the memory of his parents once again, but was hardly able before drifting off to sleep.

"Ernst," Liam said quietly to the floating head, "fade the Phantom to ethereal mode, but avoid the police anyway. Let's get these two home."

STANCHIONS HOLLOW

L ook out, Grimmond," Eralynn whispered.

Grimmond bolted upright from an uneasy sleep.

"Who's there?" he said, looking wildly through the windshield.

In the dream from which Eralynn just roused him, the police had finally found them, and were surrounding the vehicle. Hazily, Grimmond waited for the flashlights to shine through the windows.

"I said, look outside. You don't want to miss this."

Grimmond rubbed his eyes, but nothing except the vehicle's bright headlights burned beyond the windshield. The floating head of Ernst had its eyes closed on the dashboard, concentrating hard on something, and Grimmond looked past its ear to the clock. It was just after four in the morning.

"Where are we?" Grimmond asked, turning back to the thick fog clouding the windows.

"Somewhere between Maine and New Hampshire," Eralynn answered. "Never quite figured it out, myself."

"Almost there, now," Liam said. "Ernst will have us through in another few moments."

"Is this taking longer than usual?" Eralynn asked. "Or do I not remember well?"

"Your memory is fine," the man answered. "The defenses and veil have been thickened since early summer, when fighting intensified. A bit more mist for the borders, mainly, though Ernst and the others still get through it just fine."

Grimmond understood what that meant when the fog outside the windows began to lessen. A gnarled forest suffocated the car with foliage as it sped along a downward-sloping driveway. Grimmond knew Liam couldn't have seen clearly enough to *not* crash, and wondered if the floating head was somehow helping to drive the car.

Ernst opened his eyes, and spoke in the wispy voice of a ghost-butler.

"Arriving, Lord Stawlart."

Lord Stawlart? Grimmond wondered. *Did I miss something?*

"Thank you, Ernst," Liam replied.

Before Grimmond could question the man's title, the forest thinned outside the window. Then, the fog lifted completely, and Grimmond's mouth dropped open. Rising from the sea of darkness, masses of distant trees and colored shadows illuminated against the night, there stood something like a small city.

The Phantom stopped along a wall of trees, growing so closely they might have been a fence. Each passenger door then opened by itself, and Grimmond slowly followed after Liam and Eralynn, his head bobbing like a toy at the sight before him. He turned around when the Phantom slammed its doors shut, honked its goodbye, and drove away into the woods.

"Li — *uh*, Lord Stawlart — the car...."

"Don't worry about your things, Ernst will gather them for you."

Oh, okay, no big deal...the floating head will bring my bags in.

Grimmond looked between the gaps in the trees to see the glowing center of the city, prickling with spindly towers and thick stone walls.

"Is that —" Grimmond began in a small voice, "is that supposed to be a castle, or a tree house?"

"That," Liam answered, "is what we call the Hovel."

"Hovel?" Grimmond said incredulously. "I thought a hovel was like, a tiny, run-down shack."

"You can decide for yourself," Liam went on. "Come — we'll scrounge up someone to give you a better tour. Open the gate, please."

Grimmond thought Liam was speaking to him at first, until he followed his voice and raised his eyes skyward. On a pedestal next to a black iron gate was a towering creature, sitting stiffly and looking down menacingly as it guarded the entrance to the Hollow. Grimmond thought it might have been a small dragon, or maybe a bear with wings.

He stepped backward, his heart rate instinctively picking up. Eralynn tried to lay a hand on his shoulder, but Grimmond gruffly shoved it away.

"Remember, we can see him, too," she said slowly, in a slightly hurt voice. "That's one of the Gatekeepers. He's a Nightmare, like Ernst. There's a lot you'll quickly have to learn, but know that not *all* Nightmares are against us. Some are on our side, and those at Stanchions Hollow have aided us since the beginning...."

Grimmond didn't answer as the tall gate swung open, and Liam guided the trio to a winding, barely visible path. Grimmond noticed that it was dimly lit by dozens of glowing black and orange toads, chirping *'Kill-it, Kill-it'* as they sparkled. He followed closely, looking up to the starlit sky that slowly changed from black to purple, and checked that his pulse was still steady.

"Usually, we'd just catch a flight from here," Liam said casually. "But a walk might do you good, to take the entire Hollow in for your first look. I suppose we really could use a transport though, wouldn't have to take the bridge across the Bottomless Chasm —"

"It's been so long," Eralynn muttered as they walked. "The Hollow looks quiet."

"But, of course," he replied. "Business as usual inside, though — full swing at this hour, in fact. We must be awake when the Nightmares are at their worst."

The toads' chirping became a less aggressive 'Watch-it, Watch-it' as the trio reached a stony descent in the path. To Grimmond the glowing Hollow looked to be made of valleys, hills, and sheer cliffs down to nothing. Yet some parts were covered in a darkness that his adjusted eyes couldn't pierce through.

"See that off to the right?"

Eralynn pointed to a string of rickety-looking houses in one of the shallow valleys.

"That's Narcoleptic Row, the first of the four Wards. To the left — the cliff face and drop off, glinting purple — is Hollow Dwell. You can't see Marrow Mansion from this angle, as it's on the other side, but the tallest tower, just there, is called Steeple Spike. Classes are mostly within the Hovel, but your room will be in one of the four Wards."

"To live in?" Grimmond asked, mustering as much venom as possible. "Which one were you?"

"Well, there actually used to be a *fifth* Ward, on the lake," she answered, "but it's been decommissioned, since…well, it's just been gone a while."

Grimmond chose not to press her avoidant answer, his anger toward her still swelling. He focused anew on just how large the Hollow was, something he hadn't appreciated from the backseat of the Phantom, when it only looked like an oversized oil lamp. The path flattened and the chirping toads retreated, and Grimmond saw the central, stone-and-glass Hovel in the heart of the Hollow.

It might have occupied many city blocks, with a dozen jagged towers reaching into the lowest clouds. Shimmering blue torches burned beside doors so big that the Gatekeeper could stand inside them, and strange creatures Grimmond couldn't make out crept atop its stone walls, eyes shining like purple and green flashlights.

Why am I still seeing like this? My heart rate isn't up —

"Careful, there!" Liam warned, grabbing Grimmond's arm.

Startled, Grimmond looked down to see nothing but black air. In his stupor, he had come several inches from falling off the edge of a bridge that spanned the wide gap to the Hovel doors.

"Thank you," Grimmond exhaled with relief, stepping away from the bridge's edge. "Is there water down there, at least? I can't tell."

"If there is, I imagine it's not *fresh* water," Liam replied. "But I wouldn't say that to what might be down there. The bottom-dwellers probably kill anything that falls in, anyway — if the fall itself doesn't, that is. Humans have never gone down and come back. Only the Nightmares have."

Grimmond narrowed his eyes as a chill ran up his spine, and voiced his uncomfortable thought.

"How do you know nobody's ever come back?"

"Since the last person who fell in never did," Liam answered quietly.

"You didn't go down and look for them?" Grimmond asked with incredulity.

"We did, of course," the man explained, "but it's called the Bottomless Chasm for a reason. A team flew in, a few miles down, but still they didn't find the bottom, so they called it and resurfaced. We've considered putting up a railing since then, but the bridge was made for defense, so just mind your step! Besides, most of us usually fly, that being much faster."

Grimmond wondered what all the talk about flying was, and whether Lord Stawlart had a fleet of private helicopters. But when he looked up to one of the high towers, he saw several wide-winged creatures landing.

"Come," Liam said, walking forward as the doors opened.

Just stay calm, Grimmond thought, releasing his breath. *My lying godmother knows this place, at least.*

The Hovel was even larger than guessed beyond the doors. Grimmond thought it smelled like earth, clean water, and strong coffee. Immense tree trunks lined the walls, and some the middle of the floor, growing all the way up to the ceiling. Grimmond thought they were whispering as he walked by, but when he whipped his head to the left and saw a carven face in a dark gray trunk, he was *sure* that they were.

The face was there only a moment before it turned away, giggled quietly, and muttered to the next tree in line. Soon, the entranceway was filled with harsh whispering, as the gray or black skin of every tree stretched and contorted in Grimmond's direction. He jumped wildly when a branch slithered down from the ceiling to caress his neck.

Eralynn noticed and swatted it away.

"I always *hated* the Sentrees," she said cautiously to Grimmond. "Give them a good smack every time you pass, else they'll walk all over you."

Grimmond was more than just nervous or unsettled — after seeing murderous toads, glowing eyes atop the Hovel walls, and trees within having faces to whisper, he didn't know what to expect. Despite his anger, he stuck close to Eralynn and Liam when people were finally seen in a hall past the entranceway, thronging and shouting around a long, semi-circular countertop.

Anxious Canine was engraved into the gray stone wall, and Grimmond was horrified to see a small black dog suspended by strings above the cash register. Its eyes glowed blue, and it shook and snarled incessantly at the customers. But when a heckling blue orb of light ejected from it, the dog's animation faded, and Grimmond realized it wasn't alive at all.

High-school-aged teenagers jogged to work the knobs and levers of the shiny espresso machines. Several greenish-brown creatures, as tall as Grimmond's chest, bounced and snapped among them. Large, floppy ears slapped around their cruel faces, and dozens of sharp teeth rested above their pointy chins. Grimmond's ear was drawn to one of the louder conversations among them at the countertop.

"You're not LISTENING, Zolgo!" yelled a girl.

"Oh, I'm listening!" shouted the pointy-chinned barista in return, its New York accent as thick as its neck. "I'm just callin' you a liar while I'm at it!"

The girl's skin was pale compared to her skin-tight jeans, and a glittering pink hairpin in the shape of a skull kept a long plait behind her ears. Grimmond looked harder at the back of her shirt, where *'Why die, when I can kill you?'* was spelled out in sequins.

"LOOK, it was cheaper yesterday and you know it! You can't just raise prices overnight! I've got Scringoll in five minutes, Zolgo — now give it up or I'll sick the whole team on you!"

"Oh-ho! You want to make something of it, lipstick?"

The girl clenched her fists and pounded the countertop.

"I *hate* lipstick," she said venomously, reaching for the to-go cup that Zolgo was keeping out of reach. "Almost as much as I hate you! Now *give me my coffee*, you little imp!"

The barista hopped up onto the counter, spread its stubby wings, and extended its claws. Grimmond's neck hairs bristled at the creature's teeth, dripping with saliva.

"TAKE IT BACK! You think coconut milk grows on trees?" roared Zolgo, holding up the incorrect number of claws as he proceeded to count. "That's *three* Skiefs and *seven* Shards, and you'll like it! Go cry to mommy if you don't have the Marrow, and have her up your allowance for next week!"

The girl grabbed onto the barista's hairy legs and yanked him off the counter, suddenly looking more menacing than he did.

"*So help me*, Zolgo, I will Lull you so far past oblivion that you won't remember what coffee ever tasted like!"

"W-why, Viana," Zolgo laughed nervously, "you know I was only messin' with you, right? Of course it's only three Skiefs and two Shards! W-wait! I meant ONLY THREE Skiefs today — house special!"

Zolgo yipped as Viana threw him back across the counter and snatched her drink.

"Thanks, Zolgo!" she smiled pleasantly, handing him three oblong notes of what looked like paper. "See you tomorrow?"

"'Course, sweetheart," Zolgo answered, baring his glistening teeth and taking the yellowish bills. "Next in line!"

The girl hurried off down a corridor, taking a long swig of her drink as the crowd's outcries for coffee were renewed. Not understanding what the creature was, or the seemingly odd denominations of money that were paid, Grimmond was dumbfounded at the exchange. The girl and barista were either best friends, or had plans to kill each other tomorrow.

Grimmond didn't realize he was still staring, until Zolgo met his eyes and flew over, two cups in hand.

"Lord Stawlart! And — *bless my beans* — Eralynn Wintle! You've grown, missy!"

Zolgo handed over the two drinks to the adults, hideously grinning ear to ear as he hugged Eralynn around the middle. He released her to turn to Grimmond.

"What about you, punk?" he asked with a growl. "You like coffee, of course."

It was more of a challenge than a question, and Grimmond didn't dare argue.

"Grimmond, this is my friend Zolgo," Eralynn laughed. "Nobody beats his coffee in the city, and he's the best Grinds-Gremlin we've got at the Hollow."

"It's *Gar*-gremlin!" Zolgo admonished. "Like Gar-*goyle*, remember? Do we have to do this every time?"

"What's a Gargremlin, exactly?" Grimmond asked uneasily.

He stiffened like a board as Zolgo rose to his tiptoes, coming within inches of his face.

"I'm a Gargremlin, *exactly*," Zolgo said through stale coffee breath, jabbing a long claw at Grimmond's chest, "and I've got the best bean water around."

"Yep," Grimmond gulped, "got it."

"BUT," the Gargremlin pulled him in, going on in a poorly feigned whisper, "if you *do* need anything else, I've been known to trade in chai *and* foreign drinks. All for the friends and family discount, of course, you being the Errandi boy."

Grimmond tried to hide his shock at the Gargremlin's immediate recognition.

"It's *Scylent*, actually," Grimmond said timidly. "My name's Grimmond Scylent."

Zolgo scratched his pointy chin, then raised a claw to his long nose and tapped it twice.

"Of course it is! My mistake!"

"It's, uh, nice to meet you, Zolgo...."

"No, it isn't, but don't worry. I'll bet you your first cup that I'm one of the prettier things you'll see over the next few days! See you 'round, kid!"

Zolgo flew back to the counter, and Liam clapped a hand on Grimmond's shoulder.

"Randall!" the man called out. "Mind if we borrow you for a few minutes?"

A tough-looking boy with blond hair was walking away from the Anxious Canine, steaming cup of coffee in hand. He was bigger than Grimmond, but his face was anxious as he approached his caller, perhaps wishing he had pretended not to hear.

"Grimmond Scylent, meet Randall Planch," Liam introduced. "Randall's a junior, the same as you. Randall — can you show this young man around? Miss Fallstone and I must debrief at the Dread Map."

"Sure thing, Lord Stawlart," the boy replied with a curt nod, looking relieved at the simple request.

Grimmond didn't wish to be separated so soon from the only person he knew, even as angry as he was with her. Eralynn seemed to understand his stare, and fed up, she quickly grabbed him by the wrist to bring him back into the entranceway. Grimmond spun around wildly once they were out of sight of Lord Stawlart, wrenching his wrist free and crossing his arms.

"I'm *not* staying."

"You're here tonight," she returned. "And I expect you to make the best of it."

Grimmond's anger hardened, looking at his godmother, and he clenched his fists as she quietly walked toward him.

"Don't you understand?" her eyes pleaded. "*This*, the fight, the search to seal the Nightmayr Realm, it's all there is. It's the way to rid the world of that realm's evil — of what took your parents away — for good."

Grimmond cringed as the entranceway Sentrees swiped at his back.

"But — but," he stammered, struggling to rationalize the situation. "You're a *night security guard*, Eralynn!"

"A good cover," she answered softly. "I haven't slept at night since I was a little girl. But I never wanted this for you...I thought that if I could keep you away long enough, then maybe it would just be us. I tried to make you forget about the Nightmares, like most kids are able to do, but you never could. I'm sorry...I really did try to make you happy. But we're out of options now."

Silence followed only briefly, until Eralynn tried to reach for his shoulder.

"You *lied*!" Grimmond shouted at last as he backed away. "You've been lying to me since I've known you! About...about *everything*!"

Eralynn swallowed as she lowered her hand, and closed her eyes tightly.

"I'm still *me*, Grimmond...and it's still just us. Like always, right?"

"*Yeah,*" he mocked. "You, me, your old boyfriend, and the psych Wards. Can't wait."

Grimmond walked back to the Anxious Canine to find Randall waiting impatiently, but Eralynn was on his heels in an instant, shoving her cup of coffee in his hand.

"Here," she said firmly. "Might want to start drinking coffee after all — it's practically our currency — and the sooner you get used to the night schedule, the better."

Grimmond took the cup that Zolgo had brought her, and watched as Eralynn promptly stalked down the hall. He turned back to Randall, and at the same time noticed most of the Anxious Canine's lineup, eyeing him with interest.

"Look, Randall," Grimmond started, "I'm sure I can manage. You don't have to show me around if you don't want —"

"It's fine," the boy answered sharply. "And my name's Randy, not *Randall*."

"Take it easy, *Randall*," said another voice, standing up quickly from a table beside the spectating customers. "I'll help out. Malus Nebbick's the name, Grimmond. Did I hear right? You're the Errandi boy?"

The skinny, jaundiced speaker looked nothing short of malnourished as he offered a veiny hand. Grimmond shook it, but didn't like the way Malus smiled with the empty eyes of a scarecrow, or the large clap he next gave Grimmond on the back. Grimmond was sure he was supposed to wince in pain, but he didn't flinch at all as he stared back into Malus's appraising face.

"Let's go then," Randy said, eyeing Malus with the same distaste Grimmond felt.

Grimmond followed after his two guides, not noticing the boy and girl who rose quietly from Malus's table and hurried off.

Away from the Anxious Canine, and deeper into the Hovel the trio went. First they took Grimmond down a series of hallways to the Hearth: a large heptagonal room with an open fireplace in the middle, used for meals and assemblies.

"Breakfast is from four o'clock to five o'clock," Randy said. "Don't be late, because class starts right after that."

"Check," Grimmond answered, trying to lighten the mood. "That seems pretty early, right?"

"Four to five *in the afternoon*, Grimmond," Malus clarified. "Followed by an hour's lunch at nine o'clock, and supper finished by three in the morning."

"Oh, right — yeah," Grimmond said, reddening around the ears. "It'd be nighttime, obviously…."

The occasional coffee cup floated by as they walked, their liquid guzzled into invisible slurping mouths. More whispering Sentrees lined the expansive stone corridors, with colored lanterns hanging from their limbs to light the way.

Grimmond was shown classrooms for subjects he'd never heard of, as well as where the training atrium and main study library were. Malus pointed out the stable towers, along with the back and side entrances to the Hovel.

"There's always another way out of the Hollow," Malus grinned unnaturally, after showing the bone-encrusted Marrow Mansion in which he lived. "Or *back inside*. Just have to find the right door, eh, Grimmond?"

Why did that kid just give me the eyeball as he said that?

"Sure," Grimmond agreed, pointing toward Marrow Mansion. "Question: why are those skulls glowing yellow? And why does everything have to glow around here, anyway?"

"Why do you think?" Malus asked. "The entire Hollow is practically held together by Nightmares, even though Lord Stawlart technically runs the place. The Nightmares help us, and in return we don't send them back to the Nightmayr Realm, where *all of us* truly belong."

"That said," Randy went further, "Nightmares always embody what humans fear. Some more successfully than others."

Orbs of light passed them in the corridors, gliding or bouncing into various objects that sprang to life. Grimmond ducked a bright blue globe of the earth, spinning toward his head, and Randy booted a burning red cat that lunged at him as they passed it.

The next time a glowing object sped at them, Randy slipped a pair of brass knuckles over his fingers — much like the ones Eralynn had — and punched them outward. A bright yellow flash like a camera dazzled the air, and Grimmond stumbled as the purple, slithering bearskin rug retreated.

"What the heck was that?" Grimmond asked, staring in awe.

"A *Flare*. Sorry, should've warned you," Randy apologized. "Doesn't really hurt them if it's a quick flash, just lets 'em know to back off."

"Doesn't really hurt *what*?"

"There are three classes of Nightmares you have to worry about," Randy explained, "Minor, Major, and Total. We call the Minor ones *Terrors* — they're these little balls of light flying around, bothering us. They don't form flesh like Majors or Totals do, but they can still freak people out by possessing objects and animals. They're basic enough to deal with, once you learn your Terror Wheel and how to Flare."

Grimmond thought of the floating heads along the Charles River Esplanade, and wondered if they were Terrors, like those in the Hollow. They certainly didn't feel very *Minor* to Grimmond at the time.

"So, what's the Terror Wheel —"

"Like I said," Randy cut him off, "you'll learn about it."

"I have an idea — why don't we show Grimmond up to the terrace on the sixth floor?" Malus offered suddenly, turning to Grimmond. "You have to see it before the sun comes up. It's really something, I promise."

Randy stopped walking.

"I don't think that's a good idea, Nebbick," he said, his jawline tightening.

"No? Why not?"

"Because, I'm sure he's tired," Randy went on, "after Lord Stawlart *himself* brought him in. We should show him where he'll be staying —"

"No! I'm good, really," Grimmond assured him, knocking his coffee cup. "I'm not tired at all yet. I wouldn't mind taking a look at it tonight."

A thought entered Grimmond's mind when he got in the Phantom and left Boston a few hours earlier. For once, he wasn't the crazy kid, and he might actually have a chance to make some friends. He could have a fresh start here, knowing that the idea — the *lie* — of his hallucinations was gone. They were just called Nightmares now, and he wasn't the only one who saw them anymore.

"You see, Randy? He *wants* to go up."

"Fine," Randy said resignedly, "but I'm not going. Later, new guy."

Grimmond wondered if Randy was trying to signal something with his flickering eyes. But Grimmond couldn't be sure, not yet knowing him. Grimmond turned to his remaining guide as Randy left.

Malus took them to a large room, a crossroads where a dozen staircases met. Some led up, others down, and several straight into the wall. Malus chose one leading up, and Grimmond followed anxiously, wishing that someone else was with them.

They stepped off onto the darkest floor Grimmond had been yet. No Sentrees with lanterns or Terrors could be seen.

"The sixth-floor terrace," Malus said quietly, pointing to a set of doors. "Go have a look. I'll be right out, just gonna use the bathroom over there."

For a moment Grimmond thought Malus's eyes were pure black, but he dismissed it. It must have been the shadow of a passing Nightmare he didn't see.

"Okay," Grimmond said, "I'll be out there."

Grimmond opened cracked glass doors to walk outside, causing several pairs of glowing eyes to scutter away or take flight. He found there more of a parapet than a terrace; vines ran across the floor, enclosed by crumbling, waist-high walls Grimmond knew to be called battlements. He walked carefully toward its end, where a raised platform took shelter under a sharply pointed steeple, like some gothic gazebo.

From the high point, Grimmond examined the illuminated grounds and structures, from the path he had taken down into the valley, lit by the black and orange toads, to the four Wards that Eralynn pointed out. A dark green lake on the backside of the Hollow stretched long and wide. Grimmond tried to adjust his eyes better at the many pairs of wings rapidly darting over the water.

What am I doing? I can't stay, this is crazy — these people *are crazy. I need to get the heck out of here....*

Grimmond turned to walk back inside, but froze dead in his tracks. Standing in front of the glass doors was a tall, dark figure in a cloak, with nothing but a white face visible beneath it.

The Ending had found him.

Grimmond could barely breathe. His palms flashed with sweat, and his heart was choked by the blood flooding through it as his pulse skyrocketed. In a rush of memory, the murder of his parents crashed to the surface in fresh images: pleading screams, cracked gravestones, and a white face in the darkness.

The colorful lights of the Hollow had been nothing compared to now. Once the edges of Grimmond's vision turned bluish-white, every bit of the Hovel was almost see-through. He saw the glowing Terrors bouncing about, larger things creeping through the towers and grounds, and the flying things above the lake with greater clarity.

But the Ending didn't change at all.

"Grimmond Errandi," it said in a hoarse whisper. *"I have come for you! Muhuhahaha!"*

Grimmond tried to summon his courage, to steel his mind against the thing that killed his parents. But if Eralynn couldn't do anything against it, what could Grimmond do, when he knew nothing of fighting? White flashes of light on either side of the glass doors suddenly blinded him, and his vision spun.

Take cover! THINK!

The Ending suddenly charged, voice cracking as it screamed. Grimmond raised his hands in panic, stepped backwards, and tripped on a long vine stretching across the floor. His backside crashed into the crumbling battlements as he caught himself, but the wall gave way, and he tumbled over the edge.

Grimmond looked at the Ending once more while he was able.

He'd never know the reason why, but it had won. It killed his parents, and now him. He closed his eyes as the ground approached, withholding his scream in his only defiance: he wouldn't give the Ending that, too. But when the wind was knocked out of him, it was from two giant claws that caught him by the midriff.

This time, Grimmond screamed.

Flailing his arms and legs, he lashed out wildly at the creature about to eat him.

"Oh, *shut UP!*" someone yelled.

A few moments later, Grimmond was dropped upon a sandy beach. Heart still beating out of control, he looked up to the giant thing that had plucked him out of the air. Crouching beside the dark green lake, it looked similar to Zolgo the Gargremlin, only ten times larger and meaner, and more akin to an angry, silvery dragon.

Its eyes burned green, long claws raking at the sand as it eyed him hungrily.

"Can I eat him?" it asked.

A girl walked out from behind it, taking off her helmet to look at Grimmond and roll her eyes.

"*No*, Qinella," she said. "That's not funny anymore! He doesn't even know you're kidding!"

"Am I?" the massive beast replied.

It was hard for Grimmond to see the girl's face at first. But as his senses cleared, the pink skull hairpin became visible, and Grimmond recognized her as the girl from the coffee shop. She offered him an unsurprisingly strong hand up. Grimmond was brought shakily to his feet, only to lean over and put his hands on his knees.

"What happened?" she asked. "We saw some flashes of light, and flew over in time to see you falling like a ragdoll."

Grimmond panted from his hunched-over position.

"I was getting a tour when Malus left me," he started, "then this thing showed up and I tripped, and —"

"Yeah," she cut him off. "I'm willing to bet Qinella that that was *Malus*, not whatever you think it was. Nightmares don't attack students here in the Hollow. You're new, right?"

Grimmond lifted a hand off his knee to give a thumbs-up, trying to process what happened. When he finally stood straight, he hoped the night hid his embarrassment. The girl's dark hair fell behind her shoulders, and her armor-like vest glowed faint green. On her fist were the metallic knuckles Grimmond continued to see the Nightmarists wield.

Several thoughts ran through him at once: this girl had saved his life, and he was grateful; she was very attractive, but could likely beat him up; and, though he hoped he never had to see her again, she obviously attended the Hollow.

"My name's Viana, and only people who like getting punched in the face call me Vi. This is my Glass Wing, Qinella."

"Thanks for saving me," Grimmond answered meekly, brushing the sand off his pants. "I'm Grimmond Scylent...what's a Glass Wing?"

Viana looked him up and down before answering, her eyes squinting as she took another step forward. Grimmond realized that the flowery scent he was breathing in wasn't coming from the plants around him, but from her. He tried to breathe through his mouth.

"It's a type of Gargoyle. See how her wings are so thin you can see through them?" Viana pointed to Qinella, who spread her wings a good fifteen feet in response. "They're good for projecting a Flare across a wide area. The Gargoyle behind you is a Nerve-Neck, by the way."

"Hmm?" Grimmond turned around and did all he could to not cry out in shock.

Staring at him with another set of bright green eyes, the face of a second Gargoyle was only a yard from his head. Slightly larger than Qinella, it was dark gray, had a thick neck and head like a battering ram, and was impossibly quiet. The black boy riding it jumped off its back with a drink in hand, giving a jittery laugh as he approached. He wore a similar outfit as Viana, but seemed to be enjoying himself much more than her.

"I almost had him, Vi!" he said with an English accent.

His long braids bounced, still smiling as he dodged a punch from Viana. Grimmond didn't know how the boy was able to hold a cup of coffee while he flew, whether it had a lid or not.

"Gettin' slow, Viana!" he jested pleasantly, then humbly offered a free hand to Grimmond. "Tristin Finitude. Sorry 'bout the joke. Looks like you've had one too many tonight, yeah?"

"Yeah," Grimmond answered, "I think I'm good for today. So, this is a Nerve-Neck?"

"That's right!" Tristin answered. "Another species of Gargoyle. Pride of the sky, me and him! Don't be rude, Flynn! Say hi!"

"Hi," said Flynn deeply, his eyes still burning into Grimmond's.

Grimmond wondered if the two Gargoyles would've torn him to shreds if their owners hadn't been standing there. Viana dug a hole in the sand with her foot while staring at Grimmond, her eyes darting from his shoes to the blue streaks in his hair.

"You were lucky the Black Wings had Scringoll drills at all tonight, Grimmond Scylent," she said. "Straighten up quick, because there's no room for sissies here. Worse than *you* dying would be getting someone else killed."

For someone he'd just met, her words stung more than Grimmond would've admitted. Even Tristin let out a low whistle, turning to Grimmond as Viana hopped atop her Gargoyle's back and returned to the sky.

"Isn't she great?" Tristin said happily, sipping his coffee. "Don't worry, just catch her in the daylight sometime. You're a transfer student, right?"

"Yeah," Grimmond answered. "I just got in from Boston —"

"No, I meant a transfer from another *Hollow*," Tristin laughed. "You're pretty clueless then, I take it?"

"More than you know," Grimmond said, downcast. "What's a Hollow even supposed to be?"

Tristin spread his hands wide.

"This is a Hollow. *Our* Hollow. Didn't anyone tell you anything about it?"

"Kind of," Grimmond mumbled, "but Liam didn't tell me much — we haven't had a whole lot of time to talk yet."

"Time to *talk*? With *Liam*?" Tristin asked incredulously. "Do you mean *Lord Stawlart*? That man has maybe said ten words to me my entire life…he's a pretty big deal around here — hence the 'Lord' part. If I were you, I wouldn't let anyone else hear me call him by his first name."

"Good tip," Grimmond said, scratching his head, "thanks."

"To answer your question, then," Tristin continued, "a Hollow is just a place where Nightmarists can work with would-be bad Nightmares. Keeps them out of trouble, sometimes. We're not the only Hollow out there, of course, but we cover our area…. Anyway, Flynn and I've got to get back to Scringoll drills with the Squadron. See you around?"

"What's Scringoll?" Grimmond asked, desperate to have more questions answered. "And the Squadron?"

"It's kind of a war game for the Gargoyle Squadrons," Tristin answered. "Me and Vi are with the Black Wings. You could try out in a few weeks, I'm sure. *If* you can find yourself a Gargoyle, first. All the Haunted ones have already been claimed for the season."

Tristin remounted Flynn, who spread his wings wide.

"Take that path behind you back to the Hovel, and don't fall into the Bottomless Chasm! Last time someone did, we never found them!"

Tristin was gone in a few giant flaps of wings, and Grimmond was left alone. He stumbled over to a tall tree, thinking of the fact that he almost died several minutes ago.

This is a dream…it has *to be. A realistic, super long dream….*

Grimmond yanked on his hair, steadying his breathing. He was furious with Eralynn for bringing him to the Hollow, and furious with her for keeping him away. For lying, for making him think he was crazy for ten years, and for keeping all of this secret from him for so long.

But pressing above it all were more flashing images of his parents: crossing the bridge in Boston Public Garden, hopping the fence to the cemetery. All after Grimmond did something that Eralynn never knew about; something only Grimmond's dead parents would ever know. And that *thing*, the Ending.

That secret's safe…for now.

But if it *was* Malus who dressed up like the Ending, how did he even know what it looked like?

A stifled giggling met Grimmond's ears, followed by a quiet breathing on the back of his neck. He turned to see a crudely shaped face in the tree trunk, and jumped away just in time. Chunks of bark flew through the air as it missed biting his arm off, and Grimmond retreated to the path that Tristin indicated.

"Great first impression today," he said to the toads hopping along beside him.

"Kill-it, Kill-it!"

Grimmond followed them all the way back to the bridge. He walked inside and asked Zolgo where the guest rooms were. Following his directions, he took a few turns down the dimly lit corridors, dodging the flying objects possessed by Terrors, and swatting Sentree branches grabbing onto his shirt. He found the rooms Zolgo described, confirmed by Randy Planch's presence. He stood up quickly as Grimmond approached.

"I tried to warn you," Randy said.

"You did?" Grimmond answered angrily. "You *warned* me that Malus was going to scare me off that terrace to fall to my death?"

Randy's eyes widened.

"You *fell off?*" he sputtered. "And you're *all right?*"

"Yeah," Grimmond sighed, "I'm all right. One of the Gargoyles caught me — someone from the Black Wings Squadron?"

"Good thing they were drilling tonight," Randy said, eyes still wide. "And I'd bet Biff and Bianca were with Malus. They're *almost* as bad as he is."

"Do you mean to tell me," Grimmond went on, growing angry again, "that punk regularly scares new kids into falling off the sixth-floor terrace, and no one has done anything about it?"

"No," Randy said. "They've never gone that far before. Look, Grimmond — I'm sorry about all that. But there's a reason I couldn't warn you outright. It's just...be wary of Malus Nebbick, okay?"

Grimmond looked Randy up and down, his previously tough demeanor unsettled.

"You've got three inches and at least thirty pounds on Malus. What could he *possibly* do to you?"

"There's something *not right* with that guy," Randy shifted uncomfortably. "I know it, trust me. Being on the receiving end of him isn't good for your health."

Grimmond felt a wave of shame washing over him, realizing that everyone at the Hollow would know of the prank by morning, and that he'd been rescued by a girl.

So much for a fresh start.

"Well, thanks for the tour."

"Sure thing," Randy answered. "No hard feelings?"

"Yeah, we're good," Grimmond answered, deciding that having more friends than enemies was a good thing. "Let's just work on a signal for the next time you need to warn me about something."

"Sounds like we might need one," Randy agreed.

He shrugged his shoulders and started to walk down the hall, until Grimmond halted him.

"Hey. One last question for you — what do you know about a girl named Viana?"

Randy actually laughed as he blasted a floating red doll with green light.

"I know you should keep dreaming," he said, walking away once more. "Oh, and Grimmond, in case you hadn't heard it yet — welcome to Stanchions Hollow."

NIGHTMARE CLASSES

Grimmond wanted to hide in the guest room all afternoon after he woke up, but it proved difficult.

Eralynn checked in on him once, suggesting he explore the Hovel during the daylight, but he decided not to mention the incident with Malus. More annoyingly, the colorful orbs of light — the Terrors — continued to pop through the walls, possess objects around the room, and harass him.

Ducking beneath the bed frame at one point, Grimmond found a racket for defense. It was quickly taken over by a bright red orb and turned against him. Without having brass knuckles to Flare the half-dozen objects flying about his head, he was surprised that yelling *'GET OUT!'* made them at once fall to the floor.

Grimmond decided to sneak out and find breakfast before they returned.

He dead-ended once into the sleeping bearskin rug from the night before. A second time he opened a door that led outside, but then dropped off above the Bottomless Chasm. When he smelled food wafting from a corridor, he followed it all the way to the Hearth, and entered the seven-sided room.

"Finally," he muttered, relieved to find the hall empty with only a few minutes of breakfast remaining.

Typical dishes were on the tables, not the bugs and roasted fingernails half-expected, and Grimmond ate ravenously. But with his head down, he didn't see the infantile creature floating down to his table. With yellow eyes, two nubby horns in its forehead, and flaky red skin, it looked like an evil baby. Swooping in, it opened a large mouth of gnarled tusks, and breathed fire a foot from his face.

Grimmond gasped, dropping his fork to recoil from the stream of black flames, and narrowly avoided losing his eyebrows. The fire-breather floated away, giggling, and Grimmond looked down to see his food steaming.

Might have to get a to-go plate from now on....

"Rebbigone," a voice said over Grimmond's shoulder.

He turned to see Tristin approaching in blue jeans and a tee shirt, long braids bouncing, and swigging from his coffee.

"Sorry?"

"The little guy's called a *Rebbigone* — fire baby," Tristin said, setting down a second coffee cup. "They're all right, just keeping the food warm. Not technically Nightmares, but they've been around the world forever. I do suggest looking upwards now and again, though."

Tristin pushed the second cup forward.

"You partake?"

"No, not really."

"You do now," Tristin slid the cup further. "You'll love it. It's the only drug I'll ever push on people."

"Caffeine isn't a *real* drug," Grimmond answered, taking the cup.

"It is here, believe me. Have you seen that line at the shop? Who knows what Zolgo really puts in this stuff?"

Grimmond smiled for the first time in what felt like days. He looked from the grinning Tristin to the overfed body of the Rebbigone, then upward to the ceiling that spiraled into a hole like a spider's lair. How could a place like this possibly hide him from the Ending? Or the police looking for him?

"How do you guys do it?" Grimmond asked in wonder.

"Handle all this?" Tristin asked, understanding the meaning behind his question. "By doing it for years. And, by making that first choice to face your fears. You can be frightened of them — or not."

"Frightened?" Grimmond whispered, aghast. "I saw a kid get *eaten* last night after a party! My oldest school bully!"

"No way — that's *awesome*!" Tristin cheered, raising his cup in salute. "Congrats!"

"No, *not* awesome!" Grimmond continued in a fluster. "I was arrested, thrown in jail, then escaped when some creepy Nightmare named Kremaya set me free."

"Kremaya, *Kremaya*...." Tristin muttered. "Name sounds kinda familiar, but I can't place it. Probably only a Major Nightmare, not a Total —"

"I'm a fugitive! They're gonna show up on Stanchion's doorstep any minute to arrest me!"

Tristin shook his head and chuckled good-naturedly.

Does this kid take anything seriously?

"Did you keep your eyes closed all the way in last night?" Tristin asked. "Didn't happen to see that mist separating us from the rest of New England?"

"I guess, but I didn't realize —"

"*Only* Nightmares," Tristin went on, "like those driving the Phantom vehicles, can get through the mist of the Sleepless Orchard and into the Hollow. And there are enough defenses and watchers around the borders here for any bad Nightmares that might find their way through. That's why nobody knows where Stanchions is — you just drive around this huge area, until you find the mist."

"What about people?" Grimmond asked. "Nobody ever stumbles in? Hikers, or hunters maybe?"

"Dreamers? They turn around when the mist gets so thick they can't see their hands in front of their faces. But our

Nightmares know what to do. That's why you really don't need to be worried. As long as you never step foot in Boston again."

Never go back to Boston? Ever?

Grimmond took a deep breath, trying not to lump Tristin in with his anger at Eralynn. Tristin was just trying to be friendly. It was Grimmond's godmother and Lord Stawlart who'd uprooted him from the only life he'd ever known, troublesome though it was, and led him to believe he could rid himself of the Nightmares that plagued him.

But what was Grimmond supposed to do in a place crawling with Terrors and things like the Rebbigone?

"It's just...this time *yesterday?*" Grimmond replied. "I didn't even know I was headed to that party yet. I still thought I was crazy. As in, seeing stuff that wasn't real, taking medication, *insane.*"

"Yeah, some people take that route," Tristin answered with a smile. "Me? Nah. I was never given the choice. My parents were Nightmarists, and they trained me up pretty early on everything, though obviously I couldn't come to Stanchions until high school. What about you? What's your story?"

Grimmond felt a sense of panic. Did Tristin know something? Did Nightmarists read minds? Grimmond could almost hear the words of his six-year-old self as he walked his parents to their deaths.

"My parents were killed," he swallowed. "Murdered."

Tristin swore, the smile immediately fading from his face.

"I had no idea — I'm really sorry to have brought it up —"

"Don't worry about it," Grimmond spoke over him. "Really. I was just a kid when it happened. I only remember certain things about that night."

Tristin leaned in.

"You were *there?*"

"Yeah, I was there...." Grimmond trailed off. "The thing is, whatever it was that did it — this 'Ending' — I guess it's coming back for me. That's why Eralynn and Liam brought me here last night. To hide from it."

That's true enough....

Tristin looked at him seriously, an expression Grimmond already knew was rare for him.

"Only," Grimmond went on, "I don't *want* to run anymore. I want to know how to fight back."

Tristin bowed his head, nodding slowly.

"You're in the right spot, if ever there was one. But for now," he stood, finishing off the last of his coffee, "I'm gonna show you around a bit more. Properly — no pranks or attempts on your life. But let's start with a refill."

"Stay away from Grizzly Grove until you know how to deal with Major Nightmares," Tristin said, finishing the list of things Grimmond should avoid. "Oh, and maybe the stable towers, too, where the Gargoyles live."

"Is there anywhere I *can* go?" Grimmond asked.

"Coffee shop seems safe," Tristin said, pointing to a cup that floated by, its holder greeting them with a disembodied voice. "Just don't go walking off with Malus again."

They approached the largely empty Anxious Canine, where only a few students sat at the tables and chairs scattered around the hall. Grimmond saw no sign of Malus.

"Just missed the morning rush!" Zolgo shouted. "What'll it be?"

Grimmond was sobered, realizing he didn't have any money. He was about to tell Zolgo so, until Tristin spoke up.

"This one's on me," he said. "First-day treat for the new guy."

Grimmond looked at the menu, trying to choose between 'Fresh Cut Copse', a honey and pine latte, and 'Wrigglebits', a peanut butter and coconut mocha. He went with the latter and stood back for Tristin to pay.

"How much today, Zolgo?"

"Ya see?" Zolgo beamed with approval. "*This* one knows how the game is played. The market's always changin'! Uh, see here…fresh peanut butter…kill the nine, carry the one…that'll be five Skiefs, four Chips."

"Sure," Tristin answered, pulling out five oblong notes and a handful of small coins.

Grimmond leaned in to whisper.

"What are those? Pearls?"

"Try again," Tristin replied quietly. "The money's called Marrow, even though it's not *all* made from bone."

They took a few nearby seats to wait, and Grimmond watched as Tristin laid an example on the table.

"The oblong sheets are called *Skief* husks — tough skin of some creature, I think. Then there're different types of bone, valued differently, and carved into coins. Circular whites are *Chips*, rectangular yellows are *Shards*, and the triangular brownish ones are *Flakes*. Just remember: five, seven, eleven. Five Chips for a Skief, seven Shards to a Chip, and eleven Flakes to a Shard."

"Okay," Grimmond nodded. "A little gross, but I think I've got it."

Tristin waved as Viana walked by, looking better rested than the night before. Grimmond noticed she was wearing a green skull hairpin today, and muttering something about her mother.

"Just black," she told the barista.

The freshman boy at the register blushed, moving so quickly to pour her cup that he knocked it over and had to start again.

She rolled her eyes and turned around, arms folded. Her eyes bounced from the tables to the ceiling, then to Grimmond, and finally back to the tables again. Grimmond's eyes lingered.

"Eyes up, ice brain. Trust me," Tristin whispered, eyebrows raised. "You wanna die before classes start tomorrow?"

"I wasn't *looking*, looking…." Grimmond muttered.

He averted his eyes regardless, looking up to the high domed ceiling of the hall. He'd quite forgotten about the following afternoon, the start of classes. At least some normalcy could exist within the Hollow, even if the hours were strange.

"That reminds me," Tristin continued, pulling a folded half-sheet of paper from his back pocket. "Lord Stawlart wanted me to get this to you. It's your class schedule. I'm afraid your '101' classes will be with the other newbies, but the rest should be with us juniors."

Grimmond saw blocks for Mathematics, World Studies, and English & Literature. But every day he had a *Nightmares* class, switching on and off from *Minors* to *Majors*. On Fridays he had *Total* Nightmares as his final class.

"*Total* Nightmares?" Grimmond asked.

"Looking forward to that one this year," Tristin replied. "Total Nightmares are the hardest to deal with. No Flaring of light, no Lulling command words against them — they're a different beast entirely. Most Nightmarists never see them, *but* we'll be learning from Boogey himself."

Grimmond scanned the sheet again.

"Professor B. Manning?"

"Exactly," Tristin answered. "Boogey Manning — *the* bloody Boogey Man."

He's got to be joking. The Boogey Man isn't real.

"That's just a figure of speech, right?" Grimmond asked. "He's not really the Boogey Man…."

Viana approached the boys' table quietly, at the same time Zolgo flew over to drop off their drinks. Grimmond immediately took a sip of his Wrigglebits, and felt a surge of energy course through him.

"What do we think?" Viana asked.

"We think you were too harsh last night," Tristin answered with a stretch, "and that he'll actually be okay after some wising up."

"I agree," Zolgo said with a toothy grin. "There's some fight in there, maybe."

"You think?" Viana pondered.

All three now looked to Grimmond.

"Wait, you're talking about *me*?"

"Ah, see there," Tristin defended, "he might not *seem* too bright, but we can work on that a bit, too."

"Work fast," Viana said, shaking her head, unconvinced. "Because I'm not sold, otherwise. See you 'round, guys."

Viana and Zolgo promptly left, and Grimmond raised his hands to Tristin, bewildered.

"What just happened?" he asked.

"I think you're *in*," Tristin winked.

The next day came quicker than Grimmond wanted it to, and he was growing nervous. Tristin helped him move his few things into Steeple Spike, where Lord Stawlart informed him he'd be staying.

It was mostly like an open dorm room, Grimmond found, and he shared the large floor with Tristin and two other boys. In one corner was Black Wings' team leader Wynn Felt, a sophomore from Ohio with hair as long and smooth as Viana's, and in the other was Keokuk Jacy, a junior with roots in the Native American Iroquois Nation.

Grimmond was introduced to a few of Tristin's friends living on the other floors, but it was mostly a blur. Some were friendlier than others, and Grimmond could have sworn he heard *'the Errandi boy'* and *'terrace'* muttered as he left several of them.

Now the first day of class, Grimmond was determined to get the basics down quickly. He refused to be known as the Errandi boy: loser transfer student with blue hair, so scared of a prank that he fell off the Hovel and had to be saved by a girl.

At least Minor Nightmares should be with students who are as clueless as me.

Grimmond climbed to the fourth floor of the Hovel, and entered a classroom that overlooked the sleepy Narcoleptic Row. Only several desks remained unoccupied when Grimmond arrived, close to the open window and sinking sun, but adjacent to a few harassing Sentrees. The eyes of the classroom followed Grimmond as he walked to the open seats, kicked the nearest snapping tree trunk into submission, and sat down.

Shining Terrors by Kau Ward was lying on every desk in the room, and Grimmond nervously flipped the textbook open to peruse its pages. He scanned a few, absorbed nothing, and contracted his eyebrows to look around at the students whispering behind their hands.

News really does travel fast here, I guess.

All eyes turned when a man quietly entered the room and shut the door. He was intimidatingly tall and muscular, with an ashy face and red eyes that burned like coals in a fire. Smiling at a few of the students, he walked to the front, and leaned back against the desk.

"Good day," he began. "I'm Coach Maurs. I'll be your teacher for the introductory class here at Stanchions Hollow, and I'll be showing you the ropes in gym class later...pun *intended.*"

Several students nervously exchanged glances.

The reddish-orange glow of the teacher's eyes grew brighter as he smiled and proceeded to call roll for the classroom. He checked for pronunciation, stopping on Grimmond's name a moment too long and looking up before continuing.

"Terrors," he said, dropping his clipboard on the desk. "The basic form of manifestation from the Nightmayr Realm. Who can tell us a little about them?"

Coach Maurs waited patiently. He slowly drummed his fingers together, which Grimmond noticed were charred black down to the nail. Nobody raised their hand.

"Okay, let me try," said Coach Maurs, extending a long index finger. "Terrors are considered *Minor* Nightmares because they manifest in the Nightmayr Realm from mankind's *least* horrible dreams. Showing up late for work, missing an exam, a crazy ex, you name it. But Terrors never manifest from serious things, say, phobias or death."

There it is again, Grimmond thought confusedly, *the Nightmayr Realm. Everyone keeps talking about it like it's a* real *place —*

"So," Coach Maurs continued. "People have bad dreams, and when enough of that same type of dream has occurred, it is manifested into a Terror. If a Terror finds a rip in the veil separating us from the Nightmayr Realm, it may escape through it, returning to our world as an orb of light. Able to possess inanimate objects, animals, and wreak havoc. Yes, question there from —"

"It's Keith, sir," said the boy next to Grimmond. "I was wondering — can Terrors possess Nightmarists?"

"Good question," Coach Maurs commended, "but no, they cannot — and neither can they possess the Dreamers. Even though Terrors are entirely made of light and have no flesh like *Majors* or *Totals* do. No Nightmare can enter a human body while the soul is within it. Their capabilities are reserved to the small objects you see flying around the Hollow, or the occasionally glowing-eyed Chihuahua."

The class giggled, loosening up with the good-natured coach despite his sinister eyes. But Grimmond didn't like how the man phrased *'while the soul is still in it'* concerning the human body. He tried to keep up as the man continued, and opened his book as requested.

Grimmond's head was down when something hard clanked near his ear, and he nearly jumped to look up. A pair of metallic knuckles rested on his desk, the same that Eralynn, Randy, and Viana had. Coach Maurs walked around the room, dropping the shiny objects in front of each student.

"Bright knuckles," said Coach Maurs. "Try them on. I'm sure for most of you, this'll be the first pair you've ever worn. They're yours for the duration of your training at Stanchions Hollow, so don't lose them."

Grimmond picked up the bright knuckles and ripped off the tag to read:

Narcolex Model One
Depatsy's Bait & Wares
Boston's Below Bazaar

The weighty polished knuckles felt no less awkward over his left fist than his right, and the colored stones embedded in each ring made him wonder how expensive they were. Still, a spark kindled in his gut, watching the stones glisten in the sunlight.

"These are the very basic tool of the Nightmarist," Coach Maurs continued. "Bright knuckles emanate the wavelength of light needed to banish Terrors. All the way back to the

Nightmayr Realm, once you're good enough. A good Nightmarist recognizes the origins of a Terror by its color, and shines it with the proper wavelength of light. This is called a *Flare*."

A hand raised across the room.

"Yes — Ally, was it?"

"Yes, sir," she answered. "How are we supposed to use these?"

"All you have to do is close your knuckled fist very tightly, and concentrate hard on a particular emotion. I'm sure you could guess what many emotions would yield: sadness for blue, jealousy for green, passion for red. Any emotion will do for now, so let's give it a try. Raise your hand to the sky, squeeze very tightly, and think as you should. On the count of three."

Each Nightmarist-in-training raised their hands up, and Grimmond followed suit, feeling silly.

Piece of cake.

"One —"

Squeeze hard, think of an emotion.

"Two —"

Any emotion will do, Grimmond. Come on....

"THREE!"

Twenty differently colored lights flashed around the room: blood red, forest green, vibrant yellow, and more. But nothing came from Grimmond's bright knuckles, and his vision was dazzled so badly by the other lights that he wanted to throw up. He attempted once more before everyone else lowered their knuckles, thinking happy, sad, and even angry thoughts. But none of it worked.

He lowered his arm, removed the bright knuckles disappointedly, and hoped no one had noticed.

"What'd you all think?" Coach Maurs asked. "A quick flash of proper wavelength against a Terror will scare them off. Flare hard enough, and they'll wither away, back to the Nightmayr Realm. Please keep in mind, the Terrors we have causing chaos around here *do* serve a purpose. So please, don't have the staff wondering why half its Terrors are gone by tomorrow."

Grimmond didn't join in the class's giggling. Why hadn't his knuckles worked?

"For the rest of our time, I'd like you to let your emotions rise to the surface of your minds. Let's see how many different wavelengths of light you can come up with…."

Grimmond left *Minor Nightmares* with an extreme headache that afternoon, and wasn't any happier to push through math class and world studies before lunch. When it was time to eat at eight o'clock, he entered the Hearth to the general roar of animated voices. Avoiding many eyes, he quickly sat at the most isolated table there. But as soon as he finished piling food on his plate and took a bite to eat, someone spoke.

"Hey there," said a boy. "I'm Keith Tychus."

Grimmond looked up, recognizing the boy from his morning Nightmares class. He was a freshman like all others in the class besides Grimmond, and was a few inches shorter and much younger looking, with knobby elbows and keen eyes.

"Mind if I sit?"

"Sure," Grimmond said after swallowing a mouthful of macaroni.

"You're Grimmond, right? Everyone's been talking —"

Keith stopped at the look on Grimmond's face, his own flushing slightly.

"Sorry, never mind."

"It's all right," Grimmond said. "You can go on. I wouldn't mind hearing it officially myself — what's everyone saying?"

"Um…well, they keep calling you the *Errandi* boy. But your last name's Scylent, right?"

"Yeah. Errandi was my parents' last name. They went here too, but I'm not sure how everybody knows that."

"Right...." Keith trailed off. "So, why do you have a different last name than your parents?"

"Just made things easier."

"Easier for what?"

"For pretending they haven't been dead since I was six."

Grimmond continued eating, regretting his decision to let the boy sit.

"Right," the boy said again. "Um, is it true too that you jumped off the sixth-floor terrace last night?"

Grimmond choked on his cider.

"*W-what* — no!" Grimmond answered. "That's not what happened at all!"

"Figured," Keith nodded, taking a chunk out of a dinner roll. "I didn't think anyone would do that right after getting here."

"I was taking a tour and lost my balance," Grimmond explained. "*Nobody* should be up there, really. Whole place is a death trap."

Keith nodded again seriously, seeming satisfied enough to continue eating.

"Cool," Keith went on. "Well, if you want, I can set people straight if they ask me."

Grimmond wondered if Keith meant it, and told him it would be nice if he did indeed tell his side of the story.

"What'd you think of the lesson?" Keith asked.

"Not bad," Grimmond lied, though glad for the change of subject. "Flaring should be pretty useful once we get the hang of it."

"Yeah, for sure," the boy answered. "But why are you in the freshmen class? Is it because your parents are dea— sorry, hang on...Liv! Over here!"

Keith looked past Grimmond's shoulder and called out. The girl who sat beside Keith in class came bustling over to their corner of the Hearth and immediately began talking.

She was blond-haired and petite, with crystalline blue eyes and a lost look about her. She was nearly as pretty as Viana, Grimmond thought. But assuming this was Keith's girlfriend, he quickly tossed the thought from his mind.

"Kiki," she whimpered, "I *told* you I had to use the bathroom...why'd you leave so fast? I could barely find my way here!"

Keith blushed furiously and shushed her. She turned to notice Grimmond.

"Kiki?" Grimmond asked with a slight grin. "Best pet name I've heard in a while."

"Oh — no! Nope. Uh-uh," the girl giggled, sitting down and tucking a strand of hair over her ear. "I don't have a boyfriend. *Totally* free, actually."

Keith rolled his eyes, shoveling another forkful in his mouth as the girl kept talking.

"This is my older brother, Kiki. Just found out this morning that he's too cool to walk with me after class. Wasn't that nice of him?"

She elbowed Keith in the ribs.

"Oh, uh, Grimmond Scylent, meet my baby sister, Olivia," Keith said dryly. "She's pretty awful, even if we're only a few minutes' difference in age. Being a twin is *so* great. At least we're not identical though. Liv would have to be a dude."

"Or, *you'd* have to be a girl," Olivia retorted, holding up her fingers. "You're *this* close, already."

Keith scowled and gathered some more food on his plate as Olivia joined the discussion about Coach Maurs. Grimmond learned that the twins were in Hollow Dwell, and their Nightmare class tomorrow, *Major Nightmares*, was the other they had together. Grimmond looked between them, grinning at the new argument arising.

"It's the *Gargoyle* Games, you idiot!" Keith chastised. "What did you think it was going to be? Who can mouthwash the fastest?"

"I never said *'Gargling'* Games, Kiki, and you know it! You're just trying to embarrass me in front of *him* —"

"Hate to cut in," Grimmond interrupted. "But what are the Gargoyle Games?"

"Something you won't ever need to worry about," said a new voice.

Grimmond turned in his chair to see Malus Nebbick, smiling from ear to ear like a spider that had caught a fly. Behind him were a boy and girl Grimmond hadn't met yet.

"You're unstable enough as it is, Errandi," Malus sneered to the delight of those behind him, "you should stay on the ground. Have you met these two, by the way? Biff Grouse and Bianca Nosté. They tried to help me stop you from jumping the other night. No matter how bright they flashed their lights, you just wouldn't snap out of it…lucky one of the second-rate Black Wings was there to catch you. I heard it was that prude girl. *Viana*, is it?"

Bianca, who was even shorter than Olivia and ugly with arrogance, heckled with stupid glee. Grimmond stared at her with disgust until Biff — who looked like a Midwestern computer nerd that recently learned to wrestle — blocked her from view and ground his teeth menacingly. Already at his limit, Grimmond stood from the bench and turned around to face Malus fully.

They were roughly equal in height, but Grimmond was the stouter. Biff took a step closer.

"Level ground right now, Nebbick," Grimmond said in a low growl. "Care to try your luck? There's no costume to hide behind — I can see you this time."

"Can you now?" Malus smiled evilly, his sallow skin stretching over his thin face. "Think you know it all after a few hours here?"

The Hearth grew quiet. Surrounding students stood up, waiting to see who would strike the first blow. Malus came within a foot of Grimmond's face, and he whispered strangely.

"Can you *really* see, Grimmond?

Malus's eyes turned black with his clenching fists, and Grimmond's heart jumped in his chest. He tried to bend his knees, or back away, but couldn't move at all. Malus's lips curled wider, trembling as the room began to fall out of focus.

What the heck — how is he doing this?

All else around Malus grew darker in Grimmond's vision. He took a step toward Grimmond, smiling wider.

"What's all this, Nebbick?" Tristin asked, approaching with Viana and Randy behind him. "Spreading the holiday spirit a little early aren't we?"

Malus's black eyes diminished as the room came back into focus, and he stepped away from a dazed and perplexed Grimmond.

"Mr. Gross," Viana said with a nod at the boy and girl behind Malus. "Miss Nasty."

"Just checking to make sure the Errandi boy is comfortable," Malus said loudly. "Didn't want him heading to any high floors again."

"The way I heard it," Tristin said, "you three pushed him off."

"Wouldn't want the teachers to find out about that," Viana added. "You'd probably be banned for life from the Skeleton Crew."

The smile melted from Malus's face at last, and he turned his eyes to Viana. As soon as he squared off with her, however, nearly a dozen other students at the surrounding tables stood up behind her.

"Don't think you're off limits," Malus snarled quietly, "just because of who your mother is."

Viana's eyes flashed, and Malus waved over his shoulder to push through the crowd with Biff and Bianca. Grimmond turned to the three newcomers who now sat at his table.

"Thanks guys," he began gratefully. "You didn't have to do that."

"You're in Steeple Spike now," Viana replied immediately. "*That's* why we did that."

"Oh," Grimmond said, his sense of camaraderie deflated, "right."

Tristin was suddenly enjoying the high ceiling, but Viana continued staring.

What is this girl's problem? Seems like she and Malus should get along just fine.

"What'd you mention to get him to back off, Viana?" Olivia asked. "The Skeleton Crew?"

"It's *our* Squadron," Randy offered, grabbing a dinner roll from the bowl on the table. "Your guys' Gargoyle Squadron is the Black Wings, ours is the Skeleton Crew."

"Hold on," Grimmond said, holding up an accusatory finger. "*You're* in Marrow Mansion with those three jerks?"

"Unfortunately, yeah," Randy answered, running an uncomfortable hand through his blond hair. "But there are some good Nightmarists there. Don't think where you live makes or breaks your stay here. I try to keep Malus in check, but it usually doesn't work."

"Are you on the Skeleton Crew, too?" Keith asked Randy.

"No. I hate flying, even if I could find a Gargoyle to ride. I'll go to the Squadron tryouts, though. You three should come, too. It's still fun to watch."

Grimmond finished up the day, exhausted after his next round of classes and two-o'clock-in-the-morning 'supper.' He returned to Steeple Spike, got ready for sleep in his corner of the room, and crawled into bed. He thought again of his failure to Flare, and wondered if his bright knuckles were faulty. He thought of Malus and how he made his eyes turn black, and wondered if his true intention the night before was for Grimmond to fall off the terrace.

Hoping he'd had the worst of it that afternoon, Grimmond tried to sleep. But deep down, he knew he was wrong. He knew his time at Stanchions hadn't even started yet. And he didn't see the boy looking in through his high window in the dark.

Grimmond closed his eyes, and Malus Nebbick glided away from Steeple Spike tower.

Malus's Gargoyle quickly set him down before Marrow Mansion, but after looking left and right, he passed its doors and quickly slipped into the Hovel. Walking to the large room with many crossing staircases, Malus descended until he reached a passage that led into a very dark chamber. He entered, fell to his knees, then pulled something from his pocket.

The dim black outline of a door appeared in the chamber, and a deep, indiscernible voice spoke.

"There was nothing else I could have done!" Malus pleaded in fear. "I tried the moment he arrived, but he was saved —"

The deep voice behind the door boomed over him.

"O-of course you are right, m-master!" Malus stammered. "That is an even better way…but it may draw more attention to you…."

A hairline crack glowed like a black light across the door, and a renewed rumbling filled the air. Malus bowed his head, and his hands shook as he listened.

"Do not fear, master," he trembled. "I *will* succeed where your Ending failed."

WARNING WILD

A woman was sitting at her front desk when Grimmond entered the classroom.

She wore smart eyeglasses, long hair over her white lab coat, and appraised each student as they walked in. Grimmond, Keith and Olivia sat strategically in one of the middle rows. Not too far away to seem uninterested, but not too close to appear eager.

Grimmond was still thinking about the vivid dream he had the night before.

In it, Malus's straw chest lay in front of Marrow Mansion, skin peeled down from his face to his bellybutton like an inverted hood. A bloody letterman jacket lay nearby, but Grimmond swore to Detective Tippins he didn't do anything, even though Patrick kept insisting that Grimmond did. When Detective Tippins sent the Terrors after him, Grimmond was suddenly back in the park in Boston, using Erik Beese's mutilated throwing arm to beat the Nightmares away.

"Good evening," the woman said, shaking Grimmond from his thoughts. "Call me Dr. Knight."

Grimmond found the woman familiar as she looked out at the students, but couldn't place her.

"I trust that Coach Maurs gave you an extensive introduction into the lesser manifestations, Minor Nightmares. But you are now Nightmarists-in-training, and must learn to deal with all manner of creatures. *Major* Nightmares are immediately different for three reasons. Does anyone know what they are?"

Like the previous morning with Coach Maurs, no one raised their hand. Grimmond wished he had something to say. But how on earth could they know the answer when they hadn't been taught anything yet?

"Major Nightmares have the ability to speak human language. Secondly, they aren't made of only light, like Terrors, but have formed flesh and bone. Thirdly, within the Major class, there are a number of different Nightmares to deal with, not just one."

Dr. Knight took attendance, and like Coach Maurs, her eyes peeked up to Grimmond after calling his name, though with much distaste. Lips pursed and eyes narrowed, she eyed him suspiciously while continuing the lesson.

"*Haunters* can imitate human skin, but only partly — the rest of their bodies will still be light, like the Terrors. One could be walking with a face on one side, and nothing but a purple glow on the other. But, it's also possible for them to forego forming flesh and merge with objects."

A girl raised her hand behind Grimmond.

"Miss Knight?" she asked. "Isn't that what *Minor* Nightmares do, too?"

"My daughter is Miss Knight, Drala," she answered. "I am *Doctor* Knight. But you are partially correct. Terrors possess common objects or animals. Haunters, on the other hand, can *merge* with things of much higher complexity: vehicles, statues, or even Gargoyles. Terrors do not have that ability."

Drala Zhen, Olivia's roommate in Hollow Dwell, sheepishly muttered her thanks and sank back into her chair. Olivia gave her a sympathetic grimace as Dr. Knight continued.

"The *Brute* and the *Prowler* are also among the Majors, both made of light and flesh. We will learn about them later, and will likewise learn quickly. Things have changed this year, and Lord Stawlart has expressed his desire for us to train and teach more vigorously."

After explaining how Major Nightmares are manifested from more serious human nightmares and fears, Dr. Knight discussed the technique to fight them. Grimmond leaned in closer as she spoke, anxious to hear more, and already guessing what some of the Nightmares he had seen in the past were.

"Terrors are banished by attacking with the proper wavelength of visible light, yes? Much like a child's bad dream goes away if the bedroom lamp is turned on. Haunters, Brutes and Prowlers, however, must be faced — dealt with to be resolved. You cannot simply turn the lamp on; you must speak truth. Nightmarists do this by using command words, through the process of *Lulling*.

"Speaking the words will temporarily 'Lull' the overwhelming fear of a Haunter to inefficacy. Then their flesh can be destroyed, and they'll be drawn back through the veil to the Nightmayr Realm. Lulling may even be used to aid you against creatures that aren't Nightmares at all. That aside, mind that defeating *any* Major Nightmare is done in two steps: Lulling first, and attacking second. Hopefully, most of you will be able to do the first part successfully, as it does take some finesse."

The woman's eyes met Grimmond, and he sensed again her dislike for him. Where else had he seen those eyes? He felt as if they were from someone new in his life; perhaps someone he'd recently met.

"There are many command words," she explained, "but the cost must always be considered. When commanding a Haunter to sleep, you temporarily offer your alertness to subdue them. And if commanding a Brute to be pacified, you sacrifice your sense of calm. In either case, using command words provides a short window in which to attack and destroy Majors in the flesh.

"Ernst has provided a staff member for us to practice with, but first, let's try one together," she said, writing a word on the board. "Pronounce the word as I do, like this: Saum-noose. You'll know it worked if a change comes over you, and you grow and feel sleepier than you are now. Take heart, the physical change is only temporary, and lasts no more than a few seconds. Everyone ready?"

What physical change?

Grimmond prepared himself to perform his first Lull, determined to do better than when trying to Flare the day before. Dr. Knight counted down, and all together the classroom boomed.

In revulsion, Grimmond watched as Keith's skin suddenly turned old and wrinkly, and Olivia and Drala gasped at one another as their long hair became white and brittle. But instead of Grimmond changing, too, his stomach turned upside down like a spiraling airplane. He closed his eyes, steadied a hand on his desk, and placed the other over his mouth.

Don't even think about throwing up, Grimmond!

He opened his eyes to see Keith's skin tighten, and the girls stop panicking as their hair became youthful once again. But Dr. Knight was staring directly at Grimmond. Hastily he wiped the perspiration beading on his forehead, and tried to act calm.

"An adequate first try," she commended the room. "Most of you, anyway. You — Mr. Scylent. Try again with a real Haunter."

Perfect.

At the teacher's word, another tall woman dressed entirely in black entered the room. She was one of Ernst's Phantom drivers, the *Haunters* which merged with the fancy cars in order to drive them. Grimmond immediately knew something was off about her, aside from her sloppiness. The hair around her chauffer's hat and sunglasses wasn't pulled back, but hung loosely forward to shroud her face.

"Okay, Greta," Dr. Knight said, "let's begin."

The driver reached up, removed her hat and sunglasses, and Grimmond's stomach lurched again.

Parts of her were *missing*.

No hair, flesh, or skull was present on the left side of her head. A glowing purple brain was squishing and pulsing, and several students around the class joined Grimmond in covering their mouths. Grimmond realized that other parts of her face weren't formed yet either: she had no eyes at all, but only forehead to cover all the way down to the two nostril slits where her nose should have been.

"Try again now, Mr. Scylent," Dr. Knight prompted.

Revolted at the sight of the half-headed driver, Grimmond tried to keep his heart in check. Still staring, he carefully pronounced the command word to Lull.

"*Somnüs!*"

Nothing happened to the driver. But as before, Grimmond was washed over with an overwhelming nausea. With difficulty, he did his best not to show it.

"That's disappointing, Mr. Scylent," Dr. Knight sighed.

"Sorry — I don't feel well," Grimmond answered truthfully, clutching his stomach beneath the desk.

"That won't change a Haunter from ripping your flesh off, and making a hat from it to cover the rest of the skin they can't grow. No offense, Greta."

"None taken," said the driver in a muffled voice.

Dr. Knight allowed each student to try the command on the Haunter. Every time the Lull was used, for several seconds the user was tremendously aged, and the light in Greta's glowing purple brain would temporarily fade away. This was the window, the teacher explained, in which to physically attack a Haunter to destroy it.

"Again, good work to all of you," she said with a plastic smile at the end of the class. "Only one person not passing tonight. That'll be all. Mr. Scylent — a word before you go."

Keith whispered good luck, and Grimmond miserably walked past the exiting students to Dr. Knight.

"You failed," she said, her eyes piercing through him. "Try harder next time."

Grimmond felt that calling him a useless trash bin would've had the same effect. What could he have possibly done to this woman?

"I'm sorry, Dr. Knight," Grimmond apologized, "I guess I might be coming down with something."

"And I don't care," she said coldly. "I've been teaching this subject for nearly ten years, and every Nightmarist that's ever been here has been able to do that basic command. Except for you, that is. Figure it out before the next class."

"I'll keep trying, Dr. Knight, I promise. But I don't know what else I can —"

Dr. Knight abruptly stood up from her desk. She was slightly taller than Grimmond and much more intimidating.

"No *Errandi* will talk back to me in my own classroom. Is that clear?"

Grimmond's nausea diminished, replaced by a kindling anger.

So THAT'S what this is about? The 'Errandi' name again?

"I'll talk back to anyone treating me like dirt," Grimmond said coolly. "I told you I tried. And my last name is Scylent. *Not* Errandi."

"Oh," she leaned in dangerously, "but you *are* an Errandi.... I knew it before I read your name. And I'll tell you child — that's *not* a good thing."

Grimmond's blood boiled. *Child?* And just what did everyone at the Hollow know about his parents that he didn't? He returned to his desk, picked up his backpack and made for the door.

"You better toughen up quick, Grimmond Scylent," Dr. Knight called, "because that weakness will get you killed! I'll not allow for *sissies* in my classroom!"

Grimmond stopped and turned, a light bulb clicking on in his brain. Now he knew why Dr. Knight looked familiar.

"You said you had a daughter," Grimmond said. "You're Viana's mom, aren't you?"

Dr. Knight stepped out from her desk, approached him, and jabbed a finger in his chest.

"You *stay away* from my daughter if you know what's good for you. I'll tell her the truth about your parents — so help me, I will. You've been warned."

Grimmond stepped away, looking at her widened eyes and maniacal smile with trepidation.

"Are you *crazy?* What are you even talking about?

"What your parents made that poor girl go through...how they ruined her life.... If Viana knew the truth, she would kill you herself."

Grimmond was grateful he only had to see the unstable Dr. Knight twice a week.

After his second round of Nightmare classes on Wednesday and Thursday, he still hadn't been able to perform a successful Flare without getting dizzy, or Lull without becoming severely nauseous. Coach Maurs assured him that nothing was wrong with his bright knuckles, but to keep working at it. Dr. Knight, on the other hand, dismissed him after ordering a summary of the first three chapters of their textbook: *Facing Your Fears* by Tuffin Braeve-Lee.

Every teacher aside from Dr. Knight had been quite nice to Grimmond, in fact, but he still hadn't met the Total Nightmares professor. Grimmond returned to his room Thursday evening, disappointed when Tristin told him their first Totals class, scheduled for Friday night, had been cancelled.

"Figures," Grimmond said dejectedly.

Tristin picked up on his strange mood, and pried out of him what was going on in class.

"Hmph. I wonder why she'd act like that," Tristin said. "Dr. Knight always seemed okay to me. I promise you — Viana's not like that at all."

"Yeah," Grimmond nodded from his bed and rubbed his face. "Yeah, I'm sure you're right. I probably overreacted...."

But Grimmond knew he hadn't, and wondered if he'd ever speak to Viana again after her mother's stern warning. He also didn't mention Dr. Knight's comment about his parents. For the little Grimmond remembered of them, he was sure they wouldn't do anything wrong intentionally. That was Grimmond's department.

He wished he could talk to his godmother about it, but they'd done a good job of avoiding one another all week.

"C'mon," Tristin said, attempting to cheer Grimmond. "Let me show you the top of Steeple Spike. We call it 'Fire Watch', because that's what people used to be looking out for up there. But you can see how we do it now."

Grimmond was resignedly dragged up to the top level of his Ward, but was immediately impressed upon entering. Thick glass formed the walls and ceiling, so those present could see the glowing grounds and sky of the Hollow. A double set of doors led out onto a wide balcony that circled the entire floor, and a bright fire burned in the north wall.

Flanked by two small Sentrees, their branches wiggling happily next to the fire, the stone hearth blazed with merrily crackling flames. A girl wearing a long-sleeved tee shirt sat on one of the couches before it, reading a book with her back turned. Her hair was dark and shiny as she ran a pale hand slowly through it.

Grimmond was strangely inclined to curl up next to her and go to sleep.

"Yo!" Tristin called. "What's new?

The girl angled her head as the boys approached, flicked her hair back, and revealed two small earrings shaped like ghosts. It was Viana Knight.

Oh, come ON, Grimmond....

"What's up, Tristin?" she called, closing the book. "Hey, Grim."

"Uh — *ahem* — hi, Viana," Grimmond blushed at the nickname, already smelling her flowery scent as he approached. "Didn't recognize you without your skeleton hair thingy."

Viana raised her eyebrows.

"You know. The different colored skulls you always have in your —"

Tristin coughed.

"I mean," Grimmond continued, "Tristin made this floor sound like a guard station. I didn't think you'd be up here."

"Yeah?" she retorted. "Girls can't be guards?"

Grimmond was speechless until she laughed.

"I'm *kidding*," she said, gesturing to the couch across from her.

Grimmond shared a quick glance with Tristin as Viana looked away, nodding a thank you for saving his blunder.

"Yep, this was a lookout station for the Hollow," Tristin said, sitting next to Viana. "Though not even really for fires — for Nightmares. But between the Gargoyle Squadrons, we have enough riders flying around now, keeping watch. This is just a backup anymore — a gathering room for us Steeple Spikers. Now 'Fire Watch' means just that, sitting here and watching the fire!"

"And fair warning — don't ever fall asleep up here," Viana added. "The Sentrees love to mess with you if you do. I heard a student was dangled from the balcony until somebody found them."

"Yep," Tristin agreed. "And Vi here woke up with a mustache once."

Viana slugged him in the shoulder, then turned back to Grimmond.

"Don't ask," she said.

Tristin and Viana both laughed as Grimmond cast a wary look at the dancing Sentrees. Then, he leaned back to soak in the mesmerizing flames. Despite both his instincts and multiple warnings that week, Grimmond found his eyes drifting several times to Viana's dark hair and smiling lips.

He needed to distract himself.

"Keith Tychus mentioned the Gargoyle Games at lunch the other day," Grimmond said. "But you two said you were practicing for *Scringoll*, right? Is that what the Squadrons are for? These games?"

"Not exactly," Tristin answered. "Well, not at all, actually."

"Freshmen," Viana scoffed.

"The Squadrons are kind of like assault teams," Tristin continued, "and we train to fly, Flare, Lull and fight during Scringoll scrimmages. Viana and I are on the Black Wings, and Malus is with the Skeleton Crew, but those aren't the only two Squadrons. There're four in total, just like the Wards. *Aurora Blights* is the Squadron for Hollow Dwell, and the *Sleepwalkers* are for Narcoleptic Row."

"But Scringoll keeps us sharp for the real thing: subduing whatever escapes from the Nightmayr Realm," Viana added. "We compete once a year in the Gargoyle Games here to see who's the best among the four Squadrons. *We* are, of course."

Twinkles of firelight reflected in her hazel eyes as she finished, and Grimmond forced himself to look away before she noticed him staring.

What is wrong *with you, Grimmond? This girl will KILL you!*

A large boy approached, covered in scars and wearing a shirt that was too small for his muscles.

"Hey, Tristin — Viana," the boy said. "I heard you talking just before heading back down. What've you got here? New recruit?"

"Maybe so," Viana answered. "Need to get him a ride first, then we'll see if he can fly. But the stables are cleared out, aren't they?"

Tristin reached up to issue a brief yet complicated handshake to the newcomer.

"All right, Cap'n?" Tristin said, gesturing between the new boy and Grimmond. "Drek Heeder — Captain of the Black Wings, meet Grim Scylent, blue-haired Gargoyle enthusiast."

Grimmond shook the boy's massive hand, and scooted over for him to take a quick seat.

"We could always use more riders, Grim," Drek said. "Even if you can't try out in a few weeks for lack of Gargoyles, you should come anyway and get an idea of what we do. Nothing better than being up there, I'll tell you —"

"But," Tristin stopped him, "we need people who know how to Flare, Lull, *and* fight...."

"True," Drek countered, "but having an extra body never hurts. Ever heard of learning on the job?"

Drek smiled, stood up from the couch and headed for the stairs.

"Nice to meet you, Grim," he called over his shoulder. "Hope to see you around!"

Once he cleared the stairwell, it was only Tristin, Viana and Grimmond left in Fire Watch.

"Sorry if that came off harsh, mate, but it's not all rainbows and sunshine up there," Tristin said quietly. "We get in some real sticky situations. I'd hate for you to get hurt if you weren't ready."

Nodding, Grimmond looked at Viana, who said nothing, having gone back to silently staring at him. But Grimmond didn't care; he already had a plan forming, and was growing all the more excited. He would prove he could at least do *something* at the Hollow, and clearly it wasn't Flaring or Lulling.

He'd learn to become a rider, and join the Black Wings. He just needed to find a Gargoyle first.

Grimmond had only seen two Gargoyles up close before, and wasn't convinced they didn't want to eat him then. But with Total Nightmares cancelled, Friday night found him sneaking alone to the stable towers, too embarrassed to ask anyone for help. And when Grimmond was alone in Stanchions Hollow, it no longer seemed interesting, but cold and creeping with dark things.

Ducking through doorways, into classrooms and under desks, Grimmond helplessly hid from passing Terrors and Haunters. Something he didn't yet recognize howled as it ran across the ceilings of the fourth floor, and a disemboweled body with spiders crawling out of the stomach was blowing blood bubbles from the foam in its mouth.

The stairs to the stable towers were taken by two.

Grimmond climbed until he was nearly out of breath, all the way until the ascent leveled off into a wide, open platform.

Grimmond was relieved to see the night sky after crawling through the Hovel. He expected a smell — to see a dozen shacks filled with manure and food — but there was nothing of the sort. What was he thinking?

These aren't horses! Of course they don't need stalls.

Lining the tall battlements were a number of impossibly large Gargoyles, wings folded back, and completely motionless. For some reason, Grimmond found he was less frightened there than with any Nightmare in the Hollow. He walked to the center of the platform.

"Can you hear me?" he called timidly.

At once the green eyes of the Gargoyles burned to life, and each turned their towering bodies toward the speaker. Grimmond thought he recognized the shape and size of one, and hoped he remembered her name correctly.

"Qinella?" he called. "Is that you?"

The silvery Glass Wing jumped down, shaking the stone floor, and crawled toward him.

"Greetings," she answered.

The tips of her translucent wings shimmered magenta in the glow of an approaching Terror, but she roared violently and it retreated. Grimmond heard a sniff behind him, and turned to see the thick head of the Nerve-Neck, Flynn, already coming upon him. He sat back on his haunches, and stared with bright green eyes.

"What trouble brings you here all alone, young Grimmond?" Qinella asked. "Where is Viana?"

Grimmond dared to take a sigh of relief, pleased at least that she remembered his name.

"I didn't tell her I was coming up," Grimmond shook his head, "or Tristin."

"Oh?" Flynn spoke in his gravelly voice, getting within a foot of Grimmond and sniffing again. "They don't know where you are?"

Grimmond stepped backward when two more Gargoyles hopped down from the battlements. They looked much different than Flynn and Qinella. Slinking along as dragons' skeletons would, they were covered in knobby white plates, like interlocking bones.

Grimmond swallowed hard. Even when crouching low, the smallest Gargoyle present reached up to his chest.

"I mean, they've *probably* figured it out by now," Grimmond said. "Tristin and I are in the same room, so eventually he'll know if I...you know, if I don't come back."

"Who are you, Grimmond Scylent?" Flynn asked, sniffing the air a third time. "Your scent is...*strange* for a Nightmarist."

"Well, that's just it, you see," Grimmond said, taking another step toward the tower door. "I'm not really a Nightmarist yet, because I can't do anything a real Nightmarist is able to do. I — I was hoping to learn to become a rider on one of the Squadrons, like Tristin and Viana...."

More Gargoyles jumped down to inch toward him, blocking his exit from the tower and beginning to whisper amongst themselves.

Why did I come up here again?

"Leave the boy!"

Swooping down to land in the center of the platform was another silver Glass Wing, though more tarnished than Qinella, and larger. It wouldn't have fit in Grimmond's old bedroom.

"Grimmond Errandi, at last," said the Glass Wing in a deep voice. "It's been far too long."

Grimmond didn't dare act annoyed, but the gathered Gargoyles grew quiet after hearing his parents' name.

"My last name's actually...." he began. "Never mind. Who are you?"

"I am called Nelton," the Glass Wing bowed.

Grimmond got the impression that Nelton was older than most of the other Gargoyles, and didn't know if he should shake his wing or his claw, so he bowed awkwardly in return.

"Nice to meet you, Nelton."

The Glass Wing cocked his head to the side, and narrowed his eyes.

"Does my name mean nothing to you?"

"Um," Grimmond pondered, "should it?"

Nelton stood to his full height and growled to the other Gargoyles. It seemed to Grimmond that Qinella and Flynn said something in return, in a language he'd never heard.

"It appears there are matters that have not yet been revealed to you, Grimmond Errandi. I am a friend of your godmother's. But as your guardian, it is her prerogative to tell you more, not I."

Friend of Eralynn's?

"Yeah," he responded more coldly than intended. "Not the first time I've heard that this week."

Grimmond was too nervous to argue with anything that could swallow him in a single mouthful.

"But that's okay," he continued. "Nelton, I came to ask — what do I need to do to become a rider?"

Nelton considered him a moment.

"Why do you not ask your friends?"

"Because I'm still not one-hundred-percent sure who my friends are," Grimmond answered. "At least I know a Nightmare when I see one now."

"Ah," Nelton bared his teeth in a frightening, would-be smile. "Not all Gargoyles are Nightmares — these bodies are creatures that we *Haunters* possess. Some still remain wild in the world, few that they are. Humans have never found them, though some have claimed to. Large Legs, I think they call them."

"Oh," Grimmond muttered, "I have a lot to learn still, I guess. Anyway, can you help me?"

"Every available Gargoyle at the Hollow bears a rider. There are none remaining to assist you."

Nelton bowed his head in apology, and Grimmond was crushed until Qinella cleared her throat.

"There is *one* of course, if the boy wishes to risk —"

"No," Nelton answered sharply. "There are none."

Nelton looked from Qinella to Flynn, speaking again in the language Grimmond didn't recognize.

"Wait, hang on!" Grimmond said eagerly. "There *is* one that can take me, or there isn't? Please — I'm really willing to work hard! I have to prove I can do *something* here!"

"Alas," Nelton sighed resignedly, "there are no *Haunted* Gargoyles to assist you, Grimmond. Qinella speaks of the single wild Gargoyle remaining in the Hollow."

Grimmond wondered if Nelton was making a joke, but didn't know if Nightmares had any humor.

"I don't understand."

"The Gargoyles we possess are the Glass Wings, Nerve-Necks, and Bone Crawlers. But there is one Gargoyle that not even we have been able to approach. It is of the Blood Onyx species, and has been in the Sleepless Orchard for many years. It remains alone, and rather violent. In good conscience, I must advise against this path."

Good conscience? That's rich, coming from a Nightmare....

"I see," Grimmond said, still scheming in his mind. "Well, can you at least *show* me where it is?"

"If you wish it," Nelton said. "But do not hope for anything. Flynn, Qinella, let us go."

Nelton approached Grimmond and lowered his left wing. "Climb on."

Grimmond turned around as if Nelton was speaking to someone else.

"How's that? Climb on where?"

"We must fly to the Sleepless Orchard," Nelton growled. "Climb on my back, sit between my two spinal columns, and grasp onto the horns that protrude from my neck. Riders use these characteristics of Gargoyles to make use of them."

Grimmond's limbs were frozen, realizing anew how large the creatures were up close. What was he supposed to hold on to again?

"Um, you know what Nelton?" Grimmond said in a weak voice. "On second thought, I'm good."

But Grimmond was gently grabbed from behind by a pair of scaly fingers, and dropped onto Nelton's back. Flynn then retreated, jumping up to the battlements with Qinella.

"Hold on," Nelton said needlessly.

Grimmond's hands were already tacky with sweat as the Glass Wing leapt to the wall beside Qinella and Flynn. Each Gargoyle then leaned forward, tucked their wings, and went into a full dive toward the bottom of the tower.

Grimmond's heartbeat blew into overdrive. He closed his eyes and resisted the primal urge to scream. But when Nelton flared his wings and leveled out, Grimmond's vision clicked in place.

Together they rose into the sky, and suddenly Grimmond felt the lightest he'd ever felt in his life. The fear that iced over his heart the past week melted, and he was filled with pure adrenaline. There wasn't *anything* he couldn't do. A gust of wind blew his hair and shirt askew, and he thought he might jump off and fly around the bright Hollow himself.

The three Gargoyles circled back up to the highest level of Steeple Spike, where the glowing Fire Watch shone like a lighthouse. Members of the Ward sat around the burning fire, playing games, or lounging on the balcony as the Gargoyles passed. Grimmond removed his hands from Nelton's back and shouted.

"WOOHOO!"

The Nightmarists on the balcony cheered and waved as Nelton made for the forest past the lake. Grimmond looked over his shoulder at the Hollow from his heightened view. From the ground he didn't realize how majestic it was, like a giant sculpture made of blown glass, lit from beneath and alive with splendorous color.

Nelton softly passed into the Sleepless Orchard, flared his wings, and landed in a clearing amongst the dark trees. Grimmond unsteadily dismounted and walked forward.

"Go," Nelton said softly. "The Blood Onyx is there amongst the trees, if you wish to see it."

"Okay," Grimmond answered.

Giddy with adrenaline, vision pulsing from his throbbing heart, Grimmond walked confidently into the clearing. He stepped into the middle — still smiling, still unwisely underestimating what he had asked for. Nothing but a ring of trees surrounded him: dark red, light gray, and one tall, gnarled black tree stump.

Grimmond turned around to face the three Gargoyles.

"I don't see it," he whispered. "Where's it supposed to be?"

But a deep growl behind Grimmond answered his question, and with it was shattered all the confidence he'd gathered in the past few minutes.

"Turn around," Nelton advised. "Slowly."

Grimmond was glad his heart was already racing so he could see the brighter, but when he turned his head, the Blood Onyx didn't need to be sought. The gnarled black tree stump Grimmond had seen among the others was gone: it *was* the wild Gargoyle.

The Blood Onyx stretched its wings and moved into the clearing.

It was just as massive as Nelton was, but with a long snout, black fangs, and ridged horns curling around its ears; it looked more evil than any Nightmare Grimmond had yet seen. Its charcoal eyes didn't glow green like the Haunted Gargoyles, and its glittery black underbody was smeared red from its latest kill.

Grimmond turned around, but his legs almost gave out when he saw Nelton and the others had gone. The Blood Onyx growled like a starting engine and quickly crouched low, preparing to lunge. But in the next moment, it ceased growling, slowly rose to its full height, and sniffed in Grimmond's direction. Just like Flynn continued to do.

Grimmond waited with bated breath as the Blood Onyx merely stared at him.

Why isn't it attacking?

Before he could question further, the wild Gargoyle was flattened by Flynn and Qinella.

"Time to go, Grimmond," Nelton said calmly as he landed behind him.

Grimmond didn't need to be told twice. He hopped atop Nelton's back and they took to the sky. When Grimmond turned his head to see Flynn and Qinella had escaped, he saw the Blood Onyx take off after all of them.

"It's following us!" Grimmond yelled.

Nelton required no encouragement. They weaved in and out of the Hovel's tall towers, into the pit of Hollow Dwell, and flew a hundred yards into the Bottomless Chasm to lose the Blood Onyx. Grimmond heard the wild Gargoyle roar in frustration behind them. As they passed Fire Watch, a shrill whistle sounded, and Flynn and Qinella immediately broke away from Nelton.

"Where're they going?" Grimmond called.

He looked up when a noise like a freight train sounded. The Blood Onyx was diving straight toward them, closing fast, until a bright yellow light flashed across the sky. The wild Gargoyle barely missed, and angled its wings to turn around. But Flynn next crashed into it, Tristin cheering from his back.

Viana zoomed by on Qinella.

"Grim!" she shouted. "You're gonna need to hold your breath!"

He was so dazed by her yellow Flare, he nearly couldn't grip Nelton any longer.

"Hold my breath?" he shouted in return. "Why would I need —"

Nelton was already plummeting toward the glowing green lake behind the Hovel. Just as Grimmond gulped in a massive breath, the three Gargoyles and their riders entered the water.

Ears popping with pressure, and cold shocking him so he wasn't dazed anymore, Grimmond let go of Nelton's horns. And though knowing a worse fate was at the surface, he was quickly out of breath and went for air.

He breached, gasping.

"You must work on your breathing, Grimmond," Nelton said as he likewise surfaced. "That is key for any Nightmarist."

Grimmond looked to the skies as he tread water, and saw a glitter of black wings returning to the Sleepless Orchard. He swam over to the roots of a dead tree, and used them like monkey bars until he found a sandbar. He crawled out, putting his hands on his knees as the others joined him. Tristin stumbled out beside him, laughing raucously.

"That was bloody brilliant!" he shouted. "*AMAZING!* Let's go poke that thing again!"

Viana came out next.

"What — the — *hell* — were you thinking?" she demanded.

Grimmond looked between the two of them, then to Nelton and the other Gargoyles.

"Thanks for helping me, Nelton," he said genuinely. "I know what you mean now about there being no Haunted Gargoyles left. I guess I'll wait until there's another one."

Viana raised her head from the sand.

"You mean to tell me you *wanted* to ride that thing?"

Grimmond shrugged.

"Not after I saw it," he said embarrassedly. "I just wanted to be able to try out. You know, for the Black Wings...."

Viana rose to her feet and got close enough for him to see her eyeliner running in the dark. He had no idea how she still smelled wonderful after coming out of a lake.

"That's the dumbest thing I've *ever* heard," she scolded.

She shook her head back and forth, but Grimmond saw a smile teasing the corners of her mouth.

"Well," Tristin laughed, clapping Grimmond on the shoulder. "Now we know you can fly. If a Nightmarist bites the dust before Squadron tryouts in a few weeks, their Gargoyle is as good as yours!"

BLACK WINGS

Even though Grimmond had been spending most of his time with Tristin and Viana, he didn't realize he was friends with them until his godmother asked him about it.

Eralynn had been gone much, working closely with Lord Stawlart, and Grimmond hadn't spoken to her since classes began. She'd left the Hollow with Nelton several times, but Grimmond hadn't forgiven her for keeping secrets, and hadn't yet found the right time to ask about his parents and the *Errandi* name.

Over coffee and a begrudging walk through the swinging nooses of Grizzly Grove, Grimmond regaled his godmother on the past few weeks. Normal classes had been going well, and Coach Maurs had taught Grimmond the basics of using a *drifter's glaive* — the Nightmarists' long, collapsible staff with one bladed end. He told her of his desire to join the Black Wings, of his close shave with the Blood Onyx, and how Malus tried to spin it as Grimmond goading the wild beast to attack the Hovel.

It turned out that Eralynn already knew about it, and she wasn't altogether pleased.

"I knew you'd be okay here, eventually," she said. "Just be more careful about things, okay?"

Grimmond ground his teeth — his reputation *had* received a much-needed boost after the incident with the Blood Onyx — but he nodded nonetheless.

Drinking more coffee than he thought possible, Grimmond even dared to enjoy his freshmen Nightmare classes with the Tychus twins. Once, alone in his room, he was able to coax a quick red Flare from his bright knuckles before he fell over with dizziness. Another day, he thought that Lulling a Brute to be calmed — using the command *'Pæcief'* — stopped it from tearing another Brute to even smaller pieces.

Grimmond had to lie down afterward due to his nausea, but it was encouraging nonetheless.

Total Nightmares class was to finally take place the last Friday of September, the day before Squadron tryouts began, and after being cancelled nearly the whole month.

"Who better to teach Totals than the Boogey Man?" Tristin said as they walked together to class. "He keeps out of the action now, but we're lucky to have got him. Rumor was that the Europeans and Russians lobbied for him, but he liked New England's fresh superstitions best."

"Go ahead, tell him then," Viana whispered. "You appreciate him staying in and teaching us. Just make sure I'm nearby when you say it — I always told myself I'd be there when you die."

Tristin stared at her flatly, but Grimmond was still distracted as they neared the lowest levels of the Hovel, mulling over how he might accomplish a single successful Flare or Lull before the Squadron tryouts.

It doesn't matter, he thought. *I still can't try out for the Black Wings without my own Gargoyle to ride.*

The air was heavy with must as they entered the classroom, if the most oppressive, dark and damp room in the Hovel could be called that. Grimmond thought it looked more like a large and abandoned water cistern. He was reminded of every basement he was scared to enter as a child.

A hundred white candles burned around the wet walls, providing a small amount of light but no heat, a few passages trailed off into even darker chambers, and a desk like an ornate coffin was at the front of the room.

"I heard he's not that bad," Tristin whispered. "Really!"

Viana shivered next to him despite her jeans and thick hoodie, and Tristin grew silent. The rest of the juniors — including Malus Nebbick — piled in to take their seats.

"Where is he?" asked Linda Danners, another junior from Steeple Spike.

She gasped as on cue, a stylishly dressed man materialized from the shadows behind the desk. Grimmond couldn't immediately tell what color his skin was, as it swirled from black to white, then back to gray. He was already walking slowly amongst the tables, hands behind his back, high-collared white shirt buttoned beneath a black sweater.

"Please, tell me more about Professor *Boogey* Manning," he said in a silky, drawling voice. "I just *love* to hear the rumors."

Grimmond heard Tristin swallow next to him. Averting their eyes, most students did what they could to look small and hidden; even Malus lost some of the straw color to his face.

"The rumors, the gossip," Professor Manning whispered. "Insecurities, and fear...."

Grimmond accidentally looked directly at him, and if he'd maintained contact with the swirling white eyes for long, he might've fled in terror. But Professor Manning gave him the smallest, almost imperceptible wink. Grimmond was certain that's what it was; he just didn't know what it meant.

"I daresay I already know more about you than you know about me. The secrets — oh the secrets I've heard from the Dreamers...from the Nightmayr Realm, from *you all*. You'd pluck your ears off if you knew what your friends truly thought of you. The moral is: do not needlessly upset me, or you will regret it forever."

Accusatory looks sprang up around the classroom. Grimmond was impressed at how much discord was spread in a single speech.

"SO!" Professor Manning barked, causing everyone to jump. "Let's begin."

Learning about Total Nightmares for nearly two hours went faster than Grimmond thought. There was no textbook, since the instructor knew enough about Total Nightmares to fill several volumes. The students took notes furiously.

"Atrocities are born from people's worst fears of loss, pain, and death, and none have ever worked with the Nightmarists. They are large and powerful, and mind that no amount of Flaring or Lulling will banish them; they must be physically destroyed. And know that they are again escaping from the Nightmayr Realm, despite the work that was done to keep them all there...."

"Professor Manning, what do you mean? What work?"

Grimmond was shocked when he realized he was the one who asked the question.

"Stanchions Hollow was built several hundred years ago," Professor Manning told him. "Some creatures of the Nightmayr Realm sought a new purpose, away from the Dark Naught that ruled them. With the first Nightmarists, they created a door to trick the Dark Naught, and trap it in its own realm. But no one now knows where the door is, or the key that might lock it forever."

The professor's eyes flicked from Grimmond to the other students.

"Wherever the door may be, it is either thin and cracking — as the evil manifestations continue to escape — or it's being opened from *our* side. No handle was made for the other to use.

The Dark Naught itself has not yet escaped, but before it can, the door must by any means be found and sealed forever."

Grimmond tried to remember Kremaya's exact words in the jail cell a month ago.

She was telling me to find some sort of key, right? And to seal up the door, too...is this what she meant? But how could she know about either of them?

Class ended, but not before Professor Manning called Grimmond to the front. Grimmond gulped, telling Tristin and Viana to send a search party if he wasn't out in five minutes.

"Good question, Grimmond," Professor Manning smiled as he approached.

His entirely white eyes continued to swirl like clouds.

"Thanks, sir. I didn't mean to interrupt your lesson —"

"Be *serious*," he said. "Call me Boogey. So? Classes going well for you?"

Grimmond looked at him apprehensively.

This is THE Boogey Man, right? Why is he being so nice? He almost sounds like a normal person....

"They're okay, Mr. Boogey," Grimmond answered.

"Oh? That's not what I've heard."

"Well," Grimmond went on sheepishly, "I *do* still have trouble Flaring and Lulling, but gym class with Coach Maurs is going good, I think. I've learned to block and attack well with a glaive."

"That *is* good," Professor Manning said. "Facing a Total Nightmare is mostly weapons work. Be calm but fast, and find where they keep their heart to kill them. Sometimes, it pumps right next to their brain. What's the hold up with Flaring and Lulling?"

Being alone with the Boogey Man by his coffin-desk, and in a room lit by candles, made Grimmond feel like he was about to be used as a human sacrifice. So why was it easier to talk to him than Grimmond expected?

"I don't know," Grimmond answered. "It kind of makes me sick. Dizzy or nauseous sometimes."

Professor Manning waved his hand as if it were a small matter.

"You should've come to me sooner! That's nothing more than requiring different concentration than the other students. For someone like *you*, try singing to yourself next time. Think of music to still your mind, *then* give a Flare a go."

"Thanks, I'll try...." Grimmond scratched his head. "Can I ask you a question, Mr. Boogey?"

"You may now ask a second one," he answered, "so go on."

"Why were you acting so intimidating at the start of class, but now you're nice to me?"

Professor Manning laughed so loudly that half the candles around the room blew out, but he clapped his hands and they immediately relit. When he saw the look on Grimmond's face, he grew more serious.

"Why, Grimmond," he started. "Of course you wouldn't think that your —"

"BOOGEY MANNING!"

Grimmond jumped and turned to the open door. Eralynn was there, out of breath, hair askew, and looking feral.

"That's. *ENOUGH.*"

Grimmond stared bewilderedly between Eralynn's raging eyes and Professor Manning's stunned face. What on earth was he about to tell him? Professor Manning stood and cleared his throat, hopefully about to finish his sentence.

"That'll be all, Grimmond," he said. "Until our next class, then."

* * *

Sunset would begin the Squadron tryouts that evening, and Grimmond almost considered not going. He was still shocked at the exchange between his godmother and Total Nightmares professor, and had come up with no plausible explanation. Neither had Tristin or Viana, the ones who had inadvertently run into Eralynn and tipped her off by saying that Professor Manning had asked to speak privately with Grimmond.

"Either way," Tristin said, "looks like you've won teacher's pet. I don't know what kind of pets the Boogey Man would have though. Monsters, I suppose?"

Grimmond shrugged, shoving his hands in his pockets as they made for the lake.

"I think you'd make a *great* pet, Grim," Viana said, poking him in the side. "You'd be my little blue iguana, and I'd have a heat lamp for you, some rocks, feed you bugs...."

"Gee, thanks," Grimmond returned with a patronizing glance. "I would have that sweet tongue for catching stuff — but what about the key Professor Manning was talking about, to seal the Nightmayr Realm? Think it really exists?"

"'Course," Tristin laughed. "For a while, the Dread Map picked up a tip once or twice a year! The key's always hidden at such-and-such place, then the Squadrons race to look for it before the location changes or the map fizzles out. Gargoyles fly fast, but we never manage to get close ——"

Two Gargoyles nearly took their heads off just then, landing on the path to the lake.

"Geeze!" Grimmond yelled at Flynn and Qinella as they turned around and tucked their wings. "Don't worry about us — we're fine! Just thought you were about to carry us off to be eaten, as usual."

Flynn reared up, ripping a branch off of an antagonizing Sentree, while Qinella picked up a toad — which Grimmond learned was called a *Lightwart* — and held it to glow against an outstretched wing. Tristin and Viana hopped on their backs.

"Good luck," Grimmond said, trying to sound upbeat. "Hopefully you can find some good recruits tonight."

Viana looked at him sympathetically.

"We're really sorry, Grim," she said. "Next time. There's just nothing left for you to ride...."

Sure, Grimmond thought, *but if the Blood Onyx wasn't an evil little —*

"See you mate!" Tristin called.

The two riders flew off as Grimmond trudged, downcast, to the shore of the lake where the rest of the spectators were seated in the grass. He found Randy and the Tychus twins already there, sitting on a large blanket, with coffee and donuts from the Anxious Canine. Grimmond took a seat next to Olivia, while Keith tossed him something golf-ball sized, baked to a crispy yellow and red.

"What's this?"

"Dunno," Keith mumbled through a mouthful. "But it's either salted caramel and strawberry, or just a regular, deep-fried eyeball. Actually not bad, either way."

"Try a finger, too," Randy advised. "Zolgo made some of his cronies learn to bake!"

Grimmond took a bite, surprised to find it quite tasty. He took the box from Randy and rummaged through, trying the recommended coconut ladyfinger next — decorated like a *real* finger, of course — followed by a bat-shaped pastry filled with cream.

"What's wrong?" Olivia whispered.

Grimmond turned to see her leaning in, concerned. He looked away, nodding to the edge of the shore where the seven members of the Black Wings were assembled.

"I see," Olivia answered, her face taking on a slight pink. "Viana doesn't know, I'm guessing?"

"Oh, she knows — she and Tristin both do. I told them I wanted to try out weeks ago, but no Gargoyles ever became available."

Olivia squinted at Grimmond in quiet contemplation, then turned away to sip her coffee.

"Well, I heard you almost rode a *Blood Onyx*, and if the team can't appreciate that then — oh, damn...."

Grimmond followed her eyes to the edge of the dark water. Biff and Bianca were there, and now walked toward the grass where the rest of the spectators were. Grimmond had almost forgotten Malus was a team leader on the Bone Crawlers, second in command to the captain.

He sighed as Biff laid the blanket right in front of them. Then, he did his best to ignore the sight of Biff and Bianca sprawled on the blanket, making out. Olivia quietly cleared her throat as she stifled a nervous laugh, playing with her hair and trying to catch Grimmond's eye.

"EARTH TO LIV," Keith shouted, causing her to turn in alarm. "Toss me the little square donut, would you? I asked you like *three* times!"

Olivia swore, then grabbed the donut and threw it at her brother's face.

"I hope you *choke*, Kiki!"

Grimmond watched ruefully as the event began.

One by one, the recruits were staged on their Gargoyles, among whom was Grimmond's floor mate, Keokuk. When Drek Heeder sounded the whistle blow, they zoomed across the lake. Randy kept a constant stream of information in Grimmond's ear, which he found to be distracting on a good level.

He learned that the *Aurora Blights* had the most Glass Wing Gargoyles, were the best at Flaring, and handled Terrors with ease. Bone Crawler Gargoyles — those that looked like draconic skeletons — largely filled the ranks of the *Sleepwalkers*, who were more adept at Lulling. Training for worst-case scenarios, like facing Total Nightmares, the Skeleton Crew and Black Wings competed for which was the more balanced Squadron.

Grimmond wished he could be up there among them, to be doing *something*. He wanted to help look for the key that Professor Manning talked about. The same, perhaps, that Kremaya had warned him to look for. But the tryouts were nearing their end.

Grimmond's hair was blown back as Malus landed in the grass with his Bone Crawler. He dismounted and motioned with his finger to Bianca. She jumped off of Biff, ran over to him, and wrapped her lips around his.

Mid-swig of his Wrigglebits mocha, Grimmond turned to spit it out in the grass.

"Yeah," Randy muttered beside him, "one of those, uh, *arrangements*. Dual privileges for her. I'd advise not to ask."

Malus opened his eyes, pushed Bianca away, and strutted over to Grimmond.

"No Gargoyle, little Errandi?" he said with a sneer. "For the best, I'd say."

Grimmond stood, his face already heating up.

"And why's that?"

Malus came closer and put a hand on Grimmond's shoulder, causing him to tense with repulsion. Grimmond had never seen Malus's sickly yellow skin this close before, never smelled the sour meat on his breath, or seen the bloodshot red in his frenzied eyes.

"Five minutes to get to the other side of the lake and back. Flare through the Terrors barring the tunnel once you get there, Lull the Haunter to steal the silver ring off its belt, then bring the ring back here on the tip of your glaive."

"Doesn't sound bad," Grimmond said, throwing Malus's hand away. "Give me your Gargoyle and maybe I'll show you how it's done."

"Oh?" Malus mocked. "But I heard you can't Flare, Lull, or fight yet. And I bet your glaive isn't long enough to hold the ring, either."

Grimmond's blood boiled as he heard snorts of laughter from the blankets around them. He remembered the warning Randy gave him — that something wasn't right with Malus Nebbick — and Grimmond believed it after seeing Malus's eyes turn black a few weeks ago.

"Come on, Nebbick," Randy attempted to intervene, "just lay off."

"Quiet, *Randall*," Malus scolded. "This doesn't concern you."

Randy quieted, and the twins looked on apprehensively as Malus stepped close enough for Grimmond to feel his body heat.

Come on.... Another inch closer and I'll knock your stinking teeth out.

"For the best, like I said," Malus whispered so only Grimmond could hear. "What if you lost your balance and took another fall? Go back to Boston where it's safe. Pretend like you've never heard of Stanchions Hollow, and let the *real* Nightmarists take care of things."

Grimmond shivered as Malus's eyes darkened like they did in the Hearth, and his voice became deep and gravelly.

"Trust me, little Errandi," Malus's changed voice said. "I'll fix it so you can't ever fly — let alone walk — again."

Without Tristin and Viana there to back him, Malus may have thought Grimmond would crumble in fear. But he didn't. With all his strength, Grimmond shoved Malus backward, and he tripped over the box of donuts and fell flat on his back.

Malus gasped pitifully, wind knocked out of his diaphragm, but was on his feet in a flash to unsheathe the collapsed glaive on his back. Malus flung it open and leveled the bladed end at Grimmond. But just as Olivia sucked in a breath to scream, Nelton landed between the two boys.

"Enough," said the Gargoyle calmly.

"You're done, Errandi!" Malus choked, smoothing out his hair.

Grimmond's ears were ringing, still ready to fight, but Malus put away his glaive and turned around. With rotten breath he offered another kiss to Bianca, then jumped on his Bone Crawler and flew back to the lake. Fuming, Grimmond likewise stormed away, despite the twins and Randy asking if he was okay.

He barely made it back to the path to the Hovel before Nelton landed in front of him.

"That was unwise, Grimmond."

"You should have let me!" Grimmond yelled. "I'm sick of this! Sick of being *useless*! I'm not able to do anything here!"

"Kill-it, Kill-it," chirped the Lightwarts illuminating the path.

"I know what you —"

"No, you DON'T!" Grimmond yelled. "You don't know — none of you do! Malus is *right*...I'll never be a real Nightmarist. I should just leave!"

Grimmond wrung his hands in frustration, leaning against a Sentree and swatting its branches away.

"I have to help, somehow," Grimmond said. "To do something. *Anything.*"

Nelton growled low, approaching and speaking quietly.

"Are you so certain of what you ask, Grimmond?" Nelton asked cryptically. "There are only two candidates left for the Black Wings. You may have a chance, if we hurry — or you may die this time. Are you ready for *anything?*"

"Of course I'm ready!" Grimmond said quickly. "But what was the part about dying —"

Nelton picked Grimmond up mid-sentence, threw him on his back, and took to the sky toward the Sleepless Orchard. Grimmond thought about protesting, but was already too full of adrenaline to care. He had to beat Malus, and step one was getting a ride.

"I will not intervene this time," Nelton said as they grazed the trees of the forest. "Good luck."

Nelton slowed as they entered the clearing, and Grimmond hopped off. He nodded his thanks to Nelton, and was left alone as the Glass Wing flew away.

Gnarled and black still, the tall, false tree stump was on the edge of the clearing as it was before. Grimmond approached slowly, but it sensed him immediately. Unfurling its wings, it fell forward into a crouched position, and Grimmond's anger toward Malus was dampened by rising panic.

The Blood Onyx looked more malevolent than he remembered. Its ridged horns had curled deeper; its fangs were longer and sharper than before, and its eyes blacker than coal.

If Malus were a Gargoyle, he'd look like this. I wonder if it remembers me....

When the Blood Onyx sniffed in his direction and growled deeply, Grimmond knew it did. His heart rate kicked in, and the night lit up for him. The creature's mouth opened wide to reveal dripping fangs, and it lunged.

"WAIT!"

Grimmond was knocked to the ground like a dead plant, and could do nothing but wait for his head to be removed. But the Gargoyle's teeth didn't immediately snap. It sniffed Grimmond as it had on their first meeting, then turned its head toward him, glossy eyes looking him over.

Inexplicably, it closed its mouth and slowly removed its claws from his chest. Grimmond looked down, breathing hard, rubbing his hands over his body as he tried not to hyperventilate. He was uninjured.

"Do I smell so bad?" Grimmond asked stupidly.

What are you doing? SHUT UP AND RUN!

The Blood Onyx spread its wings, opening its mouth and roaring ferociously.

"No, no!" Grimmond yelled, throwing up his hands. "Please! I need your help!"

Closing its giant jaws, the Blood Onyx turned its intelligent yet malignant eyes on him. Grimmond nearly choked on his own tongue. Did it actually understand him? Grimmond was acutely aware that one swipe of its wing would snap him in two.

"Please, I — I need you to *help* me...." Grimmond stammered. "You're the only Gargoyle left. I promise nobody else'll ride you, and no Nightmares will try to possess you."

The Blood Onyx growled again, more softly this time.

"I know you're as alone as I am," Grimmond said quietly. "Please...I have to show them...I need to prove that I'm not what they think I am."

Grimmond's legs shook as the Gargoyle turned to the right, and averted its eyes.

That's it then...I'm about to die....

But then it turned back, blinked quietly, and lowered its wing for Grimmond to climb up.

* * *

"Well!" Drek shouted. "It looks like that was the last candidate. We'll let you all know when we've decided...."

The Black Wings team captain quieted as he saw a large black Gargoyle drop out of the sky. Several people screamed when they saw it was the Blood Onyx, and the Squadrons unsheathed their weapons to defend the crowd. But then Grimmond hurriedly dismounted, whispered something to the Blood Onyx to settle it, and ran up to Drek.

"Got time for one more?" he panted.

Drek stared, his expression completely blank. He pointed at the Blood Onyx, growling threateningly at the other Gargoyles surrounding it.

"You...you brought a *Blood Onyx*," he muttered. "You're riding *the wild* Blood Onyx?"

Tristin and Viana raced up next, their expressions equally bewildered as they looked between Grimmond and the wild Gargoyle.

"Grim," Viana gasped, "is that the same —"

"Yes," Grimmond answered quickly, turning back to Drek. "I could try out as long as I found a Gargoyle, right? Well, I've got one now. Call him Brax. Blow the whistle when you're ready! I already know what to do."

"Heads up, Grim!" Tristin called, tossing him a glaive to use for the trial.

Grimmond caught it, then ran past a wide-eyed Malus who approached with the swelling crowd. Grimmond climbed up on the Blood Onyx, sat between its spinal columns as Nelton taught him, and waited for the whistle blast.

"Let's go!" he called to Drek.

The whistle blew, and Grimmond urged the wild Blood Onyx high into the sky. It was fast, but its flight and movements rougher than when riding Nelton.

"Straight ahead!" Grimmond called. "We've got five minutes to do this!"

Grimmond concentrated on not dropping Tristin's glaive in the lake, even though it stung in his grip. He used his other hand to grasp the chiseled, bony spike protruding from his mount's neck. Riding his own Gargoyle was too surreal to yet believe, and he tried to ignore it; the other side of the lake was fast approaching, and he needed to get the silver ring, or it was all for nothing.

A sandy beach was at the base of the tree-covered mountain range, and on it lie the biggest fallen tree Grimmond had ever seen. He guessed it was hollowed out, because a mass of Terrors swarmed around its spindly roots.

Remember, Boogey said to concentrate and think of music.

"Over there, Brax!" Grimmond shouted. "Put us down on that rock!"

Grimmond jumped from the rock into the sand, turning when he saw a bright green Flare from the opposite side of the dark lake — the signal that one minute had passed.

He donned his bright knuckles and thought of the *Terror Wheel*, which taught Flaring the opposite color of the Terror being actively dealt with. A red Terror was Flared with green light, a blue with orange light, and so on.

Rising up in a colorful swarm, they rushed toward Grimmond, but Brax roared, and they all turned swiftly toward the Gargoyle in response. Grimmond had his window to enter the base of the fallen tree. He sprinted toward it, until a single yellow Terror broke away from the swarm, shot into a large piece of driftwood, and zoomed back to attack Grimmond.

Grimmond raised his bright knuckles like he was ready to throw a punch, tried to remember the emotion to create purple light, and thought of his favorite rock song. But when he thrust his fist forward, nothing lit up, and Grimmond was slammed with dizziness like he'd just been spun in a circle.

"Come on!" Grimmond yelled, shaking his knuckles and narrowly avoiding the log smashing into him. "This was supposed to work! Come *ON*!"

The yellow orb rebounded on him, and Grimmond raised his knuckles again to no avail. This time, the driftwood caught him in the stomach. He saw stars, dropped the glaive and doubled over in pain.

Was the Terror actually trying to *hurt* him?

Grimmond looked around, but no referee was there, no other students watching, and no one to help. Another flash of light came from the starting line — two minutes had passed.

One more time, the Terror-possessed-log came soaring in for his head. Concentrating with all his might on his favorite song, Grimmond raised his knuckles, thought of every purple thing he could imagine, and hoped Professor Manning's advice wouldn't get him killed.

Bright purple light Flared from his knuckles to shoot out across the beach. The driftwood fell to the ground, the yellow orb of light ejected from it.

IT WORKED!

He didn't have time to celebrate. His head spun with dizziness as he rose to his feet, ran to the hollowed-out tree, and looked inside. In its center was a glowing silver ring the width of a basketball, waiting to be taken. But Grimmond saw no Haunter present.

He went in haphazardly, almost able to grab the ring before being launched backwards out into the sand. Confused, coughing and gasping as he rolled to a stop, Grimmond knew he was lucky not to have been impaled on Tristin's glaive.

Duh! Haunters can be invisible! Lull it first!

Grimmond jumped up and ran back with his glaive leveled before him. The ring glittered inside the hollow tree, and Grimmond focused his eyes to see better, though he could barely make out the Haunter holding it. He concentrated hard on the command word to make the Haunter sleep, 'Somnüs', and thought of the same song he had before.

"SOMNÜS," he boomed.

Immediately Grimmond knew the Lull worked as he felt his energy drained and his skin loosen, but with it his stomach grew more nauseous than ever. The silver ring began to float toward him from the tunnel, and he heard the high-pitched wail of what held it. It wasn't a Haunter.

Raising his knuckles and Flaring purple once again to light up the area, Grimmond's heart caught in his throat when he saw what was crawling toward him, upside down: a *Prowler*.

Stomach torn open, blood bubbles popping in its mouth, the Prowler typically looked like a lacerated, long-dead young woman. Prowlers didn't speak. Its face was rotted and bloated, eyes glowing silver like the ghostly flashlights Grimmond remembered from the party in Short Branch; Grimmond had learned that the three things he saw at that party were *all* Prowlers.

A distant flash of orange light indicated there were only two minutes remaining.

The Prowler jumped toward him, shrieking, and Grimmond slashed at it with his glaive to remove a chunk of its leg. He raised a hand to his face to block an acrid orange spray from hitting his eyes, and the Prowler tumbled by, shrieking in pain.

Prowlers were easily the worst of the Major Nightmares, so why would the Black Wings be testing recruits on something so dangerous?

Grimmond wiped his hand in the sand to get the burning liquid off, trying to remember the command word used against

Prowlers. He dodged it again, slashing out with his glaive in return.

Not Somnüs, he thought, *not Pæcief or Frigëra....*

The ring dangled from the Prowler's waist as it ran toward him on all fours.

"Got it!" Grimmond yelled, concentrating on the word to make it sick with vertigo. "TIMORÜL!"

The Prowler fell to the ground and its silver eyes dimmed, but Grimmond fell too. Luckily, he was used to the cost of this particular Lull, as nausea and dizziness were what usually happened to him. He stumbled over to the prone creature, ripped the silver ring from its belt, and wiped it in the sand.

A red flare shone out across the lake — one minute remained.

"BRAX!" Grimmond yelled.

Spreading its wings and roaring, the Blood Onyx spun away from the swarm of Terrors and over to Grimmond, who hopped on and took to the sky.

"We can do this! Hurry!"

Brax soared across the lake, Grimmond hanging on tightly to the glaive in one hand, and the ring and Gargoyle with his other. They had only seconds, but the finish line was in sight.

"GO, GO, GO!"

Grimmond passed over the lakeshore, dropping the ring in the sand as Drek blew the whistle. Brax banked out of the turn and glided softly in for a landing before the Black Wings Squadron.

Nearly yanked off his mount, Grimmond was deafened as Tristin, Randy, and half the Hollow screamed and cheered. He was spun around, patted, smacked on the back and even hugged.

"Yo!" Keokuk called beside a cheering Wynn. "That's my roommate!"

"GRIMMOND!" Keith ran up and crushed him in a bear hug. "You know what type of Gargoyle that is, right? They're sooo dangerous —"

"Nice one, Grimmond!" Olivia called behind him, smiling with relief.

Drek Heeder pushed his way through the crowd, reaching Grimmond and shaking his hand vigorously.

"You've got to be *kidding* me!" Drek sang with delight, his muscular, scarred arms now jolting Grimmond's entire body. "We've got the Blood Onyx. The freaking *Blood Onyx*, man!"

In the surges of adrenaline, Grimmond realized he was looking for Viana, and found her at the edge of the crowd. She stared at him with her head cocked to the side. Then she shoved her tongue in her cheek, rolled her eyes, and smiled.

"Grimmond Scylent!" Drek hushed the crowd. "I think it's safe to say, welcome to the Black Wings!"

Erupting with tumultuous applause again, the crowd almost lifted Grimmond onto their shoulders. He was beyond elated.

I did it....

For once in his life, people were *celebrating* him, not calling him a freak. They were smiling, not whispering behind their hands. And it was all over far too soon.

When Malus pushed his way through the crowd, placing a small glowing object back in his pocket, Grimmond's smile faltered.

"HEEDER!" Malus called, his voice shaking with rage. "Every Squadron has the same rules for the tryout, right?"

"Yeah, Nebbick, what's your point —"

"State the rules of the trial!" Malus yelled again, his lips trembling.

Drek sighed, but obligingly rolled his eyes and spoke.

"'The recruit will, in five minutes, travel to the other side of the lake, demonstrate knowledge of Minor and Major

Nightmare tactics, retrieve the ring from the Haunter's waist belt, and return with the ring balanced on the glaive before time is up.' Those are the rules, Nebbick."

So it should *have been a Haunter instead of a Prowler?* Grimmond thought. *And it said so right in the rules?*

Biff and Bianca laughed beside Malus, who then pointed accusatorily at Grimmond's reddened face. His spirit sank; he had an idea of where this was going.

"Grimmond held the ring the entire time!" Malus called victoriously. "He deliberately didn't balance it on his glaive like he was supposed to!"

The smiling crowd began to murmur, some shrugging, others nodding their assent. Grimmond looked to Tristin and Viana pleadingly, who understood and began to speak into their team captain's ears.

"It's true, Drek," said another girl, who Grimmond knew to be the Skeleton Crew's team captain. "Hate to say it, but I saw it myself. He didn't complete the trial by the rules. He's out."

"Come on, Harriet!" Drek said, looking between the other enraged Black Wings. "Be reasonable! There's such a thing as semantics, and I think as long as the recruit brings back the ring, that should be what counts —"

"No way!" Malus shouted. "He didn't follow the rules, so he's disqualified!"

Grimmond thought being called a rule-breaker was a bit harsh.

"Now wait just a minute," he said, "the rules themselves weren't followed! I had to Lull a Prowler to get the ring, not a Haunter. It took twice as long!"

Malus scoffed, and Grimmond watched the secret smile exchanged between Biff and Bianca.

They did this...somehow...they switched the Haunter for the Prowler....

"So you wanna play it that way? Just being a whiny, lying loser?" Malus mocked as he approached Grimmond. "Here he is — the Errandi boy! Whose dad knocked his mom up senior year, and they both dropped out of Stanchions Hollow together!"

Someone snorted with laughter, and Grimmond watched many of his former admirers raise their brows. His ears began to ring.

"Do you really want him on your Squadron, Drek? Defending us?" Malus went on, pointing at Grimmond. "He's been hiding in Boston his whole life, denying that Nightmares were real! He cried in his sheets while the rest of us were fighting and getting hurt, or worse! He'll let us down just like his parents did!"

The corners of Grimmond's vision turned bluish-white.

"Not only are you *disqualified*," Malus turned to him, poking a finger in his chest, "but I vote that the Blood Onyx should go to a team who actually knows how to use it!"

That was too much for Grimmond, especially after he promised Brax that no one else would ride him. Malus reached to place a hand on Brax's wing, but before he was able, Grimmond snapped. He grabbed Malus by the shoulders, head-butted him directly in the teeth, then kicked him hard into the dirt.

"Touch him and I'll rip your slimy little head off!" Grimmond bellowed, murderously enraged. "BRAX, LEAVE NOW!"

The Blood Onyx spread its wings, knocking a few people down, and took to the sky for the Sleepless Orchard. Malus stood up, bleeding as the Skeleton Crew came forward. But the Black Wings likewise hustled to move next to Grimmond, and Drek stepped between the two groups.

"This stops, *now*," he said authoritatively. "No more! We're on the same side, for goodness' sake!"

Drek looked to Grimmond, swore viciously, and placed a hand on his shoulder.

"Look, Grim...."

Looking at Malus's bleeding but smiling face, Grimmond saw the evil laughter in his eyes. Heart still racing, Grimmond dropped the sharp glaive at Tristin's feet — before he could do something he *truly* regretted.

"I'm really, really sorry, man," Drek said.

Grimmond was breathing sharply, closing his eyes to hide his tears of rage, and took one deep breath to calm himself. He looked quickly between his friends and his enemies, then sighed dejectedly

"Do what you want," he muttered. "I'm done with all of you."

And with that, he turned and walked back to the Hovel.

HALLOWEEN

October was mostly miserable for Grimmond, and as much as he tried, the anger from not making it onto the Black Wings wasn't eased. Friends that noticed tried to help, each in their own ways, and some more effective than others.

The twins offered to do his homework one week — which Grimmond did not accept — and Randy did his best to divert the rumors flying around that Grimmond was a loose cannon. Grimmond was glad to have at least won over his two other roommates, Keokuk and Wynn. Keokuk was apologetic for being the only recruit the Black Wings chose, and told Grimmond he was even willing to give up his spot.

Grimmond told him he'd earned his position fair and square, and that was that.

Tristin was all jokes and games in Steeple Spike, and always he avoided the subject of training with the Black Wings, which Grimmond appreciated. Viana, on the other hand, smelling of sweet flowers and wearing a blue skull hairpin one Friday night, asked Grimmond if he'd like to take a walk down to the lake.

Grimmond flatly refused, saying that was the last place he wanted to see. He hadn't even been out to visit Brax since the tryouts — something he did feel guilty for.

Viana stormed out of Fire Watch, snapping at the Sentrees as she went.

"As *soon* as he falls asleep in that chair, toss that sad idiot straight off the balcony!"

When Grimmond asked Tristin what he did wrong, Tristin shook his head and patted him on the cheek.

"There, there, sweet child," he patronized. "I'll explain when you're older."

Strangely, the only real comfort in the weeks following Grimmond's disqualification was seeing Malus. Whenever they passed one another in the corridors, Malus looked darkly at him, and Grimmond smiled proudly at the stitches holding his upper lip together. Grimmond never got into any trouble, but word of the fight only expanded rumors that he was a violent good-for-nothing.

Could what he said have been true? Did my mother really get pregnant with me in high school?

Eralynn would know, but she was gone again. Grimmond was left to his thoughts, and the question festered inside him, a frustration waiting to lash out and draw blood. Maybe the rumors about his violence weren't so unfounded after all, but that part didn't bother him.

He was back to the normal he knew: gossip surrounded his family, the majority of people wondered after his mental stability, and only a handful of peers actually cared about him. But different this time, Grimmond knew how to Flare and Lull, and on his side was the most dangerous Gargoyle in North America.

Grimmond was ready to leave Stanchions Hollow.

The Halloween Dance neared, but the Hovel didn't want much for decoration, being haunted already.

Sentrees from Grisly Grove were inside for the festivities, corpse-skeletons swinging from nooses in their branches, which grabbed and tried to smother anything that passed by. Terror-possessed-pumpkins floated down the halls, auras glowing as they heckled, and smashing into Nightmarists' heads if they walked too close. Even the Hearth's Rebbigones let their horns grow long, and Zolgo switched up the menu of the coffee shop.

But Grimmond had his plan ready for Saturday night, during the dance.

His backpack was full and jammed behind his bed, his letter to Eralynn written and waiting to be set on his pillow. Once everyone was headed to the Hearth for the celebration, Grimmond would get his things, go to the Sleepless Orchard, and run away with Brax. Together, they'd go back to Boston, and explain to the authorities what really happened in August.

He wanted to see his old house, his favorite restaurants, and his old city. Forget the consequences, along with the Ending that was *supposedly* after him. He expected he knew enough now to defend himself against it, anyway.

"Why the long face?" Keith asked him after lunch on Saturday.

Grimmond was roused from his stupor and inclined his ear.

"Hmm?"

"He asked what's on your mind," Olivia leaned in.

"Oh — just thinking about the dance tonight," Grimmond returned. "Never liked school functions much back in Boston — *especially* the dances. I usually stayed home."

"Well, you're not this year!" Keith said. "Because the party's happening *in* your home!"

Grimmond waved to the twins as they walked past the Anxious Canine and toward Hollow Dwell. Olivia quickly hurried back, however, cheeks flushed from ear to ear.

"Save me a dance?"

"Sure thing," Grimmond lied.

Olivia's face blushed deeper.

"Ok," she said. "See you in a few hours then. The dance starts back in the Hearth at supper time, if you didn't know...."

Grimmond would miss the twins. Along with his newer friends in Steeple Spike — not to mention anything of Viana. Since blowing off her request for a walk, he had tried to speak to her several times, but she'd barely give him the time of night. He still didn't understand why she was so upset with him.

As Grimmond thought to himself, he realized he had more friends in the Hollow than he ever did in Boston. Why did he want to leave again?

Someone who's done what you have doesn't deserve friends.

Grimmond cast his eyes down, turned around, and ran into Professor Manning. Or he *would* have, if the man didn't dissolve into shadow, drop his cup to spill on the floor, and reform on the other side of Grimmond. He straightened his black button-up and stepped away as a glowing green mop floated over to clean the spill.

"Had anyone *else* just cost me my favorite brew," he said, "they wouldn't sleep for a week."

"I'm really sorry, Mr. Boogey! I didn't see you," Grimmond apologized. "What can I get you?"

"Nothing," he smiled. "I must see to a few last-minute preparations, actually —"

"Just hang on — I'll get you something quick. Ally! One black coffee, please!"

Grimmond called to the barista, Ally Ians, the freshman girl from Narcoleptic Row with whom he had Minor Nightmares. She nodded in return, quickly poured a to-go cup, and winked as she slid it across the counter. Grimmond paid her a yellowish Skief from the allowance Eralynn gave him, and handed the coffee to Professor Manning.

"Thank you Grimmond, but that wasn't necessary. I daresay I make a bit more Marrow than you."

Grimmond had one more person to add to his miss-list. He thought back to a few weeks ago, when their conversation was interrupted by Eralynn. It seemed that Professor Manning had been about to tell him something important, but Eralynn never would tell Grimmond what it was.

"Mr. Boogey," Grimmond asked. "Can I ask you something? About a few weeks ago —"

"If you're asking what I think you are, I shall preemptively deny you. I must respect Eralynn's wishes, and so should you."

Grimmond nodded.

"Reason number twelve that I'm outta here," Grimmond mumbled sullenly under his breath.

"What's that? I'm not as young as I look, you know — my hearing isn't excellent."

"Nothing," Grimmond answered, "just looking forward to the dance tonight."

Grimmond sat down at one of the circular wooden tables, old scratches and stains covering most of its surface.

"I never thanked you for your advice," Grimmond said, looking up. "About concentrating with music? I've been able to Flare and Lull since then, kind of. It still hurts, but I was able to take down a Prowler for the Squadron tryouts."

The man nodded, his swirling gray skin and eyes still trying to choose a color for the evening.

"May that be the worst you see, then, wherever you go," he answered gravely.

Grimmond swallowed.

"What do you mean?"

"If you ever end up somewhere that *isn't the Hollow*, it's been a pleasure teaching you," Professor Manning raised his cup. "I'm off to help with the dance decorations for now. I hope to see you there, Grimmond."

The man turned down the corridor, but spoke over his shoulder once more before disappearing.

"No matter how bad it all seems to you, remember to look up sometimes. We always have our friends. And our family...."

Grimmond was left sitting at the table, feeling very much like a child caught red-handed. Somehow, Professor Manning knew exactly what he had planned.

At two o'clock in the morning, Tristin, Keokuk and Wynn left for the dance, and Grimmond acted as if he would shortly follow. Instead, he placed his letter to Eralynn on his pillow, and grabbed his backpack from behind the bed. Feeling within it for his bright knuckles, he'd almost forgotten the glaive that was also there, taken from the hands of a statue on the sixth floor.

He pulled out the darkly glinting weapon, its blade warm to the touch. It didn't sting his hands like Tristin's glaive did, and he believed no one would miss it. But taking it out of the Hovel permanently now felt more like stealing.

Hurrying down Steeple Spike's stairs, Grimmond immediately Flared an orange lamp that attacked him. Dizzy afterward, he then kicked a corpse-skeleton through an open window for attempting to strangle him with its cut noose. He snuck through detouring corridors to avoid the Hearth, hearing the shouts of laughter and delighted screams pouring over the music.

At least it's not robot-techno.

Glowing with brilliant colors of neon, the entire Hollow was alit as always when Grimmond stepped outside by Marrow Mansion. It was chillier than expected; fall was in the air and the first of November had technically come at midnight a few hours ago. He hadn't thought to bring warmer clothing, but it was too late now.

Wolves, or perhaps coyotes — Grimmond didn't know which — howled from the mountains in the distance. He picked up his pace to a jog, feeling like a true runaway, and headed toward the Sleepless Orchard.

Grass and leaves crunched beneath his feet once he reached the clearing, and as he hoped, Brax was there, crouched over the large wolf head he was eating and licking his lips. The Blood Onyx whipped its head up, tossed the shredded animal to the side, and crawled toward him with a snarl.

"WHOA, Brax!" Grimmond called out, raising his hands and stepping backwards. "It's just me...remember?"

Stopping before Grimmond was torn in two, the Blood Onyx sniffed the air as blood dripped from its mouth. It growled low, but allowed Grimmond to come nearer.

"Feel like helping me one more time?" Grimmond asked. "I need a way out of here."

Brax's growl grew louder, and he raised his head to the sky and spread his wings.

Grimmond looked up to see a silvery Glass Wing swooping down into the clearing. At first he expected it to be Nelton, advising him against rash action, but then he saw that it was Qinella. Still worse, jumping off her back and stomping over to him was Viana.

"Has anyone told you that you're the world's *biggest jerk?*"

Grimmond's cheeks reddened as Viana shoved a piece of paper in his face. Even angry, and wearing Gargremlin ears for the Halloween Dance, Grimmond found it hard to ignore his attraction to her. At the same time, she made him feel as small as he felt the night she saved him. She held the piece of paper to read.

"*'Dear Eralynn',*" she started in a mocking voice. "'I don't belong at Stanchions like you thought I did. I have to go back to my old life in Boston. Tell everyone I say goodbye, especially —'"

"How'd you get that?" Grimmond demanded, snatching it out of her hands.

"I was looking for *you*, and saw that ridiculous letter on your pillow instead!"

She retook the letter, crumpled and threw it on the ground, then raised a finger to poke his chest.

"Seems like you were giving Eralynn the names of anyone you'd ever met," she said angrily. "You even told her to say goodbye to Zolgo, you *loser* —"

"That *wasn't* yours to read," Grimmond said, pushing her finger off his chest.

"OH!" she yelled. "I didn't gather that from the *exhaustive* list of names written in there!"

She took a step closer as Grimmond backed away.

"You don't get it — I can't stay anymore," Grimmond sighed, dropping his backpack and running his hands through his hair. "What's the issue here, Vi?"

Immediately Viana's fist swung upward for his shortening of her name. The punch likely would have socked him in the mouth, but Grimmond caught her by the wrist. It was shaking.

"You didn't mention me," she whispered through gritted teeth. "Not *anywhere*."

Grimmond's gut sank. He released her with the expectation of getting punched again, but she didn't move.

"Why didn't you?" she asked.

"Because, I'm a jerk, like you said," he answered. "Just a violent and angry, scared, couldn't-make-it-on-the-Squadron, jerk. And I'm done pretending like I'm not any of those things."

"You think the rest of us aren't?" Viana declared. "Not angry that we only see a few hours of sunlight a week? You think we're *all* not scared of Nightmares, still? Of course we are! But we don't give up!"

"You don't have to deal with Malus Nebbick."

"Forget about Malus!" she asserted. "Don't just leave the Hollow because of a few bullies! Don't let them rot what good you have in you!"

Viana, you have no idea *who I really am...or what I'm capable of....*

She sounded close to tears now.

"And don't EVER leave without saying goodbye to *me!*"

This time Viana's punch caught Grimmond in the stomach unawares, and he fell to his knees, doubled over in pain. Viana gasped, and her hands flew to her mouth.

"Grim!" she fell to her knees beside him. "I-I'm sorry! I didn't mean to hit you so hard!"

Catching his breath, Grimmond stayed on the ground with Viana's hand on his back. The clearing was quiet otherwise aside from the distant baying of the wolves, and Brax and Qinella's quiet growling. Viana helped him up after a few moments, holding his hands tightly.

Grimmond was sure she released him after feeling his pulse double in cadence.

"You can't go," she said quietly, moving her hands to her hips. "I know what happened with that bully, Erik, and the Ending that's after you. No one in Boston will believe what you have to say. You'll be arrested."

"You don't know that for sure," he responded. "I can at least try."

"And if you *fail*, you can't return through the mist to the Hollow, even if you want to."

Grimmond lowered his gaze.

"Come to the dance with me," she said. "Stay one more night, and I won't say anything if you try to sneak out tomorrow."

"It'll be harder tomorrow," Grimmond explained. "That's the whole reason I chose tonight, while everyone is distracted with that stupid party."

"Fine, then *I'll* help you sneak out tomorrow," she bargained. "Just stay one more night. Forget about everything else. Please?"

Grimmond looked from the crumpled letter to Brax, and then back to Viana with frustration.

"Why do you *care*?" he said exasperatedly. "You haven't talked to me in weeks! I didn't think we were even friends anymore!"

With a sigh, Viana shook her head, turned on her heel, and walked back to Qinella, muttering something about the cluelessness of boys. She hopped on Qinella's back, adjusted her Gargremlin ears, and called out.

"We're *all* heading back now. If the Blood Onyx is yours, you need to have him stay in the stable towers and get used to flying around the Gargoyles. Mount up."

Grimmond took a few steps across the clearing toward Qinella and Viana.

"I will on one condition," he said. "I need a question answered."

"Okay...." she replied cautiously.

"Why do you get *so* upset," he asked, "when people call you 'Vi' instead of Viana?"

She didn't immediately answer, but Grimmond thought he saw her grip Qinella's horns a little tighter.

"Because," she answered quietly, "that's what my dad used to call me when I was a little girl."

Qinella jumped into the sky and zoomed toward the stables. After a moment, Grimmond was able to uproot his feet, which felt like they'd sunk several feet into the earth.

"Vi...." he whispered. "My mom used to call me 'Grinny', since I never used to smile. But don't tell anyone that, Brax."

Grabbing his backpack Grimmond climbed atop the Blood Onyx, who had already eaten the crumpled letter, and they took to the sky in a rush of wings.

The sleeping Gargoyles sprang to life when the Blood Onyx landed and Grimmond dismounted. Viana waited for him at the top of the stairs beside Nelton — whose presence meant that Eralynn was again back at the Hollow.

"Nobody touches the Blood Onyx," Grimmond said to Nelton. "I call him Brax, by the way. He'll be staying up here. For at least one night."

Together Viana and Grimmond walked into the Hearth, greeted by loud party music, smells of food and cider, and ridiculous outfits. Several people called out to the newcomers, but the rest of them were too busy laughing and dancing to the music. As was his habit, Grimmond searched the crowd for Malus, but didn't see him anywhere.

Drek Heeder was using his arms to flap a pair of butterfly wings taped to his back, while Keokuk and Wynn had on bicycle helmets and sunglasses. Tristin was close by, long-bearded with a shark fin strapped to his back, dancing wildly as he chanted 'wizard shark' for the Stychus twins.

Viana bit back a smile, eyeing Grimmond warily as she adjusted her headband.

"Here," she said, handing him a wet mop that leaned against the wall. "Your costume for the night, if anyone asks."

"I'm a wet mop?" Grimmond asked. "Really?"

"You said it, not me," she replied sassily. "But I was thinking *janitor.*"

Food was spread out for suppertime, but there was much more than usual, and all color-themed for Halloween.

Grimmond first saw a bowl of purple tarot rolls that had tiny, terrified faces baked into them. He realized how hungry he was as his stomach rumbled and mouth watered.

On each table were platters of still-sizzling, blackened short ribs, sausages made to look like giant fingers, and mounds of pulled pork shaped into screaming faces. Spices filled apothecary jars, and bowls shaped like skulls or eyeballs held barbecue and other dipping sauces. Cast iron dishes of macaroni or mashed potatoes were more orange than they should have been, kept warm by wreaths of black fire, and a pair of Rebbigones stoking the flames.

Grimmond immediately tried to sit at a table, but Viana yanked him toward the far wall, where the Anxious Canine had set up a booth of drinks and pastries. Zolgo greeted them with a wide grin. His face was covered red in something that looked suspiciously like lipstick, and two black and white stockings dangled from his ears.

"You're dressed up like me — a Gargremlin!" piped Zolgo to Viana. "Guess what I am?"

"Crazy?" she asked. "Or have you misplaced your laundry?"

"NO!" Zolgo shouted. "I'm a sock puppet!"

Grimmond tried not to laugh with Viana, intending to stay focused on leaving as soon as possible. But a smile snuck across his face anyway, and a happy feeling started to undermine his plans.

Good grief…do I actually want *to be here?*

Grimmond may have been having a hard time at the Hollow, but a pretty girl had technically asked him to a dance that night. A girl who may have beaten him up if he refused, but a pretty girl nonetheless.

Zolgo's curious gaze bounced between Grimmond and Viana, and he pumped his eyebrows at Grimmond when Viana wasn't looking. Grimmond shook his head vigorously, becoming interested in a strawberry eyeball on the counter as Zolgo laughed. Viana looked up from the desserts that were displayed like crime scene evidence.

"What is it?" she inquired.

"Nothing!" Zolgo spat. "Mind your business, *Gargremlin*!"

"Fine, *imp*," she returned. "I'll take my usual and go. Grim here could use a giggle."

Zolgo reached beneath the counter, bringing up a tiny black cauldron with a handle on its side, along with a thick crystal goblet of light green liquid. He slid the two steaming items over; the cauldron to Grimmond and the crystal goblet to Viana.

"Whipped it up when I saw you's two walk in. You're welcome!"

"*This* is a giggle?" Grimmond asked.

"Ghoulish Gourd Latte," Viana answered with a wink. "G-G-L, or giggle, for short. Vanilla, pumpkin, cinnamon, and not on the menu anymore. Thank me later!"

They walked away after Viana additionally chose what Grimmond hoped wasn't really a baked pig's foot, but a pink pastry dipped in chocolate. They went to a table with a few others from various Wards, who scooted over to make room for them. Grimmond immediately piled onto his plate the food he'd been staring at, and began to eat hungrily.

"Easy there," Viana whispered, nudging him in the ribs. "You're gonna make yourself sick. You're not leaving tonight, remember?"

"Sorry," Grimmond said after swallowing his mouthful. "I haven't eaten much today. A lot's been on my mind — and sneaking around is hard work."

Viana smiled sympathetically, and Grimmond slowed down to enjoy his meal.

A sophomore from Narcoleptic Row, Wayne Roarsch, was dousing the flames beneath the serving dish of macaroni and cheese, and Grimmond watched a Rebbigone keep zooming in to relight it. The third time it happened, amidst the boy's mischievous laughter with his friends, two Rebbigones picked him up, only to dump him at the top of a thirty-foot Sentree buzzing with Terrors.

Zolgo's Gargremlins ran around or jumped up on the benches to refill drinks. Spider eyes glittered across the ceiling, spinning a complex web from which to hang more screaming candles. Grisly Grove Sentrees cut their corpse-skeletons from their nooses, and the fleshy bones shoved students out of the way to begin their own line dance.

Viana told Grimmond it was called the 'Rump Rattle'. It looked like a wobblier version of the electric slide, but much more grotesque when done on pairs of oozing ankles and stump legs. The corpse-skeletons did it every year, Viana said, until the Nightmarists would get fed up and take the floor back over. Grimmond found himself smiling as he drank from his cauldron, each of Zolgo's concoctions better than the last, and he wondered.

All of this, here in the Hollow... it really works, doesn't it?

Before long, Viana had pulled him from the table to cheer on a dance-off between the corpse-skeletons and Nightmarists. Grimmond laughed openly as Tristin made swimming motions between him and Viana and loudly yelled 'WIZARD SHARK!' But despite his friends' efforts — after seeing Dr. Knight was one of the chaperones along the wall — he didn't join in the dancing.

Her eyes scanned the crowd, and Grimmond had the distinct impression she was looking for her daughter. Remembering the woman's warning, Grimmond backed off from Viana, standing partially on the wall beneath a grove of

Sentrees. One snapped at him, but he didn't bother smacking it, nor did he cower from a miniature purple mummy when it crawled out from the roots of the tree and pawed at him.

When did these things stop scaring me? Two months ago I'd have been running for my life.

Viana had told him: every Nightmarist was still scared, but it was their shared fears that made the creatures of the Nightmayr Realm bearable. Grimmond grinned at the purple mummy, Flared a burst of yellow light at it, then leaned against the Sentree to watch the dancing. He jumped when a warm hand grabbed his wrist, twirled him around, and pulled him behind the Sentree.

"Hey, sissy," Viana said. "Still scare easily, I see?"

"*No*," Grimmond gasped, annoyed. "I just thought you were out dancing."

"I was," she answered. "You should be, too."

"Don't feel like it," Grimmond said, backing up against the tree. "I'd be all limbs out there."

Why did she have to stand so close to him, smelling so wonderful? And with those ridiculous Gargremlin ears that didn't even match her hazel eyes?

"If you haven't noticed," she giggled, "there are *actual* limbs on the floor. Bianca just rolled her ankle on one of them."

She covered her mouth to laugh along with Grimmond.

"You know," she said, "you don't feel so new anymore. Not to me, at least...."

Her eyes looked at the branch above him, then scanned the crowd over his shoulder, searching for something.

"What is it?" Grimmond asked, likewise swiveling his head.

But then she reached up, gently grabbed his cheeks to turn him back, and kissed him full on the mouth. Grimmond didn't move, being backed against the tree with nowhere to go. Not that he was in a hurry to leave. Her lips injected him with a drug, a poison, a tranquilizer — maybe all three at once. Whatever it was, Grimmond was paralyzed when she pulled away a few seconds later.

He managed to jumble a few words together.

"Whussthatfer?"

Viana shrugged and pointed upwards.

"Thistletoe," she said without remorse. "Sorry, it's the rules. No idea it was there, I swear. Meet me out on the dance floor?"

"Viana, I —"

"Call me Vi," she cut him off.

She kissed him again, then pulled away, quoting the Thistletoe rule of having ten seconds to leave, or a second kiss is necessary. Grimmond didn't want bad luck, did he?

He nodded his assent, wondering how she tasted like mint after eating the same food he had. When he gazed up to the tree branches to see what the Thistletoe looked like, Viana shook her head as she walked away. Grimmond said he'd follow in a minute, but was secretly worried he might fall down; he couldn't feel any of his extremities.

Was he on fire, or freezing to death?

He looked down to find evidence of either as he walked to the bathroom, but saw nothing except skin and dry clothing. Splashing some water on his face from the bathroom tap, he exited to see the worst person possible after his first, then second kiss ever: Viana's mother.

"I *told* you what would happen if you didn't leave her alone," Dr. Knight said dangerously. "I warned you, and now it's too late."

Grimmond's face was bright red, all happy emotion or thought gassed from him like a popped balloon. He immediately searched her hands for weapons, simultaneously noticing that there were no witnesses in the hallway. Did no one else at the entire dance need to use the bathroom?

"Dr. Knight…I never meant for this."

"What will my daughter think when she finds out? When she knows the Errandi family ruined her life? I know what happened, Grimmond. Do you?"

"Do I know *what*?" Grimmond said with exasperation. "What are you talking about?"

Grimmond really wished someone — *anyone* — would come walking into the hallway to save him. He would've welcomed Malus to stroll around the corner with Biff and Bianca. Trying to walk around Dr. Knight, she sidestepped to block his path.

"It doesn't have to be me that tells her, but once she knows, do you think my Viana will still fall in love with you?"

Grimmond's voice jumped an octave, and he raised his hands in denial.

"Fall in love?" he asked. "Look, Dr. Knight, there's no *way* Viana feels that way about me."

"Her father is dead," the woman replied. "Gone nearly ten years now. Did she ever tell you? He never said goodbye to her that night he went out on the mission. Didn't want to wake her. She's never really recovered, you know."

Grimmond lowered his hands, suddenly sobered to a far lesser level than he'd been in weeks.

"She never…." Grimmond started gravely. "Viana never said anything to me."

"Yes, I'm sure," Dr. Knight replied. "She likely also never mentioned the fact — because she doesn't know — that my William was killed while trying to save you and your parents."

The feeling of Grimmond's previous numbness slowly spread through his limbs again, but not from pleasure this time. His gut turned on itself, his head flipped inside out, and his world upside down.

"What?"

Dr. Knight smiled.

"In the church graveyard that night," she reaffirmed. "When Liam, Eralynn, and William came to fight the black spot that showed up on the Dread Map. My William was murdered trying to save you and your parents, though only you were spared. That's why Eralynn raised you, of course. Even after your father left Eralynn for Misty — your godmother's *wicked* best friend — Eralynn still took you in."

Grimmond reached a hand over to the wall, steadying himself against it as Dr. Knight tut-tutted with her tongue.

"You didn't know? Pity, I was the one to have the decency to tell you," she said without sorrow. "Enjoy the rest of your evening. And stay away from Viana before you make an even worse mess of things. Not that that's possible."

At the same time the woman's sharp heels clicked away toward the sounds of laughter, a girl, face white with shock, hurried out of the bathroom. She took one look at Grimmond, then ran into the Hearth after Dr. Knight.

Grimmond's vision spun, and he was having trouble breathing as he leaned against the wall.

She's lying…she doesn't like me, and wants me to stay away from Viana. That's all. It's just a lie….

But the complete story surrounding his parents' death, the trauma, the rumors, the teachers that acted strangely around him, and the conversation with Professor Manning that Eralynn stopped — none of it added up until now. The information settled into place, while simultaneously breaking his heart.

William Knight died for me…. And my dad left Eralynn for my mom….

Grimmond stumbled down the hall, passing the entrance to the Hearth to make for Steeple Spike.

"Grim!"

He whipped around to see Viana standing in the doorway, her smile bright and wide. Perhaps for the last time ever, Grimmond thought. He tried to memorize how she looked, then and there. But she'd know the rumors come morning — the girl from the bathroom was assuredly regurgitating everything she had heard right now.

"Where are you going?" Viana asked, her smile faltering as she saw the look on Grimmond's face.

"I-I have to go…." he turned around again to leave.

Quickly Viana approached behind and spun him around, her eyes glistening.

"Don't do that — I already told you," she said, holding up a finger. "Don't ever leave without saying goodbye."

Grimmond's heart wrenched, now understanding what she truly meant. But things were clearer to him than they'd been in years, and he knew: nothing could ever be between him and Viana Knight.

Intentional or not, her mother had leaked a dark secret to the whole Hollow, and Viana would soon know it. He was doing her a favor to stop whatever they had before it really started. Tears were already forming in her eyes as she looked at Grimmond, her head slowly shaking.

"This won't work…I'm sorry, Vi…."

SMACK.

Grimmond reeled from the impact, but barely felt it. Viana sniffed once, then twice as a sob caught in her throat, but the tears wouldn't fall from her eyes.

"Don't you *ever* call me that again."

Viana walked past him, away from either the Hearth or the direction of Steeple Spike, and Grimmond was alone.

BREACH OF TRUST

Grimmond woke up with his left cheek sore and eyelids heavy. Even worse, his terrible memories of the night before weren't from a nightmare; they'd actually taken place. In the daylight, he was ashamed anew, remembering the hurt look in Viana's eyes. The girl who had saved his life, later befriended him, and then put her heart on the line. But Grimmond was even more ashamed of his parents.

Had his father really done what Dr. Knight said? And his mother, too? He had to find out the truth, but knew his day needed to start with an apology first.

Having long-missed breakfast, Grimmond quickly got dressed and headed down a few floors to the girls' level of Steeple Spike. He knocked on the door, and Sariah Lunasae answered. Second in command of the Black Wings, she turned Grimmond away, telling him she hadn't seen Viana since the dance.

Checking Fire Watch and the Hearth to no avail, Grimmond went to the Anxious Canine in the hopes of finding Viana and explaining things. Quickly he saw that around the old tables of the coffee hall, more people were staring at him than usual. The Tychus twins sat in the corner and Grimmond approached them, despite Olivia obstinately looking away, and Keith shaking his head, mouthing the word 'no'.

"Hey, Keith," Grimmond stretched. "Hi, Liv."

"What do you want?" Olivia asked coldly.

"To wish you a good morning," he replied. "And ask: has Viana come through here?"

"Sure hasn't," Olivia answered before Keith could.

Keith's eyes were now wide with warning, but Grimmond was still confused at Olivia's coldness.

"Okay, well, any idea where she is?"

"Hmm…." Olivia looked up at him, eyes full of fire, and replied in a sweet voice. "Nope. Have you checked the back of your throat?"

Grimmond stammered until Tristin came up behind him and spun him around.

"Wait over there, my clueless young friend," he offered, pointing to the adjacent hall. "Trust me. I'll grab us a few Americanos and we'll go outside."

Grimmond obliged and walked into the hall outside the coffee shop, having a suspicion behind Tristin's warning.

Everyone already knows what Dr. Knight said.

Receiving a number of nasty looks as he waited, Grimmond moved to the entranceway of the Hovel so only the Sentrees could harass him. But even they were whispering more than usual, and didn't seem to want to touch him.

Great — even beings from another realm are repulsed by me.

Tristin soon exited, handed Grimmond a cup, and they walked outside to sit on the edge of the bridge.

"Is it true?" Tristin asked with a grin.

"Which part?"

"The *best* part!" he laughed. "You and Viana!"

Grimmond felt a stab of pain in his gut as he looked down into the Bottomless Chasm.

"For about five minutes," he answered, causing Tristin to hoot with glee. "But I botched it."

"Yeah," Tristin said, "heard about that, too. She didn't want to talk, though, so I couldn't confirm anything."

Grimmond burned his lips with coffee as he perked up.

"You've seen Viana?" he asked anxiously. "I've been looking everywhere!"

Tristin made a sideways face and raised his eyebrows.

"I'd let her cool down, mate, if I were you."

"No, I can't," Grimmond protested. "I *have* to talk to her and explain things myself, before more rumors get around."

"Look," Tristin went on, scratching his chin awkwardly. "I've known Viana almost my whole life. She's lived in the Hovel since she was a little girl, and we've been friends since about then. She's a fighter, a looker, and a thinker. She'll come around once she sorts it out herself."

Grimmond thought a moment, then turned on Tristin again.

"Then you knew about her dad being killed?" he demanded. "Why didn't you tell me?"

"Right," he scolded. "Tell me exactly when that's come up in conversation, you dolt! Besides, that's not my story to tell — it's hers. I'm still not sure how the whole secret got spat out last night, though. It's a mess of rumors bouncing around in there."

Grimmond sighed deeply, already embarrassed at what he was about to say.

"I'll tell you how," he started, "but there's something else I've gotta tell you, first."

Grimmond proceeded to tell Tristin everything that had been going in his head since the Squadron tryouts, including his plan to return to Boston. He told him how Viana had stopped him, making him stay one more night, how her mother saw them kissing, and then what Dr. Knight told Grimmond about his parents.

"I knew that once Viana found out the truth, she'd hate me," Grimmond said, downcast. "I thought I was doing the right thing, saying what I did."

Tristin took a long swig of his coffee, having listened intently to Grimmond's whole story.

"First off Grim, you're *paper thin*," he started. "You've been moping around here for weeks. We knew something was up, and Vi and I had been paying a little closer attention. But going back to Boston, especially with the Ending after you — the same thing that killed *your* parents *and* Vi's dad? Honestly…."

Grimmond looked back into the Chasm as Tristin shot him a patronizing look. He hadn't thought of that angle. Was he really so arrogant to think that he was better than full-fledged Nightmarists, after he had only had a few months of training?

"Secondly," Tristin went on, "get out of your own way! Miss Mary — Viana's mum — may be the vengeful, vindictive type, but Viana isn't. You're not always what you come from, mate. And you told me that you were what — six years old that night? As if *any* of that was your fault! You can't expect Viana to hold that against you."

I wish I could tell you what happened that night, Tristin…I swear…it all happened so fast.

"And why shouldn't she hold it against me?"

Tristin slugged him on the shoulder.

"She's one of the good ones. Really sounds like you need to have a talk with your godmom, though. She's back, you know. Saw her this morning."

"What if Eralynn tells me it's all true?" Grimmond said quietly. "Everything about my parents?"

Tristin removed the lid from his cup and finished off its contents.

"Then, you know for sure," he said seriously. "No more rumors or guessing. In the meantime, try to cover your ears if you happen to pass anyone in the halls."

* * *

Grimmond knocked on the door, heard sniffles on the other side, and stood back for his godmother to open it. She didn't look surprised to see him. Her eyes and cheeks were already puffy, and she wore a thick orange sweater and low ponytail. Grimmond guessed she'd already heard the rumors going around.

"Come in," she said stuffily.

Grimmond walked into her darkened room without saying anything, and looked around. They'd only been there two months, but it looked like she'd lived there much longer. Then, Grimmond realized, she had lived there for years — long before she left to take care of him.

Lining the walls were posters of bands Grimmond had never heard of. Different colored scarves and jewelry surrounded a vanity, and a bed was covered with tissues and purple and pink blankets. On the window sat a picture frame, and Grimmond moved to it and picked it up.

Three laughing young people were frozen in it, still dripping water in full clothes after jumping into the lake. Grimmond's eyes widened when he realized who they were, and he set the picture frame down, looking around the room to see at least a dozen similar pictures with the same three smiling faces.

"All these…they're of you and them?"

Eralynn nodded, and Grimmond felt an anger hastily rising inside him.

"The one you just set down," she nodded to the windowsill, "that's when I was still dating your father. It's one of the last ones we took before they left…."

"Left?" Grimmond gritted his teeth.

"Yes," she said, "before…before they went away."

"I think what you *mean* to say," Grimmond raised his voice, "is before my dad *cheated* on you with my mom — your best friend! Then they dropped out and ran away to have me!"

Eralynn's eyes teared up anew and her shoulders trembled.

So the rumors are true, Grimmond thought as his anger boiled very near the surface. *Dr. Knight wasn't lying after all.*

"W-we all really w-were *best* friends," Eralynn said through a sob.

Grimmond scoffed, turning away.

"I never wanted you to know, a-and think…and think that they were b-bad people —"

"THEY *WERE* BAD PEOPLE!" Grimmond exploded. "How could you not tell me about this, Eralynn?"

She lowered her head, continuing to cry but saying nothing. For Grimmond, it felt good to finally have more people to blame. More people to bear his own crushing guilt.

"After all they did to you? To WILL KNIGHT? After what they're STILL DOING to all of you? Look at this place! It's a shrine for those assholes!"

Grimmond hardly knew what he was saying, giving full vent to his rage like a breaking dam. He pointed wildly to another picture, barely stopping himself from throwing it out the window.

"They don't *deserve* your sympathy. Or mine! Do you hear me? Don't give it to them! They left both of us, and now they're GONE! Trash all these stupid pictures and move on with your life!"

Grimmond's mind flashed like a camera: his parents were on the ground, his hands bloody. Another flash, and the white face in the darkness was there amongst the gravestones. Grimmond tried to crush his head with his hands. Eralynn had no idea, but did *he* even know what happened anymore?

She looked up, wiping her eyes with a balled tissue. Grimmond hadn't realized he was crying, too.

"Your parents made a *mistake*, Grimmond. They were ashamed —"

"OF ME!" he shouted, barely able to speak through angry tears. "Because *I'm* the mistake they made! I'm just…just one big mistake…."

Grimmond was now shaking as badly as Eralynn was, until she moved forward and wrapped him in a hug.

"*You* are not a mistake, Grimmond," she said through another sob. "Don't confuse their actions with your being. They made a bad decision and hurt a lot of people, but I still miss them both. No matter what happened. And look what I got out of it, in the end!"

She pushed him away to look him in the eyes.

"I got *you*," she said softly. "You hate me for lying to you, for lying about everything your whole life, but I did what I must. I had to protect you from it all. What happened to your parents, the Ending, the Nightmayr Realm…can you understand that, at least?"

Grimmond hastily wiped his eyes with the back of his hand.

"I don't hate you," he said at last. "I hate them for doing this! You're the one who should hate me. I've been a reminder for ten years of what those jerks did to everybody."

And I, Grimmond, am the one who took them from you forever, Eralynn….

"No!" she admonished, grabbing his chin. "You're a daily reminder of the two best friends I ever had. You must forgive them — people make mistakes, Grimmond. Sometimes I even regret changing your last name."

Grimmond lowered his head, sniffing and wiping his eyes once more.

"I was leaving last night, you know. I wrote you a letter, and I was taking Brax and heading back to Boston. It sounds dumb, but even before finding out about my parents…I knew I didn't belong here. Not anywhere. You don't know how people look at me. And now that they know this? What am I supposed to do?"

Eralynn closed her eyes, took a deep breath, and spoke calmly.

"If ever I meant anything to you, Grimmond, promise me you won't give up on this place, no matter what you're feeling. I don't know what I'd do if I lost you, too."

Grimmond looked up into her eyes, filled with a sadness and pain that far exceeded his own. He took a deep breath.

"All right," he answered. "I'll give it one more chance."

With the help of Malus, half the Hollow had turned against Grimmond overnight. He was the bastard child, the reminder of his parents' mistakes to anyone who had known them, and a warning of what not to be: angry, violent, and unstable. But rumors of his parents didn't matter to Grimmond's true friends, like Viana or Olivia. They only cared how Grimmond himself had treated them.

Students dressed warmer as weeks passed, spending more time indoors next to the fires, and laughing about the goings-on of the day. But Grimmond in turn decided to begin training himself, flying and practicing without a Squadron. He and Brax became hard to find in the evenings, doing maneuvers across the grounds, flying over the lake as fast as they could go, or diving into the Bottomless Chasm.

Grimmond learned how to control his vision better, steadying his heartbeat as he flew, or letting it beat wildly so he could see further. Sometimes he'd push Brax into the mist that separated the Sleepless Orchard from the rest of the world, wondering if he had the courage to fly through it. But he'd always turn around when he could barely see the lights of the Hollow any longer, remembering his promise to Eralynn.

A few days before Thanksgiving, Grimmond went to the clearing in the Sleepless Orchard, where he first sought out the Blood Onyx. There he had privacy to work on his Flares, Lulls, and weapon work, and the moon was nearly full. Its light mixed eerily with Flares as Grimmond practiced, taking aim and illuminating the somber trees.

Supper had been especially awful that evening. Making hopeful eye contact with Viana at her new table, he was crushed when she looked away, as if he was nothing more than a stranger. He Flared angrily as he thought about it, watching dizzily as different colors burned through his misty breath in the cold air.

He wondered about the key and the door to the Nightmayr Realm: those that could seal away its creatures forever. If they'd been found before, then maybe his parents wouldn't be dead, and neither would Viana's father. Things could be different. Why wasn't Stanchions trying harder to find them?

Cold breath rolled across Grimmond's neck; someone was directly behind him.

He spun quickly, heart racing, but nothing was there. A strong wind was passing quickly through the clearing, like it was fleeing something. It chilled him to the bone as the mist and his hovering breath were evacuated, and he stopped Flaring altogether once it was gone, his neck hair standing on end.

Grimmond hadn't felt that chilling feeling in months.

An unnatural stillness filled the air in the wind's wake. Grimmond Flared a steady stream of blue across the clearing, flooding the ring of trees with light. A few Sentrees that were mixed in among the normal trees bristled their branches, but nothing was out of place. No Minor or Major Nightmares were in sight, and no band of sneaking students.

He looked to Brax, but his wings were still wrapped up to look like a dead stump.

Brax hasn't moved a muscle. If he didn't sense anything, then there's no way I did, either.

So why did Grimmond feel like something was now watching him?

"Hello?" he called.

He jumped when a distant scream responded. At first Grimmond hoped it was someone on the receiving end of a prank, but Brax immediately undid himself from his camouflage, and fell forward into a growling crouch. A second scream told Grimmond that someone was in trouble: it was a girl calling out for help.

Grimmond sprinted toward Brax.

"Up!"

They cleared the tops of the trees in an instant, and Grimmond looked toward the Hovel to see where the disturbance was. From the Wards he could see on this side of the Hollow, no one was panicking, running, or otherwise concerned. A few Squadrons practiced above the lake in the distance.

Had Grimmond been the only one to hear the scream?

Odd pinpricks of light emanated within the Sleepless Orchard, just past Narcoleptic Row, like a dozen small flashlights merging together. Against them, three separate Flares shone out, followed by only two, and after another scream of pain only one remained. Howling wolves sounded across the dark forest, along with a guttural bellows Grimmond had never before heard in the Hollow.

"FLY!"

Brax raced above the Sleepless Orchard toward the glowing lights, and Grimmond pulled the dark glaive from his belt, extending and holding it at the ready as they neared.

Grimmond quickly saw that the pack of large, glowing-eyed wolves was being Flared by a single boy. Another boy was frozen with fear behind him, doing absolutely nothing beside a girl who lay on the ground, blood pooling around her legs. Her skin and hair aged rapidly as she Lulled the handful of fleshy, golem-like Nightmares trying to get to her: *Brutes.*

Skinless but covered in bloody red muscle, Brutes were like starving gorillas without heads, their mouths and eyes buried in the folds of their stomachs. Grimmond had never seen them like this, never in a true frenzy.

Terror-possessed-wolves and Brutes, both attacking? Stanchions' Nightmares aren't supposed to be hostile!

"DIVE, BRAX!"

Grimmond's heart raced, his vision and reflexes primed.

He threw his glaive with all his might, and a gray wolf with yellow eyes was skewered in the side of the head. Brax picked up another two and flung them against a Sentree. The sound of their breaking necks cracked through the air as they heaped onto the ground, but the yellow Terrors flew out of them to continue fighting.

Grimmond jumped off of Brax and braced himself for a powerful Flare.

He'd never completely banished a Terror before, and these weren't like the Terrors from Stanchions. Laughing with mouths askew and sunken, ethereal eyes, they looked like the ones from Boston.

But how could they have gotten into the Hollow?

In order to Flare violet against yellow, Grimmond concentrated hard on emotions of hurt and betrayal. Hot purple light flooded out from his knuckles as he was hit with a swoon of dizziness, and the oncoming Terrors were boiled away like evaporating water.

"I'm coming, guys!" Grimmond called, turning his head. "Just hang —"

He caught his breath when recognizing the fighting students. It was the Tychus twins.

Keith was weakly Flaring back and forth against the wolves, while Olivia, hair white and skin sagging from Lulling past her limit, was nearly passed out on the ground. Wayne Roarsch was behind them both, whitewashed with fear and standing stock-still.

Grimmond retrieved his glaive from the dead wolf's head, yelled *'PÆCIEF!'* at an oncoming Brute, and with his nausea felt his face's skin sag. He ducked as Brax leapt over him, ripping the stunned Brute to fleshy pieces.

"KEITH!" Grimmond shouted with panic. "Come on!"

"Liv's hurt!" he called back. "Get her to the Hovel and bring back help!"

Running to Olivia, Grimmond hacked at the Brute she had stunned, and was surprised when his glaive easily cut through its bloody muscle. Flesh seared with revolting smell as the Brute fell defeated, but Olivia's head rolled back, her body almost spent. Nightmarists needed to recharge between Lulls, and Olivia hadn't been able.

She trembled as Grimmond picked her frail head up, now looking like an eighty-year-old woman's.

"Grimmond?" she croaked. "Where's Kiki? *Where's my brother?*"

Grimmond turned as Keith let loose a Flare strong enough to eject two green Terrors from the wolves. The Terrors were banished to the Nightmayr Realm, and the wild wolves fled into the woods. Only one possessed wolf remained.

"I'm gonna get you outta here, Liv," Grimmond reassured. "Wayne, I need your belt! HURRY!"

The shell-shocked Wayne didn't move and Grimmond ran to him, kicking him down to avoid a bloody swipe from a Brute. Grimmond Lulled the attacker, experiencing a fresh wave of nausea before slicing it open. Stealing Wayne's belt next, he ran back to Olivia and cinched it tightly above the deep gash in her leg.

Her eyes opened to scream in pain — a good sign — and Grimmond called for Brax.

"Take her to the Hovel!" he yelled, setting her on the Gargoyle. "And *don't let her fall!*"

As Brax took to the sky, Keith yelled in pain. Grimmond turned to see the remaining wolf attached to his arm, and Wayne fleeing toward Narcoleptic Row without so much as a 'good luck'. Grimmond Flared bright red, banishing the final Terror, then drove his glaive into the wolf's neck.

It yipped and howled as it fell, and Grimmond kicked it away from Keith's prone body.

"Dammit," Keith gasped, red trickling through his fingers as he tried to stem his arm's flow of blood. "Got me good...."

"Let's go, Keith! We've got to get out of here!"

"Just need...a minute...." Keith mumbled, closing one eye. "Is Liv all right?"

Grimmond gulped, looking from Keith's pale face to his bloody arm, steaming up through the cold.

"She'll be fine — c'mon, let's go see her," Grimmond said, heaving him to his feet. *"What happened?"*

"Dunno," he said. "I just tagged along on their little date, in case that worthless piece of crap, Wayne, tried anything with my sister. Good call, huh? What a loser —"

Keith suddenly stopped talking, and Grimmond's chilling feeling returned.

The boys looked sideways as the ground shook, hoping what they felt was only a small earthquake or landslide. But the tremors were too far apart, too rhythmic, and they were getting stronger. Sentrees spread their branches out of the way, and Grimmond tried to keep his hands from shaking as he released

Keith to hold his glaive level. A Nightmare bigger than Brax, too tall to stand up straight inside the Hovel, exited the trees.

It was a Total Nightmare — an *Atrocity*. The first ever to be in the Hollow.

Fifteen feet tall, with four arms and four legs, sharp barbs of white bone poked through its skin. A long, thick neck swung hungrily from side to side, and the scant illumination of the silver moon glinted off its black eyes. Red secretions dripped from it like an oozing fountain, and the ground beneath it moved as the worms and insects tried not to drown in its pungent liquid.

Grimmond broke into a cold sweat, his stomach turning as the Atrocity slurped and sloshed. Then, one of its long arms reached up to a Sentree, broke off a tree branch, and launched it toward the two boys. Grimmond tried to push Keith out of the way, but wasn't fast enough.

Keith was knocked backward against a tree, his stomach ripped through. His mouth spat blood, crying out in pain as Grimmond watched helplessly. The Atrocity uprooted an entire tree next, and flung it toward Grimmond.

The environment appeared to slow around Grimmond as his heart cranked up faster than ever.

His vision turning even brighter, he looked around, dove behind a rock, and the tree trunk popped up to barely miss crushing him. Dazed but unhurt, he sat up quickly to see the mist of the Sleepless Orchard glowing to his eyes; his throbbing heart had taken his senses to a whole new level.

Stars were blue, the glaive in his hands was dark purple, and the Atrocity burned red.

Past the Total Nightmare, a second wave of creatures approached in the distance. The Hollow was under attack. Keith was pinned to a tree, and the Atrocity would next hit

Narcoleptic Row. Grimmond couldn't deny one simple thing: he was scared to death, and ready to run for his life.

But he wouldn't cower any longer. He wouldn't be the Grimmond Errandi who ran away like his parents, and wouldn't be the Grimmond Scylent that used to hide from his fears. Gritting his teeth, he wiped the sweat from his eyes.

"Hey! I'm right here!" he shouted, his voice a strange echo. "Come ON!"

The Atrocity moved forward toward Keith, unbothered, and Grimmond jumped to his feet. He clanged his glaive against the rock, then picked up a stick and threw it at the Atrocity's chest. Struck with a dull thud, the thing turned its sunken eyes toward Grimmond instead of Keith.

Losing his mind entirely, Grimmond sucked in a breath, yelled, and ran toward the Atrocity. He released a bright green Flare at its eyes, dodged left as all four arms tried to flatten him, then sliced one of them cleanly off. With an ear-splitting screech, the Atrocity whipped an arm out to smash into his side.

Grimmond felt like he'd been hit by a wrecking ball as he skipped across the ground, stopped only by the carcass of a dead wolf. He stood up, stumbling in pain and struggling for breath, and his ears rang as he felt the wet blood in his side. Lifting his shirt, he nearly swooned as he saw where the barbed arm struck his bottom ribs, and a glittering blue was stuck deep within his flesh.

The Atrocity lumbered toward him again, and Grimmond next tried the Lull used for Prowlers: the command word to cause vertigo.

"Timorül!"

Grimmond felt his strength temporarily sacrificed, and nearly threw up with nausea. But the Atrocity didn't stumble, and Grimmond was forced to run in again, one hand on his bleeding side, the other with his bright knuckles held high. He concentrated on every color or emotion he'd ever tried to Flare, and yelled out.

A piercing white light emanated from his knuckles, and the Atrocity stumbled dazedly in the brightness.

Letting loose its ear-splitting screech, it crashed into a Sentree and became tangled in its branches. Grimmond was given the precious moment needed to retrieve his glaive. He picked it up, raced toward the Atrocity, and sliced its long neck and head off.

Gasping in pain, Grimmond kicked the head away, teeth still snapping as it rolled across the ground. Angrily then, he plunged his glaive through the creature's chest, pinning it to the tree like it had done to Keith. It was dead.

Grimmond fell to his knees in the leaves, breathing hard and clutching his side. But howling wolves approached with the second wave of Nightmares, and Grimmond raised his head to gauge their distance.

"Keith!" he gasped. "Time to go!"

But Keith was motionless, and Grimmond ran over, shaking him until he came to. His eyes opened with rattling breaths, his skin deathly pale in the moonlight. With his sleeve Grimmond wiped the spit and blood away from Keith's mouth, and tried to keep his voice steady.

"Come on, buddy," Grimmond grunted. "We've gotta move. Gotta get you back...."

Keith spit up more blood, looking aimlessly at the sky. Grimmond picked him up, half-carrying, half-dragging him toward the Hovel. They broke through the trees to the edge of Narcoleptic Row, and Grimmond yelled for help, raising his arm to Flare red and blue light in distress.

Keith grabbed onto him.

"Wha — *cough* — are you?" he choked.

"It's all right," Grimmond soothed, holding his ribs and wincing as he spoke. "It's me, Grim, and I'm gonna get you some help."

Grimmond leaned over to try to pick Keith up again, but was pushed away.

"*N-no,*" Keith choked again. "Wh — *cough* — WHAT *are* you?"

Grimmond leaned Keith against a tree, wiping the renewed trickle of blood from his friend's mouth as the howling wolves neared. But Keith slowly reached out to Grimmond's side, lifted up his shirt, and pointed. Grimmond obediently looked down to his wound, seeing the dripping red blood.

And then, seeing the blue flesh behind it.

Bright enough in the darkness to illuminate the grass, it cast a faint glow on Keith's twitching face. Grimmond's eyes glazed over, watching as the strange substance wept from his wound and down his hip. He touched it with his free hand, rubbing the stuff between his fingers, and looked back up.

What...what did that thing do *to me?*

"I don't...don't understand," Grimmond muttered.

He attempted to form a cohesive thought, but Keith grabbed onto his collar and pulled him close, snapping him out of it. Keith was in more trouble than him; Grimmond ripped off his jacket and held it to Keith's side.

"S'alright," Keith said, shivering in the cold. "Secret's safe.... D-did we w-win, Grim?"

"Not...not yet," Grimmond replied, blinking back tears. "Not until I get you help — then we win."

Grimmond turned around, and yelled again until his throat was raw.

"Thanks for s-staying, man...I know y-you could've...could've j-just left...."

Keith spit up blood again, and Grimmond let the tears fall from his face as he looked him over. Keith managed a dying smile, knowing he didn't have any blood left to lose.

"S'okay," Keith sputtered. "S'alright, Grim...s-secret's safe...*your secret's safe with me....*"

Keith laid his head back, his eyes out of focus. He didn't stir as a dozen massive, Terror-possessed-wolves broke through the trees, nor when the Brutes and Prowlers followed behind. And Grimmond didn't move as they all rushed toward him.

He simply stared, unblinking, into Keith's eyes.

Grimmond didn't notice when Brax arrived with all four of Stanchions' Squadrons. He didn't hear the howls of decimated wolves and banished Terrors, burned in waves of light by the Aurora Blights, nor did he hear the Brutes' bellows as the Skeleton Crew tore them to pieces, nor the Prowlers' shrieks as the Sleepwalkers shouted words of command and dismembered them.

Grimmond held his jacket to Keith's side even though it wasn't really bleeding anymore, and even though Keith's hand slackened and fell to the ground.

He held the jacket there until he fell face forward, onto Keith's cold and dead body.

GUILT OF THE SURVIVOR

Vaguely Grimmond heard his name called as someone pulled him upright, and they swore softly when they saw Keith's body.

"*Grim….*" they panted, out of breath. "OVER HERE!"

Lightly Tristin smacked Grimmond's face, and tried to lift his bloody shirt up to see the wound on his ribs. But Grimmond pulled away before Tristin could see it well. Tristin instead used Grimmond's jacket to press against his wound as Brax landed next to them and growled softly.

"Thanks, Brax," Grimmond said weakly. "You were just in time."

Grimmond grunted as he tried to sit up, hissing from the pain in his likely broken ribs. He looked at Keith's vacant face, lying there motionless, until Tristin reached over and gently shut his eyelids. The Black Wings and other Squadrons came jogging over, gasps escaping from them like steam.

"You okay, Scylent?" someone asked.

"Is that *Keith Tychus?*" another demanded.

At once the voices began to stumble over one another.

"He's not moving —"

"Keith's gone —"

"*Dead?*"

"Killed!"

"Where's Olivia? Does she know yet?"

Grimmond closed his eyes, trying to block out the pain taking over his body.

Keith's gone.... He's actually gone....

Viana pushed to the front of the crowd, bruised and sweaty, and ran over to Grimmond. She fell to her knees beside him, then closed her eyes with relief. Her hand reached for his, but recoiled just as quickly.

"You're hurt," she whispered.

"Grim," Drek spoke loudly over the din. "What *happened?*"

"Nightmares," Grimmond whispered. "Bad ones. They got through the mist...attacked the twins and Wayne...."

"An *Atrocity* is back there," Drek said urgently, pointing into the forest. "Was it the only one?"

Grimmond looked over surreally at Keith: Olivia's loyal brother, now lost forever. Grimmond grunted, his eyes suddenly wide.

"Olivia!" Grimmond cried out. "Is she okay?"

"She'll pull through," Viana assured. "Mom's sewing her up in the infirmary now. Brax brought her to the entrance hall just before Wayne busted in to the Dread Map room and told Lord Stawlart you were in trouble. We came as fast as we could...."

So, Wayne did something, at least. But he wasn't fast enough, just like me...Keith's still dead.

"I have to see her," Grimmond whispered.

"She's asleep for the surgery now," Viana said, swallowing hard. "You can see her, after...after she wakes up."

Numbness spread through Grimmond that had nothing to do with his injuries. How was he going to tell Olivia that her brother — her *twin* — had been killed by a Nightmare? Drek produced Grimmond's collapsed glaive and handed it to him.

"This yours?" Drek asked. "I've never seen one like it."

"Just borrowed it for practice...."

"Good thing. I found it sticking out of the Atrocity's chest," Drek said, almost awestruck. "You cut its head off, too? How? I've never even *seen* an Atrocity in person before."

Grimmond looked at Keith once more, holding back his tears in the dark, and made a decision.

"It wasn't me," Grimmond lied. "The Atrocity hit me first and knocked me down, then got a lucky hit on Keith. But Keith picked up the glaive I dropped and saved me. He tripped the Atrocity and it fell into that tree, then…then he cut its head off before it got up."

Drek lowered his head.

"The Hollow's safe, thanks to you two," he said. "We took out the rest of the Minors and Majors easily enough…but man, I didn't know Keith had *that* in him…."

Grimmond looked away, but Malus suddenly pushed to the front of the crowd. He looked between the dead body and the survivor, then pointed an accusatory finger at Grimmond, a mad glint in his eye.

"Keith didn't have to die!" Malus shouted. "You could've gotten him out with Olivia! But you wanted to play the hero, trying to make us forget who you really were. Another Errandi who got someone killed!"

"Shut your mouth, Nebbick!" Viana stood, the rest of the Black Wings behind her.

"Out of line, Malus," Drek glared. "Get outta here before you say something you regret!"

Even members of the Skeleton Crew backed away from Malus, unwilling to come to his defense. Grimmond didn't say a word, but twisted his glaive until it sprang open, then used it and Tristin to stand up.

"That Blood Onyx was big enough to escape with all of you," Malus continued. "You made the bad call, again, Errandi."

Grimmond closed his eyes as he stood there, unsure why he wasn't talking back. Maybe he was hoping to feel something other than the numbness spreading throughout his body. Was Malus right? Should he have run?

It didn't matter. Grimmond would have plenty of time to think about that later. For now, he needed to see Olivia was safe with his own eyes.

"Grimmond Errandi, the would-be hero, couldn't even keep his friend from biting the d —"

Grimmond spoke over him with a single, softly spoken word.

"Brax."

The Blood Onyx thundered, leapt over Grimmond's head, and landed in front of Malus. Its open jaws were a few inches from Malus's face, and Grimmond knew that if he commanded it, Brax would end him. But Grimmond didn't even wish for that, he just wanted to leave.

Malus's smile melted as he shook, and the rest of the Skeleton Crew backed slowly away from the Blood Onyx, eyebrows raised: either impressed at the training of the Gargoyle, or not wanting to get splattered with guts.

"I wouldn't move," Grimmond quietly warned Malus as he stepped forward. "I've seen him decapitate a few animals already tonight — he really only likes the heads. Still hungry, Brax?"

Brax growled loudly, his breath disheveling Malus's hair, and Grimmond turned his head toward Keith for the last time. Jack Michaels, the Aurora Blights' captain from Hollow Dwell, approached beside Drek.

"Go, Grim," Drek said quietly. "We've got him."

Grimmond hobbled onto Brax's back as the crowd parted. Malus remained motionless, staring up at Grimmond with hating eyes, but not daring to say another word. Brax then snapped his mouth shut, flung Malus backward with a shove from his snout, and leapt into the sky.

* * *

Grimmond hardly left his room until after Thanksgiving was over. Eralynn was with him most of the time, and he received a few other visitors as he rested, but didn't feel he earned them. His mind was tied up with the Tychus twins, and what Malus called him: *'another Errandi who got someone killed!'* He wondered if Keith should be counted as either the fourth or the fifth death he was responsible for. First his parents, then William Knight — was Erik Beese his fault, too?

"You look terrible," Tristin said, entering their bedroom on Sunday morning.

Grimmond winced and sat up, making room for Tristin as he was handed a Fresh Cut Copse latte.

"Still haven't been sleeping much?"

Grimmond shook his head, scratching around his bandaged arm and ribs.

"I wondered," Tristin went on, pointing to Grimmond's bandages, "Vi told me you never went to see her mum in the infirmary. Who patched you up?"

"Professor Manning," Grimmond answered. "I barely remember leaving that night, but apparently I went right to Eralynn. She took me to Professor Manning, saying he knows best when it comes to wounds from Total Nightmares. But really I think things are still pretty heated between her and Dr. Knight. From letting the big secret slip, you know.... Come to think of it, I'm not sure I'd have let Dr. Knight lay a scalpel to me, anyway."

Tristin raised his eyebrows.

"Gonna have to talk to the in-laws at some point, mate."

Grimmond stared at him flatly, then slowly reached for the glaive on his nightstand until Tristin raised his hands in surrender.

"Okay, okay," Tristin grinned. "I take it back!"

He swept his braids over his shoulder, then leaned forward, elbows on knees.

"Viana *is* worried about you though."

"Yeah?" Grimmond said, tightlipped. "*She* hasn't stopped by yet."

Poking Grimmond's legs, Tristin screwed up his face in confusion.

"Did I miss something?" he asked. "Are your legs broken now, too? You both are hopeless, but for what it's worth, I think you should be hopeless *together*. You'll need to figure it out soon, anyway — I've got news."

Tristin stood up and made a grand, sweeping gesture.

"The Black Wings voted again. Even Harriet Ulrecht from the Skeleton Crew was swayed this time."

"What are you talking about?" Grimmond asked.

"You're *in*, Grim," Tristin said, stepping closer. "Drek reasoned with Harriet and the other Squadron captains that your tryout should have counted in September. Then he said that repelling the Orchard Incursion — that's what they're calling the battle that night — proved your worth more than most of them had."

Grimmond didn't answer when Tristin finished, but looked down at his covers blankly.

"Did you hear me?" Tristin said excitedly. "I said you're on the Squadron now!"

"I hardly did anything," Grimmond answered, unsure why he was still lying. "It was Keith. Why would they want me?"

"*Why?*" Tristin sighed excitedly. "Let's see. Because you managed to team up with likely the only Blood Onyx on this continent? Or because you helped take on almost a dozen Nightmares during the Orchard Incursion? Or maybe —"

"Maybe because I'm the one left alive after a fight with an Atrocity."

"*Or* that," Tristin finished. "Does it matter? We need you on the team, Grim. Always have. Drek wanted you before, too, but didn't have enough justification to get you in."

Grimmond rubbed his finger over the Gargremlin image on his coffee cup. He should have been as ecstatic as the little laughing creature was. But being on the Black Wings wasn't worth Keith's life.

"I'll think about it."

The middle of December came as quickly as Thanksgiving left, and snow began to fall in the Hollow. Lord Stawlart had instated flying patrols every half-hour to sweep across the Sleepless Orchard. But he and the professors couldn't figure out how a group of Nightmares got past the mist. Theories and rumors were rampant nonetheless.

One invented by Wynn Felt was that Stanchions' own Nightmares had turned against them, until Tristin pointed out that they never had any Atrocities on their side to begin with. Randy said he heard that the barrier itself, separating the Hollow from the rest of the world, was failing. But Grimmond's favorite rumor was that he had let the Nightmares in himself for practice.

"Why would they even try to get in here?" Grimmond asked. "Why bother?"

"Why *not?*" Keokuk replied. "There's a whole army of good Nightmares here who betray the Nightmayr Realm on a daily basis. What if they could be turned back?"

Shuddering at the thought regardless, Grimmond knew that wasn't the reason. Nightmares didn't just *get through* the mist. Someone let them in. He thought again of the door to the Nightmayr Realm, and where it could be. If only they could find it, they could close it permanently

But we'd need to find the key, too. Maybe they're together?

Grimmond had been visiting Olivia in the infirmary since the Orchard Incursion, but she always seemed to be asleep when he got there, her cheeks freshly tear-stained. She assuredly knew what happened to Keith by now, and Grimmond deeply regretted not being the one to tell her. One day when she wasn't in her bed anymore, the infirmary Haunter told Grimmond she'd been released the day prior.

Grimmond realized then: she didn't want to talk to him.

Classes moved slowly for Grimmond that week, his heart heavy with fresh guilt. Viana met his eyes in Total Nightmares class, but Grimmond didn't allow his heart to jump. He returned her sympathetic smile, but neither one of them tried to speak afterward.

Drek Heeder sweet-talked Grimmond often, working to convince him that training with the Black Wings would be the best thing for him, but Malus was less helpful. Every opportunity he could find, he mockingly honored Grimmond as the Hollow's second-best hero for thwarting the ambush of Nightmares.

"And don't forget," Malus proclaimed, "for getting our *real* hero, Keith Tychus, killed in the process."

Grimmond occasionally wished he'd had Brax bite Malus's head off that night, but holiday break was soon coming, and Malus would be gone for a few weeks. Grimmond, Tristin, and Viana were among those who would be staying at Stanchions. Drala Zhen told Grimmond that Olivia — who hadn't yet returned to classes — would be staying as well.

The Friday before Christmas, schedules were assigned for Squadron duty over break, and the Phantom fleet took students away in droves. Nightmarists who could fly went up to the stables in the cold and left with their Gargoyles, ready to return at a moment's notice if they received the call.

Grimmond stood on the icy bridge outside the Hovel's large entranceway. He watched as the final Gargoyle and rider took off into the night, and the last Phantom faded into the mist past the distant front gate. Zipping his coat up a little higher, he set off across the bridge toward Hollow Dwell.

Walking through a cold, crunchy blanket of powder, he found the snow-laden path easier than he'd hoped. The Lightwarts had grown copious amounts of thick white fur, but still they glowed dark orange to light the way for Grimmond. He soon reached the purple cliffs of Hollow Dwell, and found switchback stairs that led down to a large cleft hewn into the rock.

A double set of doors stood there, and Grimmond knocked between two evergreen wreaths. He was surprised at who quickly answered.

"Dr. Knight?" he said incredulously. "What are *you* doing here?"

"Mind your tone," the woman said, standing back to let him in.

But Grimmond stayed on the doorstep, his expression as cold as the air howling across the cliff face.

"We're not in class right now," he said angrily, "so why don't you mind *that*. Is Olivia here?"

Dr. Knight sized him up a moment.

"Yes," she answered. "I was just leaving."

She looked down to finish buttoning up her coat, then pushed past Grimmond to walk outside.

"I'm sorry about Keith," she said over the wind, turning her head. "For what it's worth, I don't think it was your fault...."

Your word isn't worth anything to me, Grimmond thought.

As she walked away by the glow of the furry Lightwarts, Grimmond wondered what might happen if he threw a snowball at her head; she was still awful to him in class, and it was her fault that he and Viana never got together. He shook the teacher from his mind as he crossed the threshold of Hollow Dwell and shut the door.

He'd never been inside another Ward before. It wasn't as expected after going through the entryway, but warmer and brighter. Red fires burned in two stoves on opposite walls, and miner-style oil lanterns emitted golden light from decorative hangers, bits of tinsel hung from them. Thick carpets lined the floors everywhere except beneath a long wooden dining table, and rows of books were packed on shelves next to couches and reading lamps.

"What are you doing here?"

Grimmond turned to a set of stairs he hadn't yet noticed.

"Olivia...." he said. "I knocked — Dr. Knight let me in as she was leaving."

"Oh," she said, crossing her arms. "Well, she was taking out the last stitches from my leg, so I know that's not what you're here for."

Grimmond gulped. He wasn't used to seeing Olivia without a smile, or a face completely devoid of emotion. She wasn't wearing makeup — not that she'd ever needed it — and her long hair was ratted, hanging lifeless around her shoulders. Her crystalline blue eyes were the most noticeable, the spark within them all but extinguished.

"Can we talk?"

"What's there to say?"

"Some," Grimmond answered. "Well...enough that I haven't slept much the last month."

"Been having a rough time, have you?" Olivia answered, a slight bite to her tone.

Grimmond lowered his eyes to the golden tinsel hanging from the oil lantern on the wall. Olivia descended a few more stairs.

"I wanted to talk to you myself, right after...." Grimmond continued softly. "But you were, like, in a coma or something. Then you left the hospital before I could see you."

"I didn't need to hear it from you," she answered. "I knew the moment I opened my eyes in the infirmary, when my brother wasn't next to me. I knew when Brax carried me off that night, that I wouldn't see him again."

"He really loved you, you know —"

"Don't," Olivia warned.

She quickly walked down the remainder of the stairs, stopping in front of him to cross her arms again.

"Don't you *dare* try to tell me how my own brother felt. He's my...he *was* my twin...my only sibling. I know what we had."

She breathed heavily, her eyes brimming with tears.

"Why did you lie about him?"

"Lie?" Grimmond repeated, cheeks flushing.

"I still hear things even though I'm not in class. I *know* what you said about what happened. That he cut that Atrocity's head off?"

Wishing to let her simply talk, Grimmond didn't interrupt her. He shrugged his shoulders, but Olivia shook her head as she continued.

"I don't believe it for a second. He'd just gotten the hang of Flaring, but he could hardly Lull or handle a glaive. You're telling me he took on, and *beheaded* an Atrocity?"

Grimmond knew she wouldn't believe any lie he tried to feed her.

"He really did do great," Grimmond started. "Few people could take on a whole pack of wolves and not run away. I watched him banish two Terrors with a single Flare. We...we would've been all right until the Atrocity showed up. It got both of us, but while Keith was down, I was able to try again...."

Grimmond looked away, swallowing uncomfortably as he rubbed his sweaty fingers together.

"I'm sorry it was me, Liv," he said, just above a whisper. "I'm sorry I'm the one who got lucky, and not him. I'd change it, if I could."

Olivia remained standing, arms crossed, but her expression slightly softened.

"You think I'm mad at *you*, Grim?" she asked. "We all would've died that night if you and Brax hadn't heard me screaming and shown up. I'm not mad at anybody except myself."

"Mad at yourself?" Grimmond said gently. "Why? You did your best...I saw. You kept Lulling the Brutes even after you were injured, and even after you looked about a hundred years old."

Olivia raised an eyebrow, but took a seat next to the stove. Grimmond pulled up a chair to sit across from her.

"I wanted Wayne to kiss me that night," she said, her voice trembling. "But Keith didn't trust him, so he came along even though I didn't want him to. Do you want to know the last thing I will have ever said to my brother? *'Go away, jackass!'*...."

Olivia sniffed between quivering breaths.

"My big brother, always protecting me — that's the last thing he ever heard me say."

Grimmond's heart rate jumped. For Olivia's sake, he decided to offer her a glimmer of masked truth.

"Last words aren't that important," he began quietly. "I said something...something awful to my parents the night they died...I don't remember exactly what, but...I know it was awful."

Liar.... You know exactly *what you said...like you know* exactly *what you did to kill them....*

Grimmond swallowed hard before continuing, not wanting to turn the conversation to himself.

"And like you said, you know what you had together, and Keith knew how you felt about him, too. You'll always be his baby sister, Liv."

Olivia sat quivering, moving even closer to the fire, but Grimmond knew that no amount of heat would warm her. He moved from his chair to put a gentle arm around her shoulder.

"I couldn't go home to our parents," she said. "I can't face them."

Grimmond gauged his words cautiously.

"Is it easier for them to miss both of their kids?"

She didn't answer immediately, wiping the silent tears from her eyes.

"Do something for me."

"Name it," Grimmond whispered.

"Join the Black Wings," she said unexpectedly. "They need you."

Grimmond hid his shock poorly, removing his arm from her shoulder. He'd already decided he wouldn't join, but hadn't told Drek yet. And out of respect for Olivia, he never planned for her to find out at all.

"How'd you know about that?" Grimmond asked.

"I told you I still hear things, even though I've been holed up," she sniffled. "It's getting pretty bad outside the Hollow, Grim. Attacks are way up in New England alone. I know you feel guilty, but you and Brax need to help."

Grimmond rubbed his ribs, sighing; though he no longer wore any bandages, they were still sore.

"If you really think so, I will," Grimmond said. "But you agree to go home and see your parents?"

Olivia nodded and rose from the couch, and Grimmond followed.

"There's something about you, Grimmond Scylent," she said, leaning forward and hugging him around the neck. "I've always thought that. You'll help put a stop to all this, someday, I know."

She released him, walking back up the stairs, and Grimmond turned toward the door.

"Grim?"

He turned to see her swiveled on the top step.

"Your parents loved you, too — no matter *what* happened," she said quietly. "But…if you could go back and change what you said somehow, would you?"

Grimmond gritted his teeth, wishing he had the ability to lie to her again, but he didn't.

"Yeah," he answered truthfully. "There's nothing…nothing I'll ever regret more than what happened that night."

Grimmond left, walking into the cold, and back across the snow-laden path toward the bridge.

He couldn't erase Olivia's empty face from his mind, the pain he felt on her behalf, or the fact that she believed he had some unknown role to play against the Nightmayr Realm. Whether he believed that or not, Grimmond wouldn't let anyone else get hurt while he stood by.

Grimmond would search for the door *and* the key to the Nightmayr Realm, to seal it all away.

Stopping by the Anxious Canine for three *Tingle Hells* — cayenne-peppermint mochas — Grimmond hurried up to the mostly empty Fire Watch. Tristin and Viana were on the couch beside the fire, playing a board game together. Grimmond promptly walked up to them, handed them each their drinks, and spoke.

"Drink up, because I'm in," he declared. "Tell Drek I accept the Black Wings' offer."

THE DREAD MAP

The holiday break flashed by as Grimmond trained outdoors.

Largely ignoring the festivities happening inside, while flying over Grisly Grove Grimmond saw what he thought was a scene reenacted from a Halloween-Christmas movie. But it was only the Terrors, kidnapping and dressing up the corpse-skeletons from Grisly Grove. Grimmond's childhood images of Christmas were forever ruined after seeing a bloody Santa Claus, hanging from a Sentree by its neck.

After Grimmond finally told Viana it was Dr. Knight who revealed the secret of her father's death, Viana was furious. She didn't speak to her mother for weeks, then hunted down the gossiper from the bathroom — the girl who originally heard Dr. Knight's story and spread it around. Grimmond saw the bathroom girl again later, wearing much more makeup around her right eye than at the Halloween Dance.

Though again on speaking terms, things were terse between Grimmond and Viana. They both acted as if Halloween night ended when Viana convinced Grimmond not to run away. The kiss they shared in secret never happened, even though the entire Hollow knew about it. To Grimmond, Viana was back to being a warrior again: beautiful, witty, and as untouchable as the day he met her.

Grimmond learned quickly that he and Brax paled in comparison to either her or Tristin's skills as Black Wings. Using her Glass Wing's translucent wings as a magnifier, Viana could press her bright knuckles against Qinella's sides and Flare ten times as wide. Tristin used Flynn's massive Nerve-Neck snout like a warhead, flying feet from the ground in silence, and breaking through anything in their path.

Expecting that all the Black Wings would be just as good when he started drilling with them, Grimmond wondered what he'd eventually be able to do with Brax. He could find very little about the Blood Onyx species in the main library, but Grimmond knew Brax was large, fast, and had hide as hard as steel. And although Brax couldn't speak, being free of Haunter possession, Grimmond thought sometimes his Gargoyle understood him.

By the time February hit, Grimmond and Brax had already become much stronger together.

Grimmond grew in confidence, learning more about Nightmare types in his classes, and riding with the Black Wings. Each Squadron was split into two teams of four, and in charge of both was a single captain, for a total of nine riders. On the Black Wings, Drek Heeder acted as captain over the two teams. Grimmond, Tristin and Viana were on the *Blue* Team under Sariah Lunasae, while Keokuk, Linda, and René Yates — a short, red-headed girl whom Grimmond didn't know well — were on the *Red* Team under Wynn Felt.

Scringoll, Grimmond learned more about, could be run with either two small teams or two entire Squadrons. One side was offensive and the other defensive, the offensive being whichever had possession of the single silver *'Ringlet'*. Grimmond thought he would immediately like the war game, but hadn't been able to make up his mind.

"Full armor's worn in competition matches," Drek explained at the lake, "and glaives are fitted with protective sheaths so nobody gets skewered. One side uses their blunted glaives to toss the Ringlet back and forth, racing it through the defense, all the way to the tall *'Spindle'* on the other side of the lake. Once they make it there, the Ringlet is tossed around the Spindle for one single point, and then the Ringlet's turned over to the opposing team."

"Kind of like football, then?" Grimmond asked.

"Sure," Drek answered. "Maybe American football — defensive players *do* try to steal the Ringlet as it's thrown from glaive to glaive. But, there aren't Gargoyles in football with three different Terrors tethered to their spines."

"Terrors are *attached* to the Gargoyles' spines?" Grimmond asked. "What the heck for?"

Tristin laughed, then cut in to explain.

"So they can be *Flared*," he said. "Every Gargoyle has three Terrors on its backside — kinda like having three lives. When a Terror's Flared, it fades away, right? If a Gargoyle loses all three of its Terrors, that Gargoyle and its rider are both out of the match. Only the side *not* in possession of the Ringlet is allowed to Flare, though."

"Cool," Grimmond summed up. "Defense can Flare the offense, and each Nightmarist gets three lives before they're out. Like baseball, I guess, but I never loved that game."

"You don't have to," Drek took back over. "Offense can't Flare to protect themselves, but they *can* Lull as they fight their way to the Spindle. So long as it's not *'Somnüs'*, of course — we don't need Haunted Gargoyles stunned and dumping their riders to fall to their deaths. Wouldn't be a problem for the Blood Onyx though, I guess.... Oh, and for that matter, any Gargoyle advantage can be used freely, so long as they don't attack a rider directly."

"Basically, Grim," Tristin spoke again, "The first team to get the Ringlet on the Spindle ten times — to reach *ten points* — wins. Unless a whole team loses all their Terrors first, of course, and are out of the match by default."

"Got it," Grimmond nodded, trying to keep track of all the rules. "Get that big silver ring across the lake and onto the tall needle-looking thingy, before my three Terrors get fried or I burn myself out by Lulling too much."

"That's about the size of it!" Tristin commended.

"So, Scringoll is basically like...*Scringoll*."

Despite his efforts, Grimmond nose-dived in the lake one night during Scringoll drills after slipping off of Brax. He didn't admit it was because his fingers were so numb he couldn't hold on while flying upside down. Fortunately his fall wasn't from a great height, and the water was deep. But it was still below freezing outside, and he had to return to Fire Watch and change before hypothermia set in.

Drek decided to call training for the night, and held a meeting around the blazing fire while Grimmond warmed himself.

"All right," Drek said seriously, stretching out his scarred muscles toward the fire, "you all know what's coming up at the beginning of April."

"I d-don't," Grimmond said, shivering.

"Gargoyle Games!" Wynn cheered, joined by the rest of his team sitting on the couches.

Tristin yipped along with them, spilling some coffee on his jeans, but Sariah and Viana exchanged an exasperated glance.

"I never did get a g-good answer on what they w-were, though," Grimmond shivered. "It's not Scringoll?"

"Tell him, Viana," Tristin said.

Realizing his blunder too late, Tristin took an extra-long swig of his drink. A Sentree beside the fire, meanwhile, reached to a tattered blanket, picked it up, and threw it at Grimmond's face. He thanked it as Viana unclenched her teeth to explain.

"It's an annual competition between all four Squadrons here at the Hollow," Viana said. "Whoever wins gets bragging rights of being best Squadron for the next year."

Grimmond nodded, locking eyes with her, and tried desperately not to turn away. He did before her, however, and didn't see her clenching teeth again. The rest of the Squadron suddenly became interested in the view outside the windows, or polishing their bright knuckles, until Tristin cleared his throat.

"Right, well, we basically have a task assigned from Lord Stawlart, that the Nightmares will set up for us. It'll either be on the lake, here in the Hovel, or...I suppose *anywhere*, really. Usually the Nightmares hide something, we decipher a bunch of clues, fight some armored Nightmares, then actually try to *find* whatever they hid —"

"In *far less* words," Sariah cut him off, "it's a scavenger hunt on steroids, Grim. You'll do fine."

Sariah shot Tristin a quick glance and winked, and Tristin upended his coffee cup once again. Grimmond was sure he had blushed.

"Well said, all," Drek agreed. "But even more so, Scringoll and the Gargoyle Games keep us sharp for the real deal, for whenever we get called outside the Hollow. We don't treat either like they're make-believe. You all should know, the Dread Map has read more activity this year than ever before, and we're getting stretched big time. We can't afford to be making mistakes out there."

He narrowed his eyes accusingly at Grimmond, who wilted and pulled his blanket tighter.

"The Aurora Blights got sent up the coast over break, to a town overrun with Terrors," Drek went on. "Easy enough, right? But last week the Sleepwalkers were in New York, for a string of forty murders. *Forty.* The media tried to tag it as gang violence, then changed their minds to say it was serial killers banding together."

"If only it were that simple, my bros," said Wynn, taking off his red knit cap and smoothing his hair back. "The Sleepwalkers confirmed it was two Prowlers that did all that. Only *two*, y'all."

"That's it?" Grimmond said in disbelief.

"Understand, Grim," Drek nodded. "Dreamers don't stand a chance against something they can't see. We do what they can't do for themselves — what nobody but a Nightmarist can do. We're fighting *for* them."

"Things really are worse than ever," Sariah added. "First it was the escalation of Dread Map activity this summer, then the Orchard Incursion. Now we can't get them fast enough, and it's hitting the news. At least there's nobody out there seeing what's really doing the killing. Not that anyone would believe it anyway...."

The Squadron drank their coffee in silence, nodding in agreement with each speaker.

"So," Keokuk spoke up. "About the *Games*. Do we know what they're doing this year?"

"Not yet," Drek answered, "but I'll find out. And as the two newest members of the team, you and Grimmond need to get some real gear before that. Wynn and Sariah will handle it."

Olivia returned to a normal schedule before February ended, though Grimmond knew she wasn't the same person she once was. She stuck with Grimmond in class and at meals, but spoke little, and almost never smiled. Grimmond thought she was even sitting physically closer to him than before Keith's death, stealing glances at him every so often, as if making sure he was still there.

He couldn't imagine what she felt like.

Never questioning how she coped, Grimmond only wished he could help her, more so than warding off people she didn't want to speak to, like Wayne Roarsch. The boy from Narcoleptic Row attempted to talk to her at supper one night, until Grimmond, Tristin and Randy all stood up. Olivia muttered her thanks as Wayne ran for the exit, but barely lifted her eyes from her plate.

"You think she's gonna be okay?" Randy asked after Olivia left. "I mean — eventually?"

The others didn't answer.

"*Wow* — just heard myself," Randy said, shaking his head. "What a stupid thing to ask."

"I never had a brother or a sister," Grimmond answered, "but I think a *twin* is even more different."

Tristin pushed around the food on his plate.

"There's nothing to be done, gents," he said with a sigh. "Just bloody make sure you're listening when she's ready to talk."

Sariah, Linda, and René walked over to the boys' table and sat.

"Did you guys hear the news?" Sariah started, pulling her wavy brown locks back with a hair tie.

"*Big* news," added Linda, reaching out for Randy's drink and taking a sip.

Grimmond looked at Tristin, who shrugged his shoulders.

"Well, get on with it," Tristin said, "we haven't heard anything."

Sariah waved the others in conspiratorially.

"The Gargoyle Games this year —" she said. "Lord Stawlart is switching things up."

"Really?" Tristin said. "Why would he do that, I wonder?"

Grimmond hid his grin, watching Tristin's change in posture; he arched his back, sat up a little straighter, and looked intensely at Sariah. Grimmond had never seen Tristin give such undivided attention to anyone.

"It's an obstacle course now — a race for a key!" René piped, trying and failing to pull her short hair back like the two older girls had. "And it's going to be set up on the lake."

"*That'll do*, René," Linda said with an air of superiority. "But yeah, she's right. Drek said that it's going to be like a real-life situation. I dunno what all he was saying, but he wants us to be down at the lake tonight to start planning."

"We'll be there," Grimmond said in return. "Does Viana know yet?"

René blushed almost to the shade of her red hair, while Linda stole Randy's drink again with a flirtatious wink.

"Oh, come on, I can't even say her *name* without people getting awkward? Viana and I are fine."

Grimmond tried to look nonchalant, but Sariah raised her eyebrows in disbelief.

"If you say so. Meet me and Wynn up at the Armory in twenty minutes. Drek reminded us that you and Keokuk still needed some gear. Tristin, would you mind showing him up? Might as well show Grim the Dread Map while we're at it."

"Oh," Grimmond said. "I think I already know where the map is —"

"Yep! I'll be there," Tristin cut him off. "I mean, yeah, I'll show him up. Keokuk, too, if he needs me."

"Great," Sariah answered. "See you in a bit."

The girls left, and Tristin slowly deflated to his normal posture. He looked up at Grimmond and Randy's grinning faces.

"Too much?" Tristin asked.

"*Way* too much," Randy answered.

*   *   *

Tristin walked Grimmond to the top floor of the Hovel, and approached Lord Stawlart's office.

"I thought you said the Dread Map *wasn't* in his office...."

"It's not," Tristin winked, walking past the doors. "The Dread Map is kind of its own office."

He turned down another hall, and Grimmond followed after him, looking around the corner curiously. Tristin smiled at the developing look on Grimmond's face when he stepped past the corner.

The next hall was a singly large, seven-sided room.

On each of the seven walls were seven separate maps, made of white, shimmery material and extending up to the pointed ceiling. Each depicted a single continent of the world, and Terrors hovered behind them like backlights, illuminating countries, regions, or geographic features in vivid colors. In front of the maps were Nightmarists monitoring, advised by Haunters that pointed out areas with glowing fingers.

Ernst, the Phantom driver who brought Grimmond to Stanchions, was pointing at the northern edge of Asia with Professor Manning and Coach Maurs. Grimmond thought it strange to see Ernst with a full body.

Or a *mostly* full body, as Ernst's neck hadn't grown skin.

Turning about to take in more, Grimmond saw Lord Stawlart and Eralynn conversing quietly before the map of North America. Beside them, something like a darkly colored, mutant half-teddy bear — more unnatural than many things Grimmond had seen at the Hollow — was breathing quickly.

Two black arms and legs sprouted from only one of its sides, spiky-haired and knobby, and long crooked pincers grew from its face. Grimmond's skin didn't start crawling until it turned its four glowing white eyes on him. When it hissed, a yellow liquid dripped out beneath its bottom end and sloshed on the floor.

It was so fast that Grimmond barely had time to react when it scuttled toward him.

"OY!" yelled Tristin, reaching for his bright knuckles.

Grimmond tried to step backwards, but stumbled on the sticky floor and fell. Just before foot-long pincers would be driven into his stomach, a second one of the creatures swung down from the ceiling and plowed into the other's limbless side. Grimmond gasped, watching in morbid fascination as the second creature stuck its oozing side up against the dripping yellow of the first one, like two halves of a rancid sandwich.

Ribbons of flesh shot between them, and then they stopped moving, rose up slowly, and stared at Grimmond. Now with eight limbs altogether, Grimmond saw that they were two halves of the same spider, now sutured into one.

"*Cyto!*" Eralynn admonished. "That's my *godson!*"

"What's this, Plasm?" Lord Stawlart came over next. "There's no need to get excited. The young man wouldn't be here if he wasn't on our side. Now both of you — pull yourselves together."

Cyto-Plasm's thorax squished revoltingly as another strand of flesh wove between its two halves.

"Ah," Lord Stawlart said, "well...I see you're in-process, so just move along for now."

With an insidious hiss, the two red and black spider-halves jumped onto the wall and scurried away up the web. Lord Stawlart beamed at Grimmond.

"Never mind them. Sometimes they're split in half to work more efficiently. Clearly, it's not always the case. Separates the brains from the brawn, I think."

"Split in two?" Grimmond grunted as he was helped off the floor by Tristin.

"Cyto and Plasm are two halves of a *Dreadachnid*. They're our Plotters, hence the name 'Dread' Map. They weave information together, after gathering it from the least of the fear manifestations — the Wispers — and alert the rest of us after putting it on the map. Cyto and Plasm are really the only ones who can perceive the Wispers, you see; without them we'd never know where Nightmares are surfacing in the world.

"Though you might not realize it, Grimmond, always we're searching, listening for rumors of either the key or the door to the Nightmayr Realm. That's partly why we allow so many Nightmares into the Hollow: to gather information. Some have been here far longer than I, of course — *ahem* — like dear Ernst here."

Ernst turned to bow quickly, then drew Professor Manning and Coach Maurs back into conversation.

"I should've warned you before, dear," Eralynn said. "Cyto and Plasm don't love new faces, but it usually takes both of them to decide to eat someone."

Eralynn placed an apologetic hand on Grimmond's shoulder, and Tristin clapped the other. Grimmond stepped further into the room, noticing that the sticky floor was soft and springy, like a tightly woven trampoline. Then he looked at the walls, and started to wonder about the other room in the castle that was heptagonal.

Isn't there a spider web forming at the top of the ceiling there?

"Hey Tristin, isn't the Hearth shaped like this room, too?"

"Yep," Tristin affirmed. "We're at the top of the Hearth now, in the Dreadachnid's web. Perfect spot to see all seven continents at once and keep an eye on the world, even though most of it's handled by the other Hollows."

Lord Stawlart guided them over to North America, where he and Eralynn had been standing.

"Do you see the little red dots around New England, Grimmond?" asked the man. "That was the Nightmare activity last year. Each of those is a separate threat — an incursion from the Nightmayr Realm into the *real* world. Stanchions Hollow deployed to and eradicated each of them. Now, here's what the end of this past summer looked like."

The backlighting Terrors changed the map at Lord Stawlart's bidding, and Grimmond saw maybe ten times as many dots in Massachusetts alone. All of them, for some reason, were forming a loose circle around Boston.

"Why did Cyto and Plasm plot them in a circle like that?" Grimmond pointed.

"Because, Grimmond," Eralynn explained, "that's where they were showing up. Remember how this past summer was the worst you'd ever seen the Nightmares?"

"You mean my *hallucinations*?" Grimmond said dryly. "Yes, I remember."

Now I know why, at least….

Grimmond moved his finger up the map on the wall, to what almost looked like another ring of red dots.

"Why are they starting to form again in this area?" Grimmond asked. "Isn't Stanchions around here?"

Grimmond thought Lord Stawlart exchanged a quick glance with Eralynn, but just then Sariah walked in with Wynn and Keokuk.

"Grim — Tristin!" Sariah barked. "I'm sorry Lord Stawlart. Miss Eralynn. I'll get them out of your hair. I told them to meet me in the Armory, not bother you."

"No trouble at all, Miss Lunasae," Lord Stawlart replied. "They're all yours."

Grimmond said goodbye to his godmother, then followed Sariah and Tristin to a door between Europe and Asia. The room held glaives of different thickness and length, bright knuckles organized by finger size, and armor like Viana and Tristin wore.

"How's your glaive working out?" Sariah asked. "I heard you already had one."

"I do," Grimmond answered. "If it's all right, I'd like to keep using it."

"Stood up against an Atrocity, right?" she answered. "Fine by me. And your bright knuckles? All good?"

"Ah," Tristin sighed, picking up a pair of old bright knuckles. "What I'd give for the Narcolex Model 3...just don't have the Marrow. We really ought to visit Boston's Below Bazaar sometime."

"Yeah, man!" Wynn agreed. "But I hear they've got stuff that, like, even the Nightmares use on *us*, bro."

Grimmond assented to Sariah's question, but after her mentioning the Atrocity, his thoughts went to Keith Tychus.

"All Grim needs today is the *Luciferin* armor," Tristin said, clearing his throat as he grabbed a vest and helmet off the wall.

He laughed at the look on Grimmond's face.

"It's not as evil as it sounds, mate. Luciferin is what makes bugs and plants glow — bioluminescence and all that. Stanchions found out that anything from the Nightmayr Realm hates the stuff, and then figured out a way to incorporate it into our buildings, weapons, armor — basically everything. It gives us the edge we need."

"At last, *there's* a straight answer," Grimmond said. "To why everything glows around here."

"Just because something's lighting up doesn't mean it's got Luciferin in it," Tristin said. "Nightmares glow of their own accord."

"Fine," Grimmond said lightly. "It's just good to know I'm not crazy anymore."

Tristin handed Grimmond the armor that glowed light green. The black vest felt like a stiff leather tee shirt as he slipped it over his neck and strapped the buckles on the sides, but his arms rubbed against the outside and he found the feeling unpleasant. He tried on the helmet next, similar in color to the vest, though more like what a medieval knight would wear during jousting. But he didn't like it either, feeling constricted, and altogether itchy and uncomfortable in the set of armor.

He didn't complain, his mind drifting back to Keith. It was difficult not to wonder if the armor could've saved his life, had he been wearing it.

"Okay!" Sariah clapped her hands together. "You've got weapons, you can fly, and now you've got Luciferin armor. We're done here. Let's head down to the practice field so you can try it out. I'll make sure Tristin and Viana get to stab you once or twice."

"Get *stabbed?*"

"I'll do my best!" Tristin chimed in. "It's good to have faith in your equipment, right?"

At last the day of the Gargoyle Games had arrived, and nervous to win, Grimmond stared at the lake in silence from the top of the stable towers. His Squadron had exhausted themselves against the Skeleton Crew, playing Scringoll several times a week over the lake. He'd learned to wear long sleeves to prevent his Luciferin armor bothering his skin, and had also gathered why *full* armor was necessary when going against other Squadrons.

Grimmond nearly had his head taken off during one game, when Malus plowed into him with his Bone Crawler, claiming he lost control. In reprisal, ramming into Malus and kicking him hard in the chest, Grimmond also claimed it was an accident. Things declined between the rest of the two Squadrons after that, and it was decided that a referee should be present in the future.

But within a few days, the lake over which they practiced had been transformed from a body of water into a massive, floating obstacle course. Wooden bridges led out over the dark depth of water, where jumbles of tunnels, ropes and small huts floated like a lost city — it was nearly the same size as the Hovel. Groups of new trees now grew tall, though beneath them were the same old gnarled stumps, burning with torchlight.

Stanchions' Nightmares have been busy to make all this....

"Hey," said Tristin, walking out onto the open platform of the stable towers.

Viana walked up the stairs behind him, holding a few cups from the Anxious Canine. She offered Grimmond a small smile and handed a cup to him.

"Wrigglebits, right?" she asked.

"Yep, still my favorite," Grimmond answered. "Though the Bloody Valentine last month was a runner-up. I do love chocolate and raspberry."

Viana smiled again, and Grimmond allowed his eyes to linger on the sunset reflected in her eyes.

Get it together, Grimmond. You burned — no, BLEW UP — that bridge months ago.

Viana and Tristin leaned over the wall between Grimmond and Brax, and Viana placed a hand on the Blood Onyx's head. He growled as usual, but quieter and non-threateningly.

"How're we looking down there?" Tristin asked.

"Unclear. I don't know how they built all that up so fast, either."

"Those are the ruins of the fifth Ward, Drift Dam," Viana said offhandedly. "Didn't you know? It used to be right on the lake, but was destroyed the only other time the Hollow was breached, some twenty years ago."

"What's it supposed to be now?" Grimmond asked, recalling Eralynn's murky explanation of the fifth Ward the night they arrived. "The world's biggest jungle gym?"

"Looks like it," Tristin said. "How're you guys on monkey bars?"

"I'll manage," Viana answered. "At least we shouldn't get wet, since we'll be flying and not swimming."

"As long as the key isn't under water," Grimmond answered.

His face darkened, his mind falling back to his thoughts of the last few weeks — thoughts of the key to the Nightmayr Realm, and the door with it that could seal away the Nightmares forever.

"We know that the key's *somewhere* on that lake. We've gotta find it before anyone else. Before things get any worse around here...."

Tristin turned toward Grimmond, seeing the concentration on his face.

"You all right, mate?" he asked. "You know this isn't *actually* the key to the Nightmayr Realm."

Grimmond returned an exasperated look.

"Yeah, but Drek said we should be acting like it's the real deal, not a game."

"You're right," Viana said, "but finding the key is just one piece of the puzzle. We still don't know where the door is, either."

Grimmond took a drink of his coffee, staring back over the lake, and the group grew silent. The air in the Hollow was beginning to warm, the snow melting, and Grimmond felt a sense of foreboding with it. Something was being readied somewhere; some *thing* was in motion that he couldn't know yet.

"Tristin — remember what Lord Stawlart showed us on the Dread Map?" Grimmond asked. "How a ring of Nightmare incursions circled around Boston last summer?"

"I've seen it before, too," Viana agreed after Tristin. "Kinda weird, I think."

"Well," Grimmond went on, "what if the door was there? *In* Boston? What if that's where it's been the whole time?"

"If that was the case, then Stanchions would've grabbed it long ago," Tristin reasoned.

Grimmond wondered, thinking back to the first time he met Lord Stawlart at his house, the night he escaped the city. He hadn't told his friends everything about that night, thinking they'd view him differently if they knew one particular truth.

"You know Lord Stawlart picked me up himself from Boston," Grimmond began tentatively. "To bring both me and Eralynn here."

His friends nodded, and Grimmond guessed that then was as good a time as any to tell them what he knew.

"Well...while we were alone, Lord Stawlart told me that my dad was the last descendant of some of the *old* Nightmarists."

Tristin took another sip from his cup, and lazily turned toward him.

"What do you mean?"

"As in, the old Nightmarists who actually *made* the door to the Nightmayr Realm," Grimmond clarified. "Those were my dad's great-great-great grandparents, or something."

"Come off it."

"No," Grimmond answered. "I'm serious."

Tristin's eyebrows nearly flew off his forehead before setting his drink down.

"Grim," he started, eyes bulging, "if *that's* who your dad is, that's HUGE —"

"Who his dad *was*," Viana interrupted. "It's who *Grim* is now. He'd be the last descendant after his father, obviously —"

"Why've you never told us before?" Tristin spoke over her, his tone still amazed.

Viana scrutinized Grimmond while he stood in silence.

"Because...that's why he finally came to Stanchions," she said, eyeing him up and down. "The Ending is after him because of his dad."

Grimmond remained pensive.

"Lord Stawlart guessed that, too. I think that's why Eralynn kept me hidden for so long...I've been feeling more off than usual the past few weeks, thinking about it all."

"You're just nervous for the Games," Viana offered.

Brax abruptly took flight toward the Sleepless Orchard, and Viana stepped closer to Grimmond to pat him on the arm. Grimmond hoped she couldn't somehow feel the chills suddenly appearing beneath his shirt.

"I won't pretend that I'm *not* nervous," Grimmond answered truthfully, "but I don't think that's the only reason. I'll know after today I hope, once the competition is over —"

"Blast," Tristin interrupted, stepping toward the stairwell. "I forgot something in Steeple Spike. I've gotta go grab it. I'll meet you guys down in the entrance hall in a few?"

The others turned to wave, but when Viana looked forward, Tristin winked conspiratorially at Grimmond.

He doesn't need anything! He just wants Viana and I to talk alone!

"You *sure* you can't get it later?" Grimmond called. "We need to be there soon!"

"Nope! Sure can't, need it now. See you downstairs!"

Tristin hurried away, and Viana turned toward the stairs after him, the hood of her sweatshirt blown back by a passing breeze. Grimmond couldn't avoid inhaling some of her sweet scent as strands of hair whipped him in the face.

"That could *not* have been more obvious."

"What?" Grimmond panicked.

"Tristin, leaving us alone to talk."

"Oh," Grimmond said awkwardly, taking another swig of his Wrigglebits to hide his blushing face. "Yeah."

He hadn't been completely alone with Viana since Halloween, and was heavily reminded of what happened last time.

"Welp," Viana said, making a popping noise with her lips, "I guess we should get going, too."

She turned toward the stairs and began to march away. Grimmond mustered his courage, hoping he hadn't already blown the first moment they'd shared in months.

"Viana?"

She turned, raising a hand to her eyes to block the sun.

"Can we talk?" Grimmond asked.

Walking back to him, Viana stood in his shadow to block out the orange sunset. She was close enough for him to smell her breath.

Is that peppermint? Spearmint? Lavender? Who cares, it's too good to name....

Grimmond saw impatience warning in her eyes, but she didn't make a move, nor did she say anything. He cleared his throat, knowing he needed to stop daydreaming before he earned another smack.

"What I meant to say was, can we *please* talk," Grimmond tried again. "Take a walk and actually catch up, maybe? Tonight after everything's over?"

Grimmond watched her expression soften. She chewed on her lip, then spoke at last.

"I'd like that."

She gestured between them, and scuffed her shoes against the stone floor.

"I'm tired of this too, you know," she continued. "But it's gonna take more than just a walk and one night of talking."

"Tonight, then?" Grimmond asked hopefully.

"Okay," she agreed. "Tonight."

Grimmond could tell she tried not to smile as she turned away, but when she did, it was a smile he hadn't seen in months.

GARGOYLE GAMES

Together the three friends walked down to the lakeshore, Grimmond feeling more encouraged than he had in weeks. He tried his best not to steal a glance at Viana more than every few dozen steps or so.

When the path opened up and the Lightwarts — chirping their usual death threats — departed, Grimmond was quite distracted, seeing far more people on the beach than he'd expected. Filling nearly a dozen sets of bleachers, wrapped in blankets, and with steaming cups in hand, the entirety of Stanchions Hollow was assembled and waiting for the start of the Games.

"I've never seen everyone all together," Grimmond said.

"Yeah," Tristin replied. "More Nightmarists than you'd think, eh? Even though most aren't on the Squadrons."

Grimmond weaved through the crowd with Tristin and Viana, looking at the various vendors' sizzling meats, strange candies and drinks. He'd never eaten smoked Jackalope or flame-broiled wolf before, though they smelled promising, and neither had he heard of Rebbigone Sweet Blood, Specter Spit or Terror-Tart Droppings. He resolved to try them all later, assuming the candy names were just a gimmick.

The Anxious Canine had its booth set up on the end, and although the line was long, Zolgo shooed his customers back when he saw the trio from the Black Wings approaching. Several people grumbled, until Zolgo and the other two Gargremlins on staff jumped up and bared their fangs.

"You see these?" Zolgo shouted, pointing to his stubby black wings. "If you're not a Black Wings fan, then get outta my line!"

No one did, even as the small black dog beneath the booth's sign — the Anxious Canine itself — glowed and snapped at anyone who dared to complain. Grimmond stared at the dog, stepping back when it likewise tried to lunge at him, and was only held back by two small chains from which it was suspended.

"Nice touch, ain't it?" Zolgo asked, leaning in. "I gave a few Shards to a Terror to hang out in there for the day and shape people up. What do you's need? Little pick-me-up? Coffee? Espresso?"

Viana eyed his sudden generosity with suspicion as Zolgo bent even closer, waving them in.

"Something *else* for a bit of an edge? Prowler Powder, maybe?"

"Oh, *please*!" Viana snapped. "You weasel! How much do you have riding on the competition?"

"DON'T INSULT ME!" shrieked the Gargremlin, though backing out of reach as Viana fumed. "I offer merely outta the *goodness* of my heart!"

"Thanks Zolgo, but we're fine," Grimmond said quickly. "We've actually gotta hurry up and get to our staging area."

"Hang on — Tony!" Zolgo called, "Three blacks, *STAT*!"

In a flash, a smaller Gargremlin flew over with the coffees, handed them off, and immediately got back to work taking new orders.

"Good luck!" Zolgo called, cupping his claws around his mouth as the trio left. "And if you lose, I'll upcharge you for a month!"

Glaive tips sheathed, bright knuckles polished, and armor clad, each of the four Squadrons was assembled along the edges of the lake. Walking past the Skeleton Crew first, Grimmond saw Malus Nebbick, and braced himself for their daily standoff. But Malus's face was sweaty and fearful as he stared out at the water. He didn't throw a single insult at Grimmond, too busy fiddling with whatever was in his pocket.

What's wrong with him? Can't swim?

Grimmond greeted the Sleepwalkers next, wishing them a sportsmanlike 'good luck', followed by the Aurora Blights. But he almost tripped when he saw who was now on their team.

"Olivia?" Grimmond spat, burning his lip with coffee.

"Surprise," she answered dryly.

She walked over to Grimmond and the other two, dressed in Luciferin armor and holding a glaive.

"What do you think you're doing?" Grimmond asked in shock.

"What's it look like?" Olivia answered. "I'm with the Blights now. They had an opening, and I tried out once a Haunter found a Nerve-Neck for me."

"No way!" Grimmond said animatedly.

"Yep," she said with a half-smile. "Just figured it was time I finally —"

"No," Grimmond cut her off, stepping forward to the general shock of her teammates. "I meant: *no way are you doing this!*"

"Yo — Scylent," the Aurora Blights captain said, standing up cautiously to walk over. "Tychus volunteered, it's not like I went out to recruit her —"

"What the *hell*, Jack?" Grimmond yelled. "You should've said no to this! What're you two thinking?"

"Don't talk about me like I'm not here!" Olivia scolded. "I'm not a *kid*, Grim. Not anymore. And Captain Michaels let me in because I can do the job — that's it. Now get out of our area so we can get ready."

Grimmond and Olivia squared off, sparks shooting between them, until Tristin grabbed Grimmond by the elbow and pulled him back.

"C'mon, mate," he whispered, "people are watching — we need to get over to our Squadron."

Grimmond relented, and stalked away angrily.

"What was that all about?" Viana asked in a tone of feigned lightness.

"I — I don't know," Grimmond answered honestly. "I just can't believe that after everything, she'd find a Gargoyle and put herself right in the thick of it. After everything that's happened...."

"She almost died," Viana said. "Her brother *did* die."

"Exactly my point —"

"So, wouldn't you want to do something about it if you were her?"

"I...I guess," Grimmond sighed. "Oh, dammit."

Grimmond realized he'd done the exact thing Tristin had warned him not to do. When Olivia was finally ready to talk at last and attempt some normalcy, Grimmond shut her down, and possibly strained their friendship to the point of breaking.

"Hey," Tristin said as they arrived at the Black Wings staging area. "No time to dwell on it — we'll fix it later. Lord Stawlart's about to talk."

Trying to shake off his rash outburst, Grimmond looked to see Lord Stawlart and Ernst walking toward a podium that stood before the first bridge to the lake. Ernst held a glowing loudspeaker in front of Lord Stawlart, who cleared his throat.

"I'll keep this short," the man began, waving his hands to silence the applause from the swelling crowd. "What's behind me is something different than anything we've ever done with the Gargoyle Games before. Amidst obstacles, dead ends, and aggressors in the scattered rubble of Drift Dam, a key like this will be searched for."

Lord Stawlart gestured to Ernst, who held high a bright red key, no bigger than his ghostly palm.

"Each Squadron will move from here to four different sides of the lake. Then, before entering the course, Gargoyles will be instructed to remain behind. All searching for the key will be done on two legs only; no flying shall be permitted this evening."

Grimmond's breath caught with the muttering crowd.

No Gargoyles?

He looked to Drek for some sort of protest, but the captain's face was solemn and unchanging; he already knew, Grimmond guessed, but the remainder of the team was crestfallen.

"What am I supposed to do without Brax?" Grimmond whispered quickly to Tristin and Viana. "He's the only edge I had!"

"Captains," Lord Stawlart's voice rang out, "take your Squadrons to your designated starting points across the lake. I'll give the opening signal at sunset in five minutes' time, when all Squadrons will enter Drift Dam at once."

Lord Stawlart made to step down from the podium, but turned again to the largely quiet crowd.

"Ah, I nearly forgot," he said into the loudspeaker. "A task without Scringoll or Gargoyles requires higher stakes. Therefore, after the starting Flare signals, the thirty-minute countdown to the floating city's renewed destruction will commence. Anyone left after the time is over may be seriously injured."

The crowd jumped to their feet in the bleachers, cheering with ear-splitting cries.

Okay, I can swim if I have to....

"The center of the city is longer than a mile from shore," the man continued, "and the water is being patrolled by corpse-skeletons of Grisly Grove, free of their nooses —"

Never tried to swim a mile while fighting rotting skeletons, though.

"So, Squadrons," Lord Stawlart said over the tumult, "please do your best to be safely back on shore before your time is up, or we may be holding Squadron tryouts tomorrow to replace those of you who don't make it."

He's kidding, right?

"Good luck all, and may the best Squadron win!"

Lord Stawlart stepped down from the podium to more applause, and glowing balloons were thrown into the air. Drek turned to the Black Wings, green-faced as the sun finished retreating.

"This is a *joke*, right?" Grimmond started.

"Yeah, Drek!" Linda added. "What are we supposed to do —"

"Black Wings need *wings*, my bros!"

"I KNOW, *now quiet*!" Drek hushed them. "Bring it in, and hurry up!"

Obediently the Black Wings gathered close.

"We're gonna do this without Gargoyles, and I know we can, but we have to be fast! It'll take us ten minutes to get out to the lake, and ten minutes back to shore, so that leaves us ten minutes to search when we get there."

"What about the other Squadrons?" Tristin asked. "What do we do about them?"

"Nothing," Drek answered. "Stay out of their way, even if they try to get in yours. Lord Stawlart didn't mention anything about fighting one another, but I wouldn't put it past some of them. We're not fighting tonight — we're concentrating on finding that key. Let's move!"

CHAPTER THIRTEEN

Grimmond quickly hopped on Brax, who had arrived during Lord Stawlart's speech, and took to the sky with the rest of the Black Wings. To the north side of the lake they followed Drek, where the shadow of the mountain was already darkening.

"Sorry, Brax," Grimmond said, dismounting him, "the rules say we can't use you tonight. Stay close though, okay?"

"Vests on — no helmets!" Drek called. "I don't want anyone drowning if they fall in the water. Get into the city, break off with your team, and search north to south as fast as you can. I'll stick with Wynn on Red Team. Sariah — watch your time. With ten minutes left you've gotta split. Clear?"

Sariah sounded her affirmation.

"Remember, we're *not* supposed to be fighting the other Squadrons, we're finding that red key!"

The Black Wings moved to the edge of the bridge, where a wall of glowing Terrors, Haunters including Greta, and Coach Maurs guarded the entrance. Linda and René quickly stretched out against one another, while Wynn and Keokuk drew a last-minute battle plan in the sand.

Sariah looked to her own teammates, nodding.

"It's been a fun year so far," she said wryly. "Let's get this key and not mess it up."

Viana and Tristin remained quiet, staring at the crowd of people back near the Hovel, their cheers echoing dimly off the lake. Grimmond gripped bright knuckles in his right fist, and his collapsed glaive in the other. He felt the glaive's cool metal against his skin, and looked at its glowing purple tip, wondering offhandedly why it wasn't the dim Luciferin-green like everyone else's.

Coach Maurs turned to the group, his coal-like eyes smoldering red in the dark.

"Thirty seconds," he said. "but first, a quick tip I am permitted to offer: any Nightmare you force into the lake will be out of the Game, and no longer hostile to you. Keep that in mind — these are just actors! We'd prefer it if you didn't banish every one back to the Nightmayr Realm. Good luck!"

Across the lake, a green Flare pierced the sky, and the wall of Nightmares before the Black Wings moved to the side.

"Keep that glaive level, Keokuk!" Coach Maurs called as the Squadron took off. "You too, Linda! And Grimmond, *remember your Terror Wheel —*"

The coach fell out of earshot as the cool wind whipped across Grimmond's face. His heartbeat began to race, and his enhanced vision kicked in. The Hovel became a glowing beacon in the distance, the water bright green, and the sky its nightmarish purple.

The countdown had begun.

The bridge was wide enough for three people to run abreast.

Drek and the team leaders took point. Nothing bothered them initially, and Grimmond thought they had caught a lucky break. But a half-mile in, they were assaulted by a horde of Terror-possessed-logs, red-eyed snakes, and stones big enough to break bones.

"Should've brought those helmets after all!" Tristin yelled. "Look out!"

The stones came in, bouncing off the Luciferin vests, but one struck René in the arm and drew a sliver of blood. Keokuk extended his glaive and cut the head off a snake as it slithered through the air.

"Onyare!" Keokuk called in his Mohawk dialect. "Snake to the left! Kill the stupid things!"

He chopped the head off another snake, ejecting the red Terror within.

"Don't waste your energy!" Drek shouted. "Everybody — give me a quick primary burst!"

As they'd drilled dozens of times before, Drek's bright knuckles Flared yellow, Wynn's team deep red, and Sariah's sky blue. Well over half the Terrors were singed by the light, and they dropped their possessed objects into the water in order to flee.

"Now — *secondary* burst for the rest of them!" Drek shouted again.

Drek then Flared green, Wynn's team orange, and Sariah's team purple.

It was a free-for-all to get the remaining unusually colored Terrors, but Drek's strategy had worked well; the horde was quickly reduced to nothing when each team focused on a specific color. Grimmond fought through his dizziness as the Squadron pushed across the rest of the bridge, stopping on the first large platform in the floating city.

Back at the cheering crowd, a yellow Flare illuminated the dusky sky.

"Okay, that's ten minutes burned!" Drek called between gasping breaths. "Time to split! Stick with your team, and sweep for that key!"

Grimmond and Tristin fist-bumped their other roommates, then ran off with Sariah and Viana.

Through the swinging nooses of Grisly Grove Sentrees they went, but nothing jumped out as expected. The team felt momentary safety, until the nooses themselves silently struck. One caught around Grimmond's throat, and another Sariah's, lifting them into the air; the others didn't notice until they heard choking, then spun around and unsheathed their glaives.

"Actors *my butt*, Coach Maurs!" Grimmond coughed, massaging his throat after being cut down.

"Come on!" Viana panted, slicing the remaining nooses in her way. "The first place to search is just there!"

She pointed toward a stone hut, and the broken bridge and dark tunnel that led to it. Their feet pounded on the wooden path as they ran toward the bridge, but as soon as they cleared its several missing planks, they were again assailed. Terrors swarmed, corpse-skeletons reached out from the water to grab their legs, and a Prowler exited the tunnel ahead.

"UGH!" Tristin grunted, kicking the first rotting skull in the head.

His boot was stuck in its squishy face, until Grimmond extended his glaive to remove the ballooned neck and head altogether. Grimmond then dismembered another corpse-skeleton, dodging the expelled yellow and green bile from getting in his mouth or eyes. Viana Flared the blue Terrors overhead with bright orange light, and Sariah rapidly Lulled the Prowler's bloated body before kicking it into the water.

"You and Viana go check out the hut!" Sariah called to Grimmond through her sagging jowls.

Her skin and gray hair quickly normalized, and she slashed out at another corpse-skeleton.

"We'll stay and watch for more!"

Nodding, Grimmond ran through the tunnel after Viana, and then up the stairs of the hut. They kicked open the front door, glaives leveled, and saw an old chest sitting in the middle of the room. The Rebbigone atop it didn't waste time, opening its large mouth and blowing out black flames for them to dodge.

Grimmond could smell singed hair as he shoved Viana to the right and dodged left himself. The Rebbigone's yellow eyes squinted as it laughed, rolling onto the floor and preparing to blow fire again at Viana.

"FRIGËRA!" Grimmond boomed.

He didn't brace himself for the cold in addition to his queasiness, never having Lulled a Rebbigone before. Immediately he felt like he'd been dropped in an ice bath, but he watched as the creature was slowly frozen solid. Shivering, he grabbed the creature by its wings, walked to the door, and threw it into the lake, hoping he wouldn't throw up at the same time.

"Quick thinking," Viana said, rising to her feet and approaching the chest. "Thanks."

"D-don't...m-mention it," Grimmond shivered.

She flung it open, but both of their faces fell when they looked inside.

"Empty?" Grimmond said, rubbing his cold chest and upset stomach with his hands. "Nothing at all?"

"It was just a decoy!" Viana cursed. "We have to keep looking for another chest!"

Running back to the others, they left the broken bridge behind and chose a new path through the Sentrees. It wound through several turns and then to a four-way crossroads, but Sariah chose one that eventually brought them to a dead end. She pulled her hair in frustration, Flaring at a Sentree that tried to tickle her leg.

"There's no way around it," she said. "We've gotta split up further. Back to those crossroads, and we'll each take a different path this time. We've probably only got three or four minutes before we have to go back to shore!"

Sprinting to the crossroads, they stopped in their tracks when coming face to face with two other teams. Olivia with the Aurora Blights approached from one path, and Harriet Ulrecht, captain of the Skeleton Crew, stepped out from the other team.

Each person's eyes narrowed, fingers twitching and bodies tense.

"Any luck?" Tristin panted.

"*Obviously* not," Olivia retorted. "You?"

"Dead end," Viana said coldly.

"Hey —" Harriet interjected. "Anybody seen Nebbick? Lost track of him as soon as we got here."

"If I do, I'll let him know he's a bag of trash," Grimmond said menacingly.

Fists clenched, glaives were slowly reached for, and stances widened until Harriet stepped forward.

"No *way* we're doing this," she said.

"Says who?" Olivia retorted, eyeing Viana.

"Says a Squadron CAPTAIN, little girl!" Harriet thundered. "We've only got a couple minutes before this place blows. Now…on the count of three, we all go our separate ways — all right?"

Some participants of the standoff nodded, but not all as Harriet began counting down. Sariah subtly nodded to the left for Grimmond, indicating for him to make for that path when the countdown ended.

"*Three — two — one —* break it off!"

Grimmond immediately sprinted down the path to the left, but with his sudden movement, a concentrated red Flare was startled out of the Aurora Blights.

"*Are you kidding me?*" Viana yelled, crouching low. "You almost burned my face off!"

"S-sorry!" Olivia said, aghast. "It was an accident —"

"SOMNÜS!" Viana and Sariah yelled together.

The situation devolved into an explosion of light, Lulls, and extending glaives, but Grimmond didn't have time to break his friends up. He needed to find the key before time ran out.

His path became an open bridge amongst the gnarled stumps that reached up from the lake's depths. There were no more stone huts in sight. He thought about turning around and braving the fight at the crossroads, until something caught his eye.

Hovering across the path in front of him, small and glowing red, was a shiny metallic object.

Grimmond stopped running, catching his breath and wiping the sweat from his brow to get a better look at it. It was about the size of the key Lord Stawlart held, though Grimmond couldn't see it well, even with his enhanced vision. As soon as he tried to get closer, the object dove over the side of the bridge.

"Wait!"

He ran to the edge where the object entered the lake, watching as it sank into the water. But then it shot forward beneath the roots of a tree stump that was the size of a school bus. Grimmond was freezing already from his recent Lull, but he knew there was no time to lose.

Lord Stawlart never said the key couldn't be under *the water....*

Removing his Luciferin vest, he took several deep breaths and jumped in.

* ~ * ~ *

In the dim of the rotted bedroom, Malus stood defiantly in the black light. He cringed as the rumbling voice echoed around him, but he didn't cower from it.

"You can't enter Stanchions Hollow from within yet," Malus said, pacing back and forth, "not without the key. And the mist remains vigilant in keeping your servants away."

Sound rumbled through the arched black outline of the door before Malus. Several cracks running across its wispy face glowed greedily, and black ribbons of smoke leaked from them, sizzling as they slid through the air and dissipated.

"The Nightmarists aren't any closer to finding this door, and have never suspected it to be under their stupid noses for years. I mean: the clue is there in the name! *Stanchions* Hollow! Might as well have been called *Gated* or *Door* Hollow...."

Malus continued arrogantly, pacing back and forth as water splashed around the floor of the old Drift Dam bedroom, which was submerged just beneath the surface of the lake.

"But they're still searching for the key, and harder than ever. You say the trap is set, my lord — but I don't understand why the Errandi boy is needed at all, beyond revenge's sake."

Malus flushed in the darkness as he listened to the rumbling door.

"Forgive me, *Master*," he said through clenched teeth, "but I've given everything — *everything* to release you — and no one else has gotten as far as I. What will you do with that pathetic boy that you could not do with me alone?"

The black cracks in the door rumbled, but Malus continued, heedless of the warning.

"No longer my concern?" he asked. "He has been more resilient than I thought possible, considering his past, but I hoped he might be *scared* out of the Hollow if I couldn't kill him outright. After the Atrocity I managed to let in through the Orchard attacked, and especially after the idiot Tychus boy was killed —"

A black ribbon of smoke lashed out to caress Malus's neck, and the door shook at the edges.

"O-of c-course, Master!" Malus whimpered in pain, falling to his knees. "*Your* Atrocity!"

His neck sizzled as the black ribbon seared his flesh away and then disintegrated, leaving a long, angry red mark.

"Y-yes!" Malus responded to the unintelligible rumblings of the door. "The Errandi boy will be lured out tonight with the rest of them. But he won't be easily convinced once the Ending finds him."

Malus cowered again like a swatted puppy. He skittered to the wall of the windowless bedroom as the black light brightened, and another ribbon crept through the cracks in the door.

"Never — I wouldn't pretend to give *you* counsel, my lord!" Malus asserted. "I will have them out tonight as you order. Your plan will be successful, and after you are through with him, even his mother won't recognize him...."

A quiet plop broke the sound of Malus's breathing in the room, followed by a glowing red object appearing beside him. A larger splash was then heard outside, and the black ribbon stopped a few inches from Malus's forehead.

"The Errandi boy is coming."

Quickly Malus walked to the arched doorway standing freely in the air, twisted its doorknob, and removed it.

* ~ * ~ *

Flailing when he broke through the surface of the water, before Grimmond was the glowing red object, floating in the air of the sunken bedroom. And standing right beside a broken bedframe was Malus Nebbick, his face reflected evilly in the red light. Grimmond thought he saw the outline of a black arch fizzling away as Malus stuffed a strange-looking doorknob in his pocket.

"Took you long enough," Malus said quietly. "If only you could just give up here, now, it would be easier for all of you. All of *us*."

Grimmond clambered out of the water, catching his breath as he rapidly thought. The damp smell of rot blurred his senses, along with something that smelled vaguely of burned flesh.

"Give up?" Grimmond panted. "That's the key, then? Why haven't you turned it in and won?"

Malus smiled, the light of the floating red object glinting off his teeth.

"It's not the key — but I figured a wannabe hero like you would think it was."

Grimmond already knew the only way out of the bedroom was swimming back through the hole in the floor. He readied himself for whatever Malus was planning.

"Your team's looking for you," Grimmond said quietly, slowly reaching for his glaive. "I promised I'd let you know you're worthless, by the way."

Malus took a step forward, but Grimmond backed away, quickly extending his glaive.

"That's far enough, Nebbick," Grimmond said simply. "If you're not here for the competition, then why are you?"

"I wanted to chat," he said in a strange voice, taking another step toward Grimmond's glowing purple glaive. "Remember last fall, how I gave you a chance to go home? I'll offer it to you once more."

"I *am* home. What are you talking about?"

Grimmond wiped the water from his forehead, and could've screamed in frustration when he verified that the floating red object was nothing more than tin foil twisted up like a toy.

I need the key — the real one!

"You're crazier than my time is worth," Grimmond spat, collapsing his glaive. "I'm leaving. You should, too — this whole place is about to fall apart. Stay and drown if you want, though. Makes no difference to me."

Grimmond stepped back into the water, but froze when Malus laughed a deep, gravelly laugh. It wasn't his — and it couldn't possibly have come from him. Something *else* laughed through his throat.

Something that didn't use a normal voice.

Skin prickling as he slowly turned around, Grimmond expected to find a third body in the room. But only Malus was there, the red light accentuating his eyes; they were pinpricks of black, just like they'd been in the Hearth, months before.

"Go back to Boston yourself. Now, and willingly," Malus said. "It'd be *so much* easier…go see your old friend, Patrick. Tell Stella you're sorry about Erik. You are sorry, aren't you? I know she is."

A cold dread dropped into Grimmond's stomach as he listened to the strange voice, and the feeling spread to his fingertips as he reopened his glaive and pointed it at Malus's chest.

How does he know who they are? I've never even mentioned them to Tristin or Viana….

"How could you even know about them?" Grimmond asked, trying to keep his voice steady.

Malus took another step closer, and cocked his head to the side; if Grimmond twitched his glaive, he could empty his guts into the water. Malus's sideways smile made it clear: he was out of his mind. His black eyes barely held back tears of mania as he fiddled with the strange doorknob in his pocket.

Grimmond wanted to jump in the water and swim away as fast as he could.

"Remember how she treated you that night?" Malus continued, a faint, darkly hued light leaking through his pocket. "After Patrick outed your secret to the whole school? *'He's for real, pill-popping nuts!'* Stella didn't even turn around when she went back into the house, did she? You looked so foolish standing there, wallowing in pity as your world crumbled."

Grimmond nearly dropped his glaive in shock with the realization. How was it possible?

Malus was there.... He was at *the party that night....*

"I gave you two chances to go back on your own, without any incentive. Remember that in the end. Now, I just can't wait to find out what you're really made of. To see if it's all true."

Incentive?

Grimmond's shock quickly turned to rage as the threat settled in his mind, and he was done listening. He yelled, swinging the blunt end of his glaive toward Malus's head, but Malus quickly dodged to the side. Grimmond saw stars as a bright yellow Flare was shot in his face, and a punch in the stomach brought him to his knees.

Keeled over, he struggled to regain his breath. Malus mercilessly laughed as he kicked him over, but the room then began to shake, and a rending noise filled the air.

Grimmond had been with Malus long enough to finish out the full thirty minutes of the Games.

"Hope you can swim," Malus said.

He laughed again before diving into the water. Grimmond scrambled for his dropped glaive, collapsing it as the room's stability shifted. He then felt motion in his gut, and fought the urge to panic: he and the bedroom were sinking to the bottom of the lake. Still recovering the wind that was knocked out of him, he gulped in several massive breaths, and dove through the hole in the floor.

The purple tip of his glaive provided just enough light to avoid the spindly tree roots and swim free of them. But the water pressure threatened to burst his eardrums as he pumped his legs, looking toward the glow of flames above the water. Lungs and muscles burning, Grimmond breached the surface and sucked in air as if they were his very first breaths of life. He grabbed his floating Luciferin armor before paddling to the closest sand bar.

Prowlers and Sentrees jumped into the safety of the water behind him, while glowing Terrors and Haunters lunged into boards and buildings, ripping them apart piece by piece. The Rebbigones blew black flames to ignite the rest.

Grimmond looked at the Black Wings' starting line in the distance, seeing a small blob of bodies sprinting toward it along the bridge. It seemed they had made it back in time. Or, at least, they wouldn't have to swim as far as him when the rest of the bridges collapsed.

Back by the distant Hovel, screams of delight were heard, along with muffled congratulations by Lord Stawlart. He was honoring Narcoleptic Row through the loudspeaker. The Sleepwalkers had found the key, and won the competition. Grimmond heard the chant even from where he was.

"We found the key, we found the key!"

Grimmond sat in the sand and placed his head in his hands. He breathed hard, eyes smarting, stomach hurting from where he was punched. But the chills on his neck had nothing to do with the cold.

Malus's laugh still echoed in his ears.

What was he going on about? And what'd he mean, he can't wait to find out what I'm made of?

If Malus hadn't distracted him for so long, Grimmond could've kept searching for the key. Looking down morosely to the water, splashing revealed a dozen corpse-skeletons sloshing toward him. He didn't have the energy left to deal with them, but a pair of dark wings was already falling toward him.

Grimmond hobbled to his feet, sighing as he lumbered onto the Blood Onyx's back.

"Thanks, Brax," Grimmond said quietly. "Let's get back to the others."

A single corpse-skeleton made it out of the water. Brax looked at it curiously, twisted his tail toward it, then swatted it into fragments before taking to the sky.

Gliding slowly across the lake, out of Grimmond's gloom he heard the celebratory chant changing in the distance. It wasn't happy, as it was at first, but now disjointed and panicky. He looked to the crowd, seeing people run from the bleachers.

A sense of warning stirred in him, and he quickly forgot his sorrow.

"Pick it up, Brax," Grimmond urged, "something's not right!"

They rapidly flew to the lakeshore, where people were running back and forth, some of them looking anxious, and others excited. Had the Sleepless Orchard been breached again? Grimmond heard someone yelling out loudly as he grew close.

"They've found it! WE KNOW WHERE IT IS!"

Grimmond saw his friends where the Black Wings had assembled before the competition, and quickly put Brax down next to them.

"Tristin — Viana!"

Grimmond weaved through the chaotic mass of bodies.

"GRIM!" Tristin yelled, grabbing him by the shoulders. "You're okay!"

"Yeah, I'm fine! Got caught up, but never mind for now!" Grimmond responded loudly. "What's going on — what's happened? Is the Hollow under attack?"

"They found the key, Grim!" Viana exclaimed, her eyes wide with excitement.

"I heard!" Grimmond said. "The Sleepwalkers won!"

"*No*, Grim —" Tristin said, "not talking about the Sleepwalkers —"

Too many people were talking, and Grimmond was continually jostled by passersby.

CHAPTER THIRTEEN

"What do you mean?" Grimmond said. "What are you talking about?"

"Grim!" Viana pulled him close. "Cyto and Plasm believe they've located *the key* on the Dread Map — the key to the Nightmayr Realm! And you'll *never* guess where they think it is."

MIDNIGHT RETURN

Boston…the key's in *Boston!*"

"Been there this whole time, maybe —"

"Could seal the Nightmayr Realm for good —"

The words were repeated over and over again inside the Dread Map room, where Grimmond sat in a wooden chair with his head in his hands. He didn't care that the Black Wings lost the competition, or that Malus might have a psychopathic dual-personality; he only tried to process the same words repeated on everyone's lips.

This is it, Grimmond thought to himself, *it has to be! The odd feeling I've had the last few weeks, the same feeling I felt when I was in Boston last summer — this is what it all meant! It's about this key!*

"Hey, Grim —"

The Nightmares finally figured out the key was in Boston, too, and they're trying to find it for themselves. That's why I saw so many last summer! Doesn't explain why Malus was at Stella Matterson's party, though —

"Grim!" Drek called again. "You look like you're gonna be sick…you okay?"

Grimmond was summoned from his thoughts and answered in the affirmative.

"Yeah, just thinking that it's been a long night already," he said, looking around at the anxious faces in the room. "Is everybody going out?"

"Looks that way," Drek muttered. "We usually wouldn't deploy all four Squadrons at once, but considering what we're after, and since half the Squadrons are already exhausted from fighting *each other* —"

"Right," Grimmond said quickly. "All hands on deck, then."

"More hands than that, even," Tristin added, leaning in from the other side of Viana. "Coach Maurs said volunteers are being called up to triple the perimeter watch. The Hollow doesn't need to be caught off guard while we're gone."

The movements in the room were even faster than people's speech, as Squadron members and Nightmarists hurried to and fro. Everyone was gathering needed supplies from the Armory, checking in with their leaders, or packed near the Dread Map of North America, awaiting Lord Stawlart.

No one understood the plan yet, nor did they understand how the key was discovered in Boston. But the awaited man soon entered the room from his adjacent office, followed by Professor Manning. Lord Stawlart stopped before North America and rolled his dark sleeves up.

Grimmond bumped Tristin and Viana to look up.

"An opportunity has come upon us," Lord Stawlart began. "Captain Qojiala and the Sleepwalkers' victory was impressive, but we must put off celebration in order to search for *another* key. Though perhaps coincidental, it seems the Gargoyle Games were fortuitously prepared for."

He paused, and the listeners waited with rapt attention for him to continue.

"We have received rumor of the key to the Nightmayr Realm — rumor that it is likely in Boston, and that tonight the Nightmares plan to seize it."

Mutters broke out, many acting as if Lord Stawlart saying it aloud finally made it true.

"We do not know where the door is, or whether the enemy has it; therefore, *we must get that key* to prevent the enemy from possibly having both. I need not remind you what the consequences would be, if the Nightmayr Realm was reopened, and the Dark Naught returned."

Shadowed looks passed across the faces of the Nightmarists, but Grimmond wasn't certain what the Dark Naught even was. He'd heard it mentioned before, but it was always glazed over, as if it was *too* awful to teach about.

"Lord Stawlart, sir," Elaine Qojiala asked from the back, "how do we know for sure that the key is there?"

The man looked up to the ceiling and nodded. Cyto and Plasm quickly descended at his prompt, and came to rest a few yards apart from one another on the floor. Then, as moving pistons of an engine, hairy legs between the two halves of the Dreadachnid fired rapidly. A woven map like a large orb began to form between the sticky floor and ceiling.

At first like a shaken white snow globe without glass, bright Terrors entered the web to transform it into a glowing hologram. It continued to expand with the Dreadachnid's manipulation, and Grimmond recognized the silky silhouettes and thin lines of Boston's cityscape.

Dozens of bright red dots appeared as the map slowly revolved.

"Cyto and Plasm are hearing things from the Wispers — rumors that the Nightmares have at last located the means to fully reopen their realm," Lord Stawlart said. "That might've been unremarkable news, if not for the influx of Nightmares to the city. They're after something, and regardless of what, many Dreamers shall die tonight if we don't stop them."

"Do we know what we're dealing with yet, sir?" Drek asked. "Terrors, Brutes, Prowlers?"

Cyto clacked his pincers together, and the glowing map zoomed in near Boston Public Garden — the same place Grimmond witnessed Erik Beese's murder. Several large red dots were there now, along with at least one black one. Grimmond swallowed. Why did it have to be *there*, of all places?

"Worse than Majors," Professor Manning answered, taking over for Lord Stawlart. "The large red dots are confirmed *Atrocities*, and we know of at least one *Sangmanger* present —"

'Sangmanger', Grimmond thought, remembering the name from Professor Manning's class. *That's the fat and bloated Total Nightmare that ate Erik Beese....*

"There are several more Total Nightmares, shown as black dots. And as you know, a black dot signifies that something's unidentified, meaning we've never encountered it before."

More muttering spread through the crowd, and Drek exchanged a concerned look with Harriet. Grimmond looked over as well to see Malus, and was unsurprised to see him sitting still, his face calm.

"Most of you have been taught to face Total Nightmares," Professor Manning continued. "Remember: Flaring or Lulling will not be effective. Each has a central fear from which it manifested in the Nightmayr Realm, and you must find this to destroy it. Demonstrated last November, Totals *can* be killed."

Professor Manning whipped a swirling white eye on Olivia before continuing. She didn't so much as blink as she stared back. Grimmond was reminded of her decision to join the Aurora Blights, but concern for her grew with his anger. Professor Manning cast a meaningful glance at Grimmond before continuing.

"Keith Tychus was incredibly brave, and he proved: removing an Atrocity's head, coupled with a glaive through its center, will kill it. On the other hand, Sangmangers must be drained of their blood before they can be dismembered and destroyed. As for the unidentified Nightmare, you must find out its weakness, and quickly."

Tristin leaned in again.

"No problem," he whispered. "I hear the Totals are usually pretty easy to figure out."

Grimmond gave an obligatory smile, but didn't laugh. His head was low, his mind jarred as Keith's death was brought to the forefront of his memory.

"We don't know where the key may be in the city," Lord Stawlart spoke again, "if that *is* what the Nightmares are searching for. Follow the heaviest groups of them, and put them down while searching yourselves. Spread out to search, but not too thin. You're stronger together than apart.

"Drek — cover downtown and Old Boston while Jack assaults East Boston with the Blights. Harriet, concentrate the Crew above the Charles River. Elaine will start south of the zoo, then come north to meet everyone else."

Of course we get Boston Public Garden! I'll be fine…I only saw someone eaten there….

"You are to leave at once," Lord Stawlart finished. "Captains, a final word."

The rest of the Nightmarists prepared to leave, but Grimmond looked around, not knowing what he should be doing. He'd already changed from his wet clothes and into long sleeves so his armor wouldn't irritate his skin. He couldn't do much about the helmet, but he would surely need it that night.

Am I nervous, or just not used to feeling like a coward anymore?

He didn't have time to decide before someone grabbed him by the arm. He turned to see Eralynn.

"I have to talk to you," she said urgently.

"We're leaving in just a few minutes," Grimmond protested. "I need to finish getting ready…."

The look in her eyes warned him that something was wrong, and he stood up to follow her to the privacy of the hallway.

"Is everything all right?" he asked after catching up with her.

"I'm not sure," she responded, wringing her hands together. "But this doesn't make sense. It doesn't make sense that the key would just show up out of thin air tonight — *tonight* of all nights."

"What's so special about tonight?"

Eralynn averted her eyes, but didn't answer. Grimmond noticed she looked as if she'd been crying again, but he couldn't guess why.

"Remember why we had to leave Boston in the first place," Eralynn said. "That thing — the *Ending* — might be waiting for you there, if you go back."

"I won't let the Squadron go without me," Grimmond answered firmly. "And I *have* to go help if Cyto and Plasm are right — the Wispers say the way back to the Nightmayr Realm will be in Boston tonight!"

Eralynn blinked her swollen eyes, swallowed hard, and looked up at him.

"That's what I'm afraid of."

She rubbed her hands together, looking as if she was struggling with some detail of information. Something she didn't want to tell him.

"Eralynn — *what is it?*" Grimmond asked. "Have you at least told Liam your concern?"

"No. I don't want to burden him any more than I do you."

What's wrong with her?

Drek called into the hallway for the Black Wings. Grimmond cupped his hands to shout back, but Eralynn unexpectedly wrapped him in a hug.

"Eralynn," Grimmond struggled. "It's time...I have to go."

"You'll be with the Black Wings, and I trust them — but promise me you'll be careful."

"Okay," he grunted. "I'll be careful."

Eralynn released him to turn down the hallway, and Grimmond jogged to the Dread Map to collect his things.

Finally, I can start to make things right....

The Gargoyles flew with impossible speed, and Grimmond tightly gripped the spike on Brax's back as he lie flat against his body. He didn't know how he hadn't slipped off yet, was worried he wouldn't be able to release his hands when they landed, and was terrified in the meantime that the breaking sound barrier would tear him to pieces.

He looked to the left and right through his helmet visor, his racing heart lighting up the night sky.

The Sleepwalkers led the other Squadrons, and the eyes of each Haunted Gargoyle was a glowing blur. They flew like fighter jets across the hills and fields toward Boston, with the Atlantic Ocean glowing bright green to the left, and the moonless April sky its foreboding purple. Grimmond wondered at what Eralynn said before leaving.

The stakes are big, but this isn't the first time I've fought. It was just Keith and I before, and we held our own, for a while...but this time I've got nearly forty riders with me. What could Eralynn be so worried about?

The lights of Boston drew near, the Sleepwalkers slowed their pace, and Grimmond found he was able to loosen his grip. Exchanging salutes, the captains broke each of the Squadrons away from one another, and made for their assigned portions of the city. Grimmond looked out over the buildings and water, momentarily flooded with reminiscence.

But then, block by block, each building, lamppost and billboard lost its power.

"The Nightmares know we're here!" Drek shouted. "*This is it!* Stay low!"

Soaring in from the northwest, they swooped through the low arches of Longfellow Bridge that crossed the Charles River, and nearly grazed the water. Grimmond saw the shadow of the Hatch Memorial Shell, and silently thanked it for hiding him from the Nightmares the summer before. He wished the orchestra were there now, playing classical music to calm his nerves.

"LOOK OUT!" yelled Sariah.

Brax banked hard to the left as something came careening out of the sky toward Grimmond. He felt the pulse of air push him as the dive-bombing aggressor narrowly missed its mark, crashing into the water like a missile. Grimmond berated himself.

STAY FOCUSED!

With a gulp, he extended his glaive as a white body resurfaced from the river, and flew through the darkness with eyes that didn't glow. It was a Bone Crawler. But not from Stanchions Hollow, and seemingly not possessed by an enemy Haunter.

Why was it there and attacking if it wasn't being driven forward by a Nightmare?

"Get ready!" Grimmond called nervously, more to himself than Brax.

Just as the enemy Bone Crawler flew in again, the wide head of a Nerve-Neck smashed into it like a falling tank. The enemy Gargoyle folded and dropped into the water, and Grimmond knew it wouldn't resurface. He exhaled with relief.

Tristin gave him the thumbs up as he zoomed by on Flynn, and Grimmond almost put his glaive away. But as soon as the Black Wings turned to continue into the city, a dozen Terrors and formless Haunters shot up from the water to attack the Squadron.

Brax dodged with expert ease, whipping in every direction as Grimmond shot his bright knuckles in wide Flares, or Lulled at the top of his voice. Enemies dropped back into the water one by one as the team attacked, until Drek called for them to break away.

"Save your energy!" Drek called. "We need to move on!"

He led the Black Wings away from the water, and Grimmond's wrinkled, weakened hands struggled to recover from his Lulls as he braced himself for the real fight.

Loud screams of pain and hysteria echoed downtown. Hordes of Terrors flooded side streets and apartment buildings, turning animals into snarling beasts that ripped into their owners. Prowlers crawled up the walls like ants, and Grimmond's stomach turned as he saw a Brute holding half of a person.

How are there so many? It wasn't this bad on the Dread Map....

"Viana — Linda — Wynn!" Drek shouted. "Circle overhead with your Glass Wings for aerial Flares! The rest of you, to the ground! Concentrate on the Majors!"

Grimmond glided toward the street with the Black Wings, but his head snapped in the direction of a scream. A woman hung from a window ledge, crying shrilly, and Grimmond got his first true glimpse of the Nightmarists' burden: none of the regular people — the Dreamers — could understand any of this; they couldn't even see what was attacking them.

Grimmond turned Brax so quickly that he was nearly thrown off his back.

"HANG ON, LADY!"

The woman's scream didn't relent as Grimmond caught her. He was barely able to get them both to the pavement and dismounted before she ran down the street, maddened. Leveling his glaive at the group of Brutes coming toward him, Grimmond quickly boomed '*PÆCIEF!*' Nauseous and drained from the Lull, Grimmond ducked as Brax leapt over him and tore the Brutes to pieces.

Lights Flared overhead for the next few moments: objects fell to the ground, and fiercely attacking animals ran in fright as the Terrors possessing them were banished. Brutes and Prowlers were Lulled and shredded by the Gargoyles or Nightmarists' sharp glaives, but the enemy Haunters proved most challenging, attacking in ways the Black Wings hadn't trained for.

Statues and vehicles were animated to glowing life, speeding forward to run the Nightmarists down. Grimmond dodged behind a parked sedan to avoid a motorcycle driven by a colonial statue, and Linda pulled René out of the way before she was flattened by a garbage truck. The Black Wings were forced to the skies again to avoid the Haunted vehicles, and finished them off with a series of Lulls before cutting the Haunters down.

"Is that it?" Sariah asked, wiping the sweat from her forehead.

"Not even close," Wynn panted. "Check it."

From their refuge on a low rooftop, Wynn pointed down another street, where more hordes of Nightmares were congregating and running toward Boston Public Garden.

"Perfect!" Keokuk said. "I'm up for another round."

"Attaboy," Drek praised, clanging his glaive on the rooftop. "Just getting warmed up!"

Emergency vehicles' red and blue lights sparked across the city. Grimmond breathed deeply, looked outward, and focused his eyes past them; Flares were coming from the south.

"The Blights are moving north to the Public Garden," Grimmond said. "The zoo must be cleared."

"Or, they're just driving the Nightmares toward *us*," Sariah countered.

"Either way," Drek declared, cracking his neck, "let's go meet up!"

Leaping from the rooftop, the Black Wings raced toward the other Squadron, looking down on the streets aglow with Nightmares. But when they neared the Aurora Blights at the Public Garden, they saw that they weren't driving the Nightmares away; the Hollow Dwell Squadron was being driven back themselves.

Limbs like a combine and leaving behind a trail of red secretions, Grimmond saw the two Atrocities.

A body count of Dreamers lay in their wake, and Grimmond's shock gave way to anger. He then looked closer at the lone Nightmarist flying in and out of the Atrocities' reach, and his thoughts froze entirely. It was Olivia, fighting alone like Keith had done — like Keith had died, months before.

A long Atrocity arm reached up, its barbs catching in her armor. She was unseated from her Gargoyle, and tumbled to the ground. Grimmond's heart stopped with his scream.

"OLIVIA!"

Breaking away from the Black Wings, Grimmond pushed Brax with everything he had.

Not again...I WON'T let this happen again!

"HEAD ON, BRAX!" Grimmond cried, bracing himself for the impact.

Like an axe into the Atrocity's thick neck, Brax crashed into it with his full weight. The Atrocity was lifted off its four legs and blown backwards, and Grimmond almost bit his tongue off as he was launched from Brax's back and rolled to the ground.

But immediately he was on his feet, glaive extended and heart racing.

He ran in, decapitating the neck that Brax's teeth latched onto, and stabbed the Atrocity through the chest. Its barbed arms swung in the air with its last bits of life, incidentally swatting several incoming Prowlers. Brax turned on the rest as Grimmond retrieved his glaive and went to Olivia.

"LIV!" he cried, rolling her over and violently shaking her. "Olivia! *Wake up!*"

She didn't stir as Grimmond removed her helmet, and he thought his throat might close up. Gritting his teeth, he reared back, closed his eyes, and slapped her in the face.

Olivia came to beneath him as Grimmond straightened up to Flare a group of moaning red Terrors. He dizzily looked down at her, giddy with relief, but her eyes quickly narrowed over his shoulder. Grimmond barely turned in time to see all four arms of the second Atrocity, swinging downward to crush them.

He grabbed Olivia, and rolled through turf that was flying like shrapnel. Ready to stand and fight again, in the next instant, Grimmond watched the entirety of the Aurora Blights swarm the Atrocity. Following Grimmond's example, they managed to remove its head and stab it through the chest.

It fell dead next to the other, and Captain Michaels dismounted his Gargoyle to Lull and bisect an incoming Brute.

"SCYLENT — that was *awesome!*" Captain Michaels shouted with a look of wild amazement.

"Jack!" Grimmond yelled. "Olivia's still out of it — watch her! I've gotta get back to my Squadron!"

Captain Michaels nodded, and Grimmond sprinted across the dark Garden toward where the Black Wings landed, calling for Brax as he went. But Brax was nowhere in sight, even as

Grimmond saw someone lying on the ground within a protective circle. It was a girl with long and dark hair.

Oh no...please, please, *not her....*

Grimmond grew closer to see not Viana on the ground, but Sariah, and Tristin and Viana protecting her. He was ashamed to admit his relief, though still he ran to Sariah's side as she Flared and Lulled the incoming attackers.

"Terror crashed a log into my leg," she said bitterly. "Of all the stupid things to take me out...."

"Can you stand?" Grimmond asked, slicing through the neck of the silver-eyed Prowler she Lulled.

Its head rolled across the ground, mouth and teeth still gnashing.

"Maybe," Sariah winced, "but I think it might be broken."

Trampling and biting through a group of large, snarling dogs, Sariah's white Bone Crawler came over. Grimmond helped her on its back and handed off her glaive.

"If you can still fly, get airborne," Grimmond advised. "You're a sitting duck down here!"

Grimmond watched Sariah get safely into the air before looking back to Tristin and Viana. Then he looked to Drek with the Red team. Then the Aurora Blights.

You can't protect them, all, Grimmond...whose death will you be responsible for tonight?

Brax landed behind Flynn and Qinella, screeching loudly. Grimmond looked in his direction, but past his wings saw the pinnacle of a single building, glowing green in the distance, and standing out from all others that were still without power.

"Drek!" Grimmond called. "Look!"

Drek turned his head to see at what Grimmond pointed.

"You three go check it out!" he said in return. "We'll keep them busy...."

His voice faded away as something passed overhead. Grimmond looked up, trying to ready himself, but had completely forgotten about the same thing that Drek had: the black spot on the Dread Map. The Total Nightmare they'd never encountered before had arrived.

And they had no idea how to defeat it.

Wide-winged and pale, strips of skin fluttered beneath it like hair drifting through water. It looked like the ghost of a great sea beast, covered and marred by hundreds of meaty scabs. It was bigger than either one of the Atrocities, but with two appendages only, ending in openings that chomped with sharp teeth.

It landed with a squish, and Grimmond watched as its scabs cracked open and looked out. They were each of them iridescent eyeballs, opening up as if to taste the air, with thousands of sucking tendrils where eyelashes should be. Rearing up and spitting like a snake, its challenge was immediately answered by the swarming Aurora Blights.

"Grim, get to that light!" Drek yelled, dodging one of the eye-covered appendages from latching onto him. "Take the Blue Team and go!"

Grimmond spoke quietly, as if to himself.

"We can't just leave you to fight alone...."

He knew the amount of Lulling had taken its toll on both Squadrons, and the Glass Wings were smoking from refracting the Flares. Olivia and Sariah were hurt, and none of them yet knew how the Skeleton Crew or Sleepwalkers were faring. Grimmond couldn't stand the thought of which one of his friends would be hurt next, or worse.

"GO!" Drek roared, running forward to Lull and dismember a half-fleshed Haunter.

"Come *on*, Grim!" Viana urged. "Remember why we're here! We have to find the key!"

Tristin grabbed him, yanking him toward Brax until Grimmond caught on and jumped atop the Blood Onyx himself. They launched into the sky and soared toward the lit building by the harbor. Terrors and wild Gargoyles chased after them, attempting to head them off before they could get there.

"It's Custom House Tower!" Grimmond called as they neared. "One of the oldest skyscrapers in Boston!"

They circled the tower, trying to see inside its upper windows while dodging Nightmares.

"Need a hand?" called a voice.

Grimmond turned in the air to see the Sleepwalkers crossing over the water with Captain Qojiala.

"Elaine! We need a perimeter up while we check —"

He was cut off as Brax flipped in the air, and a ribbon-like piece of flesh missed wrapping around his neck. The pale Total Nightmare from the Garden had followed them.

'Impaler' — that's what I'll call you....

Like a rainbow of fireworks, a dozen flashes of light and Lulls threw the Impaler off course, and it crashed through the windows of a darkened office building with a boom. Glass, steel and concrete exploded into the air, but the Impaler changed its course and soared in again.

The Sleepwalkers took up the fight, and Grimmond looked to the base of Custom House Tower. It appeared at first to be sinking, but Grimmond realized the situation was worse: a wall of Nightmares was crawling up the base and toward the top level.

With little time, he flew in closer to peer inside the bright upper levels of the building, and saw a shining object.

Could that be the key? Here in the tower this whole time?

"The guard rail!" Viana called out. "It's ripped open at the edge there! And the window's broken — something's already inside!"

"Come on!" Grimmond shouted.

Bracing himself, he crashed through the hanging window shards of the observation deck. Amidst the shattered glass Brax slid into a landing, with Flynn and Qinella close behind him. Grimmond opened his eyes and saw what was in the center of the room, glowing with a faint green glow.

It was a key, sitting on a pedestal like a showcase.

Immediately the riders dismounted, and the Gargoyles were bidden to return to the fight that raged outside the building. No one spoke for a moment as they stared at the key. It looked as if it had been there a millennium, though Grimmond knew the building was only a few hundred years old.

"NO WAY!" Tristin giddily shouted at last, albeit with exhaustion. "That's it! That's the key!"

Blasts of light illuminated the room in different colors, and Grimmond felt them fill him with a warmth and happiness he'd never known. They had found the key to the Nightmayr Realm, the way to seal away the Nightmares forever. It would all be over soon.

"Could that be it?" Viana asked quietly.

She held a hand over her heart in reverent wonder, staring at the object that had been sought for years. All at once, the three friends ran toward it. Not realizing how exhausted he truly was, Grimmond slipped on a piece of broken glass, and crashed to the ground. He smacked his head hard, and was saved from injury only by his helmet.

He looked up dazedly, and without knowing why, suddenly felt that everything was wrong. Very wrong.

The room became oppressive, the flashes of light outside warnings, and the hairs on his neck stood on end; the chilling feeling he hadn't experienced in months resonated within him. He began to understand: it had all been far too easy. He looked up to Viana as she reached out to touch the key.

"Viana — *no!*"

"What is it?" she asked, her hand recoiling to her glaive.

"Something's wrong...*this* is wrong," Grimmond tried to explain, standing back up and wincing. "A beacon lit in the middle of the city for us to come find? Why would it be here — this place is a hotel now! The key to the Nightmayr Realm has just been waiting up here for hundreds of years? No way!"

"Grim, I'm sorry, but we don't have time for this!" Viana said. "The key is right here! We have to take it and go!"

"No, please — wait!"

But without another word, she picked it up. Nothing happened. She held it to her eye, like a glowing green diamond, and tossed it next to Tristin. He looked at it a moment, then turned to Grimmond.

"Here you are, mate," Tristin said, tossing the key. "Nothing to be scared of."

Grimmond stretched out his hands, caught it fully in his palms, and immediately knew pain.

Searing pulses shot through his entire body, and he screamed, dropping the key to the floor. To his great surprise, the seemingly solid key shattered into dozens of small shards, and in seconds they began to smoke like dry ice.

"It — it *burned* me!" Grimmond sputtered as the room darkened. "I couldn't touch it!"

Exchanging looks of complete shock, the three friends watched the shards dim from green to black, then diminish completely. They barely heard when a Haunter emerged from the shadows of a wide pillar. Running toward the shattered window, it yelled out in a deep and hollow voice.

"WE'VE *FOUND* HIM! THE KEY IS HERE!"

Tristin and Viana squared off to face the threat, but Grimmond felt something else watching from the shadows. He could sense it before he saw it, dread clouding his senses, and his heart rate picking up.

When a set of bone-white fingers felt out from behind the pillar, his fear was confirmed.

The Haunter was sucked toward the white fingers with a choking gasp, and disappeared into something Grimmond couldn't see. Moving from the shadows into the open, the white fingers materialized a second hand and face to go with them. Without introduction, Grimmond knew what the approaching dark figure was: the Ending. The *real* Ending.

It had found him at last, and Grimmond fallen right into its hands.

Its skull-like face was without skin and dripped an evil Grimmond had never imagined, floating toward him out of the darkness as if suspended by strings. Suddenly he was six years old again, but more frightened now than his memory as a child allowed him to remember. Grimmond was flooded with images of his brutalized parents and paralyzed by terror, believing he was about to die.

He tried to back away, but could barely shuffle his feet. Soaked in ice-cold sweat, his eyes flooded with tears, yet they wouldn't fall down his face. Viana grabbed his arm.

"Grim," she whispered, close to panic. "What is that thing?"

"*It,*" Grimmond breathed. "The Ending."

Grimmond tried to turn and run. To hide, to flee, but he couldn't — the Ending wasn't letting him. He couldn't move, like the way he couldn't move that day in the cafeteria with Malus, as if he had been glued in place. Tristin and Viana stood by his side, but Grimmond had never felt more alone.

"*Come with us....*"

Grimmond didn't expect the Ending to be able to speak. He didn't see a mouth, but its very voice infected him, making him want to curl up in a ball and cover his ears — what he'd do as a child during a scary movie scene.

"Seventy sevens is long up, and ten years have passed since you were left behind, forgotten.... Come with us...the Ending has the answers you seek...."

Grimmond knew what the hissing whispers of the Ending meant, as he looked into two black holes where its eyes should've been.

Eralynn — she knew my parents were killed, ten years ago tonight! How could I have forgotten?

Grimmond swallowed hard, trying to convert a smidgeon of his terror into some sort of plan. He needed to get his friends out of there before the Ending hurt them.

"Your last words still echo in your mother's ears...do you not wish to apologize?"

It wouldn't be long before it attacked, Grimmond knew. His eyes darted around the room. What could he do?

"Grim," Tristin started. "Let's get this thing —"

Tristin was cut off by a wave from the Ending's hand, which threw him against the wall in a tangle of shadowy tendrils. Viana tried to scream a Lull next, but was likewise thrust backward and pinned beside Tristin.

"Go willingly, like your mother did...or we will take the key and your friends."

Grimmond glanced at the ground.

It doesn't realize the key's already been destroyed! It's my only chance!

All the key shards had evaporated except for the largest one. Grimmond tried to hide it with his foot as he looked back toward his friends.

"L-let them go f-first!" Grimmond said in a trembling voice. "Then I'll give it to you!"

The Ending raised a hand, and Grimmond braced himself to be thrown against the wall next to Tristin and Viana. But his stomach lurched at what he next saw.

In the far corner, bloodied and gagged but awake, were Patrick Gusset and Stella Matterson, and at the feet of a bloated Sangmanger. Patty's eyes flew wide as he saw Grimmond, but Stella was beside herself with terror. The Sangmanger picked them up, walked to the edge of the observation deck, and held them to dangle out over the open air. The Ending reached a black tendril of shadow over to Grimmond's old friends, pulling down their gags.

Stella screamed at the top of her lungs, but Patrick spoke, his eyes streaming frightened tears.

"Grim!" Patrick cried out. "What the *heck* is going on? WHAT ARE THESE THINGS, MAN?"

Grimmond's very soul wrenched, but not for his old friends. The Ending had approached him, raising a bony white hand toward his chest, and Grimmond's heart began to rage like the Ending was trying to rip it out of him. Tristin and Viana were dropped to the floor, the Ending's attention off of them, and they began to Flare and Lull the Nightmares that swarmed out from the shadows.

With a twisting of the Ending's fingers, Grimmond felt his foot lifted, and the key fragment revealed.

"Fool. No Nightmare may touch pure Luciferin…the key is here — your beating heart…."

Grimmond still couldn't move, and was overwhelmed with cold as the Ending placed its fingers softly against his chest. He wondered if blood could turn to ice as his body began to shake, but several things then happened at once.

Crashing through an unbroken windowpane, Brax and Qinella came flying in to rescue them. Grimmond was freed from the Ending's hold, and stumbled backward to the ground.

But almost faster than his eye could move, the Ending reached a white hand up, pinned the large Glass Wing to the ground, and plunged its other wispy hand inside the Glass Wing's chest.

Wailing, the purple Haunter *within* the Gargoyle — Qinella — was unwillingly dragged out and swallowed into the shadows of the Ending.

"QINELLA!" Viana screamed, turning after Lulling a Prowler.

But Qinella was gone, and the Glass Wing, now free of Haunter possession, fluttered on the floor before dragging itself to the window and flying out. Brax flew in next, but the Ending smashed him to the floor as it had the Glass Wing. Only when the Ending plunged its wispy hand inside the Blood Onyx, nothing happened.

"Brax isn't possessed by a Haunter — you can't take anything from him!" Grimmond yelled. "And you won't be taking my friends, either!"

A rumbling tremor shook the tower, and Grimmond whipped around to see the defeated Impaler crashing through an entire side of the observation deck. Brax quickly smashed his tail into the Ending with the distraction, and in a gust of wings, tossed Grimmond on his back and scrambled out of the way before they were crushed.

The massive Impaler slid across the floor, knocking down the pillars, the Ending, and even smashing into the Sangmanger. Grimmond watched the air glistening with flashes of light, reflected off the flying shards of glass. And he watched as every one of his friends was swept off the deck and into the night sky.

Time might have stopped as he yelled.

"GO, BRAX!"

The Ending wailed in anger as Brax and Grimmond jumped off the edge of the building, tendrils of shadow reaching out to grab them. Before they were clear, the tendrils unseated Grimmond from Brax's back, and he began to free-fall behind his friends.

Stella and Patrick were snatched out of the air by two separate Gargoyles, and Brax latched onto Tristin and Viana beneath him. Only Grimmond was left, and only a few stories separated him from splatting on the ground. A Gargoyle swung in to catch him at the last moment.

Expecting to thank Flynn when he looked up, Grimmond instead saw Olivia and her Nerve-Neck.

"That makes us even!" she called over the wind.

Grimmond was almost limp as they flew several blocks away, landing opposite a police precinct; the same one that Grimmond was taken to the previous summer. Brax touched down, releasing Tristin and Viana, while Flynn and Keokuk dropped Stella and Patrick to the pavement. Stella had passed out as they flew, and rolled to the ground, but Patrick stood speechless and white-faced.

"Who are *they*?" Olivia asked brazenly, pointing to Patrick and the unconscious Stella.

Grimmond rushed over to them, placing his hands on Patrick's shoulders and speaking loudly.

"*Patty!*" he said manically. "Take Stella into the precinct and wait for Detective Tippins — he's a good cop. Tell him what happened, and tell him that what he saw ten years ago tonight was real! He'll understand — and he has to get you and Stella out of town before the Nightmares take you again!"

"I-I don't...don't understand...." Patrick repeated in a daze. "I thought I'd never see you again. They say you killed Erik, and that you escaped from jail...but what are these things, Grim?"

Now Grimmond was confused. Patrick was assuredly a Dreamer and couldn't have seen what happened.

"Patty — did you *see* what had you?" Grimmond asked. "Did you see what carried you here?"

Grimmond didn't need Patrick to nod; he could tell by the look on his face that he *did* see. But how was that possible?

"They're what I've always seen, Patty," Grimmond answered. "I was never crazy. They're called Nightmares, and we fight them."

"I...I can fight...."

"You *can't*," Grimmond declared. "Dreamers like you can't Flare and can't Lull, because you've all trained yourselves to be blind since you could talk. Not like us — only we can drift between the Nightmayr Realm and this world, to see and fight against —"

"No time for this, Grim!" Tristin interjected. "Unless you killed that Ending while I was doing a half-gainer, we need to get out of here! Keokuk and I'll carry them to the station. Off we go, Pat!"

Keokuk picked up Stella, and Tristin dragged Patrick away.

"Grimmond," Patrick started. "I'm sorry, man — I'm sorry I never believed you...."

Olivia ran over to help up Viana, as Drek, along with René, Linda and Wynn landed next, followed by the remainder of the Aurora Blights. Grimmond saw the Sleepwalkers and Skeleton Crew land atop the buildings across the street, forming up a perimeter.

Grimmond looked back and forth, but didn't see who he was searching for.

"Where's Sariah?" he asked.

Drek didn't answer, but spun his head wildly back and forth, examining the rest of the Squadron.

"Drek — *where's Sariah*?" Grimmond asked again, more loudly.

"She's gone," Olivia said hollowly. "I saw a Sangmanger take her out."

Grimmond's mind spun with Olivia's short words. He leaned his head against the brick wall.

Gone, Grimmond repeated it in his mind. *Gone.... Sariah is dead.*

"THE KEY!" Drek shouted as Tristin returned from the police station. "Did you three at least find the key?"

Grimmond exchanged looks with a defeated Viana and panting Tristin.

"No," Grimmond answered in a shaky voice. "No — it wasn't there."

Drek looked like he was about to crack, and placed his hands on his head.

"No? NO? Then *what was up there?*"

"A trap," Grimmond answered quickly. "And we've *got* to get out of here before whatever was up there comes down. It's not a Total Nightmare — it's something worse. We need to return to the Hollow."

Drek didn't like the answer, until Viana backed Grimmond's story.

"Trust me, there's no key up there," she said flatly. "Grim's right."

Resignedly Drek ordered the Black Wings to mount up, and Grimmond helped Viana onto Brax's back. She wrapped her arms tightly around his waist as they took to the sky.

Boston was still in chaos, Grimmond saw, but it was now only from the Dreamers. The Nightmarists had defeated each Total Nightmare, and the remainder of the Minors and Majors had suddenly fled when the Impaler crashed into the observation deck. Grimmond looked over the cityscape as he held onto Brax, Viana held onto him, and his brain threatened to split apart.

"Grim!" Viana called. "What happened up there — was that the real key that we broke?"

"No!" he said over his shoulder. "At least, I don't think so!"

"Well, if it was, looks like there's not a real key to the Nightmayr Realm anymore!"

Oh, but there is....

Grimmond didn't answer her, wondering if she and Tristin had heard what the Ending said to him.

And according to the Ending, that key is me.

ADVICE IN THE DARK

Grimmond watched Boston's news from the *ectoplasma* television in Fire Watch. Sometimes he forgot that he didn't have his own cell phone anymore to know what was going on in the world; he'd be tracked by the police if he ever left the Hollow with it, anyway.

Power had been restored to Boston the day after the mission, though the city was at a loss to explain how so much damage could have occurred during the blackout. No reports of looters went out, but in the hundreds were reports of dead or missing persons, vicious animals loose, and family members attacking one another.

The Dreamers didn't know what hit them, and they couldn't begin to explain it.

"This is just the beginning, if the Nightmares got to that key," Drek muttered.

The mood of the entire Hollow was low: downcast at the key they weren't able to recover, and somber with pain and loss. Though the Aurora Blights were without injury, the Skeleton Crew was beaten up, and the Sleepwalkers had several riders in the infirmary. The only presumed losses were Sariah Lunasae, whose body was never found, and Qinella the Haunter. As the Black Wings' captain, Drek felt responsible for both, and took their losses the hardest.

Tristin nudged Grimmond's foot.

"What did Lord Stawlart say after the debrief, when you told him about the Ending?"

"Nothing," Grimmond answered. "He muttered something, then went to the infirmary to check on the injured Squadron members."

Viana shook her head, wrapping her arms about her knees.

"Okay," she said, "what about Eralynn?"

Grimmond rubbed his chest in the place where the Ending had touched him. He was distracted, despite everything else going on. He felt different — his *heart* felt different. Was it bigger, or smaller? Bruised, or stronger?

"Grim?" Viana asked again.

"I didn't say anything to her," Grimmond responded, casting an awkward glance at Viana. "Things...haven't really been the same between us, since Halloween...besides, I don't think she could handle it."

Tristin nodded in understanding, though Viana pursed her lips. She and Grimmond never got the chance to take their planned walk after the Gargoyle Games. Viana turned her head around, checking that the nearest pockets of conversation were out of earshot, then leaned in.

"What is it?" Grimmond said.

"Grim, what really happened up there?" she asked. "When the Ending let Tristin and I go, and we went after Patrick and Stella, did something else happen that you're not telling us about? You've just been...*rattled*, ever since we got back."

Swallowing, Grimmond looked to Tristin, but received no help.

Grimmond *was* still trying to warm the Ending's deathly cold touch from his skin, and trying to shake the memories of his slaughtered parents. He had hoped, too, that he'd be able to keep the Ending's words to himself, but he couldn't make heads or tails of them.

"It said something to me, before...before we got away," Grimmond began, rubbing his eyes. "I think the Ending told me that it couldn't touch the key because it was a Nightmare."

"That's right," Tristin affirmed. "Nightmares hate Luciferin, and I'm pretty sure that's what that key was made from, seeing how it was glowing that same green light as our glaives and armor."

Grimmond thought hard, knowing he was missing something, but couldn't quite pinpoint what.

"Right...well, then it said — I *think* — that *I* was the key."

Viana leaned back in her seat, but Tristin twisted his head in confusion.

"Either you misheard," Tristin said, "or that Ending is as crazy as it was scary. You're not a hunk of metal."

"I realize that," Grimmond said dryly. "I don't know what it meant. But right after that, Brax and Qinella busted in. If they'd come even a few seconds later, I don't think I'd be here."

Viana lowered her eyes, and Tristin nodded toward her, clearing his throat.

"Oh, geeze, Viana," Grimmond berated himself. "I'm sorry...I know you and Qinella were together a long time."

Viana stared at the ground blankly, but spoke.

"Hasn't really hit me yet," she said. "She was my friend for years, and always made me feel better. Ever since that morning he didn't come back...."

Her voice fell away, but each of the boys knew she was speaking of her father.

"Kind of strange, I know," she went on. "How could anyone love a Nightmare?"

Tristin patted her back as Grimmond looked away, but Viana quickly changed the subject to the key.

"So, the key we — *ahem* — the key we *broke* up there," she finished in a whisper. "That was all the Ending's doing just to lure us up there? And the Nightmares kidnapped Patrick and Stella, too? Why?"

Grimmond filled in the others on Malus's deranged antics at the Gargoyle Games, and how Malus knew about Grimmond's old friends in Boston.

"You don't think *he* had something to do with this?" Tristin asked. "He's a weasel, but he's still a Nightmarist like one of us. How could he have possibly kidnapped your old friends and handed them over to the Ending?"

There was more to it than that, Grimmond knew. But how was he to describe it?

"You should've seen his eyes," Grimmond whispered, rubbing his hands. "They were black, and his laugh was...*off*. I don't even know how he knew who Patrick and Stella were. He *did*, somehow — and he knew a lot more. My only guess is that he was there the night I left Boston."

"Maybe the Skeleton Crew was patrolling the city that night...but *murdering* that bully, Beese?" Viana questioned. "That seems too far, even for Malus."

Grimmond rubbed the pain in his chest again, thinking quietly. What *was* Malus Nebbick capable of?

Scaring me off of the terrace, threatening, bullying.... Murder doesn't seem too far off.

"Do you think I should tell Lord Stawlart and Eralynn about all this? About Malus, and the Ending saying I was some key?"

"*No way* can you tell Lord Stawlart that," Tristin said suddenly. "The Ending was just messing with you, trying to get in your head!"

"Yeah, well, it worked —"

"And what do you think Lord Stawlart will do?" Tristin went on. "He might never let you leave the Hollow again in order to keep you safe. Or worse, all of Stanchions Hollow will try and figure out if you're actually some key. Lord Stawlart's a good man, but sometimes I wonder how far he'd go to close the Nightmayr Realm."

Grimmond turned to Viana, looking for her to weigh in.

"I'm leaning toward Tristin on this one," she said. "Let's just wait and see what happens."

Waiting was easier said than done once things got worse.

Brutal attacks and killings were on the rise, according to the news. Red dots on the Dread Map began to erupt everywhere in New England, and a different Squadron was being sent out almost every night. The four Squadrons were stretched thin, and new recruits were even being trained for a fifth.

Worst of all, rumors of the key that broke atop Custom House Tower had spread. Grimmond didn't know how; there wasn't a doubt in his mind that Tristin or Viana had said anything. But soon Grimmond couldn't even eat in the Hearth anymore, being ridiculed just short of having food thrown at him.

"Is it TRUE?" shrieked Captain Qojiala one morning. "Did you really have the key in your hands in Boston?"

Grimmond was flabbergasted, looking from Tristin to Viana.

"Elaine, who told you that —"

"And then you dropped it like an idiot? Ruining the ONE CHANCE we had?"

Grimmond opened and closed his mouth, as the entire Hearth stared in silence.

"Look, that's *not* how it happened," Grimmond said quietly, his face bright red.

"Daña Esperanza has been in the infirmary for *over a week!*" Captain Qojiala continued. "She might not walk again, and right after she won the Games for the Sleepwalkers!"

Grimmond lowered his eyes, but they came level with Malus Nebbick across the room. He smiled, and Grimmond knew: he was the one spreading the rumors.

How does he know? No one was up there but us....

"Daña deserved better!" Captain Qojiala shouted. "And it's *all because of you!*"

Viana spoke in a much softer voice, but her eyes glinted dangerously as she rose from her seat.

"Grimmond wasn't alone, Elaine — we were all there," she said. "If you have a problem, you have it with all three of us. Go cool off, before you upset someone."

Elaine took a challenging step forward, but Drek walked over next.

"I'll handle my own Squadron, Captain Qojiala," he said, steely-eyed. "Thanks."

Elaine left unwillingly and the Hearth returned to its bustle, but Drek faced Grimmond and the others.

"Why didn't you tell *me*, of all people?" he asked. "You said you didn't find anything...."

Grimmond swallowed. He would've much preferred Elaine to come back and continue yelling.

"It wasn't the real key, Drek," Grimmond started.

"And how do you know that for sure?"

Grimmond thought about what the Ending said: *Grimmond was the key.* But he wasn't ready to say that to anyone aside from Tristin and Viana, and certainly not in front of everyone there.

"I guess...I don't know for sure."

Grimmond expected Drek to begin yelling like Captain Qojiala, to pick up the lunch table and throw it in a rage. But Drek's eyes only saddened, and his scarred arms seemed to deflate in defeat.

"That's what I thought," he said.

Drek stood there dejectedly a moment before walking away, and left Grimmond feeling far worse than Captain Qojiala had made him. His appetite gone, Grimmond gathered his things and stood up from the table.

Rumors of the failed mission continued to spread that week, and blame shifted to Grimmond.

Some said that he broke the key on purpose: Grimmond *liked* fighting the Nightmares, to feed his violent side, and didn't want their Realm sealed off. Could Stanchions trust a boy who'd only been with the Black Wings a few months? What kind of person was able to tame a *Blood Onyx*, anyway?

Just whose side was the Errandi boy on?

Grimmond was running out of places to hide in the Hovel, away from the angry stares and loud whispers following him. Normally he would've been able to escape to the Sleepless Orchard with Brax, but for the first time since Thanksgiving, Nightmares were again getting through the mist.

The week after the 'Boston Calamity', the Sleepless Orchard was again breached.

The Aurora Blights were already drilling, fortunately, and destroyed the handful of Prowlers with ease. But during another trespass later in the week, the Skeleton Crew wasn't so fortunate. Two Nightmarists were put in the infirmary after fighting an Atrocity and Sangmanger, and were in worse shape than anyone injured in Boston.

Grimmond knew they wouldn't be the last to be hurt, and wondered at his responsibility.

The Ending was on the outside, waiting for him to surface, but was it sending the Nightmares in to try to get him, too?

Tristin was right. The Ending said all that stuff just to mess with my head…but it is working….

Grimmond lay in bed Thursday night, wondering if he should tell Lord Stawlart or Eralynn the full truth. Who else could help Grimmond with what such an evil thing might really want? He grew hopeful when an answer suddenly came to mind, and he sprang up to put his clothes on.

The Boogey Man!

Having gone to bed early, Grimmond knew his friends were still awake in Fire Watch. But for some reason, he didn't wish to bring them just yet. Quietly he left his room, hurrying down the stairs of Steeple Spike and toward the lower levels of the Hovel.

Somber organ music played as Grimmond approached the closed classroom door.

He knocked to no answer, and entered into darkness. The usual hundred or so candles on the wet walls were absent, but a faint light was coming from one of the back passages. Coupled with the sound of distantly singing voices, Grimmond walked curiously toward it.

When the passage opened up, a cavern like an underground cathedral was before him.

Professor Manning was at its base, playing a derelict organ that stretched from floor to ceiling. Twisted white roots choked the brass pipes as they rang out coldly, and Grimmond was eerily reminded of the Ending's white fingers. He looked around for the singing choir, but didn't see any students — only the tall white candles that were usually in the classroom.

Each of the candles was *singing*.

Yellow flames flickered back and forth, brighter and dimmer as Professor Manning played his sad music. Grimmond recognized the melody as he snuck in, or so he thought. Walking past flat boulders presumably meant for seating, a voice sounded through the cavern and stopped Grimmond in his tracks.

"Do you know why I'm not the Boogey Man any longer?"

Professor Manning hadn't even turned around yet, continuing to play as he spoke.

"I took no pleasure in it anymore. I used to get a kick out of scaring people's pants off, but I got tired. Tired of the pain…tired of all the death…."

Grimmond suspected there was more to it than just that, but didn't want to pry after he'd already intruded.

"Everything dies, Professor Manning."

"Indeed," he called over the organ. "Your friend, Sariah, for example. Another girl, dead…another *human*. I just never liked the death part about you all."

"And you?" Grimmond asked. "Are *you* dead, professor?"

Professor Manning might've laughed, but Grimmond couldn't tell over the choir of burning candles.

"Yes," Professor Manning answered. "And no…."

Grimmond considered for the first time: he had never wondered whether the Boogey Man was ever human. He stepped downward toward the booming organ, wading through the sea of flat boulders.

"What do you mean, professor?"

"I mean that Nightmares never really die," boomed Professor Manning.

So he is *a Nightmare, after all.*

The song ended at last, the candles quieted to whispers, and Professor Manning turned around in his chair. Dressed in a black tuxedo with the bowtie undone, he allowed the skin on his hands and face to remain black, but his eyes swirled like milky white clouds. Had he not known Professor Manning well, Grimmond would be reliving every nightmare he'd ever had of the dark.

"Don't mind my appearance," he said ominously, "but it takes effort to put on an acceptable face for guests, and I don't feel up to it."

"Sure," Grimmond answered with a chill. "No problem."

Unnerved at the white eyes dancing in the candlelight, Grimmond tried not to show the trepidation in his voice. Undoubtedly, the man could sense his fear anyway.

"Professor Manning, I came down because I have a question for you."

"*Boogey*, if you please."

At once the candles along the wall began to twirl and bounce up and down. Several Terrors Grimmond hadn't seen also fell down from the ceiling, and grotesquely shimmied back and forth.

"NOT YOU!" Professor Manning shouted, immediately flaring up in anger.

The dancing candles froze or blew out, the Terrors shot away into the walls, and the white eyes turned calmly back to Grimmond.

"Please, continue."

Grimmond swallowed.

"Well, I'm sure you've heard the rumors about what happened in Boston. Some of them might be true, but most aren't. I wanted to talk to you about that night, since *you're* the
—"

Grimmond stopped himself before saying the obvious.

"I just think you're the only one who can help me, Boogey."

"Oh?" he said with an unseen smile to his voice. "When the sun rises, dark secrets told in dark spaces tend to be regretted. Be quite sure, before confiding in another, Grimmond."

Grimmond swallowed again, feeling as if even the candles were listening now.

"Did Eralynn ever tell you there's a Nightmare after me? It calls itself the *Ending*. It's the thing that killed my parents, and it found me in Boston. I...I think it was waiting for me to go into that tower so it could do something to me...."

Grimmond quieted, his words sounding lame even to him.

He has *to know you're not telling the whole story. He's the Boogey Man!*

"I do not know the Ending," Professor Manning prompted. "What happened?"

"There *was* a key in that tower, but it burned me when I touched it. I dropped it, and it shattered into pieces...but I didn't do it on purpose, like everyone thinks. After that, the Ending appeared out of nowhere and told me to come with it, saying I could apologize to my mom. It told me: *I* was the key."

Grimmond blinked for only a fraction of a second, but Professor Manning was suddenly standing directly in front of him. Grimmond unconsciously stepped backward.

"Remember *carefully*," the man said in a strangely urgent voice. "Is that *all* the Ending told you?"

Grimmond thought back a week prior to the night in the tower, and realized there were some minor details he'd forgotten. He was so scared at the time, he knew he wouldn't remember all of it, but one part he now did.

'The key is here — your beating heart....'

"You're right, that wasn't all," Grimmond said slowly, raising a hand to the left side of his chest.

"The Ending said the key was *here*: my 'beating heart'. It touched my chest, and I thought I'd be frozen solid.... Do you know what the Ending could have meant by it, Boogey? How could my heart be a key? Or did it mean something else altogether?"

Professor Manning smiled again, satisfied as he returned to his seat before the organ.

"You know, I wasn't the first Boogey Man," he said. "That was my great grandfather. It was I who broke away from the mantle first, and helped start the Hollow."

Grimmond should have been more surprised at the news, but he was bothered that his questions remained unanswered.

"I never knew that. Why'd you help?"

"As I said before, I no longer believed what I stood for," he said calmly. "My father and grandfather killed by the hundreds, but I? I didn't want that. I broke away — I *chose* to be good. That's very important to understand, Grimmond."

Finding it almost hard to believe, Grimmond didn't quickly respond.

"Why are you telling me this?"

"Because *it doesn't matter* where you came from, or how you got to where you are now," he answered. "You can turn yourself to do good at any point; it's always a choice. But whether that absolves me from a lifetime of evil, I do not know."

HE KNOWS, Grimmond nearly choked. *He knows I'm the one who killed them....*

Swiveling in his chair, Professor Manning struck up his melancholy song once again.

"Professor Manning, what about the Ending?" Grimmond edged closer. "And my heart that it wants for whatever reason?"

"It seems you are incredibly lucky," the man replied. "The Ending failed a second time to get what it needed."

"Do you think I'm safe *here*, then?" Grimmond asked desperately. "Staying in the Hollow?"

"Of course not!"

Grimmond sighed, now downright annoyed at the lack of answers.

"Then what do I *do*? I know it's after me for a reason, and I can't stop it! I'm barely a functioning Nightmarist as it is!"

"Tell me something, dear boy," Professor Manning said over the reverberating music. "Why did you come to the Hollow?"

No one had ever asked Grimmond that before, and he had to think about it.

"I was in jail — a murder suspect — the night I came here. A Nightmare named Kremaya broke me out, telling me to flee to the Hollow. To find the key and seal up the Nightmayr Realm. But really...I didn't want to be afraid anymore. I wanted to face the Ending myself."

"And how did that go for you, when you faced it?"

Grimmond looked away. The Ending was more frightening than he'd ever imagined it to be. If it weren't for the Gargoyles and his friends, he would assuredly be dead.

"Pity you don't know more," Professor Manning said.

"*Pity?*" Grimmond cried. "No 'seize the day, young man, you'll get through this'?"

"You believe you've been defeated since losing your parents...why should I think differently?"

"That Ending *slaughtered* my parents like animals!" Grimmond exclaimed, a rage boiling within him. "I'm already defeated! So why should it want to kill me, too? TELL ME!"

The organ playing stopped at last, and Professor Manning turned and stood. His white eyes swirled, and his mouth smiled dangerously.

"Professor...I-I'm sorry, I don't know what I was —"

"I told you, boy-oh," he said sweetly. "I don't talk to the dark anymore, not for years. I only listen. You seek an answer *I* do not have."

Grimmond gritted his teeth. He knew he was pushing his luck, sure that if Professor Manning wanted to make him disappear forever, he certainly could.

"*Please*, Boogey, tell me what to do. How do I defeat something that can't be killed?"

Professor Manning tapped a finger to his head.

"*Think* like a Nightmare. Dream like one, too."

"Nightmares dream?" Grimmond asked, confused.

"In a manner of speaking. But what is it they need? What's this war all about? Live and let live, some say."

With another blink of his eye, Grimmond lost sight of Professor Manning, until he next appeared by the candle choir to pick one up and set it ablaze.

"Nightmares want this world, Grimmond. Not just Stanchions Hollow, mind you, but the whole world. They won't stop until every resistance is killed. If the cracks in the door continue to widen, if the door isn't resealed, mankind will be lost one day. Me? I don't mind mankind so much; they make me laugh. That's why I left the Nightmayr Realm."

"I thought it was because you didn't like death."

"Exactly. Living side by side with fear itself is not a way to live for most — Stanchions Hollow being the exception, of course. But, say the Nightmayr Realm was sealed up...then *all* its creatures would be gone forever, yes?"

Grimmond felt a flame kindled within him.

"*Including* the Ending?" he asked.

Professor Manning stared at him darkly, and Grimmond believed he had his answer. He faltered, however, realizing what it could fully mean.

"But...you're a Nightmare, Boogey. If your old realm was sealed up, wouldn't that mean that you'd be gone forever, too?"

The man slowly replaced the candle in its holder.

"I once had a sister, years ago," he began. "She failed at a task much like that of your Ending's — stealing something that didn't belong to her. The boy's heart she was to take stole hers instead. I drove my sister away, in the end, for my own foolish reasons, and I never saw her again. She's gone from this world now, but if I were banished back to the old realm myself, there's a chance I may still find her."

Grimmond was speechless, imagining what it would be like to have lost family for a reason other than death. Professor Manning pushed his sister away on his own. In another blink of an eye, the man dissolved into shadows by the choir and reappeared directly in front of Grimmond.

He moved far too much like the Ending for Grimmond's comfort.

"How badly do you want answers, dear boy?"

"Bad enough to do what I need to. People are dying, Boogey. I've lost friends."

"We've all lost those, one way or another. Are you prepared to lose yourself?"

Grimmond had a strange sensation as Professor Manning spoke, and felt the cold in his heart again from the Ending's touch. The man held out a hand, and one of the floating candles rushed into it, flame first. It sizzled out as he caught it, but he next breathed onto it. The candle yipped in pain as its wax darkened from white to black.

"Burn this the next time you sleep, but do not do so lightly. They say you should never sleep with an open flame, but this one's special. And do old Boogey a favor — keep this between us. Strictly speaking, I don't like to be very...*involved.*"

Grimmond wasn't sure he wanted the blackened candle.

"Is this like a — a séance or something? Because I'm not into that sort of —"

"Don't be a fool!" Professor Manning cut him off. "The Nightmayr Realm isn't the afterlife! But it is the Nightmayr Realm where you must go for answers, yes? Take the candle, if you wish. But tell no one."

Grimmond tried not to cringe as he took the candle in his hand. Even though it had just been lit, it was already ice cold. A feminine opera voice continued singing in a foreign language, until Grimmond stuffed it deep into the pocket of his jeans.

"Boogey...."

Before Grimmond could ask more questions, someone ran frantically into the cavern.

"Professor Manning, come quickly!" said a boy from Narcoleptic Row. "We don't know how, but she's still *alive*, and she's back! We thought she was an incoming Nightmare at first — she just walked right through the mist —"

"Calm yourself, Stephen!" Professor Manning demanded. "*Who* is still alive?"

"That girl from the Black Wings — Sariah Lunasae!"

CHAPTER SIXTEEN

A COLD WELCOME

The entire Hollow was in shock, but none more so than the Black Wings.

Sariah Lunasae lay in the whitewashed infirmary, thick blankets wrapped tightly around her, but looking none the worse for wear. Dr. Knight stood nearby in her white lab coat, almost blending in with the walls, and asking questions in hushed tones. She had removed most of Sariah's other friends, but after Viana's persistence, allowed her, Tristin, and Grimmond in.

"I just don't understand," Dr. Knight said incredulously, ticking a few more boxes on her clipboard. "It's a miracle you made it back at all, and with hardly a scratch on you."

With a frosty look at Grimmond, Dr. Knight warned Viana they couldn't stay long, then left them alone. As soon as the door shut, Viana squealed with delight and leaned in to hug Sariah. She made room for Tristin next, but Grimmond took a few steps backward to be safe.

He hadn't known Sariah nearly as long as the others, after all.

"What *happened* to you?" Viana asked, releasing Sariah from a second hug. "Stephen Adamski said the Sleepwalkers picked you up in the woods. You were just wandering in the Orchard?"

Sariah sighed deeply, but regurgitated the story Grimmond was sure she'd already said a dozen times.

"My Gargoyle was hurt pretty bad when we went up against that unidentified Total," she began in a flat voice. "He couldn't fly anymore and dropped me into a dumpster. Next thing I knew, I woke up in the hospital yesterday. I got out of there, first chance after dark, but never found my Bone Crawler. I hitched rides all the way back until I came upon the mist. Then, I just started walking."

"But only the Nightmares can get through the mist," Tristin blurted out. "How'd you manage?"

Viana shot him a venomous look.

"What he *means* to say," she said emphatically, patting Sariah's leg through the sheets, "is that we're *so* glad you're okay."

Sariah smiled weakly, but Grimmond noticed it didn't reach her eyes.

"No thanks to you two," she declared suddenly.

She leveled her gaze at Tristin and Viana, but didn't laugh — was she *not* joking with them? Viana's smile faltered, and Grimmond's lips parted in shock as he listened on.

"Didn't bother looking for me at all, did you?" Sariah said coldly. "Never checked the hospitals, never sent out a Squadron to comb the city. Did the Black Wings even have a memorial for me, or did Drek start tryouts for a new team leader right away?"

Viana's face grew bright red, and she looked close to tears as her mouth moved inaudibly. Grimmond had never seen her quite so speechless before, and he gulped when Sariah next turned her gaze to him.

"Grimmond was the only one who really tried to help me that night," Sariah continued. "He got me onto my Bone Crawler, and tried to get me to take cover."

"Sariah," Tristin said softly, "we were told you were *dead*."

Sariah threw off her covers, shoving away Viana's hand as she sat up in bed. Then she hopped down, walked over to Grimmond, and wrapped him in a tight hug.

"Thank you, Grimmond," she whispered.

Now it was Grimmond's turn to become beet red. Doing his best not to meet the others' eyes, Grimmond looked around the room, embarrassed and uncomfortable. He was surprised when Sariah knew his name half the time; now she was thanking *him* while scorning the friends she'd had for years?

"Your leg," Grimmond said stupidly. "I thought it was broken that night."

"Nope," she scoffed, "I got lucky. Probably just sprained it. It healed okay when I was at the hospital, I guess, otherwise they would've put a cast on it."

Shooting a final, cold look upon Tristin and Viana's flabbergasted faces, Sariah said 'see you' to Grimmond, then left the room in disgust. Tristin turned to the others, raising his hands in confusion.

"What was that all about?" he asked. "I can't believe she thinks that's what happened — like we didn't care about her at all!"

"She has a point, though," Grimmond said quietly. "We were on her team. Someone else told us she was gone, but we never really checked ourselves...."

At the look on Viana's face, Grimmond immediately regretted his words.

"*What?*" she breathed. "You're siding with her?"

"Sorry —" Grimmond answered, rubbing his eyes. "It's only...I have a lot on my mind."

"A lot on *your* mind?" Viana said angrily. "One of my oldest friends just came back from the dead! And she blames *me* for getting her killed in the first place!"

"I said I'm sorry, all right?" Grimmond defended again. "Forget it — I need to get some sleep. I'll catch up with you guys later."

Following Sariah's lead, Grimmond turned on his heel and left his friends in the infirmary.

Over the next few weeks, Grimmond found Sariah sticking close by him, yet still she remained cold to almost everyone else in the Hollow. Edging into his conversations with Tristin or Viana, walking with him to classes, or sitting at his table in the Hearth, she was a constant presence; a presence the old Sariah never pressed upon him.

Finding their newly begun friendship strange at first, Grimmond soon grew to see things that he'd never noticed about Sariah. Her smile was wide, her teeth white and straight, and her wavy brown hair went well with her blue eyes. He'd never thought she was attractive before, and wondered what had changed. She seemed to be smiling at Grimmond almost every time he looked at her.

By the way Viana mutilated the sandwich on her plate one day at lunch, Grimmond suspected she noticed him smiling back.

What am I doing? Grimmond chastised himself. *I don't have feelings for Sariah...I barely know her! Get it together and stop smiling like an ass, Grimmond....*

Having lost her Bone Crawler in Boston — as Viana had lost Qinella — Sariah wasn't able to rejoin the Black Wings for the first few weeks of her return. A Haunter eventually found a new Gargoyle for her to ride, however, and she approached Grimmond atop the stable tower, asking if he'd be willing to help her regain her confidence to fly.

"Me?" Grimmond asked. "Why not get Tristin or Viana, or even Drek? You know they're way better riders than I am."

"Grimmond, you're being modest again," she said with a flirtatious laugh. "You know you've taken down more Total Nightmares than anyone at the Hollow. And nobody else is riding the Blood Onyx, are they?"

Grimmond blushed, but answered with a proud smile.

"No, I guess they're not."

They walked over to Brax, but when Sariah tried to touch his wing, he turned sharply to snap at her.

"Whoa!" Sariah said, recoiling.

"*Brax* — take it easy!" Grimmond pacified. "You know Sariah! What's gotten into you?"

"It's okay, Grimmond," Sariah said, walking back to her newly Haunted Gargoyle, a timid-looking Nerve-Neck. "He's protective of you. I'm still just amazed that you were able to tame such a beast."

Beast? Sure, Brax looks like an evil, black-eyed dragon. But he's my friend, not a monster....

"Still working on the tame part, I guess," Grimmond muttered, shaking his head. "Right, Brax?"

Sariah turned away, covering her mouth to laugh.

"What is it?" Grimmond asked, flattening his hair after checking his zipper.

"Nothing," she answered. "You're just...easier to talk to than I ever knew. I feel like you understand stuff that nobody else here does. Nobody I used to call my friends, anyway."

"Yeah?" Grimmond asked cautiously. "Like what?"

Stepping a little closer to him, she spoke softly.

"Like *me*."

She swept her hair behind her ears, and inched still closer — close enough for Grimmond to smell her perfume. He found his heart beating a little faster than he wished it to.

"C'mon, Sariah," Grimmond said, "you know you've still got friends. They just don't know how to apologize for what happened that night."

Sariah scrutinized him, her eyes looking deeply into his. Grimmond tried to turn away, but she quickly grabbed onto his hand.

"Grimmond, there's something I want to tell you — something I've *been* wanting to tell you since I got back."

Despite Brax's low growling of warning behind him, Grimmond found himself moving back toward her. She didn't release his hand.

"What about?" he asked, his eyes narrowed.

"About what happened to me in Boston," she continued seriously. "About something to do with the Nightmayr Realm. I think...I think I know how we can find both the door and the key at the same time. To seal the other Realm."

Grimmond's eyes widened.

"What?" he said wildly. "What do you mean? Have you told Lord Stawlart yet?"

"Grimmond, *nobody* can know about this. Not Tristin, not Viana, not anyone. You have to promise me."

Desperately wanting to find out what she knew, Grimmond hastily agreed.

"Okay, I promise — but why all the secrecy? We're all on the same side."

"Maybe," she answered. "But I've heard the rumors about you, Grimmond, and I'm starting to put the pieces together. I'm not sure whom I can trust yet...but I *really* want to trust you."

Slowly she moved their held hands to his chest. Grimmond's heart began to beat faster as words fell from his mouth, unbidden.

"You can trust me, Sariah."

Her mouth moved in toward his lips.

What the heck are you doing, Grimmond? SNAP OUT OF IT!

Coming to his senses, Grimmond cleared his throat, dropped her hand, and quickly hopped onto Brax's back. Sariah gave him a strange look, perhaps one of annoyance, but Grimmond only smiled nonchalantly.

"Come on, we'll talk about it later. Let's knock the rust off your flying reflexes, first."

Her face flipped from annoyance to determination, and she mounted her new Nerve-Neck to follow Grimmond to the lake. Weighed down with guilt at what *almost* happened, Grimmond wondered how badly he had just screwed up. He had feelings for Viana, not Sariah. What was he thinking? He may have missed out on whatever information Sariah had, but he'd never willingly hurt Viana.

Maybe it was a bad idea to spend alone time with a girl who came back from the dead.

Practice with the Black Wings was renewed. But even with the Squadron whole again, they lacked the ferocity and teamwork they once had. Grimmond felt as if he was working with friends he hadn't seen in months.

Wynn's hair was longer than ever, Grimmond called after 'Rhonda' instead of 'René' during one maneuver, and Tristin and Viana only half-complied to Sariah's commands as Blue Team leader. In order to remain on the team and with a Glass Wing she knew, Viana had been working with Nelton under Eralynn's suggestion.

Prior to a Scringoll scrimmage amongst the Black Wings in early May, the first since before the Gargoyle Games, Eralynn came down to the lake.

"Hello, dear," she greeted Grimmond brightly.

"Hi, Eralynn," he returned, released from her embrace. "What brings you down?"

"Fresh air," she said, taking a deep breath, "It's a nice night for flying. Are Nelton and Viana working well together? Everything going okay?"

"Yes and yes," Grimmond answered. "We all just need to get back into the swing of things, now that Sariah's back."

Eralynn smiled, but Grimmond saw her nervously drumming fingers against her leg.

"Tristin and Viana?" she asked. "How are they? I haven't seen much of you three together the past few weeks."

Grimmond realized with a start that she was right. He hadn't really spoken to them, or anyone except Sariah, in several days. He wasn't even sure why.

"Yeah, I guess you're right," Grimmond replied awkwardly. "It's just been a little weird the last month. Sariah's still adjusting to being back at the Hollow, and some of her older friends like Tristin and Viana aren't making it easy."

"It seems new friends sure are helping, though," Eralynn said pointedly, her eyebrows rising. "You've stopped spending time with your old friends, as well, just for Sariah's sake?"

"I'm helping her get back on her feet," Grimmond said, feeling heat rise in his cheeks. "That's all. Tristin and Viana will get over it. Look, is something *wrong* here, Eralynn?"

Eralynn pursed her brows at Grimmond's rudeness, but didn't address it.

"No, I just want you to be careful," Eralynn warned, shaking her head. "I've seen the way that girl looks at you."

Grimmond wasn't certain why he was put on the defensive so quickly, but an unfounded anger sprang up within him.

"*That* girl?" he asserted, his face reddening further. "What's that supposed to mean?"

"You know what it means, dear," his godmother went on gently. "She wants to be more than friends. If you pursue a relationship with her, don't forget about the other friends that have been there for you all year."

Grimmond scoffed, pushing past Eralynn to mount Brax.

"I *won't*. But Sariah knows something important about what's going on with the Nightmayr Realm."

"*What?*" Eralynn immediately questioned. "What is it? Why hasn't she come forward?"

"She made me promise not to tell, but she never told me anyway. She said she doesn't know if she can trust me yet, and I guess I know why, with everyone constantly butting into my business! Why can't you trust me, either?"

"I *do* trust you, Grimmond," Eralynn responded in a hurt tone. "Just *please* don't push those who love you away, simply because a new relationship no longer accepts them."

"Whatever you say," Grimmond snorted, extending his glaive. "It's not like *you* ever cast away your friends after they did you wrong. Wait a minute — that's *exactly* what you did. Leave me alone before you come up with more lies, *godmother*...."

Grimmond flew into the air as tears began to stream down Eralynn's face. Confused and rejected, she walked back to the Hovel. Grimmond turned in his seat to watch her go, and was immediately flooded with remorse.

"*Eralynn?*" he said to himself. "What the hell's wrong with me...did I really just say all that?"

Before Grimmond could turn Brax around to beg forgiveness, Sariah quickly met him in the air.

"What was that all about?" she asked.

"I'm not really sure," Grimmond answered truthfully.

"It was about people not minding their own business, that's what," Sariah said. "Don't worry, Grimmond, you're better off without them."

"Am I?" Grimmond replied. "I don't know anymore…."

"Just stick with me and you'll see," she said with her flirtatious smile. "They just want to use you and what you're capable of —"

"Hey, you two!" Drek interrupted, zooming by on his Bone Crawler. "Let's GO — we're starting!"

At the interruption, Grimmond watched Sariah's face grow angrier than he'd ever seen her. He thought she might fly after Drek, her face going from red to almost purple. But quickly she closed her eyes and began humming to herself: a calming, childlike melody that Grimmond thought he recognized.

"What's that?" he asked. "I think my mom used to sing that one."

"It's an old song," Sariah answered. "Clears my head. You should try it next time you try a Flare or Lull. You said you get sick when you do them, right?"

"That's right."

Grimmond scrunched up his face as they flew back toward the Squadron; he didn't remember telling Sariah that. He had only ever told Professor Manning, who in turn told him to think of music when he Flared or Lulled. Music had made his bright knuckles and command words more effective, but he still grew dizzy and nauseous when using them.

"You can't just think of an old song, though," Sariah continued. "It's gotta be specific, like that old song your mom sang. Just twist it to be a little *darker* in your mind. The way an evil orchestra might play it."

Sariah shot him a mischievous grin, but Grimmond was shocked at the suggestion — how could she know that's what he was already thinking of? The orchestra at the Hatch

Memorial Shell, and the music Eralynn turned on in the Phantom ride from Boston: both were classical, almost ghostly songs that calmed Grimmond.

The scrimmage began, Blue Team against Red, with Drek sitting out to referee.

Grimmond quickly felt as if both teams were against him and Sariah. If on offense, Tristin and Viana retained possession of the Ringlet between them alone, and Sariah and Grimmond were forced to fly and block the defensive players from intercepting it; Grimmond quickly lost two of the Terrors on Brax's spine.

Grimmond and his team were losing five to nine when Wynn stole the Ringlet in mid-air from Tristin's pass. The Red Team jetted up the lake to return to their Spindle for the winning point, and Grimmond tore after them, now on defense.

He wasn't sure why, but it made him angrier than it should have. Wynn was his friend, after all.

Or he used to be.

The Sariah-like voice in Grimmond's head made him urge Brax forward. He quickly rose above Wynn's slower Glass Wing, took aim with his bright knuckles, and braced himself for a bout of dizziness. But he then remembered to think of the orchestra, making it dark, depressing, and evil in his mind. His bright knuckles kindled, and Grimmond Flared more intensely than he thought possible.

Black light blazed through his fist like a dark sun flare.

For once, Grimmond didn't grow dizzy at all, but his eyes, chest and fist stung as the light burned outward. At once, all three of Wynn's Terrors sizzled away to nothing, and the Flare shined through the translucent wings of Wynn's Glass Wing, sending the surface of the lake beneath it into a boil.

"AHHH!" Wynn cried out.

His Gargoyle writhed in pain, sending Wynn into the water, but Grimmond kept Flaring. The black light refracted through the Glass Wing, next hitting Wynn's teammates that came in to save him. One by one, their Terrors were likewise burned away, until none were left.

Blue Team immediately won by default, but still Grimmond couldn't stop Flaring.

"Stay back!" Grimmond cried as Tristin and Viana flew toward him. "I can't *stop* it!"

Pointing his fist toward the sky, the dark light stopped at last when Grimmond ripped his bright knuckles off with his other hand. He lowered his eyes, breathing heavily as he looked at his teammates — his *friends* — staring back in fear.

Wynn was pulled from the lake and taken to shore, but Grimmond didn't have the courage to approach him. He landed far past the Squadron to dismount Brax, and fell to his knees in the sand, though someone quickly approached behind him. Hoping it was one of his friends telling him that Wynn was all right, Grimmond turned around to see Sariah.

"That was *incredible!*" she praised, a hungry look in her eyes. "You *did* it, Grimmond."

Grimmond shook his head morosely.

"No — what the heck *was* that? I almost *killed* Wynn!" he croaked. "I have to go check on him!"

Grimmond tried to walk past her, but she grabbed his wrist and spun him around with surprising strength. Her face darkened again, as when Drek had scolded her and Grimmond earlier.

"Come *on*, Grimmond," she said through gritted teeth. "Stop being so noble for a minute, and realize the power you could have if you weren't such a good guy."

Light footsteps approached behind Grimmond, and Sariah looked past his shoulder. Then, smiling maliciously, she jerked his neck forward, and kissed him full on the mouth. It took Grimmond a moment to realize their lips were touching, but only another millisecond to realize he wasn't kissing her back.

"Whoa!" he said, pushing her away. "What do you think you're doing?"

"What every other girl in this lousy place should be trying to do!" she retorted, replacing her hands around his neck. "I *thought* I could trust you...."

"You can," Grimmond answered slowly, removing her hands, "but not like this."

He turned abruptly to see Viana hurrying away from him, back toward Nelton. His stomach jumped into his throat. Had she seen what just happened?

As Nelton took flight, Viana's face turned to Grimmond a moment, and he knew. A mixture of rage and sadness was evident in her tears as she made for the Hovel. Grimmond looked down to Tristin next, who was standing beside Flynn with his mouth and eyes wide, taking it all in. Grimmond felt like he had been shrunk to the size of a small toy, as insurmountable shame bubbled in his gut.

He swore loudly. Why hadn't he shoved Sariah away sooner?

"Uh — be right there, Tristin!" Grimmond said in an effort to escape.

But Sariah stepped back in front of him, once again standing between him and his friends.

In one corner of Grimmond's brain she smelled and tasted completely wonderful, but in another part, he might as well have just drunk battery acid. A third part of him wanted to kiss her again just to be sure, but he knew it wasn't the *real* him. At least, not the Grimmond he used to be.

What am I doing? THIS ISN'T ME!

"I want the key, Grimmond," Sariah said sweetly. "And I'll do what I have to in order to get it."

"You know I don't have it," he replied, his eyes narrowed. "What do you mean?"

"That dark light came from *you*," she said emphatically, "not your bright knuckles. Didn't you feel how easy it finally was to do? You *are* the key to the Nightmayr Realm, Grimmond. And I finally know where the door is, too. Come with me — we'll get the others, and we'll go right now!"

Sariah had to have been wrong, but Grimmond didn't have time for her right now. He needed to see Wynn, and explain himself to Tristin.

"No, Sariah. Look," he said, stepping around her, "I have to get over there and apologize…I have to fix this, first."

He walked past her, but stopped dead when a strange voice whispered behind him.

"Don't you wish to apologize to your mother?" it said harshly. *"You can still fix that, too…you did awful things to both your parents that night, after all…."*

Grimmond shook his head, confused, and slowly turned around.

"What did you say?"

"Huh?" Sariah said. "I didn't say anything."

Without another word, Grimmond walked toward the rest of the Black Wings to face what he would.

HOSTILE INTERVENTION

The next morning Grimmond couldn't find Sariah anywhere. After apologizing to Wynn the night before, Grimmond watched her depart on her Gargoyle, but she never returned to the stable tower.

Grimmond sat alone at the breakfast table.

He looked around to see Olivia and Randy sitting with their own Wards, and Tristin and Viana sitting with a group from Narcoleptic Row. Even the Rebbigones hadn't floated by to heat the plates since he'd arrived. Realizing he still needed to speak to Viana about what she saw, Grimmond made to stand up and go to her. But immediately Tristin locked eyes with him across the room, and shook his head vigorously.

Not the time, I guess. At least Tristin's still on my side, perhaps?

Grimmond sighed, deciding he wasn't so hungry after all. He slid the other way in his chair, planning to check the Anxious Canine for Sariah. But as he tried to stand, a firm hand pushed him back into his chair.

"Trouble at the loser table, little Errandi?"

"Malus," Grimmond snarled. "Seriously not a good time."

Malus plopped down to the right of Grimmond and Biff to the left, so Grimmond was boxed in. Bianca stood watch.

"Sariah got you down?" Malus asked mockingly. "Or is this just your general air of being pathetic? I see you've lost most of your company. I thought I'd drop by for a not-so-friendly warning."

"And I'm *really* not in the mood today," Grimmond warned in return, "trust me — today of all days."

Malus smiled, but continued anyway.

"Maybe that's why I came to see you," he said. "I was curious to know what lies the new girl has been filling your head with."

"Sariah?" Grimmond demanded. "She's not new, you idiot."

"Whatever you say," Malus said with another sticky smile. "How is *Sariah*?"

Grimmond wondered at the wisdom of his next words, but relished the idea of catching Malus off guard. He answered in a cheery voice.

"She's really good. We were just talking about how she knows where the door to the Nightmayr Realm is. We're meeting up with Lord Stawlart in a little bit to hash it all out."

To Grimmond's amusement, Malus's scarecrow face turned completely white, but his hand jerked unconsciously to his pocket. Satisfied at whatever he felt there, his face then began to flush as his teeth were bared.

"Think you're pretty funny, I bet," Malus said. "Not for long."

He nodded to Biff, and Grimmond's arms were quickly pinned behind his back.

"Hey!" Grimmond grunted. "What are you —"

Grimmond saw a flash of silver as Malus withdrew a collapsed glaive and pressed it against his shirt. But at the same time, Bianca tumbled across the floor with a grunt, and Grimmond heard the familiar grate of an extending glaive, reaching out to touch Malus's throat.

"Do it," said a cold voice. "Do it and I swear I'll pin you to the table like an ugly butterfly."

Grimmond looked up, completely taken aback at Olivia's unwavering face. She held her blade to Malus's throat, a thin trickle of blood already running downward where she nicked him.

"You know I don't have anything left to lose," she said flatly.

Grimmond watched Malus's hand twitch against his glaive, contemplating, but then he nodded to Biff. Grimmond was released, and the two bullies stood up and hurried to take Bianca away. Olivia quickly looked around for teachers, then collapsed her own glaive and walked away without another word.

Major Nightmares was even drier than usual, teaching Grimmond about things he'd already experienced first-hand as a rider on the Black Wings. He didn't need this class anymore. He tried to remember the last time he'd actually been afraid of a Nightmare, but couldn't pinpoint when.

The Ending doesn't count, though...I don't know what it is, but it's not like any Nightmare I've seen. I just wish I knew how to get rid of it, before it gets rid of me.

Someone quietly nudged his side, and he lazily turned to be handed a note by Olivia. He opened it on his lap, and saw that she wanted to talk privately after class.

"As do I!" Dr. Knight suddenly exploded from beside him, ripping the note out of his hands and crumpling it into a ball. "Miss Tychus will have to get in line behind *me* and the rest of your conquests!"

"Nice one," Olivia whispered as Dr. Knight returned to the front, her white coat swishing angrily.

Grimmond hurried to the exit after class ended, but as his seat was the furthest away, he was still the last one there. The door was slammed shut behind Olivia, and Viana's mother rounded on Grimmond, fuming.

"I *warned* you not to toy with my daughter's heart!" she spat. "And I know about your relationship with Sariah Lunasae!

Now you seek Olivia as well? How many broken girls do you need at your beck and call?"

Grimmond wondered if he was about to have another glaive pressed against his chest.

"You could not be *more* wrong," he said in return, reaching for the door handle. "I'm not playing anyone! I just need some time. I'll smooth everything over as soon as people stop butting in where they don't belong!"

Dr. Knight shook her head sadly.

"Are you happy? Now that my Viana had to learn about your family the hard way?" she asked. "Your actions are splitting apart more than just your Squadron, Grimmond Errandi. You're weakening the entire Hollow!"

"Great," Grimmond said. "Looks like I'll have to fix that, too. Now *get out of my way!*"

Dr. Knight hopped out of the way as Grimmond threw the door open and exited into the cool hallway. Fuming himself now, he nearly lashed out at the next thing that dared to cross him: Olivia's arm. Reaching out from an empty classroom and grabbing onto his chest, she yanked him inside.

"Geeze, Olivia!" Grimmond protested, stumbling into the dark room. "What are you trying to do aside from give me whiplash? Dr. Knight would freak out if she saw us like this — so would Viana! Or Sariah even!"

"This is the only place we could talk in private," Olivia said dryly, taking a seat in an empty desk. "But *wow*, I guess you really do have a list. Are you so full of yourself that you'd think I would want in on the action after *Sariah*? Pull your head out of wherever it's stuck, and you'll see she's not who you think."

Grimmond crossed his arms, glaring at Olivia as he leaned against the wall. A Sentree branch inched toward him in the dark, but he shot a bright green Flare and it retreated.

"You don't know her like I do."

"I know that no matter how much she thinks she's your girlfriend," Olivia replied, "you don't want to be her boyfriend. So there's that."

Grimmond scuffed his feet against the floor, listening to the Sentree whispering in anger beside him.

"Well," he answered, "I'm glad *somebody* realizes it."

He shifted uncomfortably, fidgeting with the bright knuckles still on his fist. He scrunched his face up as he looked back at Olivia.

"By the way, thanks for this morning."

Olivia offered a rare smile, but it quickly diminished.

"Malus will get his, eventually. But, there's something else I needed to talk to you about."

"Yeah?" Grimmond asked, standing up straighter. "What's that?"

In the darkness of the classroom, Grimmond heard her fidget in her seat and swallow nervously.

Grim, you and I...." she began, standing up and wringing her hands. "I know stuff's been weird since I joined the Blights, but we've been through a lot together, haven't we?"

Grimmond held up his fingers to count.

"Thanksgiving, then Boston — me saving your life, and you later saving mine...yeah, it's safe to say we've had each other's backs."

Olivia shifted awkwardly.

"I know it might be weird for you to hear," she began, "but I think of you like Keith sometimes — like a big brother, almost. The way he always tried to protect me? That's how you are, too. I'll admit, I didn't *always* think of you so platonically, but I do now."

Now it was Grimmond's turn to shift uncomfortably.

"I know," he answered quietly. "I promised myself, Liv, after Keith died, that I'd do right by him and always look out for you. That's why I was so upset when you joined the Blights in the first place — I just wanted you to stay safe. I should've talked to you sooner, but I wasn't sure how you'd take it."

The room grew silent as understanding passed between the two of them.

"Okay then," Olivia declared. "So, if I told my big brother something that was hard for me to say, he'd believe me? Even if what I had to say was about Sariah?"

Grimmond pushed off the wall, but sank into a more defensive stance.

"I'm sure it would depend," he answered, arms still crossed, "on what that was."

Olivia took a deep breath and resumed her seat.

"Look, Grim. I saw her in Boston Public Garden that night...I *saw* when she died...."

"Sariah?" Grimmond asked.

"No," she retorted testily, "Lazarus."

"Huh?"

"*Yes*, dummy," Olivia said. "The woman of the hour, Sariah. I saw a Total ripping her in ha —"

She stopped mid-sentence, looking very much like she was trying not to vomit.

"I watched a Sangmanger rip her *in half*," she finished. "When I told you that night that Sariah was gone, I meant it. There was nothing left, Grim."

Grimmond felt like a bowling ball had hurtled into him, but he stood his ground.

"That's not possible, Liv," Grimmond obstinately deflected. "Sariah got knocked out and went into the hospital. It's as simple as that."

Olivia immediately stood back up.

"Wake *up*, Grim," she said adamantly. "Everyone else knows something's off about her. She's a different person. Whoever that girl is walking around — it's not the Sariah Lunasae you knew."

"You're wrong," he said irritably. "Why would you even say that?"

Olivia sighed, but decided to change tactics.

"How well did you know her before, *really?*" she pleaded. "Why's she been ignoring her old friends and their feelings, and suddenly all over you? And getting back here without a Phantom ride or Gargoyle, just stumbling through the woods of New England until she found the Orchard?"

She has a point... how did *Sariah get back into the Hollow in the first place? She never answered Tristin when he asked.*

"It doesn't make sense, and you know it," Olivia finished. "That's why you can't defend her. How badly do you really want answers?"

Olivia's cold tone of voice sounded exactly like Professor Manning's, and suddenly Grimmond remembered the black candle he was given the night Sariah returned: what he was supposed to use to get answers about the Ending. It was in his bedside table, lying completely forgotten. Maybe it could help him with his new problems, too.

I'll need to get it and find another place alone, though....

Looking as if she knew she wasn't getting through to him, Olivia elevated her tone.

"Just *think* about it, okay?" she huffed. "Stuff is weird enough around here without you losing your mind, too."

"Fine, I'll think about it," Grimmond said, knowing full well he was about to run to his room for the candle. "Um, do you have a lighter by the way?"

"You *smoke* now, too?" Olivia snorted. "Really, grow up soon. Okay, Grim? We all miss you."

"'We all'?" Grimmond said stupidly. "Who's that, exactly?"

Olivia's eyes narrowed to slits as she stepped closer to him.

"The people you *used* to call your friends, jackass."

Indignant at the two-years-younger girl, Grimmond stared as she stomped out of the room. He hadn't seen so much emotion out of her since Keith's death. Not wishing to lose another friend in the mess of the week, Grimmond hurried out of the empty classroom after her to apologize.

He nearly ran directly into Viana and Tristin.

Olivia stalked past them, shaking her head as if to say, '*don't bother with him*'. Grimmond stood speechless as Viana's eyes bounced between Grimmond and Olivia.

"Viana," Grimmond breathed. "I'm sorry, I've been trying to talk to you and explain —"

"Stop," she said with a shuddering breath, holding up a finger. "*Just stop....* See you, Tristin."

Making a wide berth around Grimmond, so as not even to touch him by accident, Viana stormed off. Grimmond looked after her, but was suddenly spun around by an aggressive Tristin.

"*Mate*, I think it's time we had ourselves a little chat," he said through clenched teeth.

"Tristin — I'm sorry," Grimmond answered hurriedly, "but I've gotta do something. I really will explain, but this is important!"

Grimmond tore off through the Hovel, all the way back to Steeple Spike. He knew he'd miss his next class, and would have to deal with the consequences later, but he couldn't wait anymore. Things were starting to get out of control; he knew somehow that it all came back to the Nightmayr Realm, he just didn't know *why*.

He only knew that he had to find out before it was too late.

Bursting into his room, he opened up his bedside table and pulled out the black candle. He turned and made for the stable towers next, and quickly climbed up the stairs to get to Brax. As soon as he came out onto the sky-high platform, he saw Tristin blocking his way.

"Tristin?" he said, surprised. "What are you doing here?"

"Figured you'd find your way up here, Grim, seeing how you said it was something really important. Where is she, anyway?"

"Who?" Grimmond asked.

"Your new girlfriend, Sariah," he answered. "Or did Olivia get up here before me, too?"

Tristin's fingers balled into fists, and he smiled grimly.

"What's going on, Tristin...." Grimmond replied cautiously. "No one's up here but us."

"Good."

In a swift movement, Tristin grabbed Grimmond by the scruff of his shirt and pinned him against the wall. Grimmond had never seen him so angry, and never knew that his happy-go-lucky, coffee-loving friend was so strong.

"We're *friends*, right, Grim?" Tristin spat.

"I thought so," Grimmond said, struggling in his grip, "but you have a weird way of showing it!"

"Right then — instead of throwing you off this tower, I'll talk to you like a friend for the next minute."

Tristin released him and backed away, but his assault was far from over.

"What the HELL has gotten into you, mate?" he roared. "First Viana, then Sariah, now *Olivia*, too? I care too much to let you destroy yourself, Grim, along with every other girl in Stanchions Hollow!"

"Tristin," Grimmond cautioned, "don't make me do this with you — this is like the tenth time I've been cornered today and I don't want to explode. It's not like that with Liv, I promise you —"

"But it *is* like that with Sariah — I saw it with my own eyes, and so did Viana!" Tristin yelled over him. "How could you do that to Viana? It's *wrong*, Grim!"

"Sariah kissed *me*! I didn't even kiss her back —"

"And you have to rub it all in Viana's face that much more by completely cutting her out?" Tristin continued to shout. "By cutting all of us out? We're your *best friends*, Grim!"

At last, the familiar anger Grimmond had been experiencing the last few weeks ignited in his gut, taking over his better judgment. His anxiety went away, replaced by a desire to fight.

"Is *that* what this is about?" Grimmond suddenly laughed, spreading his arms wide. "You have a thing for *Viana?*"

Tristin flexed his arms and cracked his knuckles. He was a little bigger than Grimmond, but Grimmond stepped forward anyway. Something inside him almost *wanted* Tristin to throw a punch, just to see who would win between them.

"Don't make me hit you, Grim," he threatened. "Viana's like my little sister, and you know it."

"And Olivia's like mine," Grimmond retorted. "Satisfied? Any other pressing things you need to say?"

"Arghhh!" Tristin grabbed his own hair and bellowed in frustration. "You're a different person, Grim! Ever since the Ending told you that you were the key to the Nightmayr Realm, you've had this air about you, like — like you can do whatever you want and hurt whoever in the process!"

"You're projecting your own crap on me — DON'T!" Grimmond countered. "You have no idea what this has been like!"

"Then for the love of SLEEP, talk to me!" Tristin shouted in return. "Talk to Vi, talk to Liv, talk to Eralynn for pity's sake! Just don't talk to *her* anymore!"

"*Her?* Sariah?" Grimmond mocked. "You're just jealous!"

"Grim — something's wrong, something's not right about her being here, I know you've noticed —"

"Yeah, I have," Grimmond cut him off. "She almost *died*. People tend to be weird for a week or two after that happens, but everyone else forgets and turns them into an outcast. We *left* her there to die Tristin, ever think of that? It's our fault she got hurt, and I'm the only one trying to make it up to her."

Tristin didn't respond, Grimmond's heightening rage now far exceeding his own. Tristin lowered his eyes and quieted to continue talking.

"My dear friend, you *must* listen to reason —"

"We're done," Grimmond warned, fingering his glaive. "Get your priorities straight before you come to me again. Until then, *stay out of my way*."

Grimmond quickly walked over to Brax, mounted, and took off toward the Sleepless Orchard. Tristin watched as he flew into the darkness, muttering to himself in defeat.

"Grim…what's happened to you?"

Grimmond knew only one place he could be alone: Brax's clearing in the Sleepless Orchard. He flew over the edge of the eastern forest, where cherry trees were in bloom amongst the Japanese maples, and touched down to find the area almost unrecognizable.

Now warmer, the Sentrees around the clearing were coming into their haunting blooms of tiny red eyeballs and dripping fangs. Grimmond could hear them whispering to one another as he walked to the center. He plopped down onto the ground, still upset as Brax lumbered away from him.

"Why can't you talk like the other Gargoyles, Brax?" Grimmond asked bitterly. "I know you'd agree with me."

The Blood Onyx growled low, and Grimmond sensed the feeling wasn't mutual. Seething, Grimmond sifted through the numerous confrontations of the day, each one concerning Sariah. Nearly every friend he had was warning him about her, and even Brax wouldn't let her get near.

Certainly that had to mean something.

No, there's nothing wrong with Sariah! They're all just jealous that a girl like her, surviving such a terrible experience, has chosen me to be her friend now. And she believes in me — she's the only one who believes that I'm the key...we'll show them all when we close the Nightmayr Realm together!

Grimmond hastily fished the black candle out of his pocket, wedging it between a few stones on the ground, but then swatted himself on the forehead. He'd never gotten matches or a lighter, and had no way to light the wick. He stopped himself from immediately chucking the candle in the woods, wondering if Professor Manning had just been messing with him, anyway.

"I don't suppose you can breathe *fire* or something, Brax?" Grimmond said, annoyed.

Brax didn't answer from his gnarled stump camouflage, but the feminine opera voice struck up within the candle on the ground. Grimmond turned to it, reminded of the music he thought of to create the black light over the lake — the dark light that was hot enough to boil the water.

He had a sudden idea, though one against his better judgment.

No one's around this time to get hurt, Grimmond thought. *I could try the Flare again, safely.*

Withdrawing his bright knuckles, he concentrated on the dark, evil orchestra, and aimed at the candlewick. His mind remained clear as the stinging sensation filled his body, and he flooded both the clearing and candle with black light. Ignoring the tortured opera scream as he vaporized half the candle, he removed his knuckles once its wick sparked to life.

Ecstatic at his initial success, a twinge of concern likewise ignited in him.

Professor Manning advised him to sleep as the candle burned — did it matter that he was awake? Or that he didn't use regular fire? The flame was becoming taller and darker by the passing second. Alarm shot upward in Grimmond as he looked on, and realized; the candle's growing black flame wasn't providing light at all.

It was *consuming* the light of the clearing.

Expanding shadows emanated around him, and both the clearing and Orchard darkened until they disappeared entirely. Grimmond's heart picked up as all around him hoarse whispers echoed and shadows danced. He was reminded of the Nightmare, Kremaya, slithering into his jail cell.

He closed his eyes and covered his head, his heart racing like it hadn't since the previous summer. A strong jolt pulled him forward, and unable to withstand it, he fell to his knees.

What's HAPPENING?

Frantically he felt around in the dark for the candle, hoping dearly he could still blow it out. He gripped onto it at last, but before he blew, the shadows lifted and his eyes began to adjust to dim lights above him. The clearing was gone, as were Brax and the Sleepless Orchard.

Grimmond wasn't in the Hollow any longer.

An alley, high-walled and filled with dark mist surrounded him. At the same time his ears heard squishing and chewing, a charred black face swiveled in the dark. A wispy body and folds of skin followed it, and two slimy optic nerves whipped toward him.

"ACHHH!" screeched the face in surprise.

Breathing in a heavy stink, heart pounding in his eardrums, Grimmond only whispered in return.

"Kremaya."

"How — *SLURP* — are you *here,* boy?" she squealed in agitation.

Grimmond breathed heavily despite the choking stench, and tried not to recoil as she swirled around him, chewing on the wriggling object in her mouth.

"You...you *found* me...."

"All Nightmares know where you are, boy!" said Kremaya. "Stanchions Hollow — *squelch* — where Endings don't follow! Someone thought you'd be safe there, but they were WRONG...."

Grimmond closed his eyes again, shaking the candle stuck in his grip, but its black flame would not go out. He smacked himself in the face to wake up.

"Boogey's black candle...I should've just thrown it away!" he cried out desperately. "Now I'm stuck in this séance with *you?*"

Kremaya laughed wickedly, eyeballs bouncing on the tips of their slimy nerves.

"Oh, BOOGEY, YOU GOODIE!" she bellowed through her full mouth. "No candle séance — *SQUELCH* — you are where I am now, flesh bag! Not like last time...."

Grimmond tried to step away, filled with sudden fear, but ran into the wall.

"What do you mean, *not like last time?*"

Coughing and squelching, Kremaya's mouth laughed so widely that it swallowed her floating body until she was inside out. Undissolved bits of what she'd just eaten crawled out from her guts. With a disgruntled clicking, Grimmond watched a series of yellow legs scuttle up the wall and out of sight.

"Am I dead?" Grimmond whispered shakily.

"You're with *me,*" Kremaya hissed, jabbing a black finger against his chest. "Like I said — *slurp* — not like last time, when I was with *you.*"

Grimmond felt a wriggling behind him, and began to sink backward; whatever hard wall he leaned against had become soft, and was trying to suck him in. Pushing off the fleshy sponge in revulsion, a thick and sticky red substance like old guts peeled away from his jeans.

He scurried away from both the wall and heckling Kremaya, but found he had nowhere to run.

Panic-stricken, he twitched to the left and right, now seeing the ghostly structures towering over him like condemned houses. Shadows, beams, and purple webs connected them together as far he could see, and high above them the sky was illuminated with black light — the same that Grimmond Flared from his bright knuckles.

"If you're trying to scare me, you're losing your touch!" Grimmond lied, his flesh crawling at the thousand smells of rot.

"Have I?" she laughed darkly, contorting grotesquely and reaching out with a single eyeball.

"ENOUGH!" Grimmond swatted her slimy tongue-eye away, trying to subdue his fear. "Just let me go!"

"This is not *my* doing," she answered, spitting black bile and slurping between sentences, as usual. "It is yours! You have summoned *me* here!"

"All I did was light this candle!" Grimmond protested. "And then…then I was reminded of you, right before I got here."

"I'm *flattered*," Kremaya cooed hideously. "Thinking of your old partner in crime — *slurp* — right before bed?"

Grimmond shuddered at the thought as she continued to heckle.

"But how kind of you — *slurp* — to visit me here! The plane of horror and land of languished! The world of the Dark Naught — *SQUELCH* — yes, *naught* better to rule the Nightmayr Realm!"

Grimmond felt the cold sweat dripping from his armpits and down his back as she laughed sickeningly; he was terrified anew as comprehension dawned on him. He spoke slowly and shakily in return.

"I'm in the *Nightmayr Realm?*"

"Of course — *SLURP* — where else, *stupid* boy!" she said harshly. "No place for flesh — *squelch* — flesh won't last! See for yourself!"

She pointed to the corner of the alley, and Grimmond took a cautious step toward it.

Peering through the darkened streets, he covered his gasp when he saw hundreds of colorful Nightmares hovering about. Creeping things screeched in the shadows of buildings, fleshless Haunters walked in and out of shops with glowing windows, and flying creatures chopped their wings through the air. Grimmond couldn't believe what he was seeing; the Nightmayr Realm was more than he ever imagined.

It was an entire *world* of Nightmares.

Mostly every Nightmare he could see had no flesh, but Grimmond recognized what some would become. Dozens of Majors and Totals walked, crawled, or flew across the wide street, like it was a demented, bustling city. And more Nightmares than Grimmond recognized continued to surface.

"Why are you here — *slurp* — flesh bag?" Kremaya asked, roughly prodding him with her squishy purple tongue.

Grimmond was brought back to the present, but his legs felt like rubber, and his dripping sweat had made him quite cold. He was in the Nightmayr Realm, and surely its endless creatures would sense his presence any moment. Why *was* he there?

Answers…Boogey sent me here to get answers about the Ending! And I don't have much time!

Looking down to his closed fist, Grimmond saw the black flame burning low. With effort, he summoned his courage again to speak.

"I-I need to know about the Ending, Kremaya!" he said quickly. "You told me to get to Stanchions Hollow, and made me think everything would be better there!"

"Yes — *slurp* — someone thought it would!"

"*Who?*" Grimmond cried. "Are they here?"

Kremaya went to chewing on something in the dark and didn't answer, but an eerie voice echoed through the street of Nightmares, reaching Grimmond's ears like a warning. He almost found it familiar, calling his name through the dark, but Kremaya then answered him.

"Yes, of course they are here — *squelch* — someone cannot leave!"

"Then take me to them!" Grimmond demanded. "My friends are hurting, and I need to know how to defeat the Ending and seal shut this realm for good, like you told me! What does the Ending even want with me?"

"Always the Nightmares are looking for cracks," said Kremaya. "Cracks to escape — *slurp* — gaps to abate! Sew, sew, sew them up closed! Use the key!"

"I found what I thought was the key in Boston," Grimmond protested, "but it broke!"

"You have — *slurp* — broken?" Kremaya asked, all three of her whirling eyes narrowing at him.

"What? No!" Grimmond responded, confused. "Of course *I'm* not broken!"

"But you have found the key — *squelch* — yes?"

"No — well, I don't know," Grimmond said shakily. "The key wasn't real, then the Ending told me that I *am* the key. What does it mean, Kremaya?"

The voice echoing down the street reached Grimmond again, this time more clearly.

Grimmond! You must leave!

"Silly, silly boy sweating in your flesh bag — *SLURP* — the key you have always had!" Kremaya bellowed. "That's why the Ending wants you! Now, time to find the *door* — *SQUELCH* — to seal or open, the choice is yours!"

"But *where* is the door for me to be able to close it?" Grimmond asked.

"Doors, doors, *doors*! Doors open here, doors open there — *SLURP* — the dark door can be opened anywhere! It's not a where, blue-haired boy, but a what! You already *have* the key — *SQUELCH* — and they have the door. Find the one with the door!"

"But I don't —"

Time is running out, Grimmond! They know you're here — GO NOW!

Grimmond stopped talking, and peered his head back around the corner to look down the street.

"Kremaya — whose voice is that?"

"I am *your* Nightmare," she shuddered with laughter, "not — *squelch* — the other way around!"

Lurking in another dark alley down the street, a bright red Sangmanger suddenly stepped out, slowly turning to sniff in Grimmond's direction. It was dragging what looked like a burlap bag of pointed, sloshing objects, but Grimmond didn't want to know what they were.

He quickly drew back further behind the corner, but it was too late. Opening its fat mouth wide, the Sangmanger let out a wail of hungry rage. And in the distance, a sound Grimmond had only ever heard twice before resounded like awaiting doom.

The Ending was calling back.

Grimmond was shaken to his core, and couldn't even move. Where could he go, here in the Nightmayr Realm? The Sangmanger lumbered toward him, but one of Kremaya's slimy optic nerves suddenly wrapped around Grimmond, then tossed him forcefully through the air.

Grimmond didn't feel the pain as he smashed into a far wall, and slid down into a heap of cold limbs and dried blood. The smell was unbearable, but the Sangmanger's bloated body sloshed by him and onto the next street, unable to discern Grimmond from the mass of carcasses he now laid still in.

He closed his eyes tightly as Kremaya picked him back up; he didn't want to know whether anything in that pile was human.

"They know you're here — *slurp* — flesh bag!" Kremaya warned. "Cannot save you twice — *squelch* — you must leave!"

"Tell me where to find the door, and I'll go!" Grimmond cried. "Please! *Where is it?*"

Grimmond recognized the calls of Prowlers and Brutes mixing in with the low rumble of the Sangmanger. Kremaya hissed as she dragged him up another alley.

"Dark places, deep spaces!" she said. "Anger opens the doors wherever he makes it."

"So there's *more* than one door?" Grimmond asked hurriedly. "Tell me, Kremaya!"

The voice telling Grimmond to leave was more insistent than ever, but sounded as if it was being choked off.

"*Whose is that voice*, Kremaya?" Grimmond demanded.

"I hear NOTHING!" she said, her face contorting.

Was that worry behind her blood-curdled eyes? Grimmond grew suddenly cold, but it wasn't due to Kremaya's grotesque appearance before him. Eyes upon eyes started to glow in the walls of the alley. Whatever the Ending had sent to find him, it was there.

"Tell me where the door is, Kremaya — *please* — and I can leave!"

"How do I know?" she asked. "I am here and you are there — *SLURP* — and I'm not there! Seventy sevens have come and gone — *SQUELCH* — the Endings are mad and have sought you long!"

The Ending is there, Grimmond! Leave now!

"She's right, she's right!" Kremaya said suddenly. "Muse always knows. Time's up, life's up, it's time to go — *squelch* — turn off Boogey's trick candle, boy!"

"You just said you couldn't hear it —"

"Oh, *her?*" Kremaya squealed. "Of course I hear my Muse — *SLURP* — but there's no time for now! The door is near, find it! Find *him*. Angry boy, hateful boy — *SQUELCH* — mad, sad, never glad! Use the key — *SLURP* — seal the door or sear it through. We will all see soon!"

"I don't have the key! I told you it's broken!"

"But YOU'RE not broken, you said!" she answered. "Oh, and someone thought you should know — *SQUELCH* — *don't trust the pretty girl.*"

"*Muse*, again?" Grimmond demanded, backing away from the eyes blinking on the walls.

"Yes, my Muse," Kremaya answered. "She sings for me."

"Who is she really, Kremaya?"

"Stupid boy — *SLURP* — you've always known who!"

Grimmond caught his breath as the Ending floated into the alley, bone-white hands stretched toward him. Of all the Nightmares Grimmond had ever seen, the white hands and face of the Ending scared him the most. He was a little boy again, scared to breathe, scared to get up and go to the bathroom, scared to take his head out from under the covers.

"Close your eyes, boy — *SLURP* — our time is through!" Kremaya warned. "Don't be deceived — *SQUELCH* — they know it's you —"

The Ending waved a white hand at Kremaya and she dissolved into nothingness. Then it angled its hand toward Grimmond, overshadowing him and causing his heart to lurch strangely.

"So the key comes to us.... Look, boy...all your struggles can be over...LOOK!"

Confirming that the Ending still believed him to be the key, Grimmond closed his eyes and covered his ears as he backed into the wall. But the strange voice called out one last time.

GRINNY — the CANDLE! Put it out! Hurry!

Grimmond felt his neck hairs stand up, as the world around him went black. He *knew* that voice. No one had ever called him 'Grinny', save one person.

"Mom?"

The voice didn't answer, and the Ending reached out toward Grimmond's heart, which thrummed like a racecar. He tried to lift his fist to smother the candle, but couldn't move again. Grimmond knew he had only seconds before his heart would be ripped out.

MOM! I know you're here!

Memories of his mother flooded his mind, and he remembered the lullaby she used to sing to him. Suddenly and in contrast to the dark light of Sariah's evil orchestra, bright, bluish-white light blasted out from Grimmond's chest. The hold on his heart was released, and without a moment to lose, Grimmond lifted the candle and smashed the softened wax between both fists.

The Ending screamed, Grimmond was jolted forward, and he crashed into the unseen ground.

He was back in the clearing of the Sleepless Orchard.

Several Sentrees backed away from him in surprise, croaking and belching as they ran around in a flurry to brush the burning light from their branches. But where was the Ending? Grimmond felt for the bright knuckles in his pockets, and donned them to continue fighting.

"Mom!" Grimmond shouted frantically, jumping to his feet. "Mom...*where are you?*"

But no one was in front of him aside from the Sentrees and Brax, all standing a safe distance away. Grimmond fell back to his knees, and threw up on the ground. His heart was strange and cold. Had he just lost his mother all over again?

Brax quietly approached him, watching warily as Grimmond wiped the tears from his face.

"Let's go, Brax," Grimmond sniffed. "We need to find Eralynn, quick."

THE KEY AND THE DOOR

"She's alive, isn't she?" Grimmond asked, bursting into the Dread Map room.

He said it as more of a statement than a question, and both Eralynn and Lord Stawlart looked over from the zoomed-in map of New England.

"Grimmond?" said his godmother. "Who? What's happened to you?"

"My *mom*," Grimmond answered shakily. "She's still alive!"

Concernedly, Eralynn moved away from Cyto and Plasm.

"Dear," she continued, "you're upset —"

"I just *heard* her voice in the Nightmayr Realm!" Grimmond shouted.

Eralynn froze, then shot a quick glance at Lord Stawlart, lowered her eyes and swallowed hard. They weren't telling Grimmond something. His previous despair, waking up in the clearing, quickly twisted to anger.

"Tell me exactly what you saw the night my parents were killed," Grimmond said. "The *truth* this time."

Lord Stawlart stepped forward, and looked at Grimmond uneasily.

"The truth," he said, "is that your father, along with William Knight, were both assuredly killed. I saw their bodies with my own eyes. And your mother...she was as good as dead, the moment she went with that Ending."

Went with the Ending? But I...I thought I killed her...I remember her blood on my hands....

Grimmond swayed on his feet, looking around for something to balance him, and spoke in a breathless voice.

"What — do — you — mean, *'went with'?*"

"I mean," Lord Stawlart proceeded gravely, "that to buy you seventy sevens' worth of life, your mother went into the Nightmayr Realm *willingly*. Otherwise, the Ending would have slaughtered us all."

Willingly? No — that...that can't be right....

Grimmond stumbled over to the wall, his heart fluttering oddly. It felt stranger to him by the passing moment: full while empty, hot yet cold, and pumping something other than blood.

"I truly wish your mother could still be alive," Eralynn said slowly, "but we can't be sure — it's impossible to know. And after this long —"

"You're *wrong*," Grimmond cut her off. "Both of you!"

Lord Stawlart approached closer, and his face hardened.

"Grimmond," the man said tensely, "you must listen."

"*No*," Grimmond asserted. "You lied to me! *I'm* the one who...*who*...."

Grimmond struggled to allow the words to come out. To confess.

"But she's *not* dead now, and we *have* to get her back! I *know* we can — I'll do it alone if I have to —"

"GRIMMOND SCYLENT!" Lord Stawlart resounded. "We can do NOTHING for your mother! But we *can* help the Hollow!"

He pointed stiffly toward the Dread Map.

"Do you see?" he asked. "The mist of the Sleepless Orchard is being tested as we speak!"

Grimmond was shocked to silence as he looked over. A bright, red-studded ring surrounded the Hollow, and continued to move inward as Cyto and Plasm weaved furiously.

"I don't understand," Grimmond muttered. "What's going on?"

"Must it be spelled out for you, Grimmond?" said Lord Stawlart. "They're coming for the key to the Nightmayr Realm!"

Slamming his fist down on a table, red light Flared from Lord Stawlart's bright knuckles.

"But we *will not* hand you over!" he boomed again. "Not without a fight!"

The man relented, breathing heavily, but Grimmond's jaw tightened as if he had been slapped in the face. Lord Stawlart's eyes widened when he realized what he had let slip.

Hand ME over?

Grimmond's eyes flicked between Lord Stawlart and his godmother, waiting for her to dispute the claim. But she didn't, and only stared back sadly until Grimmond's suspicion was confirmed.

They know...they KNOW that I'm the key....

"How long?" Grimmond managed to say. "How long have you known and not told me?"

Eralynn bowed her head, and answered in an unsteady voice.

"We weren't certain until recently," she said, "but it's clear now. It's all been for you, Grimmond: your mother's sacrifice, the ruse in Boston to draw you out, and the invasion that's now upon the Hollow. You've *always* been the key."

The walls warped to Grimmond's vision, and his head began to spin as he backed away.

"I...I don't...."

Grimmond couldn't form a sentence as his chest went from hot to cold. Cyto and Plasm clacked and rubbed their legs together at him, and the webs on the floor and ceiling seemed to be laughing like Kremaya.

"The Orchard," Grimmond said in a daze. "Have to warn Tristin and Vi...."

"You need to sit down, first," Lord Stawlart urged. "There's *more* you must know."

"Grimmond," Eralynn added. "Please."

But Grimmond had had enough, and he was already running toward the door, determined to find the only two people he now wanted to see in the Hollow.

Hurrying toward Steeple Spike, Grimmond passed the familiar Terrors, Sentrees and disembodied Haunters roaming the halls. Viana's room was checked first, but none of the girls were there. Grimmond continued to his own floor next, staggering into his bedroom and tripping on the welcome rug. He crashed upon the wooden planks, and something clattered away from him, though he didn't see what.

"Are you all right?" Keokuk asked from his corner of the room.

Grimmond spoke frantically in return.

"You and Wynn need to round up the Black Wings!" he urged. "Have you seen Tristin or Viana?"

"They're on Fire Watch duty," Wynn answered, turning at his desk. "What's going on?"

"The Hollow's in trouble!" Grimmond warned. "The mist is failing and the Sleepless Orchard is about to be flooded with enemy Nightmares! Get the Black Wings up and to the stable towers, *quick*!"

In a flash, the two boys leapt from their desks to grab their weapons and armor. Grimmond dashed from the room, climbing the stairs by two, all the way to the pinnacle of Steeple Spike. Bursting into Fire Watch, he found his two best friends sitting on the couches, doing homework.

"Tristin!" he cried out, running over. "Viana!"

Grimmond had never been happier to see anyone, but his feeling was far from mutual. Tristin snapped his book shut and sighed heavily as Grimmond approached, preparing himself for the second round of their previous argument.

"What do you want?" Viana said coldly, not raising her eyes to him.

Crashing to his knees, Grimmond clutched his chest — the feeling in his heart was getting worse.

"*Sorry*," Grimmond gasped. "I'm *so* sorry, Viana...for everything."

"Grim?" Tristin asked, immediately jumping off the couch. "Mate, are you hurt?"

Before he could reach him, Viana pushed her books off her lap and dropped to Grimmond's side.

"What is it?" she said, clutching his shoulders. "Grim, what's wrong with you?"

Looking up at her, Grimmond appreciated something he already knew to be true. Even if he hadn't just gotten back from the Nightmayr Realm, Viana Knight was still the loveliest girl he'd ever laid eyes on.

"*Fine*," Grimmond panted. "I'm fine...just need to say something."

Viana waited patiently, albeit confusedly so, as she and Tristin held Grimmond's shoulders.

"Tristin, you were right about me," Grimmond continued apologetically. "And Viana, I'm sorry for how I've acted toward you...not just with Sariah, but this whole year...."

Viana looked away painfully and parted her lips to speak, but Grimmond grabbed her hand.

"Please, you both have to listen!" he begged. "I just got back from the Nightmayr Realm."

"*WHAT?*" his friends said in unison.

Grimmond nodded, still catching his breath.

"Boogey gave me a black candle," he said. "I saw Kremaya again. She told me I have to find the door before it's too late! She was *so close* to telling me where it was…but I'm pretty sure my mom was warning me to leave, and then the Ending came and I barely got away again —"

"*Whoa* — hang on," Viana interrupted. "Kremaya, as in, the Nightmare that broke you out of jail? She *knows* where the door is?"

"That's the one," Grimmond answered. "She said a boy had it, and that it was *near*. But she couldn't tell me exactly where before the Ending showed up and I had to smash the candle!"

Tristin rose back up, raising his hands in surrendered confusion.

"You've got to slow down, Grim!" he implored. "I don't get it. Your mom's alive, and she's *with* the Ending?"

Grimmond exhaled deeply as Viana helped him to his feet.

"The Ending took my mom because it *needs me*!" Grimmond answered. "Guys, *I am* the k—"

He didn't finish his sentence as a long, blasting wail sounded around them.

"Ahh!" Grimmond grunted, covering his ears. "What *is that*?"

Viana's face paled.

"That's the Howl of the Hollow," she breathed. "The call to arms for every Nightmarist here!"

"Look!" Tristin said, pointing outside. "Something's happening in the Orchard!"

Rushing to the Fire Watch's windows, the three friends looked out over the grounds. A torrent of lights like ghostly fire was spreading around the woods surrounding them. Already Gargoyles were taking flight from the stable towers to find their riders, and Nightmarists within the Hovel were hurrying outside to form a perimeter beyond the Bottomless Chasm.

"It's the Nightmares," Grimmond breathed. "Cyto and Plasm just picked them up on the Dread Map! They've completely surrounded the Hollow and they're coming in! Because *both* the key and the door are here!"

Tristin and Viana ran to where their armor leaned against the wall. Grimmond reached for his glaive, but was dismayed to find his other weapon missing. He quickly searched the floor and his other pockets.

"My bright knuckles!" Grimmond said, "I don't have them!"

"Then get another pair from the Armory," Viana said, strapping her vest. "Come on!"

"No, wait," Grimmond remembered, "I bet I dropped them in my room when I tripped. That's closer — I'll meet you atop the tower in two minutes!"

"Well, hurry UP!" Tristin said, running toward the stairs with Viana. "We've gotta get the Black Wings up, NOW!"

Scolding himself for his carelessness, Grimmond felt rather vulnerable as he ran back to his room. Already the distant screeches of Prowlers and Brutes, and the deep wails of the hungry Sangmanger were heard.

How did they get through the mist?

Nearly knocking the door off its hinges, Grimmond burst into his room to find the last person he expected.

"GRIMMOND!"

"Sariah?"

Her face was filled with anxiety as she hopped up from his bed and hurried to the door. She tried to hug him, but Grimmond gently grabbed her by the shoulders instead to look in her eyes.

"I've been searching *everywhere* for you!" she said.

"My bright knuckles, Sariah — I came back for them, have you seen —"

"They're here," she offered quickly, producing a pair from her back pocket and handing them over. "I'm so relieved to see you...I thought the Nightmares might have already gotten to you."

"Gotten to me?" Grimmond asked wildly, clutching his chest and bending over. "*Don't you know* what's going on? That alarm means the Hollow has been breached! We're in trouble, and everyone's waiting on us!"

"You don't know the half of it," Sariah said in return. "I've been staying out of sight until I could find you — Grimmond, you *have* to come with me."

She grabbed his hands and tried to pull him toward the door, but Grimmond released himself.

"No, Sariah — the Black Wings are waiting *on us*," he clarified. "We've got to mount up and protect the Hollow!"

"The Nightmares will break through the defenses," she said adamantly, "and there's nothing we can do about that now. But we *can* do something about the door. It's right here in the Hovel, Grimmond, and *I know where!*"

Grimmond steadied himself against the doorframe.

"You know exactly where it is?" he asked in wonder.

"Yes!"

"Then, come on! We have to find Lord Stawlart and Professor Manning so they can help!"

Pushing past her, Grimmond ran down the stairs. Sariah followed him at a near sprint, all the while trying to stop him.

"There's no time for this, Grimmond!" she yelled over the screeches and rumbles coming from outside. "The attack is about to begin! We have to do this ourselves!"

But Grimmond didn't listen, and when the stairs leveled out, he turned toward the Dread Map room.

"Stop, Grimmond!" Sariah shouted, amplifying her voice to a shriek. "We have to save your mother now, or SHE'LL BE LOST FOREVER!"

Grimmond almost tripped as he slowed and turned in disbelief.

"You *know* about my mother?"

"I know she's a prisoner of the Nightmayr Realm!" Sariah continued to yell. "*She's not dead*, like everyone thinks!"

Grimmond's emotions flared with hope. There was nothing in the world that he wanted more than to find his mother, and beg forgiveness for that night ten years ago.

"*How* do you know this?" he gasped.

"This is your last chance to save her," Sariah quieted, reaching a hand up to his face. "Or the Nightmares will take you themselves, finally kill her, and release the Dark Naught upon this entire world! Now follow me!"

Sariah turned in the direction opposite the Dread Map room, and sprinted away. With only a moment of deliberation, Grimmond chased after her. Winding through halls and passages, Sariah took Grimmond to a corner of the Hovel that he'd never been before. It was nearly black as Sariah stopped in front of a simple door.

Grimmond's excitement mounted, he felt for his glaive, and slipped his bright knuckles over his fingers. They felt foreign in his hand, but it was too dark for him to look at them.

"This is it?" Grimmond asked through his labored breaths. "This is the door to the Nightmayr Realm?"

"The way to finish this," Sariah answered, "is in there. Go!"

Holding his breath, Grimmond pushed open the door and rushed into a small, dark room.

He waited for his eyes to adjust to a sky of black light, glowing buildings and creatures. But he saw nothing; this *wasn't* the Nightmayr Realm that the black candle had taken him to. When Grimmond noticed the wide window in front of him, and saw the Gargoyle Squadrons and shrieking Nightmares beyond it, he knew he was still inside the Hovel.

"Something's wrong, Sariah," Grimmond said over his shoulder. "This isn't it...."

The door slammed shut, and Grimmond twirled around to see Malus Nebbick, a look of hungry murder in his eyes. Sariah stood behind him, expressionless, as Malus withdrew an ancient and ornate doorknob from his pocket, its long stem sharpened to a point like a railroad spike.

"Sariah, *LOOK OUT!*"

She remained unreadable for only another moment. Then, she crossed her arms, leaned against the wall, and spoke.

"Get on with it."

Her eyes flashed purple, and Grimmond's head spun with revelation.

Malus's face stretched into an insane smile as he rushed forward, the doorknob clutched tightly. Grimmond leveled his fist at Malus's face, tried to concentrate, and attempted a bright blue Flare. But nothing happened.

As if watching from above, Grimmond heard his breath catch in surprise, and felt the piercing pressure of the spike slide into his heart. He blinked once, then twice as he backed away, staring from the doorknob in his chest to Sariah's face.

"Looks like I gave you the wrong pair of knuckles, Grimmond Errandi," she said quietly. "But look at it this way: at least now you understand."

Grimmond recalled Kremaya's words as he fell to his knees.

'Don't trust the pretty girl.'

Sariah averted her eyes as Malus approached, dropped to Grimmond's level, and turned the knob in his heart. A thunderous noise cracked, like the reopening of a sealed tomb, and an arched door exploded into existence. Wide-eyed,

Grimmond turned to see the black light seeping through its edges and cracks, then looked back to the glowing blue object in his chest.

The door opened. Tendrils of shadow tried to pull him in, but Grimmond gripped Malus's chest, eyes full of fear.

"For all the years," Malus spat. "All the years *your* forefathers imprisoned mine…they can finally be at peace."

Shoving Grimmond's hands away and standing to his feet, Malus kicked Grimmond through the open door.

Grimmond fell through bright blue light, and landed beneath the black-lit sky that he dreaded to see.

Rolling across the top of a tall, squishy gray hill he came to a stop, only to rise to his feet in shaking pain. The air was cold and smelled of rot around him. He gazed to his chest, all the more horrified: the glowing handle and long spike were still sticking out from his heart. It hadn't killed him yet.

At least, he didn't *feel* dead.

Frantically he stumbled to the edge of the hill he was on, but couldn't go beyond it. He looked down to its base, toward the sounds of echoing shrieks and wails, and saw what made them. His heart began to race even faster than it was before.

Stretched wide on a dark plain, as far as he could see, was an innumerable horde of Nightmares.

Clanging and roaring, they pushed against a crosshatch of white light that fell from the sky all the way to the ground. Cracks formed in it here and there, and Grimmond watched as several Nightmares jumped through them before the cracks closed up again. Grimmond understood where he was.

Malus had cast him into the Nightmayr Realm.

And he was looking at the veil that separated it from the human world.

Tendrils of shadow reached out from the darkness to turn Grimmond around. Without understanding how, he was suddenly in the center of a raised platform, fifty feet across, and in the midst of the Nightmares. He didn't bother pulling out his glaive or Sariah's useless bright knuckles; he wouldn't last more than a few seconds if he fought. But the creatures parted, and Grimmond looked to the corner to see shimmering black mist.

Kremaya.

The jail-breaker hovered around a defeated-looking Nightmare, who looked strangely beautiful and sad. Kremaya then turned her three eyes behind the platform — to something Grimmond hadn't yet seen through the darkness — and the Nightmares quieted their noises. One of Kremaya's eyes slowly turned back to Grimmond. For once, Grimmond saw no wickedness or mirth in it, but fear.

A black pillar like a cloud approached.

Grimmond's racing heart stumbled at the sight, and was filled with dread. Even with his heightened eyesight he couldn't see what was in it. The pillar was more than darkness; it was the absence of light, a void that eradicated anything good.

Is that the Ending?

But the Ending came hovering in from a different side of the platform. Grimmond swallowed when he saw not just one, but a dozen more Endings behind it. Thirteen skull-like faces surrounded the platform, every bone-white hand stretched toward Grimmond as they slowly closed in. If they were there, then what was inside the black pillar?

Grimmond's chest throbbed as he used every word possible to Lull the Endings, but only succeeded in growing weaker. He even put on Sariah's fake bright knuckles and tried to think of the dark orchestra, but nothing happened. At last shadowy tendrils reached out from the pillar, latched around the knob in Grimmond's chest, and lifted him up.

The pain was unbearable as the pillar sapped the remaining strength from Grimmond's heart.

He thought his screeching vocal chords would explode. He screamed so loudly that he hardly noticed the blue light bleeding from his fingers and chest, flowing into the shadowy tendrils. When the pain at last relented, no music, defiance or happiness was a thought in his mind.

Only words that ripped through his eardrums to be etched inside his brain:

"His Nightmare heart is ready, but his human heart must be broken before it can be made use of. Behold, my servants, the last Errandi falls before the Dark Naught."

The crowd of watching Nightmares around Grimmond roared deafeningly, and the thirteen Endings and Kremaya bowed before the pillar.

What…is this…Nightmare heart? Human heart?

Still emanating an otherworldly beauty and sadness, the Nightmare prostrated at Kremaya's feet cried out in torment.

"NO! YOU CAN'T!" the ethereal thing sobbed. "Not that beautiful boy…*not again*…."

"Quiet, Muse!" Kremaya hissed urgently.

Did one of her eyes just wink at Grimmond?

"BEGIN."

"Yes, Master," hissed one of the Endings. *"We will not fail you as did the Nightmare of Lost Love. You will consume the human world once again. This time, the Dark Naught will reign forever."*

With its own shadowy tendril, the Ending lifted Grimmond like a fish on a hook.

Grimmond came level with its empty eye sockets; this was the Ending from that night ten years ago. The same from Custom House Tower, and the same that had been tricked into a bargain by his mother. The other twelve Endings surrounded Grimmond, and all thirteen then hissed together.

"Your worst nightmare remembers you. We shall watch together, and your eyes will not close. Your heart will break; your mind will shatter. Face your Ending, final Errandi, and release us with your death."

The Ending that held Grimmond placed two bony hands on his face, and opened its mouth and eye sockets as wide as a tunnel. The rest of them followed suit, and uncontrollably, Grimmond's eyelids stretched until it was painful. He watched as a vision appeared within the Ending's face, ten years in the past — the night his parents were killed. Grimmond watched himself as a six-year-old boy, after the concert at the Hatch Memorial Shell.

He remembered fully what happened now, and could see it clearly.

"No," Grimmond moaned. "Please, don't...*don't* make me do it again...."

He tried to close his eyes or roll them back into his head, but they were stuck open and forward against his will. He was helpless, and looked on at the hazy vision of his father and mother walking him through Boston Public Garden.

"We should go see Grandpa Errandi," Christopher said wistfully. *"The cemetery's not far, Misty. It's been too long."*

She sighed, slowing her pace and smiling back at her husband as she took her son's free hand.

"I know, Chris," she said sweetly, *"but you're already dragging Grinny as it is...."*

Grimmond's parents laughed and smiled, more in love with each other than ever as they half-carried, half-dragged their son through the garden. They approached the church and fence of the cemetery behind it, when six-year-old Grimmond tugged on his father's pants to speak.

"Can we get ice cream?"

"It's too late for that, buddy," Christopher answered. *"Maybe next time, if we get out of the concert earlier."*

He tried his mother next.

"Mom, I want ice cream!"

"Your father's told you, dear, it's too late," Misty agreed. *"But how about some hot pancakes first thing in the morning? Does that sound good?"*

Instead of agreeing, six-year-old Grimmond looked up angrily at his mother. In his sleepy, petulant, and heart-of-a-Nightmare rage, he began to yell and stomp his feet.

"I WANT ice cream!"

"That's enough, Grinny," Misty said firmly. *"Not tonight."*

"I HATE you!" he suddenly screamed.

"Grimmond!" Christopher scolded, quickly turning and picking him up. *"Do not talk to your mother that way! Ever! Do you understand me?"*

Misty was silent and expressionless as she looked at her son, but six-year-old Grimmond continued.

"I JUST WANT ICE CREAM!"

"NO!" Christopher responded. *"You've been told more than enough. Now you don't get any dessert for a week!"*

Six-year-old Grimmond balled his fists, breathing heavily. The Grimmond whose eyes were peeled open, looking into the past, begged his memory to be wrong, but he knew what was about to be said. The last words he would ever say to his parents.

"I wish you were both DEAD!" he yelled.

Christopher almost dropped him in shock as he placed him on the ground, and the eyes of the Grimmond in the present brimmed with tears. He looked at the vision of his heartbroken mother, seeing and remembering the shimmer of her nightmarish blue eyes. It scared him to look into them, but Grimmond still had no control.

From the corner of his mind, he heard Kremaya shushing her sobbing captive.

"Someday, my son, we will be dead," Misty whispered, coming down to the six-year-old Grimmond's level. *"Then you'll have your wish...."*

Grimmond's peeled eyes were almost popping out of his head as he wept.

"Oh no, Mom! *MOM!*" he screamed in the Ending's face. "I didn't mean it! You KNOW I didn't mean it...DON'T GO!"

The vision of his mother stood back up, and stepped with her son into the cemetery. The air quickly changed, and Grimmond watched as a single Ending appeared amongst the tombstones. His father yelled for them to run, but the Ending turned to Misty and spoke.

"The descendant of those who sealed us away still breathes. You have failed to kill the last Errandi. You are forfeit. The task will now be done before your eyes."

The Ending lashed out against Christopher, slashing him several times, then stretched its face wide to reveal his worst nightmare: the slaughter of his family. Falling to the ground, Christopher's mind was addled as he watched Misty launched into a tombstone and fall into a bloody heap. Her face split apart, and Grimmond saw the glowing skeleton beneath her skin when he ran to her, along with the bright blue fluid trickling through his fingers and onto the ground.

Turning to six-year-old Grimmond, the Ending raised its bone-white hands, and a shimmering, bluish-white light was drawn from his chest. Grimmond felt his heart in real time, too.

The Ending on the platform was plunging the doorknob further into him, and began to turn.

Agonizing pain renewed, a new door exploded behind Grimmond and rose up from the platform. But instead of black light lining the edges of the door, this time it was lit by a shimmering, bluish-white light, and Grimmond knew: this door was made *from* him.

At long last, the door and Grimmond together had provided a way to release what was held captive in the Nightmayr Realm. The black pillar moved toward it.

"YES!"

"Dad...*Mom*...." Grimmond choked in pain as he watched the opening door. "I'm sorry...."

A scream suddenly filled his ears as Kremaya charged into the circle of Endings.

"AACCHHHH!"

She knocked him from the Ending's grip, and in a flash of blue, Kremaya's Muse rushed into Grimmond and lifted him away from the platform.

Roars of upheaval split the air as Grimmond was whisked away, further and higher across the dark plain. The door of bright blue trailed weightlessly behind him, a projection of his life force still waiting to be used; it was like a beacon, and Grimmond knew they wouldn't escape for long.

Beneath the bruised colors of the sky, he looked up at the thing carrying him: it *was* a woman. Her skin was nearly gossamer as she looked into his face, and Grimmond saw the nightmarish blue eyes he once knew so well. She set him down in an open field of dead nothingness. The black, purple and blue horizon looked hauntingly beautiful, and Grimmond knew why he liked it.

"Mom!"

Grimmond wrapped the wispy frame of his mother in a tight embrace, and she spoke in a soft, otherworldly voice in return.

"You must go, Grimmond," Misty said. "I've bought you as much time as I could, but you have to go back to your world."

"I *can't*, Mom," Grimmond returned. *"Not without you!"*

She wiped the bluish-white tears of light falling from his eyes as he cried.

"That's not my world, my boy," she said. "It never was. But it *is* yours."

"Don't say that, Mom!" Grimmond held her tighter. "I'm sorry for what I said...for what I d-did to you! I *killed* you both! I murdered my own p-parents...."

Grimmond sobbed as his mother held him.

"My sweet boy, our doom was not your fault!" she admonished softly. "You *must move on* from your guilt...your father and I were victims of our own actions, not yours. Your words hurt, yes, but they did not kill us. You were forgiven for them before we even entered that cemetery...."

A thunder rumbled in the distance: the black pillar was coming. Misty placed a hand over Grimmond's chest.

"Oh, my *heart*...you can never come back here. We must get you through the door, then reseal it, or the woven veil restraining the Nightmayr Realm will come undone. The Dark

Naught will escape; it will return to your world and make its war to consume the light within it. We must hurry."

The black pillar that was the Dark Naught thundered closer, shrieking Endings behind it.

"There has to be another way to get you out of here!"

"You are more than the Nightmare of Lost Love ever deserved," Misty said, tears forming in her own eyes. "I was sent to murder the last Errandi, your father, but he loved me even after finding me out. And still he gave me you. I'll *always* have you. Remember that, my beautiful boy...."

The Dark Naught outpaced the Endings, only a short distance from Grimmond now.

"We'll have only seconds after I separate your heart from the door, and I'll close it when you pass through. Remember the lullaby I taught you when you were a boy? Use its light to destroy the doorknob from your side, and the Nightmayr Realm will be sealed."

Grimmond shook his head.

"I can't Flare...I don't have my bright knuckles! *And I can't leave you!*"

"You don't need bright knuckles to create light, my son — you never did!" she called over the resounding chaos of the Dark Naught. "Nor do you need me!"

Misty gripped the doorknob, turned it the opposite way the Ending had, and abruptly yanked it from Grimmond's chest. Grimmond buckled in pain, but didn't fall as she handed the knob to him. The shape of the door immediately began to flicker and fade, but the Dark Naught had arrived.

Shadowy tendrils shot out toward Misty, but an intense blue light rushed back from her, keeping the tendrils at bay.

"GO NOW!"

Grimmond concentrated on the lullaby his mother used to put him to sleep as a little boy. He thought of only his parents and their love, and together he and his mother made a light so bright that the Dark Naught was pushed back still further. But Misty's body slowly began to be drawn away into the black pillar.

"MOM!"

A shadowy tendril latched onto Grimmond's leg, pulling him away from the door as it tried to push through Misty's fading blue light.

"You're my little Nightmare, Grinny," she whispered, *"and I love you more than anything."*

In a final flash of light, she rushed forward and shoved Grimmond through the door.

TRUE COLORS

Grimmond came into the lights and sounds of the Hovel, crashing onto the floor of the small room.

The doorknob fell from his grasp to clatter across the wooden planks, and he looked up into four very stunned, very surprised faces. Tristin's and Viana's were the more horrified, their glaives already extended and leveled at Malus and Sariah, as they put the pieces of what happened together.

Shadowy black tendrils began to reach through the open doorway behind Grimmond, and the room went into flurried chaos. With a shout, Malus and Sariah leapt for the rolling doorknob, while the others tried to keep them at bay. Tristin held Malus off, but Viana was thrown powerfully backwards.

Grimmond crawled across the floor, hardly able to think of his mother's lullaby over the tumult and Dark Naught trying to escape. Reaching beneath a table, he grasped the doorknob in both hands, concentrated with all his might, and Flared the bluish-white light that burned within him.

Though untamed and unfocused, the glowing doorway in the center of the room began to flicker.

"NOOOO!"

Grimmond didn't stop until the ornate knob blackened and smoldered in his hands. The Dark Naught's tendrils were sucked back into the open door, and Grimmond scurried over and kicked it shut with his foot. He stopped Flaring as the glowing door faded into the air, and he again dropped the knob on the floor.

Malus yelled but recovered quickly, then stooped to the floor to dodge around Tristin's arms and fled from the room. Sariah tried to closely follow, but Viana stuck out her glaive and tripped her. Sariah fell headlong, and her skull cracked sickeningly against the wall.

When the planks beneath Sariah's head glistened red, Grimmond was sure she was dead.

"We have to get Malus!" Tristin yelled. "Come on!"

Grimmond staggered to his feet only to bend over in pain, recovering his breath and watching the blue, light-like fluid pour from the hole in his heart.

"GRIM!" Viana cried, rushing over. "You — you're hurt...I *think....*"

"It's — *cough* — nothing," he choked, "Tristin's right, we have to go after Malus!"

"Grim," Tristin said incredulously. "Did I just see you Flare *without* bright knuckles?"

Tristin and Viana stared at Grimmond in wonder, just before Sariah stood up behind them.

"He's a *NIGHTMARE*, you idiots!"

Grimmond looked at her, red blood mixing with the purple light pouring from her cracked skull.

"Just like you," Grimmond panted.

"Just like me...."

Sariah smiled in confirmation, then ran toward the window to leap and crash through it. She landed on the Nerve-Neck waiting for her, and took off into the night.

Dazed and reeling, Grimmond stumbled over to the window to see the battle rage. Bodies and glowing blood littered the grounds like wet confetti, and flashes of colored light, reverberating Lulls, and shrieks of Nightmares filled the air. Grimmond's pain and sadness were kindled to anger.

The edges of his vision turned bluish-white, and he felt his eyes begin to glow like his mother's. Grimmond thought closing the door would stop the fighting, banishing all Nightmares from the human world. But it *hadn't* worked.

Sparks of light danced at Grimmond's fingertips, and Tristin and Viana stepped away.

What had gone wrong? Was his mother not able to close the door on the other side? Grimmond shouted out the window at the top of his lungs.

"BRAX!"

"Grim?" Viana questioned apprehensively. "What're you going to do? You're still bleeding that *stuff* pretty badly...."

"Doesn't matter," Grimmond grunted, turning toward her and clutching his chest. "I'm not going to stand here and watch, even if it kills me —"

"LOOK OUT!" Tristin yelled.

As he tackled Grimmond and Viana to the floor, the window frame and wall were blasted inward. Flynn's battering-ram-of-a-head protruded into the room with a deep growl. Brax and Nelton weren't able to fit in with him, but Nelton poked his head past the wreckage.

"Apologies," said Nelton. "The Blood Onyx seemed most anxious to answer your call."

Grimmond picked Viana off the floor and turned toward the Gargoyles. The pain in his heart hurt, but it was nothing more than a leaky faucet. He knew he could still fight.

This is my world now...this is MY Hollow....

"Let's finish this," Grimmond said.

He leapt through the rubble and onto Brax's back, relishing the ability to fly as he clutched a hand to his chest. They flew away from the Hovel, searching for the remainder of the Black

Wings amongst the fighting. But with Grimmond's racing heart, the Hollow was brighter than ever to his eyes.

The Aurora Blights defended the area by Hollow Dwell, the Bone Crawlers the north side of the Hovel by Marrow Mansion, and the Sleepwalkers by Narcoleptic Row. Viana cried out, and Grimmond raked his gaze to where she pointed. At the bridge that crossed the Bottomless Chasm, Grimmond saw Coach Maurs, Dr. Knight, and the Gargremlins fighting an Atrocity.

Grimmond descended with Brax like a meteor.

Raising his empty fists, he concentrated hard, and didn't see when the Blood Onyx's eyes and mouth began to glow bluish-white with him. In a screaming light the Atrocity was then irradiated like an ant beneath a magnifying glass, Flared from both Grimmond's fists and Brax's mouth. Its arms and legs writhed until Brax crashed into it, knocking the Atrocity off the bridge and into the chasm.

"*GRIM!*" Tristin yelled as Brax pulled back up. "What the *HECK* was that?"

"I don't know!" Grimmond wildly shouted back. "Come on! We've gotta find the Squadron!"

Grimmond, Tristin and Viana circled high once again, spotting Drek and the Red Team at the edge of the Sleepless Orchard. Just past Narcoleptic Row, the Blue Team swept into the fray. Flynn bowled into Prowlers attacking a group of young Nightmarists, Viana Flared bright green and red through Nelton's wings, and Brax crunched his giant jaws into another Atrocity.

The Black Wings and Sleepwalkers became a force of lights, Lulls, and slashing weapons.

Grimmond dismounted Brax and extended his glaive toward a Sangmanger. With the glowing purple blade, he dodged and sliced back and forth, gashing the blood-bloated Nightmare until it was draining like a water tank. In a few moments, it shrank down to nothing but a flopping pile of skin, and Grimmond cut its head off.

Dripping with Sangmanger blood, Grimmond looked to a group of Brutes. Concentrating on nothing but his mother's lullaby, Grimmond boomed *'PÆCIEF!'* and a Lull like a shockwave emanated from him. He didn't grow nauseous as every Brute near him was stunned, then cut down by a dozen blades or burned up by the swooping Rebbigones. But more Nightmares still came, and the defenders were pushed back to reform in front of Grisly Grove.

"STEADY, ALL!" Drek called from beside Grimmond.

Invigorating battle music reached Grimmond's ears, and at first he thought it was his imagination.

But burning white candles began to rise above the Grove behind him, singing like a thousand-strong choir. Corpse-skeletons then staggered out from the Sentrees, cut free from their nooses, and in their midst swirled a dark gray fog, echoing with laughter and white eyes.

The Boogey Man had arrived.

The gray fog touched down, and with it Professor Manning's human form. Scores of enemy Prowlers, Haunters, and Totals rushed toward the Hollow's defenders, but Professor Manning signaled with a ready hand. A hundred singing candles turned black and shot forward like arrows, and the struck attackers disappeared into swirling shadow.

"Grimmond!" the man called. "You're needed elsewhere!"

Grimmond focused his eyes to where Professor Manning pointed: Sariah was flying for the mist across the lake, with Malus beside her on his Bone Crawler.

"We've got it from here!" Professor Manning called again, a shadow from his own body swallowing a group of enemy Terrors. "GO!"

Corpse-skeletons behind Grimmond rushed forward, and another volley of black candles shot up Narcoleptic Row. Out of Professor Manning's gray fog then rushed massive white-eyed beasts, echoing in laughter, and followed by the black-and-orange Lightwarts, ten times their usual size and rumbling like foghorns.

"KILL-IT, KILL-IT!

Grimmond called for Brax, jumped onto his back, and raced toward the lake.

Flying fast, Grimmond reached Malus first, and raised his fist to blast him out of the sky. But before he could concentrate, Sariah's Nerve-Neck veered to crash into them. Wildly she launched herself at Grimmond, unseating him, and together they tumbled through the air.

They crashed into the water, but Grimmond was able to surface quickly, albeit gasping for breath. He treaded the green water angrily, watching as Malus flew into the mist. Watching until Malus was completely gone.

Although flooded with rage, Grimmond wondered when Sariah didn't likewise surface. Being a Nightmare, could she drown?

Making his choice, he took a deep breath and sank beneath the water.

A few moments later he held onto a coughing and sputtering Sariah, and Brax plucked them out of the water. Grimmond heard a loud roar of victory echoing across the grounds as Brax dropped them on the shore. The battle was over, and the Nightmarists had won.

Extending his glaive, Grimmond held it to Sariah's throat.

"Who are you?" he started.

"The one who — *cough* — came to finish the job!" she sputtered.

Grimmond lowered his glaive and raised his fist against her chest instead.

"Your *name*, and why you're here," he grunted, his fingers beginning to glow, "before I get impatient."

"It's *Zuielle*," she growled. "And I came to fix Malus Nebbick's repeated failures. To bring down the last Errandi — what your mother couldn't do to your father! The Endings thought they completed the job in the cemetery that night, but they didn't know the *Nightmare of Lost Love* herself had a son to continue the line! Not until after she tricked them by invoking the bargain of seventy sevens!"

"Tell me what's so important about being the last Errandi," Grimmond demanded. "Why do the Endings want me dead?"

"You really don't know, do you?" Zuielle asked.

Brax growled, and Grimmond's fingers grew brighter. A bit of light flashed out to lick the imposter's neck.

"The Dark Naught was trapped in the Nightmayr Realm at a cost!" she continued painfully. "Your ancestors had to use a number of Nightmarists in order to do it, but not all sacrificed were willing. The Endings were those sacrificed to imprison the Dark Naught. But now they can't die — the Dark Naught won't allow it. Not until they've killed the last Errandi. Then, it can return to this world."

"And that's why I was the key this whole time?" Grimmond asked.

"Do not be mistaken — there is a key to the door," Zuielle continued, breathing heavily, "but your unique heart brought about an unforeseen opportunity. The Dark Naught is an Incarnate: the Nightmare of Darkness; the oldest fear of mankind. With your heart, being both of this world *and* the Nightmayr Realm, the Dark Naught could use it to likewise live in both...it could come and go as it pleased from the Nightmayr Realm once again."

Grimmond clutched his chest. It was still sore from the ripped-out doorknob, though already less so.

"How's your Nightmare heart?" Zuielle asked. "Empty?"

Grimmond ignored her.

"Where do *you* fit into all this?" he returned.

"I am my master's servant, nothing more. My task wasn't to kill you, but to bring you to the Nightmayr Realm. Do with me as you wish, for my obligation to my master is done: I *did* bring you there. Now…now I don't know what will become of me."

"How about I send you back right now to find out?" Grimmond said.

He lowered his glaive to her neck again, and his fingertips ignited more brightly. Zuielle breathed heavily and closed her eyes, but Grimmond didn't plan on killing her. After he hopped back on Brax's back, the Blood Onyx picked her up and they flew to the Hovel.

Brax dropped them at the bridge and Zuielle collapsed on the ground, still coughing up water from the lake. Olivia was there with the Aurora Blights, and the Skeleton Crew likewise began to trickle in. Before Grimmond could leave to search out the Black Wings, they landed on the bridge with Tristin and Viana, and Drek dismounted to approach Zuielle.

"I knew there was something wrong with you, Sariah!" Drek shouted wildly, apparently having been filled in by Tristin and Viana.

"Easy, Drek," Grimmond said, clutching his chest. "The real Sariah's been dead for a while now. All the same, maybe its best if we let someone aside from us handle her."

Drek looked confused, but Grimmond went on.

"She needs to be taken into the Hovel," Grimmond continued, "but watched with a whole team."

"On it, Scylent," said Captain Ulrecht humbly. "Seems like my Ward has some making up to do."

The rest of the Skeleton Crew approached Zuielle with her, along with Randy Planch. He had a slight limp and cut across his face, but Grimmond was relieved to find him still standing. A new round of cheers went up around the Hollow, but Grimmond didn't feel right, even as Professor Manning appeared behind him and clasped a hand on his shoulder.

"Come along," he said, "I'll have a go at plugging up that hole in your chest."

Stanchions Hollow stood tall, despite the damage inflicted on it during the battle.

Though losing many of its own Minor and Major Nightmares, between the Squadrons, professors, and remainder of the Nightmarists, the Hollow successfully thwarted the attack from the Nightmayr Realm. And after Grimmond explained what he knew, Lord Stawlart understood that it was Malus Nebbick who had been guiding the Nightmares through the mist.

One day after the battle, finishing his aerial survey of the Hollow, Grimmond dropped Brax at the stable towers, then went to the infirmary to check on the injured. It was full of patients, though no Nightmarists died, and Grimmond even received a respectful nod from Dr. Knight.

He next went to Professor Manning's classroom.

"So, you found out what you needed to in the Nightmayr Realm," he said as he checked Grimmond's bandage. "Was that on the first trip, or the second one?"

Grimmond narrowed his eyebrows, annoyed.

"Do you mean to say, when you tricked me into going there with the black candle?" Grimmond asked. "Or when Malus Nebbick stabbed me in the heart?"

"I don't recall advising you to Flare *black* light to ignite the candle," Professor Manning said. "I didn't think you had that in you, even with your, eh, let's call it *'darker'* side...."

Grimmond huffed, pulling his shirt back down when his bandage was changed.

"I found out things on both trips," he answered. "The Endings were only after me because of the Dark Naught. Without the real key to let it out of the Nightmayr Realm, it was trying to use my heart — a heart of both worlds — in order to escape. But you already knew all that. Didn't you: *Uncle Boogey?*"

Professor Manning's white eyes swirled, but he raised his eyebrows and smiled.

"This has been your journey from the start, not mine, nephew," he answered. "But exactly when did you figure *that* part out?"

"Zuielle — the Nightmare impersonating Sariah — said my mom failed to kill my dad," Grimmond went on. "I remembered the way you talked about your little sister: her falling in love with a boy, you driving her away, and her being gone before you could make up."

Professor Manning smiled, impressed.

"And even though Eralynn never wanted you and I to talk, she took me to you when the Atrocity wounded me. The blue light pouring from my side wasn't from the Atrocity's barb, it was from *me*...Keith Tychus understood, too, right before he died. Eralynn didn't want to risk Dr. Knight and the rest of the Hollow finding out."

Folding his hands, Professor Manning spoke.

"Eralynn and Lord Stawlart *both* knew your mother was a Nightmare, of course," Professor Manning answered, "but they say that my sister made them promise not to tell you. Do not make my same mistakes, and harbor new evils in your heart against them."

Grimmond stood up from his seat, and looked around the dark classroom awkwardly.

"What *did* happen between you and my mom, anyway?"

"Like Sariah — *Zuielle* — went after you, so the Dark Naught sent my sister from the Nightmayr Realm to infiltrate Stanchions Hollow. When I at last found her out, there was nothing I could do to deter her. Even when I warned your father of the plot to kill him, he did not heed me. Then, inexplicably, the two fools fell in love and your arrival was announced. From there, I made further mistakes. But, here we are...."

Grimmond remained quiet as his newfound uncle spoke.

"Now a question for you, nephew," Professor Manning said. "You overcame the Endings of the Nightmayr Realm, yes? How did you defeat your greatest fear?"

"I didn't defeat it, Uncle Boogey," Grimmond said slowly. "I was forced to face it: the guilt of my parents' death. My whole life...I always believed that *I* was the one who killed them — like I *summoned* that Ending with my wish...but it's not a mystery to me anymore. I know what really happened, and I can fight against my guilt now, for as long as it haunts me."

Professor Manning smiled, commending him.

"You're learning."

Grimmond started hesitantly.

"If I'm your nephew, why did Eralynn raise me instead of you?"

Professor Manning shifted uncomfortably, but spoke gently.

"And how do you think a Nightmare would turn out if raised by the Boogey Man, Grimmond?"

"But you're not the *real* Boogey Man," Grimmond rebounded.

"Am I not?"

His eyes changed from white to black, and he filled the room with shadows. Grimmond stepped back until Professor Manning laughed and returned to normal. Grimmond thanked him for changing the bandage, then turned to leave.

"If you wish," Professor Manning said, "this summer, I can show you a few more tricks that your average Nightmarist would be afraid to try."

Grimmond agreed, made for the door once more, but then thought of a final question.

"Uncle Boogey?" Grimmond asked. "What's *your* greatest fear?"

Smiling, the man replied, spreading his arms wide.

"Why, the *dark*, of course."

Grimmond found his friends helping to clean up the rubble outside the Hovel.

It was strange to see them all awake during the daylight, but everyone's schedule had been hopelessly off track. Tristin was talking energetically to Olivia Tychus, working alongside Viana and a few others Grimmond knew. But when his friends saw him crossing the bridge, they anxiously came over to hear the latest news.

"So," Viana began nervously. "The *real* Sariah is dead?"

"Yeah," Grimmond answered her, "back in Boston. Olivia saw it happen."

Tristin and Viana both looked at the ground a moment as Olivia nodded gravely, confirmed in their pre-discussed fear.

"I'm really sorry, guys," Grimmond went on quietly. "The girl locked in the Hovel is named Zuielle...she was sent here for me. Just another Nightmare looking to get my heart surgically removed. Now that she failed, she's kind of in the same boat as my mom was: a Nightmare without a mission."

The group remained silent, until Tristin shot Grimmond a look.

"And?" Tristin said. "Can we see it?"

"Actually, I'd love some coffee, first."

"Oh, me too, I'm dying!" Viana said. "We'll go, but don't say anything important until we get back!"

As Viana and Olivia ran across the bridge to get drinks, Tristin turned back to him.

"All right, monster," he said with a smile. "Shirt up!"

Grimmond did as directed, lifting his shirt and peeling away the bandage over his heart. The shimmering blue hole where Malus had punctured his chest was revealed. Tristin poked it.

"OW!" Grimmond cried out, replacing the bandage and lowering his shirt. "I'm still *mostly* human, with a recovering hole in my chest, you ass!"

"Are you sure?" Tristin tried to poke him again, but Grimmond swatted his hand away.

"Yes!" Grimmond asserted, sparks shooting from his fingertips. "Don't make me have Brax eat you!"

Tristin laughed raucously, and for the first time in what felt like years, Grimmond joined him. He felt *allowed* to join him. He was allowed to have fun, to have a life, to be at peace. At last.

Mom, Dad, wherever you are...thank you. I'm gonna try to move on now, okay? If I'm able....

Tristin quieted after a few moments, then looked toward the bridge and scratched his head.

"See here, mate," he said awkwardly. "Just curious, and don't take anything by this, but...you and Olivia. You guys never...*you know*...right?"

"Huh?"

"You and Olivia," he tried again, kicking his feet against the carcass of a dead Brute. "You two never actually *hung out*, did you?"

Grimmond knew exactly what his friend was asking, but decided to milk it just for fun.

"Well, yeah," Grimmond said brightly. "We had our 101 classes together at a minimum, so sure."

"Oh, come *on*!" Tristin at last shouted in frustration. "Did you ever kiss her or not?"

Grimmond laughed.

"No," he replied. "Never kissed, never held hands, nothing. I meant what I said on the stable towers the other day. I feel responsible for her, in a way…but now that you mention it, she *is* kind of cute, isn't she?"

Grimmond dodged an attempted chest-poke once again, and threatened to extend his glaive as Tristin ran away, laughing. They saw the girls walking over the bridge with drinks, and Tristin turned quickly to Grimmond.

"Your window's closing, Grim," he whispered urgently. "She knows now that Sariah was in your head. Fix this, or you might never be able to!"

"What'd we miss?" Viana asked.

"Nothing," Grimmond lied. "Just filling Tristin in on what Uncle Boogey told me."

"UNCLE BOOGEY?" Tristin piped.

Grimmond shushed him, and then regaled the information he learned from his uncle as they sipped their coffee.

"It's all started to fall into place the last few days," Grimmond said. "Why Flaring and Lulling always made me so dizzy and nauseous. Why Luciferin armor bothers my skin, and why that fake key atop Custom House Tower burned me — that was made of Luciferin, too, I'm sure."

"All those things," Olivia replied, "they're used to banish Nightmares back to their realm."

"Yeah," Grimmond agreed, "now I know that means *me*. It explains why I couldn't use anyone else's Luciferin glaive, too; I only ever liked this weird one I found on the sixth floor. It glows purple instead of green — it must not be made with Luciferin!"

Olivia and Tristin nodded their agreement.

"And remember how Brax Flared *with* me when we hit the Atrocity on the bridge?"

Tristin's mouth dropped.

"Grim! The *half* of you that's Nightmare — you *haunted* the Blood Onyx for a moment...you somehow possessed it!"

"I don't know," Grimmond answered. "Is there any other explanation for what happened?"

Viana suddenly stepped forward, almost angrily.

"You are *not* a Nightmare, Grim," she said hotly. "Just...just *please* don't say it like that."

Tristin's excitement diminished as he shot a meaningful look at Olivia.

"Come on, Liv," Tristin said. "Let's go see how Randy's leg is healing up."

Tristin quickly dragged Olivia toward the Hovel, but Viana didn't even have a chance to turn around before Grimmond stopped her.

"Viana," he said quietly. "Can we take that walk now? Please?"

She nodded, and together they walked across the Hollow. Their hands brushed together more than once as they talked, but neither one made the next move. They stopped when they found an area that hadn't been damaged in the battle: the cherry and Japanese maple trees, not far from Brax's clearing.

Viana quickly sat at the base of a cherry tree that was in full bloom, but Grimmond remained standing.

"Is your godmother doing okay with all this?" she asked.

"I'm not really sure," Grimmond answered. "I had to apologize to her for some stuff at the lake before that scrimmage. She said she forgives me, but I still feel like a world-class jerk."

Viana nodded, but Grimmond saw her lips tighten before taking a sip of her drink.

"I wanted to say I'm sorry to you, too," Grimmond said, clearing his throat. "For *after* the scrimmage…for —"

"Kissing Sariah?" Viana cut in. "How about: for pushing me away most of the year, not trusting our feelings for each other, or *completely* cutting me out the last few months."

"Um," Grimmond swallowed down the fresh pang of guilt shooting through him. "Yeah, for all of it at once, I guess."

He hoped the conversation would have gone more smoothly. Hadn't he just helped save the entire Hollow from the Dark Naught?

"It's okay," she answered flatly. "You were being manipulated. For *some* of it, at least."

Grimmond sat down next to her, trying to recover the flow of the conversation, but he didn't know what to say.

"I won't blame Zuielle for everything I did," he said quietly. "And I'll try to take better responsibility for my Nightmare self. I just hope that after all this, we can still be friends…."

Viana swiveled toward him, a ferocious light in her eyes.

"Friends?"

With a look of pure venom, she threw her coffee cup against a tree, stood up, and began to stomp away. Grimmond had no idea what he had done wrong.

YOU IDIOT! Do something, QUICK!

"Viana, wait!" Grimmond cried out, jumping to his feet.

She stomped back over to him. Stopping only a few feet from his face, she looked ready to skewer him on the end of her glaive. Grimmond looked around, thinking rapidly.

He saw that a Sentree had snuck over to them as they were speaking, and had stretched a branch out over their heads to grab them. In a flash, Grimmond reached his hand out, broke a vine-covered twig off, and showed it to Viana.

"Prickleneck," he made up quickly.

"*Pickle* Neck?"

"No, PRICKLE-neck," he said again, pointing to the Sentree. "Really nasty stuff."

Viana's dark hair whipped back and forth with her shaking head, her frustration slowly mounting. Grimmond caught her sweet scent through the air, and for a split-second almost forgot his plan.

"It's — uh — a *cousin* to the Thistletoe!" he sputtered. "But, like, WAY worse, I've heard...."

It was his final ploy, and he felt as if a full minute passed as Viana looked at him, her hazel-green eyes unblinking. Then, her face turned red, and she bit her lip. Grimmond was uncertain if he'd succeeded at first, until the corners of her mouth began to stretch wide, and she slowly reached her arms around his neck.

"You know how they get if we don't follow the rules," she said quietly.

She was inches from his face.

"I really am sorry, Viana —"

He didn't finish his sentence, as she pulled him in and stopped his mouth with her lips. Grimmond's heart immediately erupted into a jig of pain and pleasure, but he didn't dare interrupt the kiss until she was finished.

When she pulled away, Grimmond was only vaguely aware of where he was. He wouldn't have been entirely surprised if he had just gotten back from another world, though neither his own nor that of the Nightmayr Realm.

"My name's *Vi*," she warned. "Don't ever forget again, Grimmond Scylent."

Understanding every implication of her warning, Grimmond was still woozy as he tried to think of something to say in response.

"Okay then, Vi," he said, barely able to hear himself speak through his ringing ears. "But *seriously* — you *just* had coffee. How do you always taste like mint?"

"Hollowmint Latte," she answered simply. "*Duh*. I only ever drink that if I'm gonna be around you. Just in case...."

Grimmond smiled, but when he came in for another kiss, alarm bells suddenly rolled across the grounds. Exchanging a confused look with Viana, they broke apart and began to race back to the Hovel. Brax and Nelton picked them up halfway, and flew them all the way up to the open balcony nearest the Dread Map.

"What's going on?" Viana demanded as they burst into the room.

Followed by a fast-forming current of other Squadron members, they watched as Cyto and Plasm wove the Dread Map faster than Grimmond had ever seen them go. They shot their webs and scuttled rapidly about the room, and slowly, red and black dots began to form across the seven continents.

Grimmond felt a pang of panic in his heart, so bad that he almost fell to his knees. He then nearly ripped his hair out for neglecting to check one very important thing. How could he have forgotten?

Sprinting from the Dread Map room with Tristin and Viana closely behind him, he went all the way back to one room that was still in smithereens: the room where he was betrayed by the

Sariah impersonator, and stabbed by Malus. He began to search frantically, but couldn't find what he looked for.

"No, *no, NO...*."

Grimmond dropped to his knees, turning over stones from the crumbled wall, and kicking over chairs and desks to search beneath them.

"Grim!" Viana demanded. "What is it?"

"The DOORKNOB!" he answered frantically. "It should have been right here, but it's gone! I don't think...I'm not *sure* I destroyed it...I may have only disrupted the Dark Naught from getting out."

He remembered slamming the door with his foot, and the door fading away into the air, but what else had happened?

Malus...he stooped down to the floor before he fled....

Grimmond's voice was a whisper when it hit him.

"Malus took it — he still has the door to the Nightmayr Realm. I didn't destroy it completely...."

Sprinting back to the Dread Map room, the three friends faced Lord Stawlart and Eralynn, along with Viana's mother, Coach Maurs, and Professor Manning.

"What's happened?" Lord Stawlart demanded. "What's wrong?"

Grimmond's heart powerfully lurched, and he fell to his knees.

Without delay, an explosion burst forth from his chest, and those in his vicinity were blown back several yards. Bright blue light reached out of his heart, mixed with the black light of the Nightmayr Realm. Grimmond was thrown to his back, writhing in pain.

"GRIM!" Viana screamed. "NO!"

Though she tried, she couldn't get to him, the warring lights spreading from his heart lashing out at everything near. Professor Manning — the only one strong enough — pushed forward with dark gray shadow and placed a hand on Grimmond's chest. The light stopped leaking, and Grimmond closed his eyes and became still.

"His heart won't last," Professor Manning said, whipping his white eyes around.

He looked to Lord Stawlart, apparently continuing a conversation they had already had.

"I must take him *now*, Liam."

"Take him?" Eralynn asked urgently. "Where? Another Hollow?"

"To a place he can be helped," Boogey replied calmly, picking Grimmond up with ease. "Away from the Dark Naught pulling on his heart. There is not much time, and I will need help —"

"We're in," Viana said immediately.

Tristin and Olivia both nodded, and Viana then looked to her mother. Dr. Knight said nothing, but exhaled deeply and looked away.

"Then grab your things and meet me at the bridge!" Professor Manning said loudly. "Quickly!"

Exchanging determined looks, Tristin and Viana ran from the room, while Olivia raced to the window and jumped onto her Gargoyle. Grimmond suddenly opened his eyes and clutched a hand to his heart, holding back the pain.

What's happening to me?

"We don't have much time, Liam," Boogey said. "He was in the Nightmayr Realm too long, and the Dark Naught drained too much from him. We must go. *Now*."

Lord Stawlart nodded his head.

"So be it," he said. "The rest of you, assemble your Squadrons to deploy at once!"

"What — NO, Liam!" Eralynn protested. "He's not taking him anywhere! Boogey, how DARE you inject yourself into —"

"Stop," Grimmond mumbled. "Don't argue. I'll come back, Eralynn...."

Professor Manning carried Grimmond from the room, followed by Lord Stawlart and his godmother. Quickly they exited the Hovel, stopping in the middle of the bridge. Tristin and Viana raced out moments later holding three backpacks, and Olivia touched down next with her Gargoyle, followed by Flynn, Nelton, and Brax.

Grimmond twitched as his heart burned with light, but Boogey placed a hand on his chest once again. With effort, the light was suppressed a second time. Eralynn was nearly beside herself with tears, but Lord Stawlart did his best to hold her back.

"Please, Boogey," Eralynn begged. "Help him."

"I will do my best, Eralynn," Professor Manning said. "But I cannot promise you that this ends happily."

Professor Manning shed his human shape, dissipating into white eyes and gray furls of fog, and Grimmond was suspended in them. Then, tendrils whipped out from the fog to similarly latch onto Tristin, Viana and Olivia, along with the four Gargoyles. A voice came from the fog next.

They listened to the creeping voice of the Boogey Man in his true form.

"Do not struggle," rang the words in their ears. "And do *not* let go."

Each of the four friends and Gargoyles were slowly lifted over the Bottomless Chasm, and Grimmond next heard a whisper directly in his ear.

"This is going to be a long fall," it said. *"Hang on, Grinny...we have much to do."*

ABOUT THE AUTHOR

Author photograph © A.B. Davis
www.abdaviswriter.com

After living across the United States and abroad, A.B. returned to the Midwest where he grew up and currently works as an engineer. He loves jogging at night, any-sized campfire, and a bright flashlight. Writing has always been his great passion, back to when he was quite young and wrote a delightfully horrible poem about confused ants on a picnic.

Visit A.B. online at abdaviswriter.com to sign up for email updates on what he is working on next, and follow him on social media @abdavis_writer.

Made in the USA
Las Vegas, NV
01 October 2021

31494486R00218